To Andrew, my soulmate

STEPHANIE FAZIO

OPAL STORM

OPAL CONTAGION BOOK 3

Syafant Press

Syafant Press

New York, New York

Cover designed by Keith Tarrier

Stephanie Fazio

Visit www.StephanieFazio.com

Printed in the United States of America
First Printing: July 2020

Library of Congress Control Number: 2020910077

ISBN 978-1-951572-09-9

PROLOGUE

r. Vemfrey adjusted the face shield of his anti-contagion suit. It was intolerably hot in the airless sick ward. There were just too many bodies in too small a space. The Lagonia infirmary was well-equipped for the normal array of battle injuries and minor illnesses, but not for this. There wasn't an infirmary on the continent that could handle an outbreak of this magnitude.

Over the last two years, hardly anyone in Lagonia had given opal contagion a second thought. The immunity had been that effective. Now that the immunity was gone, the contagion had returned with a vengeance.

Two physicians just entering the ward began to gag. Vemfrey had long-since ceased to notice the putrid stench of rotting flesh, burst pustules, and death.

He'd lost count of how many hours he'd been here, but he knew precisely how many people he'd lost.

Twenty-seven. In the last hour.

One thousand since the outbreak began two days ago.

And that number was rising. Fast.

Dr. Vemfrey clenched his teeth as another agonized shriek tore through the ward. He might have gotten inured to the smells, but the screams…. Every one burrowed into his brain like a parasite. The sounds chipped away at his sanity and the reserves of strength that had kept him on his feet since the outbreak began.

He'd first become aware of the impending catastrophe when a group of farmers came to the infirmary. They'd confirmed that Lagonia's immunity to opal contagion had burned to ashes. The flowers, which had been unwittingly consumed by every person in the empire and were the source of Lagonians' immunity to opal contagion, were gone.

Even though Emperor Jaikon had tried to keep it quiet, the news had spread like…well, fire. Within hours of the flower fields burning, everyone in Lagonia had known that the source of their immunity to opal contagion had been destroyed. True panic set in when the reserves of dried flowers were depleted.

"Change their sheets," Dr. Vemfrey barked at an attendant who seemed to be frozen in a state of shock. "If their skin isn't kept clean, the pustules will spread faster."

The attendant glanced at the nearest patient, slid a guilty look to Vemfrey, and muttered something about getting fresh linens.

He wouldn't be back.

Not that Vemfrey could blame the man. The best physicians in Lagonia could slow the disease's progression a little…make the pain slightly more bearable…but that was all.

Opal contagion had no cure.

Only about one in two-hundred of the sick never progressed to the second stage of the contagion. These survivors could live out the rest of their lives without ever succumbing to the virus. If they managed to conceive before the Emperor had them killed, their children would be Extended.

Once a patient's irises developed an orange ring, it meant they had advanced to the second stage and would be dead within a week.

Vemfrey scooped out a small measure of the precious Insorsiled numbing crystals and slipped them between the nearest patient's chapped lips. He tied off his last remaining pouch of crystals, trying not to think about what the screams would be like when he ran out.

With merchants terrified of contracting the contagion, and no more of the protective anti-contagion suits, trade with Insorsil had halted.

"Get these corpses out of here," Vemfrey thundered at whoever might heed him.

Bodies were being stacked against the wall. The ones who normally attended to corpse retrieval were nowhere to be found. They didn't want to risk the contagion by setting foot inside the infirmary. And the few anti-contagion suits that were still available had been distributed to the physicians.

Vemfrey couldn't blame the citizens for their terror. After what he'd witnessed these last couple of days, he wouldn't wish the contagion on his worst enemy.

"What the hell is our emperor doing while we're here suffering?" one of the physicians grumbled.

Another nearby physician scoffed. "Off dominating the continent, no doubt. He doesn't care if our citizens are dying in droves."

"Emperor Jaikon promised us those opal-skinned demons would already be dead," the first said. "And yet, they're running around the empire unchecked."

Vemfrey didn't bother to point out that the Lagonians had terrorized the Extended for years. For the first time in recent history, the Extended had the power to fight back against their oppressors.

This was a war of sorts. And in times of war, soldiers used whatever weapons they could access. It was simply a twist of fate that the Lagonians fought with swords, while the Extended used the poison that ran through their own veins.

The relative unfairness of it all was a philosophical conversation for another time and place. A time when he could sip Lagonia's famous ice champagne, and recline in a room that wasn't full of the dead and dying.

"What is that?" Vemfrey asked, noticing an unlabeled bottle another physician was tipping into a patient's mouth.

The physician jumped, looking guilty.

"She would have suffered for her few remaining hours," the man told Vemfrey. "I did her a favor."

With a start, Vemfrey realized that the woman's bright orange eyes were sightless. She was dead.

Vemfrey snatched the bottle out of the physician's unresisting hand. He noted the sweet smell that wafted out of the bottle and quickly stoppered it.

"We're physicians," Vemfrey hissed. "We *save* people." He pocketed the bottle. "We don't take lives."

He turned on his heel, but he heard the other physician's muttered retort.

"Look around you, doctor. All we're doing is prolonging the inevitable."

Vemfrey ignored that comment. He rushed to the door to meet the new victim being wheeled in. It was a Lagonia soldier. Vemfrey's eyes passed over her once, appraising her symptoms.

Pustules blackened and scabbing. Yellow skin shiny with opal-tinged perspiration. Hollow cheeks, wasted muscles, sagging skin. Orange tint to the irises.

The soldier was in the second stage of the contagion. That meant she had anywhere from a few hours to a week to live. It meant that her insides were eroding as though she had swallowed pure acid. It meant there was nothing the doctor could do for the woman except give her a sterile place to die.

"Kill me," the soldier whispered. "Please."

Vemfrey's gloved hand tightened reflexively around the bottle of potion he'd taken from the other physician.

All at once, Vemfrey's energy began to flag. The adrenaline that had kept him on his feet, doing what little he could to ease his fellow Lagonians' suffering, abandoned him. He slumped against the wall.

"Help…me," a young man in the third and final stage of the contagion whispered.

The patient tried to raise his arm, but his bones were too liquified for him to manage it. The man turned to the side and vomited blood. His entire body twitched on the mattress as muscle spasms and fever chills wracked his body.

Vemfrey fumbled for the pouch of numbing crystals in his coat pocket. He knew the small bit of Insorsiled medicine wouldn't be enough to take away this man's pain, but he had nothing else to offer.

The man coughed wetly. Then, with little more than a final, whispered breath, he died. The man's glassy-eyed stare was fixed on Vemfrey. His expression was frozen in agony.

Vemfrey looked down at the pouch of crystals in his hand. Aside from the powdery residue at the bottom, it was empty. His hand began to shake.

His whole body trembled from fatigue and the helplessness he'd been fighting off since this all began.

We're physicians. We save people.

That was the belief that had guided him for his entire professional life. As he looked around the sick ward, he had never felt like more of a failure.

Another scream ripped through the infirmary. More corpses were stacked against the wall.

If he couldn't save his people, then he had no use. And he couldn't save them.

If these past days had proven anything, it was that. Dr. Vemfrey, renowned throughout the empire for curing all manners of illnesses, had nothing more to offer.

Through the window overhead, Vemfrey caught sight of the mob of sick people outside the infirmary. They were clamoring for entrance, begging for help the physicians inside couldn't give.

He took the small bottle of sweet-smelling liquid from his pocket and stared at it. The glass's purple tint made it impossible to decipher the color of the liquid within. Almost without thought, Vemfrey uncorked the bottle. He unzipped his hood and brought the bottle underneath his visor. He inhaled.

The scent was sugary and pleasant. When he lowered the bottle, the infirmary's stench hit him like a physical blow. He doubled over.

He was eye level with one of the corpses.

All we're doing is prolonging the inevitable.

Vemfrey looked at the bottle. He lifted it in a morbid toast to the corpse. Then, he drained it in a single drought.

CHAPTER 1

Rhett checked the number scratched into the side of the shack against the list he carried. He dismounted Silverbird and nodded to the group of soldiers already on the ground. While the soldiers approached the shack, Rhett looked out at what used to be the flower field. Now, it was nothing more than scorched earth. Nothing remained of the rainbow-colored immunity flowers that had once grown here.

The farmers who lived here used to tend the flowers. Now, they had no source of income and no other means of providing for themselves.

Rhett tamped down a surge of anger. Jaikon had left these farmers to starve.

He stayed with Silverbird while his soldiers knocked on the shack's door. When no one answered, Rhett gestured for his soldiers to go in. They didn't have time to dawdle.

"Stay back!" a voice shouted at the soldiers who entered.

Through the open door, Rhett could see an elderly woman clutching a rusted cooking knife. She stood over two cowering children.

"My grandson isn't a traitor to the empire, and soldiers already took everything of value. Just leave us alone!"

It was more or less the same greeting Rhett's people had gotten from the dozen other homes they'd entered in the last hour.

"We're not here to arrest you," Rhett called. "We're here to bring you somewhere safe where the Emperor's soldiers won't be able to reach you."

"Rhetteman?" The old woman lowered her knife. "Rhetteman Loniger?"

He gave her a short nod. "Gather what you need and hurry."

"Where's my grandson?" she asked, shooing the children into their shabby bedroom to pack a bag.

"Securing the fishermen's cape, which is where you'll be staying until the Emperor is no longer a threat."

"You're doing it, aren't you?" The old woman's eyes shone with something that looked like reverence. "You're taking the throne from Emperor Jaikon."

"That is my intention."

He didn't bother mentioning that he still had no idea how to remove Jaikon's invincibility. And even if he solved that mystery, there was another insurmountable problem.

"Oh, thank you, Rhetteman. Thank you, thank you, thank you!"

To Rhett's horror, the old woman darted out of the hut toward him. One of Rhett's soldiers barely managed to grab her arm to stop her. Rhett hurriedly backed away while his soldiers, protected by their anti-contagion suits, made a barrier between Rhett and the unprotected family.

"I meant no harm," the woman said, bowing her head. "I only wanted to bow before my true emperor."

Rhett had to swallow several times. He couldn't bring himself to tell the old woman the truth…he couldn't bear to see the way her gratitude would transform to horror if she knew.

Rhett was infected with opal contagion.

As if to emphasize how little time he had left, a stinging pain burst across Rhett's arm. He resisted the urge to scratch at it, knowing it would only make things worse. Another flash of discomfort came, this time from the bottom of his foot.

This woman's grandson, along with a thousand other of Lagonia's finest soldiers, had turned their backs on the Emperor out of loyalty to Rhett. They had been willing to sacrifice everything for him, because they believed he was the leader Lagonia needed.

And he was going to abandon them.

"Please," Rhett said, his voice coming out even gruffer than usual. "Gather your things and come with us. Quickly."

As soon as Jaikon discovered the soldiers he'd sent across the Brookgar Sea to be killed by the giants had returned without completing their mission, he would go after their families. Rhett's first priority in the short time he had left was to protect his soldiers and their loved ones.

His lookouts had seen Jaikon take off on his gold dragon a few hours ago, heading toward Insorsil. The Emperor's invincible army had followed shortly thereafter, leaving only the slavers-turned-soldiers behind to guard the rest of the empire.

The pathetic excuses for guards were busy smoking the expensive leaf that Jaikon imported from across the sea. They hadn't even noticed that the most wanted man in the empire was riding around on a stolen dragon.

Since Jaikon and his soldiers could return at any time, Rhett needed to move quickly.

For the last two days, Rhett's rebel army had been hiding out in the Insorsiled forest just beyond Lagonia's borders, waiting for their first opportunity to get into the empire. Staying hidden had been no small feat with a thousand soldiers, ten of whom were giants. They'd also had Silverbird and Lady Winnowa Umbrog's pack of enormous wolves.

Rhett's soldiers led the old farmer woman and her great-grandchildren out of the shack and toward the line of people hurrying down the unpaved road. The path would bring them from the mountain farmlands to central Lagonia. From there, it was a three-hour walk to the tip of the rocky cape where the rebels were sheltering.

Wilsean and a dozen other archers patrolled the road. They would make sure the families made the long trek without incident.

Rhett mounted Silverbird, holding his dagger loosely as he scanned the horizon in every direction.

He caught sight of Dannica, one of his most trusted soldiers, jogging across the barren flower field toward him. Her coffee-colored skin and black hair were just visible through the clear face shield attached to her suit's hood. She moved quickly and gracefully in spite of the bulky material of her anti-contagion suit covering her from head to foot.

Rhett was the only one of his soldiers who didn't wear one.

It was too late for him.

If Rhett could have saved his entire army from wearing the suits by donning one himself, he would have. But the Insorsil-made suits were designed to keep the virus from coming in through the material; it did nothing to hold in the contagion if its wearer was Infected.

"The invincibles are on their way back from Insorsil," Dannica said without preamble.

The invincibles was what they'd all started calling the soldiers who wore one of the gold pins. Jaikon had gifted the magical pins, which prevented any harm from coming to their wearers, to five hundred of his soldiers. It was likely that the Emperor's latest trip to Insorsil had been to acquire more of the pins.

Rhett mentally calculated how long it would take to get these people to the cape, and whether they'd make it before Jaikon returned.

It would be close.

"Hurry them up," Rhett told Dannica.

He needed to get back and see how the rest of his army was coming along with making the fishermen's cape defensible. It wouldn't do these people any good if he relocated them, only to have them fall to Jaikon's soldiers just the same.

"Sir." Dannica put a gloved hand on his arm. She looked at the line of rebel soldiers' families disappearing down the road. "This means the world to us."

It was hard to tell with the suit, but Rhett thought he saw the gleam of tears in Dannica's eyes.

"I'm going to make this right," he promised her. He wasn't sure if he was trying to convince her or himself.

In his mind he heard Stone's voice.

Words are cheap, Rhetteman.

Shaking his head to clear it, Rhett jumped on Silverbird's back and urged her into a canter.

Rhett dismounted and led Silverbird over the craggy landscape of the fishermen's cape. He had ridden ahead of his soldiers and their families, who were making their way on foot.

The fishermen's cape was a rocky half-moon strip of land that jutted out from Lagonia proper. It circled behind the ridge of mountains to Lagonia's north, and doubled back almost all the way to the Insorsil port. The cape was too rocky to accommodate merchants' wagons. It also wasn't protected by the Insorsiled weather charm that kept Lagonia's climate temperate year-round.

The only people who ever came here were the fishermen who hunted the rare and priceless rose-striped umberfish that lived in the shallows.

Now that it was winter and the umberfish had migrated elsewhere, the fishermen's rafts and houses were unoccupied. It wouldn't be the most comfortable fit, but it was better than staying in the Insorsiled forest.

The cape was everything Rhett and his soldiers needed. It was a comfortable eight miles from the Lagonia palace, it afforded easy access to Insorsil and Lagonia, and it was defensible. The sheer cliffs on either side of the cape ensured that Jaikon wouldn't risk attacking them from the water.

Gray clouds hovered over gray-blue water. The only real color came from the fishing houses clustered at the cape's tip. Each of them was painted a different, bold color.

The brightness made Rhett's eyes ache. He wondered if that meant he was nearing the second stage of the contagion. He hadn't noticed any orange tint to his irises yet, but it wasn't like he spent much time examining his reflection, either.

Liss and his friends were holding out hope that Rhett would be one of the lucky few whose symptoms never progressed to the second stage of the contagion. In Rhett's experience, there was little difference between luck and delusions. He didn't have time for either.

Rhett led Silverbird to the towering wall the giants had erected to block off the cape's narrow entrance. His dragon stared longingly into the distance. She turned her nose in the direction of the Lagonia stables, where the other flightless silver dragons were kept. She let out a plaintive wail.

"Sorry, girl." Rhett offered the dragon a handful of gold nuggets and a conciliatory pat.

Since Wilsean had stolen her right out from under the slavers' noses, Rhett's spies had reported that the dragon stable was kept under constant guard. Jaikon's gold dragon, the only winged dragon on the continent, was kept in a separate building adjoining the palace.

Silverbird fixed her watchful gaze on Lady Winnowa Umbrog's pack of white wolves. The beasts prowled back and forth in front of the wall. Their black eyes glittered menacingly. No one would want to be on the receiving end of those fangs and claws, invincibility pin or not.

Anyone who did make it past the wolves…and the wall…would face the ten giants under Lady Umbrog's command. As strange as it was to be allied with Lagonia's longtime enemy, Rhett couldn't deny the usefulness of his new partnership with the giant leader.

Grub, a giant who liked to tell anyone who would listen that Liss was his best friend, waved at Rhett.

"You see Lovely now?" Grub asked.

Rhett nodded.

Lovely was what Grub had started calling Liss after hearing Ciago's nickname of *Lovely Liss*. Rhett wasn't thrilled about a giant showing so much interest in her, even if Ciago had assured him the giant was harmless.

Nothing that big could be harmless.

Ciago, Lady Umbrog, and her group of nine giants were working on what Ciago was calling *Jaikon's welcome home surprise*.

From what Rhett could tell, it looked like they were digging a deep trench. Ciago's muscled frame strained against his anti-contagion suit as he thrust shovelfuls of dirt onto a growing pile.

Ciago was the biggest soldier in Rhett's army, but he appeared almost small compared to the giants he worked alongside. It was a fact Wilsean never tired of ragging on him about.

Fortunately, Lady Umbrog and her giants had natural immunity to opal contagion and didn't need to worry about anti-contagion suits. Not that there were any suits that would have been large enough to accommodate their towering forms.

Rhett's soldiers were pitching un-Insorsiled tents for the overflow of people who wouldn't fit in the houses. They had just finished securing the last one when the rebels' families began filtering in through the barrier wall.

Rhett watched from a safe distance as his soldiers greeted their parents, lovers, and children. There was laughter and tears between people who thought they'd never see each other again. One of Rhett's soldiers lifted his girlfriend into his arms and kissed her. It made Rhett look toward the Insorsiled tent on the cliff's edge, where Liss was. He was about to go to her when a sharp whistle caught his attention.

Wilsean, who had climbed into one of their makeshift lookouts and was peering through an Insorsiled glass, signaled to Rhett.

Wilsean tossed the glass at a distance that would be unreachable for just about anyone else. Rhett caught it and strode just outside the barrier's open doors. He peered through the glass in the direction Wilsean had indicated. Rhett had expected to see Jaikon and his soldiers returning. What he saw was worse.

A long line of wagons was hurtling down the cobbled road that led straight toward the cape. Rhett caught a flash of opal-hued skin from the wagons' open windows.

"Get anyone without an anti-contagion suit into the houses," Rhett ordered his soldiers. "The Extended are coming."

CHAPTER 2

Liss was wearing down the carpet in her and Rhett's beautiful bedroom in the Insorsiled tent. Even though the soldiers were all wearing anti-contagion suits, she didn't want to go outside until their families were safely out of harm's way…safely out of her way. Her very existence was a threat to all of them, and there was nothing she could do to prevent the virus that lived inside her from spreading.

If she had listened to the logical part of her brain and kept her distance from the beginning, Rhett wouldn't be sick right now.

He wouldn't be dying.

Liss paced faster, using the rhythmic thumping of her footfalls on the carpet to distract herself. She chewed on what was left of her thumbnail.

What was taking so long?

She hated that she had to hide in here while everyone else was out there being useful.

The Insorsiled tent was doing its best to sooth her. The room was dimly lit, and soft music played from a source Liss couldn't identify. A clean citrus smell, the same scent the Insorsiled tub filled with whenever Rhett bathed, wafted through the room. Little candies and other treats kept appearing out of thin air and hovering in front of her face, and then floating sadly away when she ignored them.

"Stop trying to make me feel better," Liss snapped at the tent.

Great. She had been reduced to yelling at a tent….

A muffled shout from somewhere outside, followed by another, had her stopping in her tracks. The wall of the tent, which had been solid wood before, turned transparent the moment Liss wished to see what was happening.

From the tent's position on the curved center of the cape, Liss could see all the way to the barricade where the sounds were coming from.

She bit out a curse as cold dread shimmied down her back. Grabbing her knife off the nightstand, she ran out of the room. Liss darted through the common room and past a startled-looking Samara. She threw open the tent's brass door and raced out into the cold.

Liss headed straight for the barricade wall as wagon after wagon slid through. The barrier doors were firmly shut, but the wagons passed through the solid wood as though it was nothing more than Insorsiled illusion.

Liss understood the source of the wagons' uninhibited progress when she got close enough to see an Extended woman pressing her hand to the edge of the barricade.

Extended Phasers could transform any object into solid, liquid, or gas. From the way the wagons were passing right through the barricade, it was obvious the wood's solid mass had been transformed to gas. The wall still looked the same, but the wagons met with no resistance as they slid through.

The rebel soldiers on guard had to hurl themselves out of the way to avoid being crushed beneath the churning wheels.

Two dozen wagons halted just inside the wall, where the rocky landscape prevented them from going any farther. Liss could see the bright yellow blobs of the rebel soldiers running uphill from the fishermen's houses on the other end of the cape. The giants and wolves were already facing off against the Extended, who were pouring out of the wagons. Rhett stood between the two groups.

Liss ran faster. If she was going to prevent this impending battle, she'd need to get there before someone did something stupid.

By the time she got within shouting distance, the handful of rebel Lagonians who had been guarding the wall were lying on the ground. At first, Liss thought they were dead. As she looked closer, she realized their chests were rising and falling. Their souls were cloudy in the way that indicated they were in a deep sleep.

"Liss, do something," Rhett called.

He was keeping the giants from going after the Extended. But once the rest of the rebels got to them and saw their own people down, Rhett wouldn't be able to keep them from attacking.

Liss's heart stopped beating when she caught sight of a familiar mop of burnt orange hair.

"Spence!" she cried, just as Spence reached out and touched a soldier who was waking up. As soon as Spence's fingertips touched the soldier, she was out cold.

Spence was Liss's friend from her caravan and one the kids from her old thieving crew. He was barely fifteen and had no business being here. He should be back at the hideout, where it was safe.

Spence shoved his long, tangled hair out of his face. He met Liss's gaze across the small group of unconscious Lagonia soldiers.

Tears leaked from Spence's eyes, making his opal cheeks look like they were sparkling.

"I have to, Liss," he said in a choked voice. "They killed my mom. They killed so many of ours."

Liss couldn't speak. What could she say?

Lagonia soldiers had beaten Spence's mom and left her to die by the side of the road. They had killed so many Extended and enslaved even more. How could she begrudge her people for taking their revenge?

But then she caught sight of Rhett, his hands held out to the giants and rebel soldiers who were racing toward them.

Liss felt her chest tighten as she approached Spence the way she might a skittish animal.

"Please stop," she told him, before turning to the rest of the Extended.

Most of the Extended had halted. Their eyes were turned on Rhett, the giants, and the wolves. Out of the corner of her eye, Liss saw one of the Extended slip through the crowd and bend over a sleeping Lagonian.

It took Liss several precious seconds to realize what the Extended planned to do.

"No!" she screamed.

There was a ripping sound, and then the Lagonian's hood was peeled back, exposing the soldier's unprotected face.

Another horrified shout made it out of Liss as the Extended man bent down and…licked the Lagonian's bare cheek.

"That's for my mother, Lagonian scum," the Extended man told the unconscious soldier. "Have fun dying from opal contagion."

Shock made Liss go rigid.

Rhett shouted something. A second later, an arrow was buried in the Extended man's neck.

Liss staggered forward until she was between the Extended and the group of unconscious Lagonians. Some of her people were still coming out of the wagons. The rest who were already on the field began to congregate around her, but not in a friendly way. The emotions pouring off their souls were the exact opposite of friendly.

The last time Liss had been with her people, she'd faced them with a knife in her hand as she defended Rhett.

"I'm not your enemy," Liss told them. "I'm one of you."

She faltered under the scoffs and curses that assaulted her.

"If you were one of us," an unfamiliar Extended woman spat, "you wouldn't look like the enemy. You wouldn't have chosen them over your own people."

"I didn't—" Liss began.

"Then prove it," an Extended man Liss didn't recognize said, stepping forward. "Slit your precious boyfriend's throat, just like he's done to so many of ours."

Bile curdled Liss's gut.

"I'm not a traitor," she said.

It infuriated her the way those words came out sounding like a plea.

Liss felt a comforting wall of heat and muscle at her back. The familiar storm of Rhett's emotions surrounded her.

"I've ordered my soldiers not to harm you," Rhett said, coming to stand beside her to face the Extended. "But if you come any closer to us, I'll change my mind."

He stood to his full height, and with his dagger in his hand, he looked every bit the brutal assassin he'd once been.

The rebel Lagonia soldiers and giants fanned out around them. Rhett turned his attention on the Extended.

"You will also stop attacking the Lagonia peasants," Rhett continued in a cold, commanding voice. "Go back to your hideout."

"Or what, Viper?" an Extended man shot back.

In spite of the man's brazen words, he cowered under the glare Rhett leveled on him.

More Extended were gathering around to face off against the rebel Lagonians. Liss scanned the group, searching for the one person who might listen to her.

Liss's mom leapt from one of the wagons with all the grace of a dancer. Her quiver was strapped to her back and an arrow was already nocked in her bow. She was tall and rail-thin, whereas Liss was petite and hour glass-shaped. Between that, and Liss's Lagonia pale skin and blue eyes, they looked nothing alike.

Nya's attention immediately locked on Liss.

"Liss, what are you doing here?" her mom called in a shrill voice.

What do you think I'm doing here? she wanted to retort. Instead, she said, "Mom, please. It doesn't have to be this way."

Rhett stayed at Liss's side as she moved toward her mom.

"Come back with us," Nya said letting her bowstring go slack. "You don't belong here."

Liss shook her head.

"My friends are here," Liss managed, hating the tremor in her own voice.

Rhett moved closer until their sides were touching. He stared at Nya without blinking. "Liss will always belong here."

Blame and grief flared across his soldiers' souls. Liss was the reason why they were going to lose their beloved commander and their one chance of having a peaceful future.

Liss hesitated as she met her mom's tortured gaze.

"Why aren't you wearing a suit?" Nya looked at Rhett, like she had just noticed him.

For anyone who didn't know Rhett well, he still seemed healthy. Everything except for his face and hands were covered, so none of the pustules were visible. He'd lost some muscle mass, but he'd been so large to start with that he still appeared normal. No one would be able to tell just from looking at him that he had opal contagion.

"Because I don't need one," Rhett said in a flat voice.

In a way, it was true. The anti-contagion suit worked as a prevention, not a cure. Wearing one wouldn't help Rhett now.

Panic flooded Nya's soul.

"What did you do?!" Nya all but shrieked at Liss.

It took Liss several seconds to understand what her mom was so upset about. Nya wasn't worried that Rhett was leaving himself exposed to the contagion. She thought Liss had done for Rhett what Nya had done for her husband.

A cold sweat broke out all over Liss's skin, even though a frosty wind was whipping her hair across her face. Liss's mouth went dry as ashes.

"It's time for you to go," Rhett told Nya. "All of you."

Liss's mom ignored him.

"Tell me you didn't," Nya said to Liss, her voice cracking. "Tell me you didn't make yourself weak just to protect *him*."

Liss was having trouble catching her breath. For the last two days, she'd been fixating on Rhett's declining health and Samara's assurances that they'd find what they needed to cure him in Insorsil.

Now, all of her old fears crashed back over her like an icy tidal wave.

An image of her mom, huddled under a mountain of blankets and weeping for a man who had been dead for decades, filled her mind.

This…this was the reason why she had never wanted to let herself fall in love. She had never wanted to rest her soul's happiness on another, only to lose him, and then lose herself.

"Liss?"

Rhett's hand on her lower back brought her away from the brink of true panic.

"I'm okay," she managed, sucking in a shallow breath.

"He's not worth it," Nya persisted. "Liss, please. If it's not too late, stop whatever dark magic you're involved with."

Liss's nausea and fear of becoming as weak as her mom retreated in an instant. She crossed her arms and glared.

"You always told me you didn't regret giving up your strength for my dad. Are you implying Rhett is less worthy?"

"Of course, I am! He's a murderer and a thief."

"Actually, I'm the thief," Liss reminded her mom.

"And a spy," Ciago added helpfully, reminding her that she and her mom had an audience for this conversation.

"He stole you from us!" Nya snarled.

"I'm not some *thing* that can be bartered or stolen," Liss shot back. "And Rhett's right. It's time for you to go."

The Extended on either side of Nya shifted impatiently. Liss could sense the Lagonia soldiers behind her were doing the same. If this went on much longer, she and Rhett wouldn't be able to stop the two forces from clashing.

"I can't lose you," Nya said, her orange eyes wild and desperate. "You're all that I have left." She turned away to hide the tears in her eyes.

Liss swallowed the lump in her throat. She shook her head, willing her mom to understand.

"I'm giving you one minute to get all of your people back on those wagons," Rhett said. "The next time you enter Lagonia, your welcome will be less friendly."

The rebels drew their weapons.

"Come with us," Nya urged Liss, giving Rhett an accusing glare. "Once the Lagonians are gone, we'll have a future. We'll have a real home, and land, and—"

"You have ten seconds," Rhett said.

"I'm not leaving," Liss told her mom, even as her vision began to blur.

Nya's shoulders drooped a little. To Rhett, she said, "I can't deny my people their vengeance. I won't."

Rhett didn't reply. He raised his right hand.

For a few seconds, nothing happened. Then, the giants' wolves began to howl. Quivering lips pulled back to reveal long fangs. The beasts crouched low to the ground, waiting for the signal to pounce.

"I suggest you run," Rhett told Liss's mom.

The rest of the Extended began to race back toward their wagons. Nya looked from Liss to the giant who was striding toward them.

Grub's heavy footfalls loosed rocks and chunks of ice. He swung a stone mallet in his fist. The weapon was big enough that Liss doubted she'd even be able to lift the thing.

"Leave Lovely alone!" Grub thundered, bashing a small crater into the ground with his mallet to emphasize his point.

Nya gave Liss one more pleading glance. Then, she turned and followed the rest of the fleeing Extended.

Lady Umbrog—or Winny, as Ciago called the giant leader—came to stand with their small group.

"Shall I have Ulfrath eat one of them?" the giant leader asked.

"No!" Liss said quickly.

The wagons began to hum with the Energizers' power. Liss watched as her people scrambled inside. In seconds, the wagons were moving back out through the barricade.

The soldiers on the ground were starting to wake up. They looked at the wagons, stared back at Liss, and reached up to make sure their anti-contagion suits were still in place.

Liss's attention was drawn to the one soldier whose expression wasn't full of relief. The woman's hood was torn and her face brutally exposed to the elements…to Liss.

Rhett went motionless beside Liss as the horror of realization swept over them all. One of the Extended had licked the soldier's bare face.

She was now Infected.

The woman got to her feet and ran her finger along the shredded lining of her hood. She unsheathed her knife with a trembling hand. Then, to Liss's surprise, the woman offered it to Liss handle-first.

Liss glanced at Rhett, but he seemed as puzzled as she was.

"Take it," the soldier ordered Liss. "You may as well be the one to cut my throat, since you've already killed me."

For the second time that day, Liss was speechless.

"Go on," the soldier said in a harsh voice, thrusting the weapon at Liss. "Do it. Because I'm not going to wait around for my body to rot."

Liss sucked in a breath. Her arms had turned to lead. She could feel everyone's eyes on her, but she couldn't move.

Someone spit on the ground. Liss caught the whispered insult of *Infected* on the breeze.

Rhett's arm shot out and snatched the knife from his soldier.

"Go straight to the infirmary," Rhett told the woman in a voice that sent a chill racing down Liss's spine. "That's an order, soldier."

With one last death glare at Liss, the soldier did as she was told.

Even once all of the rebel soldiers were out of sight, the blame on their souls still lingered.

CHAPTER 3

Rhett stood with Ciago and Wilsean as the Extended wagons disappeared right through the solid wooden barrier.

Wilsean nocked an arrow in his bow. He aimed at the Phaser, who kept one hand on the barricade as the wagons passed through.

"Want me to take him out?" Wilsean asked.

Yes.

"No," Rhett replied. "I'll never kill another Extended."

Wilsean sighed, replacing the arrow in his quiver. "I know they're Liss's people, but you have your own soldiers to think about."

"I'm not killing any more Extended," Rhett said again.

Wilsean went to scratch his head before remembering he was covered in the anti-contagion suit. He crossed his arms and stared out at the retreating wagons.

Rhett noticed that he, Wilsean, and Ciago were standing in the exact same pose. If they didn't look as different as three men could, they might be mistaken for triplets.

They all had the shaved haircut that was customary for men in the Lagonia army, but that was where their physical similarities ended. Like many Lagonians, Ciago had pale skin and light blue eyes. The giant blood in his family tree made him appear as though he was built out of boulders instead of flesh and bones. Wilsean, in contrast, was tall and lean. His black hair was only a shade darker than his skin and eyes.

It was strange to see his friends without the dragonhide jackets they'd worn as soldiers in the Lagonia army. Now, they wore armor of a different kind…a kind meant to protect them from the disease eating through Rhett's body.

"You know the Extended will be back, right?" Wilsean asked.

"I know," Rhett replied.

And instead of staying at the cape to defend his soldiers, he was going to be leaving for Insorsil. It was a futile mission to hunt down a rumor of more immunity flowers.

Rhett didn't want to waste time on what was most likely a pointless venture. But Liss had made it clear she was going, no matter how slim the possibility of success. He wasn't going to let her break into the most well-guarded place in all of Insorsil without him.

"Don't worry about things here," Ciago said, sensing Rhett's hesitation. "You all go on your little Insorsil vacation. Bring me back a magic toy."

Wilsean snorted.

They all turned at once and started to pick their way across the icy rocks. Rhett could just make out their Insorsiled tent on the edge of the cliff, where Liss had already returned to finish packing.

They had almost reached the tent when footsteps had Rhett turning back.

Lady Umbrog was heading toward them, her long strides unimpeded by the icy, uneven ground.

The giant leader made for an imposing figure. Even though she was smaller than the nine giants she had brought with her across the sea, she was as tall as Wilsean and as muscled as Ciago. Intricate swirls were shaved into her short hair, which was as dark as her ebony skin. Her pack of monstrous white wolves surrounded her, their tongues lolling between their impressive fangs.

"We have a problem," Lady Umbrog said as soon as she was within shouting distance. "Lagonian peasants are trying to storm the barricade."

Wilsean swore. Ciago was saying something to the giant leader, but Rhett didn't wait to hear it. He started to run back in the direction they'd just come from.

Rhett crossed the treacherous landscape as fast as he could without falling and breaking his neck. He could sense his friends following behind him, even though he didn't turn back to look.

Screams and the clash of weapons filled Rhett's ears by the time he reached the barricade. The peasants had forced open the doors and were trying to fight their way onto the cape.

"Hold your fire!" Rhett shouted to his archers.

He doubted anyone could even hear him over the sounds of fighting.

"Tell your giants and wolves to get back," Rhett yelled to the giant leader as he hovered at the edge of the fray.

He glanced up in time to see the archers in the makeshift crows' nests pull back their bowstrings.

"No!"

The archers released their arrows. Furious, agonized cries came from the peasants who were pushing and shoving their way through the narrow opening. Others thrust grappling hooks onto the wall.

Peasants and archers tussled. There was a hoarse shout, and then a peasant climbing over the wall lost his hold. He crashed to the ground head first.

There was sickening thud as his skull connected with the frozen ground. He didn't move again.

Rhett shoved his way through the line of giants who were waiting with their mallets poised.

"Open the doors all the way," he ordered the soldiers on either side of the crank.

The peasants were coming onto the cape, anyway. At least this way, he wouldn't have to watch any more of them kill themselves in an attempt to climb over the wall.

Rhett had been expecting a handful of angry peasants on the other side of the barricade. When the doors fully opened, he saw there were hundreds.

They held hammers, cooking knives, and trowels. What they lacked in fighting ability they made up for in numbers and determination. They surged forward through the opening between the two doors.

The peasants in front caught sight of the enormous wolves, but they didn't turn back. That was when Rhett caught the look in their eyes. It wasn't anger or fear, but something far more powerful. Desperation.

"Stop," Rhett ordered the sea of peasants. "You'll get the contagion if you come any closer."

That made them pause, when not even the giants' wolves had scared them off.

Rhett quickly identified the peasants' leader, an elderly man who clutched a rake as his only weapon.

"What do you want?" Rhett asked the man, taking advantage of the few seconds of quiet.

"Commander Rhetteman." The peasant man bowed low. "The Extended are comin'. The Emperor ran off and left us. You 'ave to help us. You 'ave to save us."

Rhett kept his expression cold and neutral, but his pulse was thundering in his ears.

It was Jaikon's responsibility to protect his people. Instead, he'd abandoned them.

"We have Infected here and no spare anti-contagion suits to give you," Rhett told the man.

The peasants looked from Ciago and Wilsean, both wearing their anti-contagion suits, to Rhett. He felt the moment when their realization struck.

"Y-you?" the peasant man stammered. "You're Infected?"

Defeated cries came from the other peasants.

Instead of answering, Rhett addressed the entire crowd.

"Go home. I give you my word my soldiers will do everything they can to protect you until we can end the hostilities with the Extended."

"We thought you were going to be our emperor," a different peasant said, her voice trembling from emotion.

"I am going to take down Jaikon and his invincibles so you can choose a worthy successor," Rhett told them.

The peasants murmured and shook their heads, their distress apparent on their faces.

"Then we're doomed." The peasant leader's shoulders slumped.

"You're the only blood heir," another peasant said. "If you don't take the throne, then all them rich folk'll fight over it."

"They'll make us do their fightin' for 'em," a peasant deep in the crowd called out.

"And while they're busy fightin' over the palace," the peasant leader told Rhett, "we'll starve."

A hollow feeling squeezed Rhett's chest. He knew the peasants were right. Taking Jaikon off the throne wouldn't solve the empire's problems. As the courtiers and councilmen vied for the throne, the most underprivileged members of Lagonia society would be ignored.

Rhett knew better than to dwell on things he couldn't change. Stone would have been the first one to tell him that.

A fresh wave of helplessness and grief filled him at the thought of his mentor and former guardian. Rhett couldn't stop remembering how his own failures had resulted in Stone's death.

Steel doesn't know love or despair. It can't be bent or broken. It needs no heart or warmth. I am steel.

Stone's mantra filled his head. It was no longer a reminder to keep himself separate from everyone and everything…that illusion had crumbled the day Liss stepped into his life…but it was still a comfort. It was a reminder of Stone's strength.

"Go home," Rhett told the peasants again. "We're going to do everything we can to keep you safe."

All of their anger was gone. Some of them dragged their weapons across the ground behind them, like the rakes and shovels were too heavy to hold up.

They walked like they knew they'd already been defeated. Like they were already dead.

The giant leader came to stand beside Rhett as the peasants retreated.

"You know," Lady Umbrog said without turning to look at Rhett. "You are a far better leader than the man ruling Lagonia."

"Not very high praise, all things considered," Wilsean pointed out.

"Winny isn't big into touchy-feely stuff," Ciago said.

"Not all of us can be as skilled at flattery as you," Lady Umbrog retorted, giving Ciago an irritated look.

Rhett's lip twitched at that.

"We wouldn't have made it this far if it wasn't for you," Rhett told the giant leader.

He sobered when he thought about the bargain he'd made with Lady Umbrog. The giants had kept up their end of the bargain, but they would only get what Rhett had promised if he became emperor.

Rhett had never broken his word, and he wasn't going to start now. He just needed his body to cooperate long enough for him to keep his promise.

"Lady Umbrog." Rhett turned to face the giant leader. "I'll make sure Lagonia's eastern farmlands are yours, regardless of who ends up sitting on the throne. I swear it."

Lady Umbrog stared at Rhett in a way that would make most people uncomfortable. Then, she flashed him a brief smile. "You may call me Winny."

* * *

Rhett nodded to Samara when he stepped inside the Insorsiled tent. He headed straight for his and Liss's bedroom.

Liss was looking out a window that hadn't been there the last time he'd been in the tent. Her brow was furrowed in thought as she chewed on one of her nails. It was a new habit for her—one she'd picked up the day Rhett started showing symptoms of the contagion.

They hadn't talked about any of it. There hadn't been time. In the two days that had passed since Rhett's first pustule appeared, all of their attention had been on plans for securing the cape, rescuing his soldiers' families, and getting back into Insorsil despite the entire kingdom wanting him dead. All of their planning had been a welcome distraction…a reprieve…from thinking about everything that was out of Rhett's control.

"Are you ready to go?" Liss asked, her attention still on the view outside the window.

"Just going to get cleaned up," he replied, heading for the washroom.

Liss had barely spoken the last two days, unless it was about their plans to find more of the immunity flowers. Rhett hated that she was hanging all of her hopes on something that, even if they could find it, likely wouldn't be of any use to him.

Samara had theorized there was a chance that if he ate enough of the immunity flowers, their magic might stop any more damage from being done to his body. Rhett was less optimistic.

Liss had been desperate enough to plan on waylaying one of the invincible soldiers and convince him to take his pin off. Rhett had stopped her just in time before she got herself killed.

Besides, as Samara had explained, the invincibility pins couldn't help Rhett now that he was Infected. The pins only protected a wearer from a threat outside of one's body. Since the contagion was already inside him, an invincibility pin would be useless.

When her original plan failed, Liss had only become more determined to find the flowers hidden in Gatria's underground treasure trove.

According to Liss, the flowers were just a backup plan in case Rhett ever got to the contagion's second stage, which she was still hoping he would avoid.

He shut the door to the washroom before stripping, even though he wasn't prone to modesty around Liss. Rhett didn't want her to see how quickly the disease was progressing. It was the reason why he kept as much of his body covered as he could, even though his clothes rubbed mercilessly against the open pustules.

What had been a single, open blister on his arm two days ago had multiplied. His arms, legs, chest, and back were covered. The ones on his inner thighs were the worst, but they were bearable. The expression in Liss's eyes whenever she looked at him, part hope and part heartbreak, was worse than the disease ravaging his body.

He bathed quickly, hissing in a breath as the antiseptic he'd found in the medicine chest burned his open sores. At least they hadn't reached his face. That would be harder to hide from Liss.

When he was clean and dressed, all of the ugly, oozing blisters covered by his usual black uniform, he opened the medicine chest. He grabbed a jar of quick-heal and brought it back out to the bedroom for Liss's fingers. He motioned for her to sit on the edge of the bed. Kneeling before her, he took one of her hands in his.

He didn't say anything about her bloody cuticles and ragged nail beds. He just scooped out some of the quick-heal and went finger by finger, applying the salve as gently as he could.

After his first pustule appeared, Liss had tried putting the Insorsiled medicine on the blister. It had healed up and then reopened before Liss had even capped the jar.

When Rhett glanced up, he saw Liss was biting her lip like she was trying not to cry.

He knew her emotions had nothing to do with the pain in her fingers.

"Liss," he began, but she shook her head furiously.

"We don't even know for sure that you'll even reach the second stage."

The stubborn set of her jaw stopped him from trying to argue.

"Even if you do get to the second stage," Liss continued, "you'll be fine once we have the immunity." She raised her chin and glared, silently daring him to argue. "So will that soldier who is now Infected."

"You know that wasn't your fault, right?" Rhett lifted her newly-healed fingers and kissed them one by one.

She offered him a brave smile that didn't reach her blue eyes.

There were so many things he should say to her. But Rhett had never put much faith in words. So, instead, he leaned forward and pressed his lips to hers.

Liss made a small, desperate sound that chipped away at his insides a little more. He let his fingers glide through the silken strands of her hair as he deepened the kiss, knowing all the while it was the exact opposite of what he should be doing.

With a groan, he forced himself to pull back.

"I'm sorry," he managed, his heart galloping in his chest like a runaway dragon. "I shouldn't."

"Why not?" Liss asked, her chest rising and falling as swiftly as his.

"It's not right for me to try and hold onto you."

Not when they'd soon be torn apart.

If he was less selfish, he'd be doing everything he could to distance himself from her. He should be letting her move on. Instead, he was trying to hold onto her as tightly as he could. The thought of giving her space made him sicker than the contagion.

Liss let out a humorless laugh. "I think it's a little late for that, Rhett. I'm not going to stop being head over heels for you just because you're—"

Liss looked away. Before Rhett could say or do anything, a knock on the door had them jerking apart.

"You guys ready?" Samara called.

"Ready," Liss replied, scrambling off the bed and hurrying to the door.

As an Insorsiled, Samara had natural immunity to the contagion even though she was an Empty. She wore armored pants and a heavy jacket, which she must have borrowed from one of Rhett's female soldiers. An over-stuffed cloth bag was slung over her shoulder. Her long, white-blonde hair was plaited back in the style worn by the female soldiers in Rhett's army. Even though Samara wasn't a soldier, she looked like she was ready to walk into battle. The friendly, good-humored expression she usually wore had been replaced by a determination that mirrored Liss's.

Wilsean, dressed in an anti-contagion suit, had his bag slung over one shoulder and his bow strapped to his back.

"Let's go get these flowers," Wilsean said.

It was a short walk to the steep flight of rickety stairs that led down to the dock. A raft was already waiting for them in the shallow water. As the others climbed onto the vessel, Rhett turned back. The sun was setting over the cape, and rays of pink and orange cut through the gray clouds. The colors softened the frozen landscape.

As Rhett looked at his empire, he came to a staggering realization. Unless they discovered something miraculous in Insorsil, this might be the last time he glimpsed Lagonia.

CHAPTER 4

Liss kept her eyes peeled for any sign of danger as their raft docked amid all the other small boats crammed into the narrow Insorsiled channel. Wilsean steered them through the watery traffic without drawing any extra attention. She and Rhett hunched their shoulders and kept their faces downturned. They were the two most wanted people in the kingdom, and if anyone recognized them, their mission would be over before it began.

This watery passage between the far tip of the cape and Insorsil had enabled them to cross the distance between the two realms in half the time it took to travel on the open road. The passage wasn't useful for the large Lagonia war ships or merchant vessels, but it suited their purposes perfectly.

Under normal circumstances, it would be easy for Liss to blend in with the bustling market crowds. But images of her and Rhett's faces were still plastered on just about every building in the kingdom. After their part in murdering Insorsil's former queen, they would be killed on sight by anyone who recognized them.

Samara would also be executed if she was caught. As an Empty, it was illegal for her to ever set foot in Insorsil again.

But Liss hadn't earned her title of Opal Smoke for nothing.

Within seconds of getting on solid ground, Liss had stolen Insorsil cloaks for all of them. Wilsean did what he could to cover his bright yellow anti-contagion suit with the cloak, but his towering height ensured a few inches of the suit were visible below the hem.

Liss snatched two staffs for Wilsean and Rhett, which helped make them appear a little less Lagonian…at least from a distance.

The four of them cut through the crowded alleys, which were full of afternoon shoppers.

Liss had to stop herself from cringing when a group of slavers dressed in Lagonia livery, weapons dripping from their belts, crossed the alley in front of her. They seemed to be on a mission of their own. None of them looked twice at Liss's group.

Liss was almost disappointed. She'd been hoping for a challenge…or even a fight. Anything to take her mind off all the *what ifs* that were like a crushing weight on her chest.

Liss was so wrapped up in her own thoughts that she wasn't paying attention to her surroundings. She was drawn back into the present by a painful jab in her ribs.

"Look," Samara whispered, as Liss rubbed her aching side and glared at her friend.

Liss followed the direction of Samara's gaze. A line of Insorsiled were coming down the road toward them. Everyone else was pressing themselves against the sides of shops to get out of their way.

Liss really looked at the witches and warlocks coming toward them. Their colorful cloaks were torn and filthy. Their waist-length hair was matted like they'd gotten caught in a ferocious gale…followed by a dust storm. Their eyes stared straight ahead, seeing nothing. The part that made Liss's blood run cold was their souls.

Emotions came with the act of living. There were positive and negative emotions, but everyone felt. Except, these Insorsiled didn't.

Their souls were blank.

When people were asleep or unconscious, their souls had a cloudy, indiscernible feel. These souls weren't like that.

These Insorsiled were alive, and at the same time, they weren't. A shudder traveled down Liss's spin.

"What's wrong with them?" she whispered to Samara.

"I think they're under a manipulation spell," Samara whispered back. "Gatria did something like this to her subjects when she was alive, but it was much more subtle." Her amber eyes widened as she studied the dead-souled Insorsiled. "The new king must be really powerful to have these people so strongly under his control."

Once the Insorsiled were out of sight, everyone else began to go on their way. There were a few hushed whispers, but for the most part, everyone just seemed to be relieved to be free of those disconcerting people.

"Come on," Liss muttered, ushering Samara into the crowd that was merging back into the alley. The guys hadn't stopped and were half a street ahead.

Liss was so intent on the emotionless Insorsiled that she ignored the irritating buzzing near her ear. She swatted at the insect, but it was immediately replaced by another.

The buzzing transformed to a high-pitched cackle.

Liss froze.

"Found her, I did. Found her so good," the squeaky voice said. "Honey. Gonna get me my honey. Honey, honey, honey."

Lightning fast, Liss reached up and snatched the tree fairy out of the air. The tiny creature hissed and squirmed in Liss's grasp.

"Liss!"

She spun around at Samara's cry.

The diabolical creatures were all around Samara. Two of them had yanked down her hood, and a handful of others were tugging on her long hair as they attempted to drag her in the opposite direction. They were all jabbering about honey.

A tremendous buzzing filled the air, and then a swarm of tree fairies appeared overhead.

Liss pulled out her knife as the shocked Insorsiled all around them stopped to stare. They were drawing the attention of every witch and warlock in this crowded alley.

Not good.

The tree fairies descended, chattering about honey and uttering the foulest curses Liss had ever heard.

"Shut up," Liss ordered the tiny creatures.

She should have known better. The order only incited them, making them even louder. At this rate, it wouldn't be long before the slavers came to investigate.

They had to get out of here.

Liss sliced straight through two of the fairies with her knife, wincing as the halves of their bodies flew in opposite directions. She smacked the flat of her blade across the fairies grabbing onto Samara's hair. While the little creatures were temporarily stunned, Liss grabbed her friend's hand.

"Come on!" Liss waved her blade in a spastic motion to part the swarm of fairies as she pulled Samara away.

"Is that…Opal Smoke?" a warlock asked, pointing at Liss.

Shit.

"It's her! It's the queen killer!"

Double shit.

Liss and Samara ran.

Rhett and Wilsean were shoving their way back through the crowd toward them with their weapons drawn.

"What the hell's going on?" Wilsean demanded.

"Run!" Liss and Samara both shouted.

Cries of *murderer* and *queen slayer* followed them as they bolted down the narrow alley.

Liss led their small group as they tore through the crowd. Samara screamed out a warning. Rhett wrenched Liss to the side. A burst of green sparks flew past and scorched a hole through a nearby shop.

There wasn't time to marvel over the near miss. From the looks of it, the entire kingdom was after them. Liss heard the thrum of an Insorsiled bike somewhere in the distance.

If they didn't find somewhere to hide, they were done for.

Liss wracked her brain as the four of them continued their mad dash. Her time as a thief had made her intimately acquainted with Insorsil's hidden passageways and back alleys. If there was anyone who could get them out of this mess, it was her.

"This way," she shouted, swerving down a tiny alley that smelled like fermenting potions. The others' footsteps pounded behind her.

Liss ripped a pin out of her hair and had the nearest shop door unlocked in two seconds flat. She already knew it was empty because she didn't sense any souls inside. She also knew this shop was connected to another alley, where they'd be able to lose themselves among the shoppers.

Liss's plan would have worked…if it wasn't for the goddamn tree fairies.

First came the telltale buzzing of their wings, followed by more chatter about honey. No fewer than a hundred tree fairies zoomed through a small crack in the window.

Liss noticed their eyes had a golden glow and their stomachs were distended. Even their skin had a sickly golden flush. From the way they jerked and spasmed as they flew, Liss could tell something was seriously wrong with them.

There were too many to kill, but that wasn't going to stop Rhett and Wilsean from trying.

Liss forgot all about the fairies when she heard the click of the door they'd just come through. She turned and raised her knife, just as a boy with a mop of orange hair and shimmering opal skin stepped into the shop.

"Spence?"

"Hey, Liss." Spence scratched his messy hair as he looked at her. There was a mixture of guilt and regret on his soul.

Liss tensed as another person entered the shop, but it was only Arom.

Arom had been one of the few Extended willing to help Liss free the slaves in Lagonia. His ability to create smells out of thin air had been surprisingly useful during that mission. He also had one of the gentlest souls Liss had ever encountered.

"What are you doing here?" Liss asked them.

Rhett and Wilsean stopped killing the fairies and turned their attention on the new intruders.

"Trying to find you," Spence said. "I came here to steal food after the wagons brought us back to the hideout, but then we saw the tree fairies on the hunt. We came to warn you before they found you."

"A little late on that, kid," Wilsean said as he slashed out at the fairies with his knife.

Rhett knocked the hilt of his dagger into another fairy that was trying to lift Samara up by her braid.

"Why did you come back here?" Spence ask Liss, ignoring the others. "You know everyone in Insorsil wants to kill you."

"We, uh, need to get some medicine," Liss said.

She didn't want to get into the specifics. The truth about Rhett's weakness seemed like information that should only be given out on a need-to-know basis.

"D-don't worry, L-Liss," Arom said, his opal skin rippling with color as he blushed. "I'll m-make the fairies go away."

The dusty air around them filled with the rich scent of honey. Liss breathed deeply, even though she knew it was just Arom's Extension. The tree fairies were salivating.

The fairies zoomed back out of the crack in the window without a backward glance, lured away by the irresistible smell of honey.

"Thanks for that," Liss said.

Arom's nose wiggled and he wiped at the sweat gleaming on his bald spot. He stuttered something that Liss couldn't catch.

Rhett raised his eyebrows at Liss, clearly having picked up on the way Arom was looking at her.

She cleared her throat and tried to ignore the longing in Arom's soul. "So, my mom's using the tree fairies to track me down?"

"And bring you back to the hideout." Spence nodded. "She's…really upset."

Liss cringed. They hadn't agreed on much these past few weeks, but she still loved her mom. Nya already lived with enough pain. Liss didn't want to add to that burden.

"Strange thing about the tree fairies," Spence said, tilting his head in consideration. "They've been dropping dead in droves. No one can figure out why."

"Honey is a slow-acting poison for them," Rhett said, not meeting Liss's gaze. "They get addicted to it. Eventually, it kills them."

Spence glared at Rhett. "You knew that from the beginning, and you still used honey to control them?"

"Yes," came Rhett's terse reply.

Spence's scowl deepened. "You really don't care who you kill, do you?"

"Do you know what's been going on in Insorsil?" Liss asked quickly. They didn't have time for an argument right now. "It seems like there are some strange things happening."

Spence shrugged. "Krozor Ragnor Mantis has crowned himself king, which I'm guessing you already knew."

Liss hadn't known, but even if she had, that name meant nothing to her. She turned to Samara.

"My siblings told me he was the new king," Samara said. "No one knows much about him, except that he's a reclusive archaeologist. Or at least, he was before he became king.

"Apparently, he only leaves his hut in outer Insorsil when he's going in search of some ancient artifact." She took a breath. "My brother said Krozor still lives out there and only comes to the castle for meetings. He doesn't care about jewels or possessions, and he's the first Insorsil monarch to refuse to live in the castle."

"Wonderful," Wilsean muttered. "Another insane monarch was just what we needed."

Samara tilted her head in thought. "I remember my parents talking about him a while back because of a controversial paper he published." She narrowed her eyes in disgust. "It was about how the Insorsiled should isolate themselves. He had a lot to say about how useless and expendable anyone without magic is."

"I'll show him expendable," Wilsean growled, which made Samara smile.

A bigoted Insorsil king wasn't ideal, but it was a small problem compared to the others they currently had on their plate.

Worry about today's problems now, and tomorrow's problems later.

That sentiment had kept Liss alive for twenty years and helped her keep her priorities straight. The only *today* problem she had was curing Rhett's opal contagion.

"The Insorsiled want Rhett bad," Spence continued, with another sour look in Rhett's direction. "They're not going to stop hunting you until he fries for what he did to Gatria."

Unlike Mari and Jema, the other two kids on Liss's old thieving crew, Spence had never really warmed to Rhett.

"I think Krozor is using their hatred of Rhett to unify his people," Spence continued.

"They'll need to get in line if they want to kill Rhett," Wilsean said.

Rhett seemed completely unphased that the Extended, Insorsiled, and invincible Lagonians were after his blood.

"Are you going to tell my mom we were here?" Liss asked Arom, since she already knew Spence wouldn't say anything.

"Of c-course not," Arom said, looking a little wounded.

"Thank you." Liss smiled at him, which seemed to make the Aromatic's hurt evaporate.

"What do you need from me and the girls?" Spence asked.

By *the girls*, he was referring to Mari and little Jema.

"Keep your Infected people away from Lagonia," Wilsean said, his voice hard with barely-restrained anger.

Rhett shot Wilsean a look.

"Just stay safe," Liss told him. "Don't go searching for trouble."

Spence crossed his arms and frowned, like she'd just said something deeply offensive.

"Why does everyone keep saying that to us?" Spence demanded. "If I hear one more time that we're just kids and need to stay in the hideout—"

"Okay, okay." Liss tried not to laugh. "Just keep your ears open, and let me know if you find out anything that might be important."

A mischievous grin spread across Spence's face.

"Are you saying the girls and I should become the new Opal Smoke?"

Liss matched his smile with one of her own. "That's exactly what I'm saying."

CHAPTER 5

Samara followed the others on a twisting path through the labyrinth of inner Insorsil. She'd been embarrassed to discover that Liss knew the kingdom better than she did, despite the fact that Samara had grown up here. The guys parted the crowd with their huge bodies and menacing expressions. Samara was the only one who didn't have anything to contribute.

If only she had magic—

Samara cut that thought off right there.

She managed to keep her mind clear of negative thoughts…for a few minutes, at least. The closer they got to the castle, the more nervous she became.

She had given all of them, especially Liss, reason to hope that they'd find the cure to opal contagion down in Gatria's underground treasure trove of secrets.

In all honestly, Samara wasn't even sure if they'd be able to get into the most highly-guarded place in all of Insorsil. And even if they could get in and find more of the immunity, Samara wasn't sure the flowers would even be useful.

Unless Samara's witchdoctor sister could discover a way to transform prevention into a cure, the flowers wouldn't do Rhett any good.

Still, hope of finding the cure was all that that seemed to be keeping Liss from losing her mind.

When Liss stopped without warning, Samara lurched into her back.

She heard Liss's gasp. Beside her, Wilsean's whole body tensed.

Samara looked at him and then followed the line of his furious gaze.

He was staring at an ugly wooden structure had been set up in the castle's courtyard. Looming in front of them were gallows.

The gallows were newly erected. Samara could still see where the earth was darker from having been freshly dug to anchor the wood. She could smell the wood shavings that were littered across the icy ground.

Samara's knees began to buckle. If it wasn't for the arm Wilsean wrapped around her waist, she probably would have collapsed.

Seven bodies swung in the wind, the ropes creaking from the corpses' weight.

Samara looked at the dead warlocks' faces. Her stomach curdled at the sight of their eye sockets, which had been picked clean by the crows. Their blue lips were parted in expressions of agony.

Samara began to shiver.

"Those poor people," Liss murmured. "No one deserves to be put on display like that, no matter what their crime."

"Traitors who opposed the new king?" Wilsean guessed.

"They're not traitors." Samara's voice came out as a whisper. She swallowed.

The Insorsiled used magic for all of their executions…with a single exception. There was only one type of person whose crime was shameful enough to merit this non-magical death.

"They're Empties," Samara said, her voice coming out only a little wobbly. "This is what happens when they're discovered in the kingdom after banishment."

It's what would happen to me if anyone here recognized me.

Wilsean tightened his grip on her waist. Usually, his overprotectiveness annoyed her. Now, she leaned against him, taking strength from his solid presence.

"And they have the nerve to call the Extended barbaric," Liss said, gripping her knife even though there was no target for her anger. "I have half a mind to string this King Krozor up there, and see how much he likes it."

"I like the way you think, Liss," Wilsean said, his voice tight with all of the anger he was concealing. To Samara, he said, "I'd like to see any one of these magic freaks try to lay a finger on you."

Rhett gave a solemn nod of agreement.

Warmth spread through Samara. In that moment, she didn't care that the Insorsiled hated people like her simply for the way they'd been born.

"Come on," she said, giving the gallows a wide berth.

She kept her attention fixed on the beautiful castle in front of them, even though the sight of those corpses was burned into the back of her eyelids.

The castle's glass surface reflected the winter sun. Dozens of spherical domes appeared to balance in mid-air over the main body of the castle. They were held in place by a network of unseen spells. The domes contained various meeting spaces and recreation rooms, which were accessible through Insorsiled wind tunnels that levitated a person from one to the next.

Because Samara's parents were royal advisors, she had spent a fair amount of time in the castle as a child. She and Ambrosius, her older brother by one year, had gotten to know just about every inch of the castle while their parents were stuck in boring meetings. That was how she knew to lead her friends away from all the main entrances and to a metal grate the palace guards stayed far away from.

"Phew, what's that smell?" Wilsean asked, checking to make sure the hood of his anti-contagion suit was fully zipped.

"The garbage chute," Samara said. She unlatched the grate and flourished her hands at the dark, filthy tunnel beyond. "And our way into the castle."

"You're serious?" Wilsean asked her.

In answer, Samara braced her hands on the lip of the tunnel and hoisted herself inside.

"Are you sure you weren't a thief in a former life?" Liss asked her, giving her a playful nudge as she joined Samara in the tunnel. Liss's voice came out nasal-y, since she was pinching her nose with two fingers.

Samara breathed into the collar of her shirt. Only Rhett seemed unphased by the retched stink.

The passage was narrower than it had seemed when she was a child. They all had to slither through the rank tunnel on their stomachs. Wilsean, for all his towering height, was thin enough to move through the space without a problem. Rhett, with his broad shoulders, had to twist his body from side to side to make it through the narrow passage.

"Good thing you've been on a diet the past two days," Wilsean told Rhett, his voice echoing against the metal pinning them in.

Trust Wilsean to make light out of something that was tearing him apart.

It hadn't escaped Samara's notice how, every time Wilsean looked at his friend, his body went rigid.

The garbage chute deposited them into the laundry tower, where they all took grateful gulps of soap-scented air. Since laundry was done with magic rather than by hand, there was no one inside to see the four filthy people who fell onto the mountain of sheets and clothing.

"Sorry," Liss muttered to the empty room when she got off a pile of freshly-pressed linens and saw the grime stains she'd left behind.

The pile of folded linens leapt up at the sound of her voice, let off an annoyed puff of starch, and deposited themselves into a vat of boiling water.

From there, a few narrow servant's passages brought them to the queen's suite. It was unguarded, since the queen was dead and King Krozor didn't live in the castle.

"You guys ready?" Samara asked when they reached the set of double doors that led into the queen's chamber.

"We're with you, beautiful," Wilsean said, brushing his hand down her back.

Even though he was wearing gloves, it didn't stop a pleasant shiver from going through her.

"I'm glad you're here," she whispered to him.

"I wouldn't be anywhere else," he replied.

Samara reached for the door handles, letting out a huff of annoyance when they were locked.

"Step aside," Liss said in a lofty voice, "and make way for the master."

A door at the other end of the hallway opened. They all jerked in the direction of the well-dressed witch who was standing in the open doorway. She opened her mouth to scream.

The sound never escaped her parted lips. She slid to the floor, one of Wilsean's throwing knives sticking out of her neck.

Guilt squeezed Samara's inside.

"Don't worry," Liss said as she knelt down to inspect the locks. "Her soul was rotten."

Alright, then.

A few seconds later, Liss had the doors open.

"Someday, you're going to have to teach us your secrets," Wilsean told her, shaking his head in admiration.

"A thief never reveals her secrets," Liss replied as she stepped into the dark sitting room.

"I'm not exactly sure where the entrance to the grotto is," Samara told Liss, peering into the dusty room. "I think—"

A shrill clanging drowned out her words.

All four of them exchanged a panicked look. Glass bells hanging from the ceiling were frantically ringing.

"Did we do that?" Liss asked, having to yell over the deafening sound.

Samara glanced down at their feet. Sure enough, there was a line of white powder that had been disturbed when they stepped over the threshold. She swore.

"The floor's dusted with an alarm spell," Samara told the others.

"I take it this spell is going to bring every guard in the castle here?" Wilsean asked, somehow speaking calmly and still making himself heard over the bells.

Samara could only nod as fear clawed its way through her insides.

"Well then, I guess that means we shouldn't dawdle," Liss said, clearly in her element.

Rhett and Wilsean locked and barricaded the doors, while Liss started feeling along the walls for a hidden entrance.

Samara mimicked Liss's gestures, even though she had no idea what she should be searching for.

If only she wasn't an Empty, she could conjure a locating spell. They could be down in the grotto already.

Samara jumped when the first blast of magic came from the other side of the door. The smell of burning filled the air, and the wooden frame rattled.

Wilsean and Rhett thrust their backs against the furniture they'd piled against the doors as another spell made the whole blockade lurch.

Panic clawed its way up Samara's throat. In another minute, the Insorsiled on the other side of that door would come barging in. It would be four of them against what sounded like dozens.

"How's it coming over there, Liss?" Rhett asked.

Liss didn't respond. She was staring at a life-sized marble statue in the corner of the room. The naked statue's face was a perfect replica of the late queen. Samara couldn't speak to the likeness of the rest of the statue.

"Are we admiring the artwork or finding a way out of here?" Wilsean asked, grunting when a particularly strong spell made the doors bow inward.

Liss turned toward them, her blue eyes sparkling with mischief. She grasped the statue's hand and pulled up.

The solid-marble arm lifted easily, revealing a coiled spring hidden beneath. There was a sound of stone grating against stone, and then a panel behind the statue slid back to reveal a tunnel.

Samara let out a laugh that was half-surprise and half-relief.

"Let's go," Rhett said. The furniture blocking the door scraped against the ground as soon as his weight was no longer pressed against it.

Samara could hear voices and incantations coming from the other side of the door.

"Insorsiled are a strange bunch," Wilsean noted as he passed the statue and joined the rest of them in the tunnel.

No arguments here.

Samara wrenched the lever on the inside of the tunnel just as a crash came from the other side of the room. Wood cracked. Furniture squealed in protest as it slid across the floor.

The wall panel slid shut, encasing them in darkness.

For several seconds, all Samara heard was their harsh breathing. The stone must have been very thick, because she heard nothing of the chaos that must be happening on the other side of the wall.

With a shaking hand, Samara reached in her bag for the Insorsiled stone she had brought. The stone heated and let off a soft yellow glow that brought their surroundings into stark relief.

There was a mechanical whine, and then a metal panel slid across the door.

"We're locked in," Rhett said in a calm voice that wasn't enough to slow Samara's raging pulse.

"I don't think so," Liss said, running her fingers along the lever. "I think it's only meant to keep anyone on the other side of the wall from getting in."

"Well then, we better not pull that lever until we're ready to battle with the entire castle," Wilsean said.

He started forward.

"No one move," Samara said quickly.

If an alarm spell had been used in the outer room, there was a good chance this tunnel was also enspelled.

It smelled strongly of dirt, but beneath that more overpowering scent, Samara detected a faint burning odor. That meant there was magic around, and Samara was willing to bet the spells down here weren't the friendly sort.

Removing her pack, Samara took out the velvet bag she'd stuffed full of the Insorsiled beads her siblings had sent her a while back.

"No need to get dressed up on my account," Wilsean said, raising an eyebrow at what must look to him like jewelry.

"Gatria always liked mazes," Samara explained as she broke apart the clasp on one string of beads. She took a bead off the necklace and let it fall to the ground. The stone emitted a blue glow that cut through the darkness. "In case we get turned around, these will help us find our way back."

"Have I ever told you you're brilliant?" Liss asked Samara.

Samara couldn't hold back a smile at that.

"Sexiest brain ever made," Wilsean said, making Samara duck her head in embarrassment. "Sexiest eyes, too. And body. And—"

"Focus, man," Rhett said.

Wilsean pulled two throwing knives from his jacket and started forward. Samara grabbed his arm before he could take another step.

"I'm going first," she said, holding up a hand when he started to argue.

Samara raised the Insorsiled stone and peered into the darkness ahead. There was an archway several yards in front of them. Beyond it, the path split off to the left and right. She squinted until she found what she was looking for.

"That's what I thought," she whispered. To Wilsean, she said, "Do you see that faint shimmer in the air? Beneath the archway?"

Wilsean looked at where she was pointing. He nodded.

"Hit it with a knife," she told him.

He didn't ask questions. She stopped him just before he could release the blade as another thought occurred to her.

"Lie down on the ground," she ordered the others.

"I love it when you're bossy," Wilsean said as he lowered himself to the ground and readied his knife.

Samara dropped to her stomach on the hard ground. With a shrug, Liss followed. Rhett joined them last.

If Samara was wrong, she'd have to endure her friends' weird looks. If she was right—

Wilsean threw the knife.

Seconds later, a whistling sound filled the tunnel. Hundreds of arrows appeared out of nowhere and sped down the tunnel toward them. The barbed tips slashed through the air.

Samara winced as one of the shafts came close enough to stir her hair. There was a chorus of thuds as the arrows sunk into the solid stone and metal at their backs.

Samara got to her feet and brushed herself off.

"Damn." Wilsean stood and studied the arrows. "How did you know?"

"Just a hunch," she said. The real answer was far more complicated.

As a young teenager, when she'd harbored the hope that she might force her body to produce magic, she'd learned everything there was to know about magical theory. While her siblings created advanced magic simply by following their instincts, she read about the how's and why's of every spell, potion, and charm on record.

All of her knowledge hadn't resulted in an ounce of magical energy inside her.

But her studies hadn't been worthless. It was the reason why she'd known that the counter-clockwise swirl of these particles, combined with their slight apricot color, meant it was a materializing spell. The particles had hovered in the center of the tunnel, so Samara knew that whatever came at them would shoot down the tunnel instead of coming from either the ceiling or floor.

From there, it hadn't been much of a leap to think that whatever materialized would be of the killing variety.

After that, no one argued about Samara leading the way down the tunnel.

"This one won't hurt us," she said, studying a faint pulsing light on the ground. "It's magic-seeking, and since none of us have magic, it won't give us any trouble."

"That's a rare bit of good luck," Wilsean noted.

"It's not luck." Samara shrugged. "Gatria never imagined anyone without magic would try to break in here."

"How wonderfully ironic," Liss said, delighted by the queen's oversight. "You gotta love good old Insorsiled arrogance."

They paused when they reached a juncture where the path split off.

Both paths looked the same. Neither offered any obvious clues about which one they should take.

"Any ideas?" Samara asked the others.

"Right," Liss said with confidence.

"How do you know?" Rhett asked, his gravelly voice echoing in the chamber.

"Because I can feel evil souls in that direction. Lots of them."

"And we want to go toward the evil souls?" Wilsean asked.

"Yes," Samara and Liss said at the same time.

"We're going to have to pass through a series of challenges," Samara explained. "Going toward the danger will bring us closer to where we want to be."

"And I thought this mission wouldn't be any fun," Wilsean said, smiling as he nocked an arrow.

CHAPTER 6

Jaikon signaled to his soldiers to spread out. He dismounted and gave his
reins a sharp yank, keeping his winged dragon from lifting off the
ground. The beast twisted its neck and opened its mouth. Jaikon easily
sidestepped the gust of fire that came at him.

He could have let the fire engulf him, since his pin would keep him
from harm, but it was an old habit to avoid his dragon's periodic attempts
to fry him. Besides, Jaikon didn't know whether the pin's protection would
extend to his clothes. He didn't want scorched garments to distract from
the sweetness of his imminent victory.

This moment had already been delayed, since Krozor had called him to
Insorsil to retrieve the rest of the pins. Jaikon had been less than pleased to
run his own errand, but it had been a good excuse to parade his entire force
of invincible soldiers through the streets of Insorsil.

It had been an opportunity to remind the new Insorsil king that Jaikon
had something the warlock didn't…an army.

"Where did you say this hideout was?" Jaikon asked the Extended man
at his side.

When he didn't get an immediate answer, Jaikon dealt Burk a vicious
kick. Burk whimpered and curled his cadaverous body in on itself.

"Just a little farther," Burk said in that insufferable whisper of his.

The Extended man's thinning and filthy orange hair was plastered to his
scalp. With all of the grime, the man's opal skin was barely visible. He
twitched and muttered to himself as struggled to keep up.

Jaikon looked down as something crunched beneath his dragonhide
boots. He saw with little interest that the forest floor was littered with dead

tree fairy corpses. Their bones snapped and ground into dust beneath his heel.

The creatures were so fragile. So weak. So pathetic.

"Ahead," Burk whispered beside him. "Two people."

Jaikon signaled to his Chief Assassin and drew his sword.

They all moved quietly. The sooner this slaughter was finished, the sooner he could move on to more important tasks. It would be inconvenient if his soldiers needed to chase down any cowards who tried to flee.

Jaikon was overcome by an intense urge to turn around and go back the other way. The compulsion was so strong he would have capitulated without a second thought if he hadn't known to expect it.

They'd reached the ward surrounding the Extended hideout.

Jaikon gritted his teeth and pushed through. He sucked in a breath once he was on the other side.

A towering wall appeared before him.

He barely noticed the opal-faced freaks fumbling with their weapons and moving to stand in front of the door. All of his attention was locked on the wall itself. The inelegant, double-reinforced structure had Rhetteman's imprint all over it.

That traitor had helped the Extended. And were those Lagonian weapons in the opals' hands?

Fury ignited.

Jaikon handed off his gold dragon to Elouicia, ignoring the Chief Assassin's growl at the tacit order to stay behind. Jaikon strode forward.

"Emperor Jaikon." One of the Extended guards sneered, making Jaikon's title sound like an insult.

For that alone, Jaikon unceremoniously cut the man down where he stood.

He walked around the gurgling, blood-spurting body. The other Extended guard pressed his back to the door, like he could block Jaikon's entrance by sheer force of will.

The Extended man's hands were shaking so badly he dropped his sword. Jaikon watched in disgust as the man tried to bend down to gather his weapon. The Extended man's knees were wobbling so forcefully that he couldn't even manage the simple task.

Then, to Jaikon's further amusement, the man abandoned his feeble attempts to reclaim his weapon and began to blow out air onto Jaikon.

The Extended man inhaled deeply, exhaled in Jaikon's direction, and then repeated the strange exercise.

"Are you having a fit?" Jaikon asked. "Or is this some unfortunate Extension I'm unaware of?"

Genuine curiosity stayed Jaikon's sword. There were so many useless, arbitrary Extensions, that it was impossible to keep track of them all.

"You might kill me," the weakling man said in a tremulous voice, "but at least I'll die knowing you won't be far behind me."

"What are you babbling about?" Jaikon raised an eyebrow at the man.

"Opal contagion." The man spoke slowly, like Jaikon was the dim one. "You're going to end up like all the others."

Jaikon offered the man a smile that was the honed edge of a blade. "Nothing about me will ever be like *all the others.*"

Jaikon grabbed the man by the back of his neck and pulled him close.

"There will be no opal contagion for me, or any other death," Jaikon told the stunned Extended. "I'm invincible."

Then, Jaikon skewered the weakling's body on his sword.

Jaikon stepped over the corpse slumped in front of the door and used his sword to slice right through the door's lock.

Jaikon's tolerant mood had disappeared. He wanted to kill every one of these Infected with his bare hands. Not just because they were threatening his hold over his own empire, but because it was one more blow he could deal to the traitorous Rhetteman Loniger.

The wall and stolen weapons proved Rhetteman was as dedicated to his whore's people as he was to the useless Lagonian peasants. Those simpering, impoverished fools worshipped the traitor like he was some kind of deity.

The same peasants who should be worshipping their sovereign.

Jaikon let himself into the Extended hideout and came to a dead halt. Their wagons were there, parked along the hideout's far wall. There were gardens bursting with vegetation despite the layer of snow covering the ground.

But there wasn't a single person in sight.

Without looking to the side, Jaikon delivered a swift blow to Burk's spine. The man let out a wheezing cry and toppled over.

"You warned them we were coming, didn't you, Burk?" Jaikon kept his voice soft in the way he did before he killed.

"No, Your Majesty," Burk whispered. "Even if I had warned them, the Insorsiled contract between us would have forced me to tell you about it."

Jaikon knew he was telling the truth. Burk's part of the agreement was that he had to tell the Emperor everything he knew about the Extended. The other half of that contract was the only reason why Burk wasn't dangling off the end of Jaikon's sword.

Jaikon didn't keep useless companions, and now that Burk had delivered all he knew about the Extended, he was worthless. But every time Jaikon raised his sword for the killing strike, tendrils of ink began to squeeze around his lungs, reminding him.

He was stuck with the insufferable Infected fool.

A new voice, just as whispery as Burk's, drew Jaikon's attention. A man—a Lagonian man—was sitting up against the wall of a dilapidated cottage. His wrists were tied in front of him, and he was bound to a stake in the ground. At first glance, it appeared the man was dying from opal contagion.

Even though Jaikon couldn't get the virus, he was overcome with the urge to back away.

When Jaikon looked past the scabbed-over pustules, he realized the man's skin had an opal sheen. It wasn't nearly as bright as the Extended themselves, but it was a step beyond the sickly yellow tinge of those who were in the first stage of the contagion.

Everything about the man's appearance indicated he was in the second stage. His eyes didn't have that orange ring around them, though.

"How long have you been like this?" Jaikon asked.

"Three weeks," the man replied. "Don't get better. Don't get worse."

That was when Jaikon understood. This Lagonian was Infected, but he wasn't dying. He was a survivor.

"Funny, ain't it?" the man asked, letting out a wheezing chuckle. "Thought for sure I was a gonner, but then I just kept on livin'." He laughed again. "Trouble is, now that I'm Infected, no one wants me."

Jaikon had never actually encountered one of the survivors of opal contagion. It was said that one in two-hundred survived after being infected, although the actual number seemed much lower. This was the first one he'd heard about since his father was emperor.

Survivors took on the appearance of Extended and were still contagious, but never developed abilities. It was their offspring that became the full Extended package.

"Thought the rest of the Infected would let me stay with 'em, but they didn't take to me when I told 'em I'd been a slaver."

He smiled, displaying teeth that were brown from smoking.

"Where are the Extended?" Jaikon asked the man, looking pointedly around the empty hideout.

"Went to hunt Uninfected, but they'll be back," the man wheezed.

As Jaikon stared at the Infected man, his anger grew. The Extended had deprived him of an easy victory. Worse than that. They'd evaded him and had the audacity to go after Jaikon's own subjects.

Jaikon drew his sword.

The slaver gasped as his dim brain comprehended what was about to happen.

"Please, Majesty," the slaver begged. "I've been loyal to ya. I've killed Extended."

"And now you're one of them."

"I ain't—"

Jaikon's sword slid into the man with little resistance. The slaver's eyes bulged. His opal skin flickered. Then, he slumped.

He died easily, just like the rest of the Extended would…as soon as Jaikon found them.

"Majesty?" Elouicia asked, as soon as Jaikon reemerged on the other side of the wall.

Jaikon snatched up the reins and mounted his dragon.

"Find the Extended and kill them all," he ordered. "Bring Burk and the slavers to help you."

Jaikon had more important plans for his invincible soldiers.

Elouicia ran his tongue over his sharpened canines before folding himself into a bow. "It would be my pleasure, Majesty."

Jaikon slapped the flat of his blade over the dragon's shoulder. The beast screeched fire as its wings snapped open.

It was time for the continent to know that Jaikon Horowicken, II was not just the eternal emperor of Lagonia. He was the future leader of the entire developed world.

Jaikon felt his pocket grow hot, distracting him from the enticing future. He cursed as he tried to free the corresponder from his pocket one-handed. His right hand dangled uselessly by his side.

He was going to make Rhetteman's whore pay for that, he promised himself as he finally managed to free the corresponder. The pain in his right hand would be nothing compared to what he made that bitch suffer.

"What?" Jaikon demanded as soon as a face clarified in the glass sphere. It was one of the slavers guarding the palace. Jaikon hadn't bothered to learn any of their names, since they all looked the same.

"Majesty. The peasants are riotin' and burnin' the crop fields," the slaver reported.

Like roaches, Jaikon thought.

"Well, then make them stop," Jaikon said through clenched teeth.

"There's more trouble afoot," the slaver said. "It's not just the poor folks who are talkin'. Your courtiers are sayin' that if you'd started the opal contagion procedures your Master Interrogator was goin' on about, thousands of people would still be alive."

Jaikon gave his dragon's reins a vicious yank.

"There's one other thing," the slaver carried on, oblivious to Jaikon's mounting fury. "Your advisors are turnin' on you."

"What?"

"They're sayin' you lied about who really killed the last emperor." The slaver paused. "They're sayin' you murdered your father."

CHAPTER 7

Liss wiped sweat off her face.

So far, they'd encountered fifteen evil creatures, been hit with twelve different spells, and almost died as many times. Rhett and Wilsean were covered in the blood of all the terrifying beasts they'd slaughtered. They were all bruised and sore. Rhett's sleeve was still crackling from a fire that had almost incinerated all of them. Liss and Samara were stumbling from exhaustion.

It was impossible to tell how much time had passed, but Liss guessed they'd been in the grotto for more than a day.

Samara dropped a handful of beads as they got to yet another split in the path.

"Which way?" Wilsean asked.

A whooshing sound from the left answered that question. They turned down a short passage that ended at a thick wooden door.

"One soul," Liss reported. "It's faint, though." She wasn't sure if that was because they were far away or because the person was asleep.

Rhett pushed the door open and stepped inside. The rest of them followed.

Liss stepped into a room full of....

"Ghosts?" Wilsean gave Samara an incredulous look. "Ghosts aren't real."

"They're spirits," Samara said in a quiet voice. "I'd been wondering how Gatria kept the spells down here from disappearing after she died. Now, I get it."

"I don't," Wilsean said.

Neither did Liss.

"When an Insorsiled dies, their magic and any spells they had ongoing die with them," Samara explained. "The only exception is when an Insorsiled dies while they're casting a spell. These spirits," she gestured around them, "are the ones who created all of the spells down here. They're still tied to the world by the last spell they were casting when they died, and so they can't fully pass on."

The door behind them slammed shut, startling Liss into clutching her knife.

Wilsean grabbed the latch and pulled. As expected, the door didn't budge. They were locked in.

Liss scanned the room.

"There," she said, pointing at the door on the other side of the room. The lock had a faint gold glow. Liss didn't need Samara to tell her this was no ordinary lock.

As she looked around at the spirits, Liss realized every one of them was wearing a necklace with a white key dangling from a white ribbon. All of the keys were slightly different, although they were all about the right size and shape to fit the lock on the other door.

One of the spirits floated by, close enough to touch. Liss reached up and grasped for the key hanging around its neck.

A wave of ice hit her with so much force it tore the breath from her lungs. Her arms and legs instantly went numb.

"Liss?"

Rhett was beside her. As soon as his warm fingers touched her skin, she managed to draw in a breath.

Liss's teeth were chattering so much it was a struggle to get the words out.

"D-don't t-touch them. C-cold."

When she heard Wilsean's shocked gasp, she knew he'd felt their freezing touch, too.

Rhett wrapped an arm around Liss. When one of the spirits came flying straight for them, Rhett pulled Liss closer. He used his free arm to slash the blade of his dagger across the spirit's throat.

The spirit dissolved, and its ghostly particles doused both of them with a stinging, freezing gust of air.

Liss tried to scream, but it felt like shards of glass were embedded in her lungs. Beside her, Rhett was on his knees, his skin blue from the cold.

"Get to the door!" Samara called in a shrill voice.

The ghostly creatures, which had been drifting lazily around the room, grew agitated. The closer Liss and the rest of her group got to the door, the more the spirits congregated around them.

Liss's body felt like it was encased in a block of ice.

All at once, the spirits drifted away. Liss tried to feel relief, but she was too cold. And then there was definitely no relief, because she realized why the spirits were leaving them alone. The creatures had amassed themselves in front of the door that was their only way out of this frozen hell.

Wilsean tried to barrel his way through the spirits. He made it halfway before he collapsed. Rhett and Samara didn't even make it that far. They were both standing still as statues. If it wasn't for the emotions in their souls, Liss would have been terrified they were actually frozen solid.

Liss crawled on the ground, partly because she was too weak to stand, and partly because most of the spirits were hovering a few feet off the ground.

Their dangling ghost feet scraped over her back, making it feel like she was being gouged by icicles. Liss shivered and convulsed as the spirits swirled around her. No one else in her group was moving.

They were all going to die here.

Even if they made it to the door—a feat that was seeming more and more unlikely—they didn't have the key.

Every time Liss gathered her courage to reach into the spirits' iciness to try to snatch one of their necklaces, the key dissipated right along with the spirit who wore it.

Part of Liss's body was shrieking in pain, and the rest was numb. She wasn't sure which alarmed her more.

She was trying to drum up enough strength to crawl back to Rhett, so they could at least die in each other's arms, when she felt the brush of a soul. It was the same one she'd felt before…faint and barely there. She craned her neck, ignoring the way her skin felt brittle enough to snap.

There.

The woman looked just like the spirits. Her dress and skin were white. Her eyes were cloudy and unseeing. The only difference between her and the spirits was that she had a soul.

"That one," Liss gasped.

Her arm was too numb for her to point, and she had no more energy to explain. She dragged herself across the ground inch by excruciating inch.

If the woman was real, then the key around her neck had to be, too.

"Liss," Rhett said on a rasp.

"Door," she replied without turning back. "Get to the door."

Another spirit crashed through Liss. An agony of ice consumed her. She whimpered at the sight of her fingertips, which had turned bone-white.

Two more spirits sped through her before she reached the woman with the soul.

Liss didn't bother with pleasantries. She made her arm obey through sheer determination. She reached up and yanked the key dangling from the woman's throat.

The ribbon snapped, and the key came away in Liss's palm. *Solid.*

At the moment her hand closed around the key, the spirits began to shriek. The deafening sound filled the air. If Liss's hands were less numb, she would have covered her ears.

Rhett appeared beside her. Liss didn't know where he'd come from or where he found the strength to lift her into his arms. His body was as cold as stone. Somehow, he managed to get them to the other side of the room.

Liss grasped the key in fingers that had stiffened almost beyond use. Rhett put his hand around hers, not so much warming her as shielding her from any more cold.

She forced her numb hands to fit the key into the lock. The door burst open, and the four of them stumbled through to the other side.

Liss fell to the hard-packed earth and closed her eyes. Then, everything faded away into nothingness.

CHAPTER 8

Rhett eased his pack under Liss's head and draped his jacket over her. She had finally stopped shivering. Her skin was red now instead of blue, which seemed like a good sign. Samara had said the only way to heal from spirit-induced cold was sleep, and that Liss would be fine in a few hours. Samara had then collapsed on the ground and passed out next to Liss.

Rhett sat with his back to the wall a short way down the tunnel. He was close enough to keep an eye on the others, but far enough to be able to see all the way to where the path split. If anything came at them, he'd have time to react.

He heard Wilsean's footsteps behind him.

"Sleep," Rhett told his friend. "I'll keep watch."

Exhaustion clung to Rhett, but he'd never be able to relax with the pain lurking beneath his skin.

Rhett also wasn't interested in falling asleep when he was underground, encased by dirt and stone. It felt a little too much like an early preview of his near future.

He'd get an eternity of unconsciousness soon enough.

"I'm not tired," Wilsean said, his voice a little muffled from the hood of his anti-contagion suit.

Rhett knew how oppressive those suits were, but Wilsean hadn't uttered a single complaint.

A cloak fell around Rhett's shoulders. He hadn't even noticed he was shivering until the extra warmth eased the chattering of his teeth.

Wilsean sat down beside him without saying anything.

"If you want someone to fuss over, Samara's right there," Rhett said.

"Nah, she gets prickly if she thinks I'm trying to take care of her. You don't intimidate me, though."

Rhett humphed, but he pulled the cloak more tightly around himself.

For a while, they sat in companionable silence. It was like the hundred times they'd been on watch together. Except Rhett could feel his muscles melting away as the contagion ate through his insides.

He stayed still and breathed through the pain. It wasn't the worst he'd ever felt, but given his history, that wasn't saying a whole lot.

"That bad?" Wilsean asked.

Rhett turned to his friend, wondering why Wilsean's face looked blurry.

Rhett got to his feet, mumbling something incoherent. He made it only a few steps before he started to vomit. The light in the tunnel was enough to see that what came out of his body matched the taste in his mouth.

Blood.

Wilsean's hand was at his back as he continued to heave.

Where was all of this blood even coming from? If he kept this up, he'd have none left.

He would have collapsed if it hadn't been for Wilsean. The other man wrapped an arm around him and helped him limp a few steps away from the pool of blood soaking into the earth.

"I'm fine," Rhett managed, his voice a harsh whisper.

Wilsean ignored him, lowering both of their bodies until they were shoulder-to-shoulder against the wall. When Rhett glanced at his friend, he saw Wilsean was grinding his teeth and a muscle was ticking at his temple.

Rhett knew an apology was long overdue.

"I don't want to abandon all of you," Rhett said. He raised a shaking hand and wiped his mouth. He ignored the red stain that came away on his palm.

"I know, man." Wilsean stared straight ahead. "We don't blame you."

Rhett swallowed, trying to rid his mouth of the taste of blood. He glanced down the tunnel at Liss, relieved to see she'd slept through everything.

"Will you do something for me?" Rhett asked.

"Don't," Wilsean said, his voice cracking as he followed the direction of Rhett's gaze. "We're going to get those flowers. Buckets of them. You're going to be fine." He swallowed. "Who knows? Maybe you'll never even make it to the second stage. This whole mission could be an unnecessary waste of time."

Rhett was too tired to play that game with his best friend.

"My enemies," Rhett said, taking in a small breath. "If they can't have me, they'll go after her. I need to know—"

"You don't have to say it." Wilsean turned to face Rhett. "No one will ever hurt her. Ciago and I…we'll make sure she's safe."

Rhett nodded, because he didn't trust himself to speak. His gratitude and relief went beyond the power of words.

"My jewels are in the Lagonia vaults," he pushed on. "If Jaikon hasn't remembered to seize them, will you…will you give them to her?"

Not that Liss had any need of his paltry fortune. She was a thief and the most resourceful person he'd ever met. His jewels would provide her with nothing she couldn't get for herself.

Wilsean gave a quick jerk of his head.

Rhett barely resisted the urge to laugh at himself. This was what he was leaving the woman who meant everything to him…a few jewels and a long list of enemies.

"I swear to you." Wilsean put his hand to his heart. "She'll want for nothing. Well," he slid a glance at Rhett, "she'll want for nothing that friendship and money can provide."

"Thank you."

For several minutes, they were both silent.

"This is what she was afraid of," Rhett said.

The moment the words left his mouth, he regretted them. He never revealed other people's secrets.

"Liss is tough," Wilsean said without looking at Rhett. "We'll help her get through…whatever."

If you love her, you'll walk away.

Stone had given Rhett that advice months ago. Rhett hadn't heeded it then. Maybe if he had, Liss would have been spared the pain that was coming her way.

His gaze slid to Wilsean, who was twisting the ring he wore around his index finger. The habit was something he did when he was deep in thought or deeply upset.

The ring was branded with his family's crest and identified him as the heir to one of the most powerful families in the empire. Wilsean's father had given it to him on his sixteenth birthday. When Wilsean married, he would take over his father's role as head of his family and gain all the wealth and prestige that came with that title. He'd also take over his father's position on the Emperor's council.

"Can I give you some advice?" Rhett asked.

"Advice?" Wilsean raised his eyebrows. "Who are you, and what have you done with my best friend?"

Rhett smirked at that. It was true he avoided meddling in other people's business. He wasn't exactly sure where the urge came from now, except for the fact that he knew he was running out of time.

"I think Stone only got one thing wrong," Rhett said.

He paused, letting the familiar ache at the reminder of Stone's death wash over him.

Rhett continued, "He was wrong about duty. It's not as important as—" he paused, trying to put words into what he was thinking.

"If you say happiness, I'm going to punch you," Wilsean warned.

Rhett's lip quirked at that. What he'd really been thinking was *Liss*, but that obviously didn't apply to Wilsean.

"All I'm saying is that if you care about Samara half as much as it seems, you shouldn't let anything else get in the way of being with her."

"Yeah, well." Wilsean let out a heavy sigh as he rubbed at his ring. "It's—"

Wilsean glanced at him and sucked in a breath.

"What?" Rhett asked, already having an idea about what his friend saw from the look on his face.

"Your eyes." Wilsean swallowed. "They're orange."

CHAPTER 9

L iss bit down on what was left of her nail. The pain that flooded through her raw fingertip was a welcome relief from the agony in her soul.

Rhett's irises were rimmed in orange. That meant he had moved to the second stage of opal contagion.

That meant he was going to die.

Liss could no longer delude herself that Rhett would be one of the lucky few survivors. Once an Infected reached the second stage, there was no going back…no hope for survival.

"We're going to find what we need to fix him," Samara said for the hundredth time. "I know it."

Liss nodded and bit down on the inside of her cheek. She couldn't cry. It wouldn't serve any purpose except to make Rhett feel guilty for something he couldn't control.

Rhett was going to die.

It was the only coherent thought in her mind. It circled around and around, until she was ready to scream.

None of them spoke beyond the bare necessities.

Wilsean was trying to be subtle about it, but Liss could see the way he was using his body to prop Rhett up as they walked.

It wasn't just Rhett's eyes that had changed. His whole body seemed…fragile. It was the last word she'd ever associate with Rhett, but as she looked at him now, there was no other way to describe him.

A bright light on the path ahead was a welcome distraction from Liss's other thoughts. She drew out her knife at the same time Rhett and Wilsean readied their weapons.

A man was standing at the end of the tunnel.

"Um, wow," Samara breathed as the man came into view ahead of them.

That pretty much summed things up. The man was drop-dead gorgeous. Golden light radiated from his toned, bare chest. His hair was a golden-orange color…not quite Extended, but almost. His skin was Lagonia pale, and his eyes were forest-green.

"I think even I might be attracted to him," Wilsean said, blinking.

Rhett just glared at the man and gripped his dagger.

Liss shook her head and cleared her throat.

"Don't let his good looks fool you," she said in a quiet voice. "His soul is…unpleasant."

"Ah, welcome to the end of the road." The man shifted to the side, revealing a door at his back. "It has been so long since anyone besides the queen and her sacrifices made it this far."

Even his voice was hypnotic. Liss found herself moving closer, almost like there was an invisible string pulling her toward the man. It was only when she glanced into his soul again that she remembered herself.

"The queen's sacrifices?" Liss asked.

In lieu of an answer, the man offered her a dazzling smile that displayed even, white teeth.

"The queen is dead," Samara said.

The man reclined against the door and crossed his ankles. He didn't seem alarmed by the news of the queen's death.

"Then all of the treasure within can be yours." The man inclined his head. "For a price."

"And what price is that?" Wilsean asked.

The man's eyes swept over Wilsean before swiveling to each of them in turn. When the man focused on Liss, she had the unsettling impression that he was somehow looking inside her. All at once, she understood why her Extension made people uncomfortable. She didn't like the idea that this man could see things about her she hadn't chosen to share.

"There are four of you, so I am curious to see how you decide," the man said without answering the question.

"What is the price?" Rhett asked, his voice a low growl.

The man's smile was lazy and knowing.

"The only way to open this chamber is by marking it with the blood of the dead. One of you will have to die."

CHAPTER 10

Liss, Samara, and Wilsean were still arguing about why they should each be the ones to sacrifice themselves when, without warning, the beautiful man vanished. The door he'd been guarding swung open.

"What the—"

Rhett wiped his dagger off and sheathed it.

At first, Liss thought he'd killed the man guarding the door. Then, she saw the fresh slash across his palm and the smear of blood on the door. Rhett closed his hand into a fist and met her gaze. The orange ring around his irises made his eyes pop out of his hollow face.

Liss's stomach lurched into her throat. They hadn't needed a sacrifice, because Rhett was already dying.

"Blood of the dead," Wilsean murmured, putting together what Rhett had done.

Rhett glanced away from Liss, like he was ashamed.

Liss sagged against the wall. She knew she was getting air into her lungs, because she heard the panicked little gasping sounds she was making, but she couldn't breathe.

The immunity flowers, she reminded herself before her legs gave out under her. *They were going to get the flowers.*

And they were going to heal Rhett. Somehow.

Liss was ready to barge through the doorway when Rhett caught her elbow and held her back.

"We'll be there in a minute," he told Samara and Wilsean.

As soon as they were alone, Rhett brought his hands up to cup Liss's face. The emotions in his soul were a tumult of guilt, determination, and a fierce love.

"I don't know what we're going to find in there," Rhett began.

"I do," Liss interjected before he could say another word. "We're going to find the cure."

She was hanging onto that belief, because the alternative wasn't one she could bring herself to consider.

Rhett stroked his thumb across the spot on her left cheek where her dimple always appeared. "I just don't want you getting your hopes up in case—"

"There is no *in case*," she interrupted. "Now, let's go find your cure."

Before he could argue, she took his hand and dragged him through the doorway.

As soon as they were inside, Liss's jaw dropped.

This room was a thief's paradise. Her first thought was that Spence, Mari, and Jema would be jealous out of their minds when she told them about this place.

There were towers of jewels, topped with more jewels. Priceless artifacts, artwork, and magic filled the place. The room went farther back than Liss could even see.

"Be careful," Samara warned them, drawing Liss's attention away from the mounds of treasure. "This place is enspelled, and I'm not exactly sure how it'll activate."

They all spread out, moving carefully between the stacks of riches. Even though Liss was only really looking for the gleam of opal petals, she couldn't help but tabulate the worth of some of the items she came across.

This one room contained more wealth than her people had seen in the entirety of their existence.

Liss thought about the threadbare clothes Spence wore, and Mari's too-skinny frame.

Liss's hand twitched on the handle of her knife. If Gatria wasn't already dead....

All other thoughts fled from Liss's mind when she glimpsed the flowers. A narrow wooden box balanced on a heap of sapphires contained twenty live immunity flowers. Each blossom grew from its own delicate white stem. The petals were thick and full of oily, opal-colored fluid.

It was the most beautiful sight Liss had ever seen. For several seconds, she just stared.

"I found them!" Liss called out.

She rushed forward. The toe of her boot caught on a heavy, bejeweled goblet in her path. The goblet made a hollow ringing sound as it rolled across the stone floor.

For several seconds, nothing happened. Then, a menacing roar filled the room.

Liss grabbed the box of flowers, cuddling it to her chest like it was a baby, and ran back the way she'd come.

She almost collided with Samara, who was clutching a thick, leather-bound book. Liss tightened her hold on the flowers.

One growl became two, and then four.

If she'd thought the giants' wolves were terrifying, they were nothing compared to the creature that materialized onto the path right in front of Liss and Samara.

It was a mammoth, hairless beast with bright yellow eyes. Its claws were the length of Liss's forearm. Two long tusks curled out of the creature's mouth, which was full of fangs. Plated armor stood up along the ridge of its spine. Muscles on muscles strained at its leathery, rust-colored skin.

The beast's lip curled back as it let out a blood-chilling snarl.

Liss shoved the box of flowers into Samara's arms and raised her knife. The animal let out a deafening screech as an arrow sliced right through its head.

Two more arrows found a home in each of the creature's yellow eyes. The beast stood up on its hind legs and clawed at the air.

"Run!" Wilsean shouted.

Liss grabbed Samara's arm and pulled her right under the rearing beast. As soon as they were past, Liss ducked under its hind legs and slashed at where she guessed its arteries ran.

The fluid that poured out was oily and foul. Liss gagged on the smell. The monster's blood splashed onto the floor, burning right through the solid stone.

The beast disappeared into a puff of yellow, sulfurous smoke.

Liss followed Samara between two piles of treasure that reached all the way to the ceiling. She caught a glimpse of the door that was their way out…and the four beasts that blocked their escape.

A scream lodged in Liss's throat as Rhett attacked one of the creatures. They tangled, and Rhett disappeared from view as the monstrous body engulfed him.

A battle cry tore out of Liss as she sprinted for the creature.

The beast twisted to the side, and that was when Liss saw Rhett. His left arm was wrapped around the creature's neck as he stabbed into it over and over again.

"Watch its blood!" Liss called, but she didn't think Rhett could hear her over the beast's roars.

She was distantly aware of Wilsean shooting arrow after arrow at one of the other creatures. Liss's attention was so fixated on Rhett that she didn't notice the beast that crashed right through one of the jewel towers…until it was standing directly in front of her.

Samara screamed her name. Rhett shouted something.

Liss crouched low and adjusted her grip on the knife.

When the beast's head darted forward and its jaws snapped, Liss lunged to the side. It swiped its razor-sharp claws. She rolled. A barbed tail she hadn't even noticed before lashed out, and she felt heat spread across her calf.

Liss impaled the point of her knife in the nearest leg. The creature howled.

Liss rolled again to avoid it slashing claws. When she got to her feet, she found herself under the beast's stomach. It bent its head between its great forepaws to shriek at her. Fetid air blasted Liss's hair back.

The beast dropped down and tried to swipe beneath itself with its claws. Liss leapt to the side and drove her knife into the monster's belly.

She dragged the blade through the fleshy underside, hurling herself out of the way as innards and foul liquid gushed out.

The creature writhed. Liss was almost crushed underneath its body.

She made it out from beneath the creature and leapt over its flailing tail. Then, it evaporated into a cloud of yellow smoke.

"Come on!" Rhett grasped her hand and pulled her out of the way of another falling body, this one riddled with Wilsean's arrows.

They sprinted to the door. Samara, her face white with terror, balanced the box of flowers on top of the thick book as she kicked the door open.

Rhett pushed Liss through the door behind Samara. Wilsean jumped over a stack of gold bars. He clutched some kind of pot under one arm, while he shot arrow after arrow at the beasts behind them. As soon as they were all in the tunnel, Rhett slammed the door.

For several seconds, they all leaned against the wall and tried to catch their breath.

"Good work, everyone," Rhett said. Aside from the dried blood all over him, he looked and sounded as calm as ever.

Liss pointed at the thick volume Samara seemed to be guarding as carefully as the flowers.

"What is that?" Liss asked when her heart had stopped trying to pound its way out of her chest.

"Gatria's spell book," Samara said, a tentative smile curving her lips. "Hopefully it'll tell me what magic she used to make the flowers, so we'll be able to figure out how to make a cure."

Liss wanted to kiss her best friend. She'd been too worried about finding the flowers to even consider what else they might need to save Rhett.

"What'd you get?" Rhett asked Wilsean, nodding at the pot in his arms.

Wilsean replaced his bow at his back and sheathed his throwing knives. He frowned down at the pot, as though he'd only just discovered he was carrying it.

"Something valuable?" It came out as more of a question, and Wilsean looked at Liss for confirmation.

Liss took one glance at the pot and let out a snort.

"It's an urn." Unable to help herself, she started to giggle. "And the jewels are fake." She laughed harder. "Even that gold paint isn't real."

Wilsean scowled as Samara's laughter joined hers.

"How do you know the stones are fake?" Wilsean demanded.

Liss wiggled one of the gems loose from the urn's cap. She put the would-be emerald between her teeth and bit down. She displayed the gem to Wilsean, showing off the depression of her tooth in the soft stone.

"A room full of treasure, and you grab something with fake gemstones," Rhett said, shaking his head.

"Well, how was I supposed to know?" Wilsean complained.

Samara guffawed.

"Look out, Liss," Samara managed between fits of laughter. "You're about to be replaced as our group's thief."

That only made them laugh harder.

Even Rhett was battling to keep a straight face.

"Everyone else was grabbing stuff," Wilsean said defensively. "It seemed like the right thing to do."

By this point, Liss and Samara were hanging onto each other for dear life as the sound of their mirth filled the tunnel. Tears were streaming down Liss's cheeks from the force of her belly laughter.

Wilsean clutched the useless artifact as he spluttered.

When Rhett gave in and started chuckling, Wilsean's anger only grew.

"At least I contributed something." Wilsean glared at Rhett. "What did you get us?"

"A way out," Rhett replied dryly, displaying his bloodstained dagger.

Wilsean opened his mouth to retort. Before he could get the words out, the ceiling overhead began to rattle. Dust and loose stones pattered onto the ground. A thunderous pounding came from the other side of the closed door. The stone walls bowed and groaned.

That was all the warning they got before the tunnel started to collapse.

CHAPTER 11

Ciago stood at the top of the barricade and watched the slavers march down the road that led out of Lagonia. He made no attempt to hide his disgust. Ciago had no idea where they were going, but at the moment, they weren't his concern.

Ciago's attention was fixed on the invincibles who were coming down the road in the opposite direction, heading toward the cape. Jaikon's dragon soared overhead, the beast's golden scales glittering in the afternoon sun.

"We should have killed those slavers when we had a chance," one of the rebels said, gripping his bow. "Maybe if we take the rafts to Insorsil and come at them from the other direction, we could—"

"Hold your position," Ciago interrupted in a firm voice. He gave the archers a hard look.

Nothing would be more satisfying than to go after the degenerates, but Rhett had been clear with his orders. Ciago had a more important task.

Ciago inclined his head at Winny, and they both headed for the ladder that would bring them down to the ground.

"You're really not going to do anything about the slavers?" the archer asked.

Ciago didn't mind the soldiers under his command challenging his decisions, but there was something in the archer's voice that he didn't like. It bordered on disrespect.

Ciago turned around to face the man.

"That's right," he replied in an even tone. "For now. We have bigger issues to deal with first."

He gestured for Winny to go down the ladder ahead of him.

"Must be nice to be able to so easily overlook evil," the same soldier said.

This time, there was no bordering on disrespect. The line had been crossed.

Ciago stalked over to the man, taking note of the other archers' reactions as he coldly assessed whether he would need to kill one of his own soldiers.

"What exactly are you talking about?" Ciago asked, even though he already had a good idea.

The soldier jutted his chin at Winny.

For some reason, that one action transformed Ciago's irritation to something much deeper.

"Watch yourself, soldier." Ciago rested his hand on the pommel of his sword. It was a warning none of the archers would miss.

"Is there a problem?" Winny, her hands wrapped around her mallet and looking every bit as ferocious as her wolves, came to stand at Ciago's side.

Winny was half-giant, but even though she was smaller than the full giants she presided over, there was a strength to her that made her seem larger than she was. Her dark eyes gleamed with intelligence.

This archer might talk a big game, but he'd have to be a true idiot to start something with Winny.

"Yeah, there's a problem," the archer said. "I don't like being forced to fight alongside Lagonia's enemy."

"The giants aren't our enemies anymore," Ciago said, "or is your memory too short to recall when Lady Umbrog and I signed that treaty?"

The soldier's cheeks flushed. He opened his mouth, but Ciago didn't give him a chance to say more. He drew his sword and let the tip hover a centimeter from the archer's neck.

"As your commander, I'm giving you two choices," Ciago said. "Either get over yourself and be a useful member of this army—"

"—Or I'll feed you to my wolves," Winny supplied.

All of the archers' faces paled.

Ciago hid a smirk. He'd confirmed that the wolves didn't actually eat people, which made him doubly appreciate Winny's threat. Her sense of humor didn't make an appearance often, but when it did, it was all the more rewarding.

Ciago had never expected to like the reclusive and ruthless giant leader. He certainly hadn't expected to respect her. Now, he could hardly imagine trying to get anything done without Winny's ingenuity and her giants' brute strength.

Ciago gestured for the giants manning the barricade to crank open the doors. Leaving the cape open and exposed when their enemies were coming straight for them made Ciago itch, but it was a necessary part of the plan.

"You make a much better ally than enemy," he told Winny as they climbed back down the ladder. "I'll give you that much."

"Indeed." Winny squinted in thought. "I anticipate much will change for the better once Rhetteman Loniger becomes emperor."

Ciago held back a wince. He couldn't help but recall the way his friend had looked before they parted ways. Unless there really was a cure down in that Insorsiled cave, Rhett was—

"Careful, my Lady," he said in a playful voice, needing a distraction. "If anyone hears you going all soft for the Lagonians, you'll lose your brutish reputation."

Winny looked at him in a way that made it clear she understood far more than he was saying. Then, she rearranged her face into a brutal expression. "We cannot have that, now, can we?"

They stopped together at the edge of the long trench the giants had dug. It was adjacent to the barricade wall they had also recently built, but not close enough that any of their own people would fall into it.

"Is it deep enough?" Winny asked, staring down into the chasm.

"It'll have to be." Ciago turned toward the road, where the invincibles were coming at a fast clip.

It was time to set their plan into motion.

Ciago and several dozen of the rebels lined up on the far side of the trench. The rebels, who still wore their bright yellow anti-contagion suits in case the Extended returned, stuck out amid the bleak landscape. They would draw the invincibles right to them.

Winny and her nine giants positioned themselves just off to the side. As soon as everyone was assembled, Ciago opened up a bag of Insorsiled powder, which Samara had given him before she left.

He really needed to get a formerly-Insorsiled girlfriend of his own. If Samara and Wilsean ever broke up, the entire empire would be screwed.

Ciago sprinkled the Insorsiled powder along the edges of the trench. The magical powder spread up and out, forming a hazy mist across the open part of the trench. There was a flash of white light. Then, the trench vanished from view.

It just looked like more of the frost-covered ground. No visible evidence of the newly-dug hole remained.

The invincibles were close enough now that Ciago could see the expectant and arrogant expressions they all wore.

Ciago met Winny's gaze. She inclined her head in acknowledgement and let out a long, piercing whistle.

The pack of white wolves, led by Ulfrath, bounded down the road. Their mighty legs ate up the distance like it was nothing. They made a wide circle around the invincibles, driving them closer together.

Just as Ciago had hoped—and Winny had predicted—Jaikon brought his gold dragon lower to the ground.

The invincibles' confidence was replaced by terror as the wolves converged on them. These soldiers might not be able to die, but that didn't stop the gut reaction that came from the sight of bared fangs and rumbling growls that had Ciago's own arm hairs standing at attention.

The wolves herded the invincibles, who seemed too intent on escape to remember how to use their weapons. They didn't pay attention to where they were going as they raced ahead of the wolves, and straight toward the hidden trench.

The Emperor was forced to bring his dragon to the ground to reach the crouching and snarling wolves.

Grub, the tallest of the giants, didn't hesitate. He reached over and plucked Jaikon right off his dragon. Grub threw the Emperor.

Jaikon's body disappeared from view as he sailed through the Insorsiled powder. The riderless dragon screeched and rose into the sky.

There was a flash of blue light from inside the trench as Jaikon's pin activated. If he hadn't been protected by invincibility, the force of Jaikon's fall would have broken at least a few necessary bones.

The invincibles, who were already on course for the trench, didn't have time to adjust. With their momentum, and the wolves at their heels, they barreled right over the edge of the trench.

Their shouts were music to Ciago's ears.

"Good work, Grub," Ciago told the giant who had tossed Jaikon into the trench.

The giant's cheeks flushed pink above his tangled beard.

"Tell Lovely?" the giant asked hopefully.

Ciago chuckled. "Yeah, I'll tell her, but don't get your hopes up. She's in love with my best friend."

Grub's eyebrows drew down, and his blush darkened.

Ciago pulled the vial of Insorsiled liquid out of his pocket and splashed it in the direction of the trench. Now that their prey had been captured, he didn't want to risk one of his own people taking a tumble.

Ciago almost couldn't keep a straight face at the sight that greeted him when the illusion peeled away.

The invincibles were attempting to scrabble up the sheer walls of the trench, only to slide back down on their asses. One soldier was using two knives to try and climb his way out of the hole. The dirt was just loose enough that his knives couldn't hold his weight as soon as he started to climb.

Ciago sighed in satisfaction as the invincibles snarled and raged from the bottom of the trench.

"Ciago," Jaikon yelled, craning his neck to look up at him. "I command you to release us this instant."

"My apologies," Ciago called down. "But my commander ordered me to secure you until he gets around to killing you." Ciago let just a little of his glee show on his face. "Rhett's very busy at the moment, so you'll have to forgive him for prioritizing other matters." And then, just because he could, Ciago added, "He and Liss went shopping for new curtains. They weren't happy with the color palette in the Emperor's suite."

Winny's laugh was even better than Jaikon's snarl.

This solution was only a temporary one. The invincibles might be uncomfortable without food or water, but their pins would keep them from dying from lack of either. Jaikon was also resourceful and determined enough that this makeshift prison wouldn't hold him for long. But with any luck, it would keep him out of the way long enough for them to figure out how to kill him.

The Emperor and his invincibles were still shouting threats, but Ciago's attention had strayed to movement on the road that led to the cape. An old Insorsiled bike sputtered along, staying just ahead of the slavers who were chasing after it.

Ciago immediately recognized the orange hair and opal skin of the skinny figure on the bike.

He looked up to the archers standing on top of the barricade.

"What are you waiting for?" he called up to his soldiers. "Kill the slavers!"

Ciago drew his sword as he raced toward Spence. He was a little nettled when the giants quickly outpaced him, but as it turned out, there were enough slavers for all of them.

"Get behind the barricade," Ciago shouted to the kid as his bike zoomed past.

Ciago threw himself at the slavers, hacking at the pathetic excuses for men with his sword. Beside him, Winny swung her mallet. She was slightly terrifying as she took out five slavers at once. Ciago couldn't take his eyes off her.

"Focus," she snapped at him when a slaver almost took his head off.

Ciago was almost disappointed when, only a few minutes later, the slavers were dead.

"At ease," he shouted to the rebel soldiers who were surrounding Spence's bike.

Ciago pushed his way through the crowd of rebels to Spence.

"Ciago," Spence said, sounding relieved.

"What's up, kid?" Ciago held out his fist for Spence to bump.

"You better bring your army to Insorsil," Spence said, leaning over as he caught his breath. "Liss and the others are in the castle, and apparently, they weren't quiet about it." He turned off the Insorsiled bike, so his next words came out sounding loud. "There's a few hundred Insorsiled waiting for them. As soon as they come out, the Insorsiled are going to kill them."

CHAPTER 12

Rhett sprinted after the others as the tunnel collapsed all around them. He kept his eyes trained on the ground, looking for the tiny glint of Samara's beads that were quickly being buried under dirt and stones.

Normally, Rhett's innate sense of direction would have made the reminder of their path unnecessary. But without those beads, he would have wandered around down here until he was buried alive. Rhett wasn't sure if it was some Insorsiled spell, or the fact that the opal contagion was addling his brain.

Faster, he ordered his legs.

When he stumbled, Wilsean dragged him up. Liss was pulling Samara along with one hand and using the other to cradle the box of flowers. They were all coughing as dust filled their mouths and noses.

The whole ceiling was coming down. They pressed themselves against the wall to avoid collapsing rocks.

"How much farther?" Liss gasped.

Rhett's lungs were screaming. Just when he didn't think his body could take any more punishment, the ground began inclining. Natural light streamed into the tunnel a short distance ahead. Liss fumbled with the lever, and then the metal door was sliding back.

She and Samara crashed through the doorway first, letting in a gust of clean air. Wilsean and Rhett stumbled out behind them.

They fell into the queen's sitting room where they had begun this journey. Except the room wasn't empty like they'd left it. It was filled with Insorsiled.

Some of the warlocks held staffs. Others had vials of potions. The rest wielded blunt knives.

None of them looked friendly.

"Aw hell," Wilsean muttered.

That just about covered things.

Rhett's body wanted nothing more than to collapse into a useless heap. Instead, he drew his dagger and searched for the greatest threat.

"Leave now, and we won't hurt you," Rhett told the furious crowd.

Rhett had no desire to murder civilians.

"Queen killer," one of the Insorsiled shouted back. "You'll die for your crimes."

Rhett looked at the witch, a heavyset woman whom he immediately pinpointed as the leader of this angry mob.

So be it.

Rhett leapt toward her. Wilsean moved at the same instant, heading for a warlock whose staff was already spitting red sparks.

Rhett killed the witch quickly and was on to the next before she'd hit the ground. Out of the corner of his eye, he saw Liss give the box of flowers to Samara and join the fight.

An explosion of purple sparks struck Rhett in the shoulder. He smelled burning flesh as the fire burrowed into his skin. Compared to the pustules covering his body, the flames felt almost like a caress. With a grim smile, he went for the warlock who had cast the spell.

These Insorsiled were motivated by passionate anger, and that made them sloppy. They weren't a people bred for fighting on a good day, and with the narrow space they were squeezed into, it gave Rhett's side all the advantage. He, Wilsean, and Liss were making short work of their enemies.

The only problem was that there seemed to be an unending number of Insorsiled who wanted them dead. No matter how many they put down, more poured into the queen's room.

The place stank of blood. The formerly-white carpet was covered with corpses and innards.

Rhett looked to the side and saw Wilsean was out of arrows. All of Wilsean's throwing knives were gone except for the two in his hands.

Through the open doorway, Rhett could see an endless line of Insorsiled waiting for their turn to face down the queen killer.

Wilsean and Liss still had energy to spare, but Rhett was flagging. His legs had turned to lead. His reactions were sluggish enough that he could barely avoid the curses that came zinging toward him. He was seconds away from being completely useless.

Rhett refocused as a cry came from out in the hall. The shout was taken up by others, and then the distinct thud of bodies hitting the floor filled his ears.

Rhett sliced his dagger through two more warlocks who refused to back down, giving himself a clear view. The Insorsiled in the hallway were dropping. Rhett didn't see any blood or glint of weapons to explain what was bringing them down. One second they were on their feet, and the next they were down.

Wilsean and Liss made short work of the rest of the Insorsiled in the room as Rhett moved to the doorway. Two more Insorsiled crumpled. There was a flash of opal skin, followed by a head covered in wild orange hair. Spence got to his feet and looked straight at Rhett.

That was when Rhett realized the Insorsiled weren't dead. Spence had put them to sleep.

"What are you doing here?" Rhett asked the kid.

"Saving your ass. Get Liss and come on."

Rhett had an insane urge to stand in the doorway and block Spence's view of the carnage within. It wasn't that the kid was a stranger to violence. It was that Spence had accomplished the same thing Rhett had—taking out the threat posed by the Insorsiled—without violence.

Before Rhett could think more about it, a shadow he recognized appeared around the corner. Ciago's large body filled the hallway.

Relief made Rhett sag against the doorway.

Ciago gave Rhett a quick wave and then turned back to fight a group of warlocks who had been trying to sneak up on him.

Two more warlocks appeared through a door at the opposite end of the hallway. They caught sight of the intruders and raised their staffs.

Rhett threw his dagger at the warlock aiming at Spence. When the man fell, the other warlock had to drop his staff and stumble backward to avoid being crushed.

While the remaining warlock tried to reclaim his lost staff, Rhett searched around for a weapon. He needed something…anything….

Rhett's dagger was out of reach, and all of Wilsean's throwing knives were gone.

Damnit. He needed—

The warlock in the hallway was back on his feet.

Move! he ordered himself. He had only seconds before the man reclaimed his staff. He had to do something.

Rhett was halfway out the door when Wilsean's whistle had him turning back.

Wilsean thrust the witch he'd been strangling with his bare hands at Liss. She plunged her knife into the woman's gut without a moment's hesitation. Wilsean bent, picked up the urn he'd rescued from the grotto, and tossed it to Rhett.

Rhett noted the object's heft, measured the distance, and threw it.

The urn cracked over the warlock's head just as flames erupted from his staff. Ashes and shards of pottery rained down.

The flames that had been meant for Ciago shot up, burning a hole straight through the ceiling. The warlock crumpled to the ground.

"Lucky you had an urn on hand," Ciago noted as he wrenched Rhett's dagger out of the first body.

"Hah, told you so," Wilsean gloated.

Too overcome by their close call for words, Rhett just shook his head.

"Let's just get out of here," Samara said in a shaky voice.

Wilsean immediately sobered as he turned all of his attention on her. She was staring at all the dead laid out on the floor.

Samara wasn't a warrior like the rest of them. When Rhett imagined the scene before them through her eyes, he was overwhelmed by the slaughter. He felt an urge to apologize to Samara for killing witches and warlocks who had once been her countrymen. But then he remembered that the dead

Insorsiled on the floor were the same ones who had hung people for the crime of possessing no magic.

Still, Rhett didn't need Liss's soul sorting ability to see how much all of the violence and death bothered Samara.

Liss was hugging Spence, who squirmed and complained at the show of affection.

Rhett and Ciago checked the hall. When it was clear, they motioned for everyone to follow.

"Wait," Liss said.

She pulled one of the immunity flowers out by its roots and held it out to Rhett.

There was so much unguarded hope on her face that it tore at his insides. If this didn't work….

Rhett held her gaze as he put the flower in his mouth.

It dissolved on contact, and the tasteless powder slid down his throat.

"Well?" Ciago asked.

Everyone was staring at Rhett. He couldn't take his eyes off Liss, who seemed like she was holding her breath.

"Do you feel any different?" Wilsean asked.

Still looking at Liss, Rhett shook his head.

Liss tore another one of the flowers out of the soil. Her hand trembled as she held it out to him.

"Liss—"

"Take it." Her eyes blazed with a combination of fury and desperation.

Rhett did as she asked, but only to prove what he already knew. Even if he consumed every one of the flowers, he was too far gone for it to matter.

"Maybe it takes some time to work through your system," Wilsean suggested.

Samara was flipping madly through the book of spells, muttering to herself.

"You just need another one," Liss said, her voice unsteady.

Before she could waste another flower, Rhett took her hand in a gentle grip.

"No," Liss said, struggling against him.

Ciago took the box of flowers away from her before it dropped.

"This has to work." Liss's eyes filled with tears. "It just has to. I can't—
"

Samara pulled a corresponder out of her pocket and said something about her witchdoctor sister. There was some shuffling as their friends moved farther down the hallway. Rhett stopped paying attention to anything except Liss.

Her silent tears tracked a path through the dust, sweat, and blood streaked across her face. She was so beautiful.

Rhett held her against him. Her small frame shook as she leaned into him.

"I'm sorry," he said, holding her tighter. "Liss, I'm so sorry."

There was nothing else for him to say.

"I can't," she gasped, her voice muffled against his shirt. "Rhett, I can't...."

"You can." He pulled back enough to look at her. He couldn't stand the thought of her drowning in grief. "Liss—"

"Guys?" Samara's timid voice came from somewhere behind them.

Rhett released Liss and turned to Samara.

"Lullianna's on her way." Samara pocketed the glass sphere in her hand. "She's going to examine Rhett and take a closer look at the flowers."

"Does she think she can make the flowers more powerful?"

The way Liss's expression transformed from despair to a fierce kind of anticipation tore at Rhett's insides. He wanted to snap at Samara to quit giving Liss false hope.

"Maybe," Samara said. The uncertainty in her voice was unmistakable. "She needs to examine Rhett and the flowers before we'll know anything for sure."

"Then, let's go. Now." Liss tugged on Rhett's hand, practically dragging him down the hall.

Rhett knew it would be pointless to try to argue with Liss.

If anyone could come up with a medical miracle, it was Samara's brilliant sister. But Rhett knew the ugly truth that Liss refused to see. Whatever discoveries could be made from this batch of flowers, they would come too late to save Rhett.

CHAPTER 13

Liss gave the flowers to Samara, who was pouring over Gatria's spell book with her sister. They had lost four days down in the grotto…which meant that Rhett had that much less time before they found a cure.

No matter how many gentle hedges Samara threw in, or how much Lullianna's frown deepened whenever she glanced at Rhett, Liss couldn't give up hope. With Lullianna's healing skills and Samara's knowledge of magical theory, there was no way they could fail.

"How are you feeling?" Wilsean asked Rhett.

"Maybe a little better?" Rhett replied. It came out as a question, like he knew the answer he was supposed to give but wasn't sure he could.

After the two flowers he'd eaten, he looked a little less exhausted. Although that could have just been Liss's hope making her see things that weren't really there.

Rhett raised his arm like he was testing something. His expression didn't change, but Liss felt the pulse of discomfort across his soul. For Rhett, that was the equivalent of anyone else's agonizing pain.

"I'll be the judge," Lullianna said. She hovered a hand over Rhett's chest and closed her eyes.

Liss held her breath. Her heart throbbed in her chest as she waited.

Lullianna opened her eyes. "Those flowers didn't reverse the virus, but they slowed down its progress. If Rhett hadn't taken them, he'd soon be on his way to the third stage."

Liss's heart plummeted. It was good news…sort of. And yet, it wasn't what she wanted to hear.

"Do you think if he takes more it'll make him heal?" Liss asked, eyeing the box of flowers.

The two sisters exchanged a look.

"I'm so sorry, Liss," Samara said in a soft voice.

"He's too far gone for the flowers to reverse the contagion's course," Lullianna explained. "His only hope now is if I can find a way to modify the magic in these flowers to make a cure."

"Just give us some time," Samara said, giving Liss and Rhett a look full of sympathy.

"I understand," Rhett said.

Liss bit her tongue so she didn't scream in frustration. Everything the sisters were saying made sense. But patience had never been one of Liss's strong points.

A handful of Rhett's rebel soldiers were there to meet them when their raft docked at the cape's point. They were all dressed in anti-contagion suits. None of them complained, but Liss could see the sweat streaming down their skin behind their transparent face shields. Even in the wintery cold, the suits must be stifling.

Resentment wafted off the soldiers' souls.

Infected. Liss had always hated that word. She hated how it was used as an excuse to extort and murder her people.

And yet, it was the disease inside her that was the reason for all these anti-contagion suits. It was why Lagonia was being deprived of its future emperor. It was why she was going to lose the man she loved.

"Liss?"

She started at the sound of Spence's voice. Guilt filled her when she realized she'd barely spoken a word to him, even after he'd helped to rescue them from the Insorsil castle.

"Sorry," she said, refocusing on him.

As soon as she turned her full attention on Spence, reality came crashing back.

"Why didn't you go back to the Extended hideout?" she demanded, her voice coming out shrill with worry. "It's not safe—"

Spence gave her a dirty look. "The girls and I are the new Opal Smoke, remember?"

Liss sighed. "I know you can take care of yourselves, but that doesn't mean I'm not going to worry."

"It's not like the hideout is even that much safer compared to everywhere else," Spence argued. "The peasants know where we are, and they've been coming after us."

"What?" Liss's panic spiked at the news that the Extended hideout was no longer secure.

"It's been going on for days," Spence said. "At first, it was just a handful of peasants. But more and more have been coming.

"We have the advantage whenever we get close because, you know, the contagion. But the peasants have bows and arrows."

"The peasants haven't had anyone willing to defend them for too long," Rhett said. "They're doing what they can to protect themselves."

"So are we," Spence snapped.

It was the one thing the Extended and Lagonian peasants had in common. They were both battling for their lives, and somehow, they were both losing.

"You can bunk with me tonight, kid," Ciago told Spence. "I've got a killer room in the Insorsiled tent."

The first time Ciago came into the tent, a third door had appeared off the common room. Rhett and Wilsean thought the tent's understanding of them and their every need was creepy. Liss loved it.

"Yeah, I guess that could work," Spence said with a shrug.

Liss didn't miss the little thrill that went through his soul.

Liss gave Ciago a grateful look. "You don't mind sleeping in an anti-contagion suit?"

"Nah." Ciago grinned at her. "I've been told it makes me even more irresistible."

"You really need to stop talking to yourself in the mirror," Wilsean told him.

Liss laughed. "It's true that not just anyone could pull off that shade of yellow."

"How right you are, Lovely Liss." Ciago draped a heavy arm over her shoulder.

After depositing Samara, Lullianna, and Spence in the Insorsiled tent, the rest of them headed down to the fishermen's houses where Rhett's soldiers were waiting for them.

Ciago filled them in on Jaikon and the invincibles' imprisonment as they walked. Rhett didn't say anything, but his soul filled with a dark satisfaction. There was also a kind of restless determination. Liss knew he wouldn't let himself die until he'd figured out how to defeat Jaikon and his army.

The realization was cold comfort.

Ciago led them to the largest of the fishermen's cottages. The cheerful pink paint made the icy wind that blew in from the cliffs slightly less brutal.

Twenty-or-so soldiers in anti-contagion suits were standing in the bare room. They all jerked to attention as soon as they caught sight of Rhett.

Respect and love, mixed with grief, poured off each of their souls as they took in his altered appearance.

Rhett had lost an impossible amount of weight in the six days since he'd first become Infected, and his face was gaunt. His shirt, which had clung to his muscled arms and chest before, hung loosely off his frame. His eyes were still rimmed with orange and had a feverish kind of brightness to them.

Liss swallowed the thickness in her throat and forced her attention on the report Rhett's soldiers were delivering.

"Elouicia took a few hundred of the slavers to Insorsil yesterday," one of them was saying.

Liss repressed a shudder at the mention of Lagonia's new Chief Assassin. Elouicia was more beast than man. He was more bloodthirsty and vile than any creature Liss had ever encountered.

"What's Elouicia doing in Insorsil?" Liss asked.

She would have expected him to be hunting her people along with the rest of the slavers.

"They're…digging," a soldier replied. "There's a huge hole on the western edge of Insorsil."

Rhett raised an eyebrow.

"What are the Insorsiled doing during all of this digging?" he asked.

"That's the strange part," a different soldier replied. "We saw tons of Insorsiled just standing around looking dead-eyed and lost."

Liss glanced at Rhett. They'd seen those Insorsiled with the empty eyes and blank souls.

"Whatever they're up to, it can't mean anything good for us," Liss said.

"Agreed." Rhett nodded. "I want this hole watched around the clock. Update me with any news."

The cottage door opened, and Dannica entered along with a gust of cold air.

"We need you," she told Rhett. "The invincibles have one of the giants."

CHAPTER 14

Rhett stared down into the trench. Even with all of the movement and people, his gaze locked on the ice blue eyes of the man he hated most.

"I'm glad you're here," Jaikon called up to Rhett. "I was losing patience."

"Did you lose your dignity along with your patience?" Rhett asked the Emperor.

Jaikon smirked and looked down at himself. He wore only his underclothes. All one-hundred of the human men in the trench were dressed similarly—stripped of everything except the bare necessities. The tiny gold circlets gleamed against their underwear.

The rest of their clothes and belts had been strung together to make ropes that were being used to restrain the two giants stretched out on the muddy floor of the trench.

One of the giants was the largest and most fearsome of the group. The other was Grub.

"Shit," Ciago muttered, summing up Rhett's thoughts precisely.

Twenty invincibles surrounded each of the giants. Jaikon's men held their blades against the giants' arteries and vital organs. The invincibles' weapons might seem small compared to the giants they were threatening, but that didn't diminish their sharpness. It wouldn't take more than a single slash or stab to the right place to end each of these giants.

The giants' eyes were wide with terror. All Rhett could think about as he looked down into the trench was that one of them was Grub, the giant that had befriended Liss.

Winny and the rest of her giants paced back and forth at the edge of the trench. They were cursing and waving their mallets around.

"How did this happen?" Rhett asked Winny. When she turned to face him, Rhett saw murder in her eyes.

"Allow me the pleasure of relaying the story," Jaikon said, his smirk widening. "It was a simple matter of intelligence versus stupidity. Fortunately for me, these giants are a particularly potent breed of dumb."

Winny snarled and raised her mallet. Ciago spoke to the giant leader in a hushed voice before she went charging down into the trench.

"I told the oversized oaf who was supposed to be guarding us that there was treasure down here," Jaikon explained. "I told him that if he didn't come down to get it, I would claim it for myself." He chuckled.

"The brute came right to the edge. All we had to do was throw the ropes around him and give him a tug." Jaikon flourished his hand at the two prone giants. "When a second one came looking for the first, we got him the same way."

In his periphery, Rhett was aware of Ciago using a combination of words and brute force to restrain the giant leader. The rest of the giants were grunting and beating at their chests.

"Stop," Rhett told Winny. "He wants you down there, too."

Rhett knew Jaikon's games and how they were played. Jaikon wanted to gloat about how he had gotten himself into the position of power, despite the fact that he was barely dressed and at the bottom of a trench. Then, Jaikon would deliver the news about the price that would need to be paid for the giants' release.

"Very clever," Rhett deadpanned. "Now tell me what you want."

"Simple." Jaikon shrugged. "I'll let these fool creatures go. If you come and take their place."

Rhett locked gazes with the Emperor. They both sized each other up, trying to read the other. When Rhett saw his half-brother's eyes harden, he nodded. Rhett unsheathed his dagger, which would be useless to him against the invincibles. He turned to give it to one of his friends.

"Absolutely not." Wilsean crossed his arms and gave Rhett an appalled look.

"Not a chance in hell," Ciago added.

"He is lying," Winny told Rhett. "He will kill you, and then he will kill my giants."

Rhett didn't think Jaikon was lying. The Emperor didn't care about the giants; he wanted Rhett. Either way, the point was moot. Jaikon had all the leverage.

"Did I mention I'm getting impatient?" Jaikon called.

"I'll do it," Dannica said from Rhett's other side. She put a gloved hand on his arm, pushing him back from the ledge. "Lagonia needs you."

Rhett shook his head. "Jaikon wouldn't allow it even if I did." And he wouldn't.

If there had been something solid nearby, Rhett would have driven his fist through it. The Emperor had bested him again. And now, Rhett would die before keeping any of his promises.

"How about we let you and all your soldiers out," Ciago shouted down to Jaikon, ignoring the glare Rhett gave him.

"I'll be out soon enough without your help," Jaikon replied. He held something up in his open palm. When Rhett looked, he realized it was a corresponder.

Wilsean and Ciago swore.

"I'm sorry, Rhett," Dannica said, her face going ashy behind her visor. "I should have thought—"

"It's my fault," Ciago jumped in. "I was so worried about getting him in there, I didn't think what he might have on him."

Rhett waved a hand, dismissing their apologies. They'd done exactly what he had ordered them to do. It didn't matter now, anyway.

A blood-curdling scream came from inside the trench.

Rhett looked down in time to see a geyser of dark blood erupt from a giant's neck. Rhett felt only a flash of relief to see that it wasn't Grub.

The invincibles restraining the thrashing giant tightened their grip on their makeshift ropes. Jaikon wiped his bloody sword on the giant's fur cloak and stepped back.

More blood spurted from the gaping wound. The giant gave another jerk and then went still. The only sound was Winny's keening cry.

The rest of the invincibles clustered around Grub, readying their weapons. Jaikon stared up at Rhett, and then he raised his sword directly over Grub's eye.

Rhett's limbs unfroze.

"Stay here," Rhett told everyone within hearing distance. "That's an order."

He gave Wilsean and Ciago a hard look. Then, he went to the edge of the trench.

He slid down the steep ravine, raking his fingers through the frozen dirt to slow his fall. He hit the bottom and rolled.

Rhett got to his feet more slowly than he would have under normal circumstances. Still, he didn't give in to his body's urge to limp. He walked past the dead giant and straight to Jaikon.

"At last," Jaikon whispered.

Rhett could hear his friends' shouts from above, but all of his attention was on Jaikon.

"Let the giant go," Rhett said in a voice loud enough for all the invincibles to hear. "Unless you want to prove to your soldiers that you are completely devoid of honor, and that you're as cowardly as everyone believes."

Jaikon's mouth thinned. Then, het let out a soft chuckle.

"Release the brute," he ordered his soldiers without taking his eyes off Rhett. "I have no need for the creature anymore." He stepped forward until he and Rhett were toe-to-toe. "I have what I want."

As soon as the invincibles stepped back, Grub stood up. He shuffled to Rhett with his head hanging.

"Lovely will be mad I got caught," he said mournfully.

"Nah, she won't be mad." Rhett could hardly believe that he was comforting a giant…a giant who happened to be pining after Liss.

Grub straightened a little at that, but his shoulders slumped when he caught sight of the other giant's corpse.

"Sorry, Bligthor." Grub sniffled and scrubbed the back of his hand across his eyes.

"Grub, I need you to climb back up to Lady Umbrog," Rhett told the giant.

He didn't have a chance to say anything else before Jaikon fisted his hand in Rhett's shirt. Rhett didn't resist as the other man pulled him forward. He could smell the copper tang of the giant's blood drying on the Emperor's sword.

"Any last words?" Jaikon crowed.

Rhett didn't speak.

Jaikon opened his mouth to gloat some more, but then he faltered as their eyes met. His attention dropped to where his hand was bunched at Rhett's collar. He let go of Rhett and staggered back.

Rhett watched the Emperor, not understanding.

Jaikon dropped his sword and doubled over. His hands were on his knees, and his entire body was shaking.

Rhett glanced up to where his friends stood at the edge of the trench, looking down. They seemed as confused as Rhett.

It took Rhett another few seconds to realize Jaikon wasn't in pain. He was laughing.

"Oh, that's rich." Jaikon stood back up and wiped a tear of mirth from his cheek. "Orange eyes and pustules. You're Infected."

Rhett looked down at himself and realized his collar had been yanked aside. Several of the open pustules along his sternum were now visible. Rhett pointlessly readjusted his shirt so the fabric covered his skin once again. Not that there was anything he could do about the color of his eyes.

The other invincibles were laughing now, too.

Rhett waited until Grub had scrambled back up the trench, with the help of the clothing ropes and Winny heaving on the other end. Then, he spoke.

"Finish this, Jaikon." He wouldn't give his half-brother the satisfaction of seeing any hint of emotion.

Jaikon picked up his sword from the ground, chuckling all the while. He didn't move toward Rhett, though.

"I've changed my mind," Jaikon said when his mirth had subsided. "You'll be dead in less than a week. Why would I kill you quickly, when the contagion can torture you more than I ever could?"

Rhett hated himself for the flare of desperate disappointment that went through him. He couldn't stop himself from thinking that a quick, clean death would have been so much easier. Not just for him, but for all the people who were holding out hope for an impossible cure.

Jaikon rubbed his hands up and down his bare arms. "Go." He waved a hand, dismissing Rhett. "Sleep with your opal whore one last time. And give her my deepest thanks." Jaikon's teeth flashed as he offered Rhett a wide smile.

"Careful, Jaikon," Rhett murmured, even though they both knew there was nothing he could do.

"I knew you would die because of her," Jaikon said. His lip curled in a cruel smile. "I just didn't expect she would be the one to kill you."

CHAPTER 15

Rhett had been gone for what felt like hours, but Liss suspected it had been far less time than it seemed. The tension in the confined room was growing by the minute. It felt like the whole place was about to combust.

Rhett had asked her to stay behind to get the soldiers' report. It had sounded like an easy enough request at the time, but the actual execution was like pulling teeth. These men and women all seemed like they would rather do just that than tell her anything.

Liss's frustration continued to mount when every detail she wrung from the unwilling soldiers was information she already knew or had suspected.

It was time to cut her losses.

"Thank you for your time," she told the soldiers as she started to back away from them and toward the door.

Liss's retreat was halted when her back came up against a hard body.

"Oh." She jumped a little as a man who was almost as big as Ciago crowded her further into the room.

"Are you satisfied?" the large man asked, taking another step toward Liss. His visor couldn't hide the pure hatred glittering in his eyes.

"Excuse me?"

"You people won't stop until you've taken everything from us," he sneered.

The room went quiet as everyone tensed. None of the other soldiers spoke, but the emotions on their souls made it clear whose side they were on. It wasn't Liss's.

There was a draft coming from the partly-open door, but no one moved to close it. All of their attention was on the brewing altercation in the center of the room.

"And you're the worst of all of them," the soldier continued. He took another step closer until he loomed before her. "You're taking away our only chance at a united empire."

"I'm not—"

"You've killed him!" The soldier raised a gloved hand like he might strike her. Liss's own hand moved toward the knife at her hip.

She opened her mouth to defend herself. Except, what could she say?

"I know." The words came out of her in a defeated whisper.

"He was ours, and because of you, he'll be dead by week's end. You filthy, infected, murdering—"

The man was lifted off his feet and thrown across the room. His body slammed against the wall with so much force the wooden boards splintered.

Rhett, his eyes blazing with emotion he rarely showed, stalked across the room. The other soldiers hurried to get out of his way.

Rhett grabbed the soldier who was slumped on the ground. He pinned the man against the wall, his forearm digging into the soldier's throat.

"Speak that way to her again," Rhett said in a low growl, "and I'll kill you. Slowly."

The only sound in the room was the soldier's labored breathing.

"Nod if you understand," Rhett said in that same threatening tone.

The soldier's head wobbled. Rhett released his hold, turning away as the man slid to the floor.

"Let me be very clear to all of you." Rhett spoke quietly, but that somehow made the threat in his voice more apparent. "If you are with me, then you're with Liss. If you can't handle that, then get out. Now."

No one moved. No one even seemed to breathe.

"Nothing about what has happened to me is Liss's fault," Rhett said into the silence. "The choices I've made are my own. And I regret none of them."

Rhett stared at his soldiers for another few seconds. Then, he took Liss's hand and led her out of the cottage.

CHAPTER 16

Rhett hurried away from the cottage, because if he stayed for another second, he might very well kill the man who had insulted Liss.

He should be worrying about Jaikon, and who the Emperor had called on his corresponder to come retrieve him. Instead, that soldier's ugly words about Liss circled around and around in his head. He was so consumed by his anger that it took him several seconds to realize Liss wasn't right behind him.

She was doubled over. Her face had gone terribly pale, and it looked like she couldn't catch her breath.

Rhett sprinted back to her.

"Liss? What's wrong?"

"He's right," she gasped. "That man was right about me. What's happening to you is my fault."

The expression in her blue eyes made his chest feel like it was about to explode.

"No." Rhett's voice broke. All other words failed him at the heartbreak he saw in her eyes.

He gathered her to him, just as her legs gave out. He lowered them both onto the hard ground and pulled her onto his lap.

For several minutes, they just clung to each other. They were in full view of all of the cottages, but he didn't care. At that moment, nothing mattered beyond the fact that Liss was hurting.

"Look at me," he told her.

When she did, he was overwhelmed with the sense that he was the one failing her. He had promised he wouldn't leave her, and even now, he could feel his body slipping away.

"You're my everything," he told her.

It was the truth. He needed her to know that whatever mistakes he'd made, loving her hadn't been one of them.

She reached up to touch his cheek with a trembling hand. Rhett leaned into her touch, tilting his head so he could kiss her palm.

"If I had stayed away from you from the beginning, you wouldn't be like this now." Her voice cracked. "You wouldn't be dying." She tried to pull away, but Rhett drew her even closer.

"None of this is your fault." He gave her a little shake when she refused to acknowledge his words.

He could tell she hadn't heard him, and he was desperate for her to understand.

"Before you, I was alive," he told her. "Alive, but not living."

She glanced at him.

"It wasn't until I met you that I realized there was a difference between the two."

He leaned in and pressed his lips to her cheek.

"I wish we had more time together," he said. "But I wouldn't trade in what we've shared for a thousand more years of a life without you."

"You're my everything, too," she said in an unsteady voice.

He closed his eyes as she traced the scars on his cheek with a fingertip.

"Promise me something," he told her without opening his eyes.

"Yeah?"

"Promise me you'll be happy again. I don't care what…or who…it takes." Rhett swallowed. As much as he believed his own words, he couldn't let himself picture her with another man. "Promise me, Liss."

He opened his eyes.

She nodded. She was blinking hard, like she was trying not to cry.

Rhett felt something ease inside him. He leaned forward until their foreheads were just touching.

"Thank you," he whispered.

* * *

By the time they made it back to the Insorsiled tent, it was almost dark.

They crawled through the tent flap and into the small outer chamber that was invisible from the outside. The large brass door unlocked at Rhett's touch, and they walked into…a party.

Music was playing from some invisible source. The air was filled with the scent of warm spices that would have made his stomach rumble if he'd had any appetite. A fire crackled in the hearth. The table in the center of the common area had doubled in size to accommodate everyone sitting around it.

Rhett realized it wasn't so much a party, as just another night with Ciago. Since Dannica had gone to Insorsil to try to find out more about whatever the slavers were up to, and Winny was keeping watch over the trench, there wasn't much else that could be done at the moment. It seemed Ciago was taking full advantage of the down time.

Ciago presided at the head of the table, with Spence at his side. Half a dozen rebels in anti-contagion suits were roaring with laughter and thumping the table. From what Rhett could gather, Ciago was telling a story that Liss likely wouldn't want her fifteen-year-old caravan-mate to be hearing. When Rhett turned to her, he saw she was smiling and shaking her head.

The sight of her dimple made him feel stronger.

Wilsean sat on the couch, sharpening his knives. The task was taking him longer than usual with the thick gloves from his anti-contagion suit. Samara had her head propped on Wilsean's leg as she leafed through Gatria's spell book. Lullianna sat on the floor with the box of flowers in her lap.

When Liss went to join them, no doubt to see if they had discovered a magical cure for the contagion, Rhett let himself into their bedroom.

He had never needed a bath more desperately. When he peeled off his clothes, he almost gagged at the sight of his body. There were more open wounds than there had been before. They covered him from chest to ankles. If he had any doubt whether the disease was progressing, the evidence was staring right at him.

His skin was yellow and felt thin. He glanced at himself in the mirror and saw the way his bones jutted out. His face was free of the blisters, but the three scars he'd gotten during his time in the torture cage stood out as black slashes against his garish skin.

He looked like a complete wreck.

He was washed and dressed, and feeling almost human again, when Liss came to check on him.

"Hungry?" she asked, offering him a plate of food.

He wasn't, but he took it because of that worried expression in her eyes.

"No luck with the immunity flowers, then?" he asked, even though he already knew the answer.

"Nothing yet," Liss replied, "but Samara and Lullianna will figure it out."

Rhett was just beginning to understand how cruel hope could be.

"Liss," he began, not knowing how to tell her that she was only setting herself up for more disappointment…more heartbreak.

"I'm going to get cleaned up," she announced, a little too loudly.

She shut herself into the washroom, and Rhett heard the sound of the bath filling itself.

Rhett cursed his body, which was the only reason he wasn't joining her.

When she came out some time later, she was glistening from the droplets of water that clung to her skin. She had only a towel wrapped around her, which clung to her perfect hourglass figure. His eyes were drawn to the outline of her breasts beneath the towel.

Every other thought evaporated from Rhett's mind. The rest of the world could collapse around them, and Rhett wouldn't notice or care. Nothing else mattered except her.

Liss's hair was getting longer, and the ends brushed the tops of her shoulders. She was so beautiful it made him ache.

"You keep looking at me like that and I'm going to blush," Liss said, even though she already was. It was one of the sexiest things he'd ever seen.

He tried to cling to the moment in his mind. If he held tight enough, maybe he could bring it with him into the darkness.

CHAPTER 17

Liss crossed the room to the dresser and picked up the silver comb that had appeared out of thin air.

She didn't look at where Rhett was sitting back against the headboard, but she could feel him watching her every move.

Liss grimaced when the comb snagged on a knot in her tangled hair. She yanked harder, having no patience for the stubborn strands.

"Here, let me," Rhett said. When she turned to him, he patted the triangle of mattress between his legs.

Liss gestured to his shaved head. "You don't seem like the type to know your way around a comb."

Still, her feet brought her and the comb across the room.

"Maybe not," Rhett replied. "But I know my way around you." He gave her a look that hid nothing about what he was feeling.

She climbed onto the bed and settled back against him, using one hand to keep her towel in place. They both sighed in unison. She couldn't decide if being so close to him made the burden on her soul easier to bear, or if it made the thought of losing him that much more intolerable.

As Rhett started to comb her hair with such gentleness it brought tears to her eyes, she decided she was right where she belonged.

She reminded herself of what she'd decided earlier when she was talking to Samara. There would be no pain…no crippling loss. Because she wasn't letting Rhett go.

Rhett finished with her hair and began to trace light patterns on the back of her neck with his fingertips. He moved to her bare shoulders, and then down her arms. He left a trail of goosebumps everywhere he touched.

Rhett swept her hair to the side, pressing soft kisses against the side of her neck.

When she turned her face, he was right there. Their lips met.

The kiss, and the way he skimmed his fingertips down her arms, was gentle. The emotions raging in his soul were not.

"I want you, too," she told him, locking her free arm around him and pulling their bodies closer together.

Rhett let out a harsh breath as he pressed her down onto the bed. He pulled away her arm that was holding up the towel. It fell onto the blanket, leaving her completely bare.

Rhett swore quietly, his chest rising and falling as he drank in the sight of her. His eyes darkened, and some color appeared in his pale cheeks.

Everything about him was harsher, from the sharp angles of his cheekbones that looked like they were about to cut through his skin, to his dark eyes. But the disease hadn't been able to make him any less gorgeous.

Liss reached for the hem of Rhett's shirt, but he stopped her with a hand around her wrist.

"Let me focus on you tonight," he said, his voice a low rumble.

Liss laughed, a little flustered. "If you think I'm going to let you have all the fun—" She reached for his shirt again, but he threaded their fingers together and pressed her hand back, away from him.

"Please," he said, his voice a harsh whisper. "I want you to remember me the way I was. Not…this."

Liss didn't know what expression crossed her face, but whatever it was, she could sense the way it ripped through him like a blade.

"Don't think about it," he whispered, leaning down to kiss her cheek. "For tonight, let's forget."

At her small nod, Rhett crushed his mouth to hers. All of the gentleness of a few minutes ago was gone. Liss relished every stroke of his callused fingers…every possessive thrust of his tongue against hers.

Liss gasped as his hands and mouth traveled down her body. He said something against her skin…maybe her name. She couldn't concentrate on anything except for the sensations racing through her and the emotions pouring off both of their souls.

As Rhett moved lower, Liss turned her head into the pillow to stifle her moans. With one hand, Rhett reached up and tossed the pillow onto the floor.

She lifted her head to glare at him.

"The walls are sound-proof," he told her, his lips curving in a small smile.

"How do you know?" she managed.

Rhett raised his eyebrows. "Have you ever heard anything from Wilsean and Samara's room?"

Good point.

"No holding back." He kissed a path between her breasts. "I want it all."

Liss felt herself coming apart as he moved farther south.

"Oh, and Liss?"

She almost screamed at the way he was tantalizing her.

Of all the times to turn talkative….

He propped his chin on her stomach and gave her a devilish grin. "I hope you're not tired. We have the whole night, and I'm not letting you sleep for any of it."

CHAPTER 18

The old Insorsiled bike sputtered across the cobbled road.

"Hold on," Liss warned Spence as she turned off the road and onto the snowy, uneven ground of the Insorsiled forest.

The bike gave a squeal of protest.

Liss's main purpose in going back to the Extended hideout was to return Spence, but she also needed to talk to her mom. Rhett's soldiers were reporting more and more confrontations between the Extended and Lagonian peasants. People on both sides were dying, and the skirmishes were distracting everyone from the enemies who really mattered.

If Liss could convince her mom to keep the Extended in their hideout, then lives on both sides would be spared.

There was a bite to the air, but every time she thought about her night with Rhett, Liss's entire body warmed. It had been close to torture to peel herself out of Rhett's arms when the sun rose. She listened to Spence's chatter with half an ear, while the rest of her mind continued to replay her night.

Rhett hadn't been happy about her and Spence going anywhere without backup, but the rebels had their own mission for the day. Jaikon had apparently called in reinforcements on his corresponder, which meant that it wouldn't be long before the rebels' defenses were tested. Rhett and his friends were out searching for Elouicia and the slavers, who hadn't made an appearance in Lagonia in days. The rest of the rebels had needed to stay behind to defend the cape for the inevitable attack.

The bike lurched when it hit a root hidden under the layers of snow. The bike caught air—and not because it was the flying kind—and crashed back down. There was a groan of metal, and then the bike died.

Liss and Spence scrambled off before they got tangled up in the useless contraption.

"Damnit." Spence kicked the still-spinning tire.

"It needs a magical jump," Liss said, listening to the pathetic *put put put* sound the engine was making.

"Well, we don't have one of those," Spence replied irritably.

"The hideout is less than half a mile from here," she told him, giving his arm a playful flick.

They had only been walking for a few minutes when the clean, wintery air took on a foul smell.

"Do you smell that?" Spence stopped and sniffed the air.

A wisp of noxious-smelling smoke curled out from behind a tree.

Slavers.

They were the only ones who smoked the cheap leaves that had the added bonus of rotting their teeth. And now that she was paying attention, Liss felt them. Souls. Dozens of the vilest souls she'd ever felt.

"Run." Liss shoved Spence toward the ward, adjusting her own body to give him cover.

"Too late for running," a slaver taunted as he stepped out from behind the tree. He was wearing what looked like the worst homemade anti-contagion suit Liss had ever seen. She doubted it would protect him from a light snowfall, let alone the contagion. It didn't even have a face shield. The man held his pipe between his teeth as he unsheathed his sword.

Another slaver appeared seemingly out of thin air. One second, he was invisible. The next, he was visible.

The slaver had come from the Extended hideout. The ward had kept him hidden from sight until he crossed over.

Liss's heart hammered in her chest. What had happened? Were her people dead?

The second slaver wore the same poor attempt at an anti-contagion suit, but he had a crossbow. He could kill them without coming close enough to endanger himself.

Liss started backing up, using one hand to grip her knife and the other to push Spence away from the two slavers.

"Move aside, sugar. Let me take care of that Infected for you." The first slaver grinned around his pipe. "Then you and me can have some fun."

"Only if you want to get opal contagion," Liss said as coldly as her growing panic would allow. She continued to nudge Spence backward. Slowly.

"Worth some pustules to get me a piece a you." The slaver gave Liss an ugly sneer.

"Hold on," the second slaver said. "This ain't no ordinary Lagonian lady. This here's Opal Smoke."

"No shit." The first slaver almost choked on his pipe as he let out a wheezing laugh. "It's payday, boys!"

The first slaver twirled his sword while the second cocked back his crossbow. A branch snapped as another slaver appeared. Then two more.

A seemingly endless stream of slavers stepped through the ward. They leered and bared their rotting teeth as they approached.

Each of them wore a makeshift anti-contagion suit and carried a crossbow.

"Get behind me," Liss ordered Spence, moving backward until he was sandwiched between her and a thick tree trunk.

She held up her knife, even though it wouldn't do her any good against crossbows. Rhett might have been able to deflect the arrows with his blade, but her skills lay in hand-to-hand combat.

"Why bother with the crossbows," Spence called from behind her, "when your breath's a lethal weapon."

"Shut up, Spence," Liss hissed.

It was the two of them against thirty slavers. Antagonizing them wouldn't help their odds.

"What the—"

The first slaver's sword flew right out of his hands. The crossbow was yanked out of the second's. One by one, the slavers' weapons were pulled from their grips by an invisible force.

Liss kept Spence pressed between her and the tree trunk as the slavers' weapons hovered in mid-air.

The slavers stared in open-mouthed terror as the first slaver's sword swiveled around until the point hovered at the level of its owner's eye. Without warning, the sword sped forward.

The slaver shrieked as the weapon pierced his eye…and kept going. The bloodied blade protruded from the other side of the slaver's skull before the man collapsed.

The only explanation was a Metalsmith, although Liss had never met one with the strength needed for that kind of control.

Before Liss could recover from what she'd just seen, the other weapons took aim at their owners. One by one, the weapons dispersed until each one was buried in a different slaver's skull.

Liss didn't have time to process what she was witnessing before more slavers stepped through the ward. They took one look at their fallen comrades, saw Liss and Spence still standing, and charged.

All at once, the woods were filled with sound. And color.

Extended, their opal skin a stark contrast to the white and brown landscape of the woods, appeared from behind trees and under snow-covered blankets.

Some of them attacked with their Extensions. Others used the Lagonian weapons Rhett had given them weeks ago. Slavers howled as their shoddy anti-contagion suits and skin caught fire from the Flamers.

Liss watched in disbelief as the Extended surrounded and demolished the slavers. There was nothing haphazard about the attack. Everything was coordinated and purposeful. The Extended, who had survived for decades by running and hiding, were fighting back. They were working together like a real army.

Liss's whole body tingled as she watched her people annihilate the group of slavers.

"Yeah!" Spence pumped his fist in the air.

Liss crouched down in a fighting stance and looked for a target to sink her blade into. That was when she realized there was no one in the woods except for the Extended. All of the slavers were dead.

"That was incredible," Liss began, hardly able to believe what she'd just seen. "That was—"

Her words cut off as a small, curved blade hovered in the air. It was several feet away, but its wicked point was positioned at the precise level of her face.

"Not your victory," a cold voice replied.

A muscular Extended man with a ring of orange hair exposing the bald cap of his head stepped forward. He raised his hand and crooked a finger. The knife reacted immediately, moving forward until it was only a foot from Liss.

Definitely a Metalsmith, some part of Liss's brain registered. *A powerful Metalsmith.*

And an angry one.

"This victory belongs to the Extended," the Metalsmith told Liss, "and you are not one of us."

Those words were like plunging into a frozen sea. They were enough to make Liss forget about the knife hovering in front of her.

This was what she'd always wanted for her people…for them to bind together and take action. She'd been desperate for them to do something about their retched existence rather than just complain about it. Now, they had.

Only she couldn't share in their triumph.

"Stop!" Spence leapt forward, stretching up his hands to cover as much of Liss as he could. "Leave Liss alone."

A blur of motion spun through the trees. Then, a skinny man with opal skin was standing beside Spence, blocking the knife that was aimed at Liss.

"Hey, Opal Smoke." The man, whose back was to Liss, turned to wink at her.

Even with the hovering blade that could go right through both of them, Liss couldn't hold back a surprised laugh.

The man in front of her was the Runner she'd rescued from the Lagonia torture cage months ago.

"Liss, meet Quic," Spence said, not realizing they were already acquainted.

"Pleasure," Liss managed.

"Likewise." Quic grinned at her before turning his attention back on the knife.

"Back off, Mul," Quic ordered the Metalsmith.

The rest of the Extended tensed as they hovered around Mul, who was clearly the one in charge of this group. They held their weapons at the ready, as prepared and vigilant as Rhett's rebel soldiers.

Even with the fact that the Metalsmith's knife was still poised to impale her, Liss couldn't help but be impressed. The last time she'd seen her people, they'd been cowering in the hideout and unwilling to leave, even to rescue their own people.

The Extended standing before her looked more like hardened warriors.

"N-now, no need for v-violence," Arom said, stepping out of the group of Extended and holding up an appeasing hand. The Aromatic's nose wiggled. All at once, the air filled with the soothing scents of lavender and vanilla.

The calming smells would have relaxed her under different circumstances, but Liss was angry. She maintained her glare as she faced off with Mul.

"I'm the one who brought all of you together in the first place," Liss snapped. "And you can thank me for the fact that the Lagonia soldiers aren't after you right now."

Mul crossed his arms. "If you care so much about your own people, then what have you been doing in Lagonia all this time?"

Liss opened her mouth to retort, but no sound came out. All at once, a crushing exhaustion settled onto her shoulders. All the fight was driven right out of her.

"I'm not your enemy," Liss told the group of Extended. "I'm one of you."

False. The emotion burst from her soul like a second heartbeat. She ignored it.

"You need to stop attacking the Lagonian peasants," Liss said, a little too loudly as she tried to silence the feelings coming from her own soul.

The Metalsmith shook his head. "The Lagonian peasants are unfortunate casualties in this war."

"They aren't your real enemies," Liss argued. "You should focus on the slavers." She motioned at the dead on the ground. "Hundreds more where they came from."

"I'm fighting to ensure our people are never enslaved or murdered again." Mul crossed his arms. "The only way to do that is to eliminate all the ones who would cause us harm. And that group includes every one of the Uninfected."

He was right.

In her months as a Lagonia servant…as Rhett's lover…Liss had never forgotten what her people suffered at the Lagonians' hands. But she'd also come to see the Lagonians in a way she'd never expected to. Even the superficial women she'd served in Jaikon's harem had somehow found their way into her soul.

Mul was looking at her, his knife still hovering in the air in front of her.

Before Liss could think of what to say, there was a blur of color. Quic disappeared. A few seconds later, he was back, this time with one arm around Liss's mom.

"Liss!"

Nya whipped out an arrow from her quiver, nocked it in her bow, and aimed at Mul.

"Get that knife away from my daughter," Nya ordered.

A humorless smile crossed Mul's face. "Should we see which of our Extensions is stronger, Nya?" he asked. "And then we can let our people decide which of us is better suited to lead the Extended."

The knife quivered, like it was anticipating the moment when it could pierce Liss's skin. Uncertainty flickered in Nya's soul.

"Back off," Liss's mom told the Metalsmith through gritted teeth.

"I'm sorry, Nya," Mul said. "Your daughter's a danger to our people, and that means she needs to die."

The knife started to move. Liss held her breath.

"Wait!" Liss's mom lowered her bow. "I'll make a deal with you."

"I can't be bought," Mul growled.

His knife quivered in response to his heightened emotions.

Nya glanced at Liss before fixing her attention on the Metalsmith. "If you really want to protect our people, I can give you something better than my daughter."

The knife backed away from Liss and delivered itself into Mul's waiting hand.

"I'm listening," he said.

Nya's gaze slid to Liss again. The emotions in her mom's soul were too confused for Liss to make sense of.

"Come to my wagon," Nya told the Metalsmith. "We'll talk there."

Nya motioned for him to go through the ward ahead of her. The other Extended followed, their eyes full of accusation and distrust.

Liss was about to follow, when Keela, the Green Thumb who had helped her rescue the Extended slaves in Lagonia, appeared in the thinning crowd. Liss's heart soared.

"Keela!" she called, earning more dirty looks as she pushed her way toward the woman.

"Are you alright, dear?" the Green Thumb asked, giving her a quick hug.

Liss was the farthest thing from alright, but that didn't matter now.

"I need to talk to you," Liss said.

Keela had told Liss that her Extension wouldn't allow her to help make more of the immunity flowers from scratch, since they were made from magic. But now that they had eighteen of the flowers, Liss was hoping the Green Thumb might be able to multiply them or make them stronger. Anything that might help Rhett.

Now, standing in front of the Green Thumb, Liss found herself tongue-tied. What if Keela refused to help? Worse, what if there was nothing she could do?

Keela lifted Liss's hand and examined her ragged, bitten-to-the-quick nails. She looked up to Liss's face and frowned at what she saw.

Keela was about the same age as Liss's mom, although there was a sturdiness to her that Nya had never had. Liss couldn't help but stare at the long scar that slashed diagonally across Keela's face and traveled the length of her neck. It gave her a somewhat menacing appearance that was a direct contrast to the warmth in her eyes and soul.

"Tell me what's wrong, dearest," she said.

For some reason, Keela's kindness undid Liss in a way she hadn't expected. The tears she'd been holding back for days came pouring out. She couldn't stop them.

Spence, Arom, and Quic muttered excuses and fled, leaving Liss and Keela alone.

Keela didn't seem to care that Liss was soaking the front of her shirt. She rubbed Liss's back, murmuring words that Liss couldn't hear over the force of her sobs, but which soothed her anyway.

When Liss had finally cried herself out, she was hiccupping and ashamed of herself. She barely knew Keela, and she'd just lost complete control of herself in front of the other woman.

"Tell me what I can do to make this better," Keela said, tugging on one of her frizzy braids.

So, Liss started talking.

When she was finished, she expected to have to wait for Keela's answer. The other woman didn't hesitate.

"Don't you worry, dear girl," Keela said. "The gardens I planted for the Extended are self-sustaining, so my services aren't needed here at the moment. I'd be happy to accompany you to Lagonia and do whatever I can to help."

Liss almost started bawling again from sheer relief.

"Thank you," she managed. "You have no idea how much."

"No need." Keela gave Liss a quick squeeze. "I'm a Green Thumb. We're built to heal and nurture. I can't stand to see anything living suffer, so if there's anything I can do to make these flowers grow, I'll gladly do it."

As soon as she'd finished speaking, Liss's mom and Mul stepped back through the ward.

There was a fierce look in Nya's eyes. She glared at the Metalsmith in warning before turning all of her attention on Liss.

It was still strange for Liss to see her mom striding around with a bow and quiver strapped to her back. For most of Liss's life, Nya had been huddled and shivering beneath a mountain of blankets. In just a few short weeks, she'd transformed into the leader of all the Extended. Although, by the looks of it, Mul was vying for that position.

Liss had also seen the way some of the Extended took their cues from Mul, and others waited for Nya's orders.

"I'm so grateful you decided to come back," Nya said, winding an arm around Liss's shoulder.

Liss swallowed. Her mom's smile faded at whatever expression she saw on Liss's face.

"I'm not staying," Liss said.

"I told you," Mul said, sounding smug.

Liss's mom glared at him. "We made a deal. Whether my daughter returns to the hideout or not, she is protected."

Mul glared daggers at Liss before disappearing back across the ward.

"What deal did you make with him?" Liss asked her mom.

Instead of answering, Nya replied with a question of her own. "Why are you here, if not to return to us?"

Liss glanced at Keela. For some reason, she didn't want to tell her mom that Rhett was sick. She wasn't sure why. She just couldn't make the words come.

Nya sighed. "Liss, you have to know you don't belong with a killer like Opal Slayer. Come home."

Liss bristled.

"Let me ask you something." Liss crossed her arms. "How many Extended have been killed when they came up against the Lagonia soldiers in the last few days?"

Liss's mom cocked her head, thinking. Liss saw the moment when understanding dawned.

"Not a single one, right?" Liss gave her mom a hard stare. "Why do you think that is, when our people are untrained and the Lagonians are the best soldiers on the continent?"

Nya' s eyes widened. Color seemed to leach out of her opal skin.

"Rhett," she whispered.

Before either of them could say anything more, Liss caught sight of Mari and Jema.

Mari was thirteen years old and the most beautiful Extended Liss had ever seen. Her burnt orange hair fell in soft ringlets down her back. Her opal skin had a brightness that made her stand out even among all the other Extended.

Jema, at nine years of age, was the youngest member of Liss's old thieving crew. What the little girl lacked in age, she made up for in personality.

The two girls were running through the Insorsiled forest and making a beeline straight for Liss, Nya, and Keela.

"Lissy!"

Jema barreled into Liss, hugging her with a strength that shouldn't be possible for someone so small. Mari wrapped one skinny arm around Liss and the other around Jema as they exchanged a fierce, three-way hug.

"Where are you coming from?" Nya demanded at the same moment Liss asked, "Why weren't you in the hideout?"

"It's not safe for you to be wandering around alone," Keela added.

"Mari and I went to spy in Insorsil," Jema announced proudly.

Mari gave Keela and Nya a defiant look.

"That was—" Liss began.

"Dangerous," Mari finished. The rainbow hue of her skin rippled as chagrin filled her soul. "I know we're not supposed to leave the hideout, but we weren't just going to sit around being useless."

"Well, what did you find out, my little thieves?" Liss asked, giving the girls as stern a look as she could manage. It wasn't like she could blame the kids for doing exactly what she would have done in their position.

The two girls exchanged a glance.

"King Krozor made an announcement to all the Insorsiled," Mari said. "He says he has a new spell that's more powerful than the strength of the entire Lagonia army." She swallowed. "And he's going to use that magic to kill every un-Insorsiled on the continent."

CHAPTER 19

Rhett urged Silverbird to pick up her pace. It was late afternoon, and spending an entire day apart from Liss was making him restless.

Wilsean was riding behind Rhett. Neither of them mentioned that Rhett would have fallen at least once during the ride if it wasn't for Wilsean's grip on his shoulder.

They'd spent the entire day searching for the rest of the slavers, who had disappeared into Insorsil and hadn't emerged. Their search had turned up nothing.

A day wasted, when Rhett didn't have a minute to spare.

Silverbird bounded across the icy shallows that separated Insorsil's coast from the cape's tip. Rhett and Wilsean clung to her back as she scaled the icy cliffside that led up to the fishermen's houses.

By the time they came within view of the looming barricade wall, the pale winter sun was setting.

As soon as Rhett glimpsed the unmanned barricade, with its doors hanging open, he knew something was wrong.

"Where are our archers?" Wilsean asked.

And wolves…and giants….

Rhett put his heels to Silverbird's flank, urging the dragon into a gallop.

They crested the final rocky hill before the barricade. An angry mob was amassed around the trench.

Rhett and Wilsean jumped off the dragon and ran forward on foot. There was so much chaos, no one even noticed them.

The giants were swinging their mallets through the air and trampling the stones beneath their feet into powder. Rebel soldiers were doing everything they could to get out of the giants' way.

"Rhett!"

Dannica, somehow catching sight of him amid the bedlam, ran over to him.

"Insorsiled attack," she shouted over the giants' crazed shouts. "The giants have never seen magic before. They're panicking."

"Wonderful," Wilsean muttered.

Curses zinged through the air, their red and purple sparks creating small bursts of flames and loud cracking noises.

Ciago and Winny were trying to regain control of the situation, but it was obvious the giants under her command were senseless with fear. The giants' wolves were growling and snapping at the flares of magic, but they seemed just as frightened as their masters.

Rhett's soldiers were fighting the Insorsiled as they tried to avoid being trampled by the giants or struck by curses.

What a mess.

Rhett searched the field until he found what he was looking for. A tight knot of warlocks stood at the edge of the trench as the rest of their people fought Rhett's soldiers.

"Show yourself, Krozor," Rhett called over the sounds of battle.

All fighting stopped as the group of Insorsiled standing in front of the trench spread out. Their king stepped forward.

The warlock's appearance was nothing special. Brown robes, brown cloak, unkempt brown hair. His beard was short, which was unusual for a warlock. He made up for the deficit with a veritable forest of hair sprouting from his bulbous nostrils. Krozor had a monocle over one eye that made it appear larger than the other eye. He certainly didn't look like the most powerful warlock to ever live.

Rhett grabbed the nearest Insorsiled and pressed his dagger to the man's throat. The warlock was a foot shorter than Rhett, which allowed Rhett to see straight over the man's head while using him as a shield against any other Insorsiled who might attack. Dannica, Ciago, and Winny had their own captives.

"Try anything against my soldiers," Rhett warned Krozor and the other Insorsiled, "and your people will die."

Rhett kept his captive in front of him as he stepped forward.

One step. Two.

Krozor was right there. Only the quaking warlock in Rhett's grip stood between them. The king was close enough for Rhett to reach out and touch. Close enough to slash his dagger across Krozor's throat.

Close enough for Rhett to see the gold pin glinting on the warlock king's dirty brown robe.

"You won't kill my subject," Krozor told Rhett. "Because if you do, there will be nothing to keep me from killing you."

Krozor glanced at Rhett and then turned back to the trench.

For what might have been the first time in his life, Rhett was stunned. No opponent had ever looked at him and then…disregarded him.

Rhett's soldiers outnumbered the Insorsiled ten to one, and Krozor was the only one wearing a pin. And yet, Krozor had looked at Rhett with little more regard than he might have given a stray dog.

Rhett stood there, with his dagger pressed against his captive's neck, as he stared at Krozor's back.

Krozor spread his arms out to the side, his belled sleeves dangling almost to the ground. Slowly, he began to raise his arms.

Everyone trapped inside the trench floated out.

Rhett had never seen such powerful magic.

The people inside the trench were rising in time with the motion of Krozor's arms. In seconds, every person who had been stuck at the bottom of the trench was now standing on the ledge.

Rhett tightened his hold on his captive, knowing it might very well be his only chance at living through this encounter.

"What the hell took you so long?" Jaikon snapped at Krozor. "I was down there for two days."

Krozor showed Jaikon only slightly more interest than he'd given to Rhett. The two men might be working together, but it was obvious there was no love between them.

Jaikon's cheeks reddened. His eyes narrowed into thin slits.

"You dare to ignore me, Krozor?" Jaikon asked in a soft voice that held the promise of violence.

Krozor didn't respond. He just adjusted his monocle and waited.

Jaikon reached for his sword, but he was empty-handed. That only incensed him more.

"Kill the magic freaks," he ordered his invincible soldiers.

The invincibles didn't hesitate. They started for the Insorsiled, and then…stopped. Some of them were poised with one foot in the air. Others were mid-leap and completely airborne. Rhett blinked, just to make sure he wasn't hallucinating.

As Rhett looked more closely, he saw that something was wrong with the soldiers' eyes. They had a glazed-over appearance, just like the witches and warlocks he'd seen days ago in Insorsil.

Then, all of the invincible soldiers spoke at once. Their voices had an inflectionless ring that sent a chill down Rhett's spine.

"We acknowledge King Krozor as our only master." The invincibles' limbs jerked, as though their own bodies were fighting against them. Then, every one of them turned to Krozor. They bowed.

"Holy shit," Ciago muttered.

"He's controlling their minds," Wilsean breathed.

There was no other explanation for what they were seeing. A hundred soldiers were frozen in their bowed poses, and Krozor was just standing there. He didn't give the impression of someone pushing himself to the limits of his power. If anything, he seemed mildly bored.

Samara had told Rhett that invincibility magic had been beyond even Gatria's skill. How powerful *was* this warlock?

"What is this?" Jaikon demanded, looking around at the soldiers still poised mid-attack. "What are you doing to my soldiers?"

The warlock let out a low, throaty laugh. "As you can clearly see for yourself, these are now *my* soldiers. And so are you."

Jaikon's red face darkened to a deep shade of plum. A vein throbbed at his temple.

"You conniving, pathetic—"

His words cut off. Spit flew from Jaikon's mouth and a sheen of sweat broke out on his forehead. And then, he sunk down into a bow before the warlock king.

Rhett knew Jaikon had no control over his own body. And yet, seeing the Emperor bow before another might just be the most gratifying sight Rhett had ever encountered. Ciago and Wilsean flashed Rhett an amused glance.

"You single-minded fool," Krozor told Jaikon, who was still frozen in place. "You were so worried about gaining invincibility, you never bothered to ask what other magic I might have infused into your pins. Do you honestly think I would have been stupid enough to gift you with invincibility without a means of controlling you?"

Jaikon put his hand to his chest. He grasped the pin like he was going to tear it off, but his fingers froze.

"You'll find the pins are now impossible to remove," Krozor told Jaikon, smiling a little at the Emperor's obvious distress. "The pin will affix itself to whatever you're wearing." His smile broadened. "And if you see fit to go without clothes, the pin will attach itself to your skin."

Jaikon made another fruitless attempt to wrestle the pin off his robes.

"I think the situation is clear," Krozor said. "In case it isn't, let me make myself plain. As I'm sure you're aware, Insorsil has no army. Well," he chuckled, "we *had* no army. Now, we do."

Krozor indicated the gold pin on Jaikon's chest. "I own you, Emperor Jaikon, which means that I own Lagonia."

The first tendrils of true fear snaked through Rhett. He was only beginning to grasp what Krozor could do with a hundred invincible soldiers under his command.

And there was nothing Rhett could do to stop any of them.

"And now, my faithful servants." Krozor smiled at Jaikon and the rest of the invincibles, all of whom were still frozen in unnatural positions. "Go forth. Attack the un-Insorsiled."

Jaikon turned his murderous gaze on Rhett.

Rhett didn't hesitate. He slashed his dagger across his captive's throat and thrust the body at Jaikon.

"No!" Krozor roared, reaching for the warlock who was already dead.

Wilsean, Ciago, and Winny killed their captives, earning more shouts from Krozor. For several precious seconds, the warlock king seemed frozen as he took in the sight of his dead countrymen.

Winny let out a piercing whistle, and then the pack of wolves attacked. Ulfrath and the others growled, snarled, and sunk their fangs into whatever they could reach.

Krozor let out an inhuman shriek as more of his people went down.

With everything spiraling out of his control, Krozor seemed lost. He stared around at the carnage and bellowed again.

Noticing a warlock who was bleeding out from a gash in his chest, the king seemed to forget about everything else. He crouched down beside the dying warlock. Sparks of magic flew from Krozor's fingertips as he tried to bring the other warlock back from the brink of death.

Rhett's people were taking advantage of the king's distraction. Wilsean took down two Insorsiled at once with his arrows. Dannica and Ciago used their swords with brutal efficiency. Rhett moved from one cowering warlock to the next, slashing throats and spraying blood across the icy rocks.

The giants' attention was on the invincibles. The giants might not be able to kill any of the humans, but that wasn't going to stop them from trying to get revenge for their murdered comrade. The nine remaining giants attacked.

They bashed the invincibles with their mallets. Blue light flared as the pins' protective shields activated. Both giants and invincibles were blasted into the air from the impact of the collision.

The giants roared in fury. The invincibles weren't harmed, even when they struck the ground dozens of feet away. The giants didn't give up. They planted their feet and swung their mallets over and over again. It wasn't long before every one of the invincibles was running away.

Krozor, his hands stained with the blood of the warlock he hadn't been able to save, got to his feet. His back was hunched, and he looked haggard. Then, he caught sight of the battlefield.

Every single one of the Insorsiled was dead.

Krozor's face contorted. He raised his arms.

Ulfrath, with the other wolves on his heels, bounded toward the warlock king.

In that moment, Rhett didn't think Krozor recalled that he was invincible. All the warlock saw were those fangs and blood-stained muzzles.

Krozor shouted something incoherent at the sky.

Gray, soupy smoke billowed from Krozor's fingertips. Rhett's nose stung as the air filled with the smell of rotten leaves and burnt sugar.

All at once, the smoke cleared. Krozor was gone.

All of the Insorsiled corpses had disappeared, too. All that remained were the streaks of blood on the rocks.

As Rhett met his friends' stunned gazes, he realized Jaikon and his army of invincible soldiers wasn't the only problem Rhett would have to solve before he succumbed to the contagion. If he wanted to offer Lagonia any hope of a future, he was going to have to find a way to kill Krozor.

CHAPTER 20

Samara wanted to scream.

"You look like you're about to start throwing things," Lullianna, Samara's two-year younger sister, said. She didn't glance up from the box of flowers.

"I'm not going to throw anything." Samara massaged the back of her neck, which might very well be permanently stuck in the staring-down-at-Gatria's-useless-spell book position.

"Well, if you change your mind," said Keela, "then please go into the other room. I'm trying to listen."

Right. Because plants could talk. And hear. Or at least, that was what Samara was gathering from all of the gentle words Keela kept murmuring to the box of immunity flowers.

So far, Keela was making as much headway with the flowers as Samara was with Gatria's spell book…which was to say none at all.

Samara went back to flipping through the brittle pages, even though she had all of the relevant parts memorized. There were no spells specifically about the immunity flowers, so either Samara had taken the wrong spell book, or Gatria had never written down how she'd created the immunity flowers. The latter was more likely. The queen had been suspicious and vain enough to ensure her most valuable spell never left the confines of her own head.

But that didn't mean this spell book was useless.

Each Insorsiled had his or her own magical strengths, and thus executed spells differently. Even for simple spells, like levitating small objects or brewing an illusion potion, Insorsiled approached them slightly differently.

Samara had become attuned to these slight variances during her long and careful study of magical theory. When she was younger, she'd referred to the unique imprint of each witch or warlock's magic as their *magical flair*.

By examining all of the spells in Gatria's book, Samara knew the former queen's magical imprint, much the same as she might recognize a particular Lagonian court lady from the scent of her perfume.

"Do you sense any metamorphosis magic?" Samara asked her sister.

"Hmm." Lullianna, who had been sniffing one of the flowers, put it in her mouth and closed her eyes.

Samara held back a wince. Lullianna needed to touch, taste, and deconstruct the flowers to understand their magic. Still, each one lost to experimentation felt like a permanent loss.

Of the eighteen they'd started with after Rhett took two, Lullianna had eaten one, burned another, and crushed two others for a brew she'd been working on.

Only fourteen flowers remained, and they were no closer to understanding how to replicate them or use them to create a cure.

Whatever spell Gatria had used to make the field of flowers replenish itself clearly wasn't at work for the fourteen flowers in front of her.

Once these were gone, they had no way to make more.

"Gatria also used a lot of magical properties that are usually found in poison spells," Samara continued, speaking over the anxiety churning in her mind. "But I doubt any of that would be relevant to the flowers."

"Samara, you're a genius!" Lullianna grabbed Samara's face and planted a kiss on her cheek. "I couldn't figure out why I kept sensing toxins in the flowers, but that totally makes sense now."

"It does?" Samara and Keela asked in unison.

Lullianna's eyes were bright with excitement. "These flowers must contain the tiniest bit of opal contagion. It's just a small amount that was metamorphosed into healing magic. The combination is what's giving the flowers their immunity properties."

"So, you know how to do it?" Samara heard the breathlessness in her own voice. "You can replicate them now?"

"No." Lullianna frowned down at the flowers. "I don't know the amounts or strengths of the spells, but this is the fun part." She rubbed her hands together.

"Be careful," Samara warned. "Don't push yourself too much."

"Oh, please." Lullianna rolled her eyes. "You're starting to sound like those stuffy old warlocks at the witchdoctor academy."

Even though she was only nineteen, Lullianna was already one of the most talented witchdoctors in all of Insorsil. She had outgrown her training about two years ago, and ever since then, Lullianna had amused herself by creating her own approach to healing spells.

The result was monthly suspensions from the academy and constant home visits from said stuffy old warlocks.

The door to the Insorsiled tent opened, and Ciago and Winny stepped inside.

The tent's ceiling and walls shifted subtly, so the two wouldn't have to duck to avoid hitting their heads.

"So, what brilliant discoveries have you made today?" Ciago asked. He adjusted the hood of his anti-contagion suit, which was much too tight on his hulking frame.

"We learned that Gatria was poisoning you through the flowers," Lullianna informed him in a bright voice.

Ciago's eyes widened. He put a hand to his stomach like the mere mention of poison made it ache.

"It wasn't poison," Samara corrected, giving her sister an exasperated look. "It was poison metamorphosed into healing magic. Basically, you were consuming just enough of the contagion to repel the true force of the virus when you encountered it."

"Is that how giants' natural immunity works?" Winny asked.

Lullianna glanced up at the giant leader. "Why do you ask?"

Winny shrugged. "I was just wondering if there was some way to magically replicate our immunity and give it to the sick."

"Or ours," Keela said, pointing to her opal skin.

"Or the Insorsiled," Samara added.

All three races had natural immunity to opal contagion.

"That's…actually kind of genius," Lullianna said.

"Everyone's a genius today, apparently," Samara noted.

Lullianna's lips pinched together in thought. "Magically transferring essence from one person to another is difficult, and all-but impossible across races. But maybe—"

"No experimenting on yourself," Samara warned, recognizing that gleam in her sister's eyes.

"Blah blah blah," Lullianna replied, falling back on the same retort she'd been using since she was five.

Lullianna began to murmur a spell under her breath as she held one hand over the box of flowers.

"Too much," Keela cautioned. She pointed at one of the flowers. A second later, its opal petals turned brown at the edges.

Lullianna switched to a different incantation, humming softly. As Samara watched, the brown edges of the flowers returned to their former opal sheen.

"Better," Keela said in relief.

"Did you figure it out?" Ciago asked.

Winny put a hand on his arm to stop his anxious fidgeting.

"It's going to take more time," Samara told him, knowing that frustrated-yet-determined look on her sister's face.

Ciago raised his arm to wipe at the sweat on his forehead before remembering he was covered by his suit. He dropped his arm.

"Come here," Lullianna told him, crooking a finger without looking his way.

Even though Ciago was usually the one giving orders, he didn't hesitate to do as he was told. He squatted down so he was at Lullianna's level. Lullianna rested a hand on his chest over the fabric of his anti-contagion suit.

"Why Lullianna," Ciago said in a seductive voice. "I didn't know this was the way things were between us. Not that I'm complaining."

"Oh, please." Lullianna giggled. "Wilsean warned me about you. I'm probably the only person with boobs you haven't slept with in Lagonia."

Out of the corner of her eye, Samara noticed Winny's expression flatten in irritation.

"I resent that," Ciago said. "There are definitely Lagonian women I haven't been with. Somewhere."

Lullianna giggled again. She'd always appreciated the copious amount of male attention she'd gotten since her early teens.

Of all their siblings, Samara and Lullianna looked the most alike. They both had their mother's gold skin. They also shared their father's silky white-blonde hair and amber eyes. The biggest difference was that Lullianna was shorter and thinner than Samara. While Samara's face was round, Lullianna's was more sharply-featured. *Birdlike* was the word Lullianna always used to describe herself.

The warlocks they went to school with had been interested in Samara too…until her latent magical abilities continued to stay dormant.

"You can take that suit off," Lullianna determined, giving Ciago's chest a pat. "The giants' immunity is strong enough in you that you won't be able to contract the disease."

"Really?" Ciago looked torn between his desire to remove the suit and his very real fear of the contagion.

"Promise," Lullianna told him. "Even though your essence is only one-eighth giant, you've got their immunity."

"You can tell that just by touching me?" Ciago almost ripped his suit in his eagerness to be rid of it.

Liss and Rhett were the next ones to appear through the brass door that led into the tent. The common room smoothly expanded once again to accommodate all of them. More cushioned seats appeared around the low table, and the smell of roasting meat wafted in from the empty kitchen.

"Where's your suit?" Rhett asked Ciago, his eyes widening. He grabbed Liss's hand and started backing out of the tent.

"It's okay," several voices said at once.

"His giant blood makes him immune," Samara explained.

Liss and Rhett both sighed in relief.

"Can't say I'm going to miss that suit," Ciago said, sinking down onto the couch.

Liss raised an eyebrow at him. "I thought you said it made you even more irresistible?"

"Let's be honest, Lovely Liss." Ciago grinned at her. "If I was any more irresistible, you'd abandon Rhett for me in a hot second."

Liss laughed. Rhett rolled his eyes skyward.

"Speaking of suits," Lullianna said, "Drink this." She handed Rhett, Liss, and Keela vials of potion she'd been brewing for the last twelve hours.

"Is it a cure?" Liss asked.

"No," Lullianna replied.

Samara's heart gave a painful squeeze at the expression that crossed her best friend's face.

"It'll filter the air around you and temporarily keep you from spreading the contagion," Lullianna explained as Rhett, Liss, and Keela choked down the potion. "It'll only last for a week and can't be taken more than once. It also won't do anything to help Rhett, but at least your soldiers won't have to wear their suits anymore."

The potion was just another example of Lullianna's skill as a witchdoctor. No potion like this had existed before, and Lullianna had only been working on it for a day.

If only coming up with a cure to the contagion could be so simple.

"Thank you," Rhett told Lullianna. "I appreciate it."

"Yeah, thanks," Liss said in a small voice without looking at Lullianna. Her stare was fixed on the box of flowers.

"Good news," Ciago informed Rhett, interrupting the fresh wave of tension. "The news that Jaikon killed your father has spread like wildfire, and the courtiers are muttering about throwing their support behind you."

Before anyone could speak, Ciago continued.

"Jaikon's advisors also know that Jaikon refused to implement the opal contagion protocols because he thought the panic would increase his popularity."

"The Lagonia rumor mill certainly has been busy," Liss murmured.

Ciago nodded. "My spies said two of the Emperor's women are leaking the information."

"Which ones?" Samara asked. As former servants for Jaikon's women, Samara and Liss knew everyone in the Emperor's harem.

Ciago scrunched up his face in thought. "I think their names were Jennev and Mizel. Ring any bells?"

Samara met Liss's shocked gaze. Jennev and Mizel were two of the three women Liss had served.

"Why would they spread those rumors?" Liss asked.

It was a good question. The Emperor's women knew the danger of displeasing the man who held their fates—and their very lives—in the palm of his hand. As much as Jaikon's harem loved gossip, they valued their lives more.

Or so Samara had thought.

Ciago frowned. "Jaikon murdered one of them a few weeks back. I think her name was Mireille."

Liss made a small sound.

Rhett turned to her. "One of yours?"

Liss nodded. "She was one of Jaikon's favorites," she said, her voice wobbling a little.

"Apparently, Jaikon was having a bad day," Ciago said with disgust. "Mireille had the bad luck to be with him at the time. He had Elouicia throw her body over the cliffs and didn't even bother telling her family."

"That monster," Samara whispered.

There was no grief in Liss's eyes. Only anger.

"We have to figure out how to kill him," Liss said.

Rhett nodded.

"Come here, Rhett," Lullianna said. "I need to touch you."

"Don't get your hopes up," Ciago told Rhett in a pouty voice. "She said the same thing to me not two minutes ago."

Raising his eyebrows, Rhett moved forward and crouched down so Lullianna could reach him.

Samara watched her sister's face grow a shade paler. Rhett, who had been studying Lullianna's expression, nodded in understanding.

"Oh, Rhett," Lullianna whispered. "I'm sorry."

Liss sank down onto one of the cushioned chairs, looking deflated.

Samara bit the inside of her cheek. She hated that there was nothing she could do to erase that look on Liss's face.

"Maybe there's something I can do for the pain," Lullianna began.

"No." Rhett glanced at Liss. "It doesn't hurt."

Lullianna wasn't exactly known for her bedside manner. Samara knew if her sister was talking about managing pain, Rhett must be in agony.

"Is there any hope?" Liss asked in a dull voice.

"Don't worry," Lullianna said. "I saved his life once before. I'll do it again."

Rhett nodded, even though Samara knew he wasn't fooled by Lullianna's brave face. Healing broken bones was very different from curing opal contagion.

CHAPTER 21

King Krozor Ragnor Mantis raised his staff. The crystal orb perched on top flared teal. He didn't need the staff's amplifying properties to generate his magic, like so many of his weaker subjects. Rather, he needed the staff to contain the raw magic he was collecting for his spell.

Krozor stood above the enormous hole the slavers were in the process of digging.

Some tasks were simpler to accomplish without magic. And Krozor certainly wouldn't mourn the loss of any un-Insorsiled who perished from the labor.

He had selected this location for the hole he referred to as *the pit* for two reasons. The first was because it was miles away from the kingdom proper. The second reason was more sentimental.

Krozor was standing atop an ancient Insorsiled burial ground. It was where he'd finally unearthed the artifact he'd sought for over a hundred years. The archaeologist in him had cringed at desecrating a place with so much history, but it had been necessary.

Other scholars might have scoffed at the stories surrounding the ancient artifact, but Krozor had sensed there was truth behind the legend. And he'd been right. Now, he had the magic to do what no previous ruler of Insorsil had been brave or wise enough to accomplish.

He was going to rid the world of the un-Insorsiled.

He stared at the hundreds of slavers hard at work. The filthy men before him wore no pins, but they were motivated by other means. Elouicia, the evil Chief Assassin who commanded them, watched their every move. He held a leather whip in one hand and his sword in the other.

If only controlling Krozor's own subjects was so easy, but of course, that was what he'd needed the artifact for. With it, he already had two dozen of his own people sending bursts of magical energy into the partially-dug pit.

Krozor despised forcing his people to do anything against their will.

All for the good of Insorsil, he reminded himself.

"Oh fuck!" a slaver yelled.

There were a few surprised shouts, and then a geyser of water erupted from the pit.

Slavers and Insorsiled were thrust off their feet from the force of the water. A frigid spray came right at Krozor. He jerked backward, gasping as cold doused him.

All at once, his vision went blurry. His hold over the Insorsiled wavered.

The artifact was gone.

No. It couldn't be gone.

He'd waited too long to find it.

He took no notice of the slavers who gurgled and floundered in the rising water. Krozor dropped to his hands and knees. He frantically began to pat the wet ground. He moved slowly, so he wouldn't accidentally crush the fragile object. He might be able to repair the glass if it shattered, but he couldn't replicate the ancient spell within.

"Where are you?" he muttered as he continued to search the ground.

Movement out of the corner of his eye drew his attention away from his feverish search.

The Insorsiled who had been under the artifact's control were blinking and staring around, like they had no idea how they'd gotten to this place. Some of them had begun to weep. Others were murmuring to each other.

One was running.

A furious sound escaped between Krozor's clenched teeth. He thrust out his hand. Magic shot from the tips of his dirty fingers.

The witch froze mid-stride.

Krozor snatched up his staff and stalked over to the witch.

Her eyes were wide with terror. Her mouth was partly open, like she had been in the process of screaming when Krozor's spell struck her.

"Where are you going?" Krozor asked the witch.

He adjusted his spell just enough for the woman's mouth to move. The rest of her limbs remained frozen.

"Have to tell," the witch said, her voice wavering. "Have to warn them."

Krozor frowned. "Why?" he asked, genuinely puzzled.

"You'll kill all the un-Insorsiled." Her lip curled, as though she couldn't stand the sight of him. As though he was her enemy instead of her savior.

"That's right," Krozor said, barely able to contain his mounting irritation. "And then we'll be free from those who wish to kill us and steal our magic for themselves."

"Still human," the witch said in a shrill voice. "Don't deserve to die."

Krozor felt his magic churn restlessly within him. He'd been arguing against this foolish perspective for the last century.

"The un-Insorsiled aren't people," he told his misguided subject. "They are a lesser species and weaker than us."

"You're a monster."

A single tear leaked from the witch's unblinking eye and dribbled down her cheek.

Krozor stared into the witch's wide, terrified eyes for several moments. He sighed at the deluded conviction he saw in them.

With a heavy heart, Krozor lifted his staff. He hated the idea of snuffing out an Insorsiled life. But he couldn't let his secret be exposed before he was ready.

Krozor pressed the glowing orb to the witch's neck, just above her throbbing pulse.

The air crackled. Teal flames erupted from the staff. The witch let out a shriek as her entire body was engulfed in the flames.

Krozor kept his gaze averted until the burning scent of magic and charred flesh dissipated.

He knelt beside the witch's bones. The words of the ancient death prayer were already on his lips, when he noticed the sunlight glinting off something on the ground.

All other thoughts abandoned him. Krozor dropped his staff and crawled over.

A tremor went through his entire body as his fingers closed around the artifact.

All of Krozor's tension melted away the moment the frosty glass was resting against his skin. Krozor fixed his stare on the Insorsiled who stood by. Their petrified looks vanished and were replaced by blank expressions.

Krozor smiled.

CHAPTER 22

Samara pressed the heels of her hands into her eyes. They were running out of time, and she and Lullianna were still no closer to figuring out the cure.

Lullianna was stirring a potion that was boiling and frothing. Keela was singing a song to the box of flowers. And Samara was going cross-eyed from going over Gatria's spells again and again.

Liss, who was sitting on the couch next to Rhett, cleared her throat. "There was a witchdoctor who made my Lagonian father immune to my mom's strain of the contagion," she told Lullianna. "I was just wondering if—"

"No." Rhett, who never showed any emotion, looked furious.

"I'm just asking," Liss said.

"Whoever worked that spell was deep into black magic," Lullianna told Liss without glancing up from her potion. "Those kinds of spells are unstable and as likely to kill you as they are to work. Even I wouldn't attempt it."

Samara felt her own tension ease slightly. Sometimes, she wasn't sure how far her sister would be willing to go for the sake of her experiments.

Rhett seemed relieved, too. Liss seemed to grow smaller. She wrapped her arms around her knees.

Rhett leaned closer and said something that was too quiet for anyone else to hear. His words seemed to calm Liss a fraction. He absently twirled a lock of her hair around his finger as he spoke.

They were both so in tune with each other. It made Samara think of Wilsean.

As if her thoughts had summoned him, Wilsean appeared in the doorway to the tent. His attention went straight to her. Her heart stuttered as they exchanged a smile.

She wondered if he would ever stop having that effect on her. They had been together for almost a year, and her body temperature still rose every time he walked into the room.

"Is there any news on the invincibles?" the giant leader asked Wilsean as he pulled off his jacket.

Thanks to the potion Lullianna had made, the Lagonians didn't need to wear their suits around Rhett, Liss, or Keela for the time being.

"Still in the palace," Wilsean replied. He turned to Rhett. "I don't know why they haven't attacked us yet."

"Maybe they don't want to get bashed around by the giants' mallets again," Ciago suggested.

Rhett shook his head. "Jaikon will retaliate. He won't give up a part of his empire without a fight."

"The giants will be ready," Lady Winnowa said in a low, threatening voice.

Ciago huffed out a sigh. "Not much we can do while they're still invincible."

The weight of every one of their unsolvable problems filled the room. It sat like a heavy blanket on top of all of them, suffocating them.

Liss stood and began to pace. "The kids said Krozor has a new spell. Apparently, it's going to kill all the un-Insorsiled."

Samara looked at her sister, who lifted a shoulder.

"Anyone in Insorsil who knows anything isn't talking," Lullianna said.

Wilsean raised an eyebrow. "Sounds like something worth investigating."

Rhett and Ciago nodded.

"Flowers first," Liss said, her tone leaving no room for argument.

"On that note, everyone scram," Lullianna announced. "I have some theories I need to test, and I can't do it with all of you babbling in my ear." She made a shooing motion with her hand.

"What theories?" Keela asked.

"And how many days of suspension would the academy give you for trying them?" Samara added.

Lullianna fisted her hands on her hips.

"If those old farts had it their way, everyone would die because they were too cautious to ever do anything useful." Lullianna made an annoyed sound. "I don't want to be a useless old fart. I want to be the witchdoctor who saved Lagonia's sexy future emperor."

"Witchdoctor in training," Samara reminded her sister.

"Semantics," Lullianna shot back.

As Samara looked at her sister, one of her own theories began to take shape.

"I wonder," Samara said. "Maybe we could create a synthetic kind of essence."

At the uncomprehending looks she got, she explained, "We could write a new spell that replicates our natural opal contagion immunity but leaves behind all the lethal parts."

"Why don't we write a spell to bottle up the stars while we're at it," Lullianna said. "That would probably be easier than what you're suggesting."

Symbols rearranged themselves in Samara's head as she imagined the kind of spell that would be needed to do what she had in mind.

"If I wrote the spell," Samara said to her sister, "could you perform it?"

"Duh." Lullianna cocked her head to the side. "Probably." She pursed her lips. "Okay, fine. Maybe."

"Only one way to find out," Samara said, reaching for a sheet of paper and hunting around for a quill.

"Oh no you don't," Wilsean said. "You haven't slept in two days."

"I'm not tired." She resisted the urge to rub at her gritty eyes as she continued to search for a quill.

"We all need sleep," Rhett said in a gruff voice. "Everything will still be waiting for us in the morning."

Liss seemed poised to argue.

"One night isn't going to change anything," Rhett told her. "Those flowers I ate are holding me. We still have time."

"My giants and wolves will guard the barricade tonight," Lady Umbrog said.

"I don't think Jaikon will make a move before the slavers come back from Insorsil," Ciago said. "He'll want his full force around when he faces us, since I think the invincibles have developed a phobia of enormous wolves."

He exchanged a sly grin with the giant leader.

"You go ahead," Samara told the others. She grabbed the quill that had materialized on the table. "I'm just going to—"

Wilsean crossed the room and, without warning, scooped Samara into his arms.

"So romantic," Lullianna sighed.

"Hardly," Samara replied, giving Wilsean a glare that he studiously ignored. "I have work to do."

"Tomorrow," he told her.

"Wilsean," she said through clenched teeth.

He didn't put her down until they were inside their bedroom. Wilsean turned the lock in the door, as though to make sure she didn't escape again. To be fair, she had been planning on doing just that. But as soon as they were standing in front of the crackling fire, with their turned-down bed beckoning her, Samara swayed on her feet.

"Has it really been two days?" she asked, trying and failing to stifle a yawn.

"Two-and-a-half," Wilsean said as he started to undress her.

Without Gatria's spell book in her hands and the mystery of the flowers staring her in the face, Samara felt her eyelids grow heavy. The room was so warm, and Wilsean's hands felt so good as he gently peeled away her layers.

She could have climbed into bed herself, but she let Wilsean lift her onto the mattress and pull the blanket over her. She barely kept her eyes open long enough to watch Wilsean strip out of his own clothes.

The feel of his body molded against hers was almost enough to wake her back up. But then his fingers found the knots in her neck and started to massage away tension she hadn't even known she'd been carrying. Her eyes closed against their will.

"Samara?"

"Hm?"

Wilsean's hand paused on her shoulder. "At some point when everything calms down, will you come have dinner with my parents?"

That was enough to bring Samara out of near-unconsciousness. She wriggled around until she was facing Wilsean.

"You said your parents were as warm as an ice statue during a blizzard."

He chuckled. "That unfortunate truth still stands, but if anyone can thaw them, it's you."

A dozen questions entered Samara's mind. She went with the most obvious one.

"Why?"

She felt Wilsean's shrug. "I figured it would be a good time to introduce you."

Another variation of the *why* question was on the tip of Samara's tongue. Wilsean's family was one of the richest and most influential in the whole empire. She couldn't imagine them wanting to have dinner with an Empty-turned-servant-turned-rebel.

"If that would make you happy," she said, when she realized seconds were stretching into minutes.

"It would." Wilsean pulled her to him, giving her a hard kiss. "Thank you. Now, turn back around so I can keep massaging you."

"Yessir."

He swept her long hair over her shoulder and kissed the back of her neck. She was on the edge of sleep when he spoke again.

"I love you, my beautiful, stubborn witch."

"I'm not a witch," she mumbled sleepily.

His next words were so quiet she wasn't sure if he'd actually said them or if she was already dreaming.

"Then how do you explain the fact that I'm utterly, completely, and irrevocably enchanted by you?"

CHAPTER 23

J aikon paced back and forth as he fumed.

He could feel the incessant tug of Krozor's last orders—for Jaikon to send his own soldiers to attack the un-Insorsiled. In other words, Jaikon was supposed to kill his own subjects.

Now that the warlock king had returned to his hovel in Insorsil, the pull of his command was more subtle than it had been when they were standing face-to-face. But it was still there, in the back of his mind. With every minute that passed, the compulsion to obey grew stronger.

Jaikon wouldn't be able to resist much longer.

The fingers of his good hand were aching from his unsuccessful attempts to remove the pin.

Jaikon roared in frustration. And then he beheaded a gold bust of his father, the former emperor.

If only he wasn't beholden to serve the warlock's anti-Lagonia agenda, he could raze Insorsil to the ground. He knew Krozor's weakness; the hairy old fool couldn't stomach the loss of a single magical life. All it would take would be for Jaikon's soldiers to slaughter a few dozen of those magic-peddling fools. Then, Krozor would be forced to surrender the kingdom.

If only he could take off this pin, he'd ruin Krozor the way he had so many others.

A knock came at the chamber door.

"Enter," Jaikon barked.

Elouicia stepped inside the gilded chamber and bowed.

"If you're here to tell me that my own damned advisors are turning on me, you can save your breath," Jaikon said sourly.

Somehow, Jaikon's most closely-guarded secret had been revealed, and the gossip had spread through the entire court. The former emperor had been well-loved, and the courtiers and peasants were demanding justice on the dead man's behalf.

After everything Jaikon had done for those ungrateful fools, they were clamoring for Rhetteman to take the throne. As if a lowbrow bastard could ever be good for anything besides assassinating people.

"Majesty," Elouicia said, bringing Jaikon's attention to the man standing before him. "Burk has disappeared."

It took Jaikon several seconds to process the meaning of those insignificant words. When he did, he just waved a dismissive hand.

"He's no prisoner of mine," Jaikon told his second-in-command.

If Burk wanted to go and get himself murdered by his own people, that was his affair. The whispering, groveling fool had told Jaikon everything he knew and was therefore of no further use.

Or was he?

As soon as Jaikon was reminded of Burk, and the Insorsiled contract between them, an idea began to take shape.

Burk's vague language in the contract had enabled Jaikon to torture the pathetic man for weeks on end. The language of Krozor's command had been similarly weak.

What had the warlock said?

Attack the un-Insorsiled.

Krozor had clearly been referring to the Lagonians, but they weren't the only un-Insorsiled.

Jaikon felt his grimace transform into a smile. He needed an army that was both strong enough to overwhelm the Insorsiled and couldn't be controlled by the new king. And thanks to Krozor's imprecise language, Jaikon knew exactly how to obtain what he needed.

"Gather the invincible soldiers," Jaikon ordered his Chief Assassin. "Send them across the sea to conquer the giants."

Ten—now nine—of the giants were already in the empire and had inexplicably allied themselves with Rhetteman. But the rest of those brutes were still on that frozen, forsaken land across the sea.

The giants were formidable enemies, but against an invincible army, they could do nothing except die or surrender.

Krozor was the only true threat that remained. Rhetteman's pathetic band of rebels would fall apart as soon as their leader died. Some of his soldiers would try to run. The rest would come crawling back to Jaikon.

"Tell my soldiers to kill the giants until the ones that are left agree to sign an Insorsiled contract to serve me," Jaikon ordered his Chief Assassin.

Jaikon couldn't wait to see the look on Krozor's face when Jaikon's army of giants stormed into Insorsil. They'd destroy everything and everyone in their path. And they'd continue to destroy the kingdom until Krozor revoked his hold over Jaikon and officially ceded control of Insorsil.

Elouicia swiped his tongue across his sharpened canines before sinking into a low bow.

As soon as the order was given, Jaikon felt a lessening on the strain inside his mind. He smirked to himself. He was upholding Krozor's orders while plotting against the warlock.

It was sheer brilliance.

"What orders should I give the slavers?" Elouicia asked.

"Their orders remain the same," Jaikon replied. "They are to remain in Insorsil and do whatever the warlock king tells them. I don't want Krozor to suspect we're up to anything.

"In your spare time, hunt the Extended. I want all of those opal freaks dead."

Elouicia bared his sharpened teeth in glee. He bowed again, and left the room.

As the door shut, Jaikon thought he caught a flicker of movement against the far wall of his meeting chamber. When he looked again, there was nothing. He paced over to investigate, but another knock came at the door.

"Yes?" Jaikon snapped.

Burk limped in. The smell of the sewer came with him, and Jaikon found himself reaching for his sword before he remembered his Insorsiled oath not to kill the parasite.

"Get out," Jaikon hissed.

"Majesty." Burk stood where he was, letting his grime ooze into the air around them. Jaikon's eyes watered from the stench. "I have discovered the answer to the problem you're most desperate to solve."

"I very much doubt that." Jaikon strode to the door to order his guards to remove the Extended filth from his sight.

"But before I tell you," the sniveling oaf continued, "I want your word that I will be rewarded with a *properly appointed* room in the palace."

"Guards!" Jaikon roared into the corridor.

Two mercenaries marched forward. They grasped Burk by each arm and dragged him out of the room. The Extended man's grime-encrusted shoes squealed across the granite floor.

When Burk spoke, his whisper was almost inaudible.

"But Your Majesty. I know how to end Krozor's control over you."

CHAPTER 24

Liss sat in an overstuffed chair in her and Rhett's bedroom as night inched toward dawn. She watched Rhett while he slept, squinting to see the tiny rise and fall of his chest. He was so utterly still.

Usually, the smallest sound woke him, but he'd slept on as she tossed and turned and finally gave up on the idea of sleep. Deep bruise-like rings of exhaustion stood out against the yellow skin of Rhett's face.

He had taken to sleeping fully clothed. Liss knew it was because he didn't want her to see the state of his body.

Liss went back to gnawing on her nail beds with renewed vigor. She jerked to her feet when she sensed a familiar soul outside the tent.

What was Jema doing here?

Liss ran out of the room and to the brass door. As she passed through the common room, she saw the box of flowers on the table. There were only eight flowers left, and Lullianna and Keela were nowhere in sight.

Shaking her head to clear away her growing panic, Liss opened the brass door to the outside. A compact little ball rolled across the threshold. The ball grew and stretched as it unraveled, until it became a fully-formed girl. Jema tackled Liss, bear-hugging her with twiggy arms.

"What are you doing here?" Liss asked Jema.

"I have a present for you," Jema announced as Liss hurried over to the vials of potion Lullianna had stacked on the table just for this purpose.

Liss didn't know if Wilsean and Ciago's closed bedroom doors would protect them, but she wasn't willing to take any chances.

"Drink this first," Liss said, handing Jema one of the vials that would keep her from spreading opal contagion to the Lagonians.

Jema grimaced as she tossed back the liquid, but she didn't complain. Her soul was too full of excitement from whatever news she had to share to even bother asking what the potion was for.

After she'd drained the vial, Jema pulled out a scroll from inside her threadbare jacket. She proudly held it out for Liss's inspection.

Liss decided to delay her lecture about how it wasn't safe for Jema to leave the Extended hideout, since it clearly hadn't taken the first several times she'd given it. Besides, her curiosity was getting the better of her.

Liss scanned the document. She read it a second time more carefully. She looked at Jema, who grinned at her.

"Right?" Jema bounced up and down on the balls of her feet. "I thought it was important, too."

"Where did you find this?" Liss asked.

"In Burk's room in the palace," Jema replied.

"You were in the palace?!"

"Don't worry, Lissy." Jema gave Liss's arm a patronizing pat. "I only went into the sewers where Burk lives." She crinkled her button nose in disgust and then giggled. "He must be so mad the Emperor makes him live down there. It's *really* smelly."

Liss bent down and scooped Jema into her arms. She spun the squealing, giggling child around and planted a kiss on her opal cheek.

"Nugget, you are the sneakiest, most brilliant thief of all time."

Jema's smile was so wide it stretched across her entire face.

"What are we celebrating?" Ciago asked, yawning as he sauntered out of his bedroom.

"Something potentially amazing," Liss told him as she lowered Jema to the ground. "I have to talk to Samara to be sure."

"I'd knock if I were you," Ciago began as Liss barged right in. This was too important for knocking.

"Shit, Liss." Wilsean lowered the throwing knives he had poised in both hands. He let the weapons clatter back onto the side table and gathered the covers up to his chin. "Where's the fire?"

Instead of answering, Liss thrust the contract at a tousled and sleepy-eyed Samara.

Samara examined the contract, while Wilsean read over her shoulder.

Wilsean's brows furrowed. "Let me get this straight. You barged in here in the middle of the night to tell us that Burk betrayed your people and Jaikon promised not to kill him?" He glared at Liss. "Not exactly ground-breaking news."

"I know." Ciago flopped onto the foot of the bed and stretched out like a cat. "I tried to tell her not to encroach on your sexy time, but she refused to listen."

"We were *sleeping*," Wilsean growled.

"Sure, sure." Ciago reached for a bowl of candy on the side table.

Jema was next. Ciago patted the comforter next to him, and Jema launched herself on the bed. Ciago and Jema started unwrapping the sweets on top of the covers. If Liss wasn't too on edge, she would have been right there with them.

"Which one is stronger?" Liss asked Samara. And then, realizing she was about ten steps ahead in her own mind, she clarified, "If Jaikon were to break his end of this contract, would his invincibility protect him?"

"Liss?"

Rhett stood in the doorway, giving their group a quizzical look.

Wilsean let his head fall back against the headboard. Hard.

"Come on in," Wilsean drawled. "Make yourself at home."

"Binding magic can't be overridden by any other spells," Samara said after considering the scroll for another minute. "Otherwise, it would be too easy for people to get out of oaths they'd made."

"Can Samara and I please have some privacy so we can get dressed?" Wilsean asked through gritted teeth.

Jema glanced up from her pile of empty wrappers. "Are you naked under there?" Her voice was a little garbled from all the candy wedged in her cheeks.

"As the day we were born," Wilsean replied.

Samara gave him a *seriously?* look as her face turned crimson.

"But what happens if you touch?" Jema's nose wrinkled.

"It's been known to happen," Wilsean said.

Samara smacked a palm to her forehead.

"But what if—"

"Eat your candy, kid," Ciago advised.

Liss felt a smile tug at her lips, but she was too intent on the contract to be distracted just yet.

"So, the contract is stronger?" she asked Samara, needing to be sure.

"Yes, the contract is stronger," Samara confirmed. "If either of them breaks their side of the agreement, they'll die."

Liss started to laugh. She sounded a little crazy, and judging from the way everyone in the room was staring at her, she looked it, too. She didn't care.

"I don't see what good this does us," Rhett said, taking the contract from Samara and scanning it. "The only way to get Jaikon to break his part of the bargain would be if he killed Burk."

Liss finally got a hold of herself enough to string together a coherent sentence.

"I have a plan for how we're going to take down both Burk and Jaikon." She met Rhett's fierce gaze and felt her glee cool just a little. "But you're not going to like it."

CHAPTER 25

Not a chance." Rhett crossed his arms and glared at Liss. "It's not even up for discussion."

"You're right about that part," Liss said, giving his glare right back to him.

She'd just finished telling all of them her brilliant plan for taking down Jaikon, and Rhett was just about out of his mind at what she was suggesting.

"I've got a pound of gold on Liss winning this lover's spat," Ciago announced, digging a handful of coins out of his pocket.

"My money's on Rhett," Wilsean announced. "And if you all don't get the hell out of my room, knives are going to start flying."

"Be nice," Samara ordered him.

"Do you have any more of that red candy?" Jema asked.

Rhett let Liss take his arm and pull him out of the room and into theirs. Liss shut the door and turned to face him.

"Save your breath," he told her, knowing there was no point in controlling his features when she could feel the fear in his soul. "I'm not letting you do it."

"This plan is guaranteed to work," she argued.

"It won't matter if you get yourself killed!"

Rhett couldn't keep his voice down. The thought of Liss inside the palace…of facing Jaikon…was more than he could stomach.

"I know Burk and Jaikon's souls," Liss persisted. "I can read their emotions the whole time and know what to say to make sure they do exactly what I want. It's the only way to make sure everything works out right."

"No." Rhett shook his head hard enough that it left him dizzy. "I'll do it."

Liss crossed her arms. "It won't work if it's you. Jaikon wants you to suffer from the contagion, so he isn't going to kill you."

"And that's supposed to make me feel better?"

Rhett's head was beginning to pound.

"You won't even be able to get into the palace without Jaikon's guards seeing you," he pointed out.

Not that logistics had ever stopped Liss before.

A crafty smile curved Liss's lips. "Leave that part to me."

"Liss, if anything happens to you—"

Liss took his hand and put it against her beating heart. She was so warm and alive. It was both comforting and terrifying.

"Trust me," Liss said in a quiet voice, leaning closer until they were breathing the same air. "I'm not going to leave you. I promise."

"Sometimes thieves lie," Rhett reminded her.

Liss smiled at those words, and Rhett's resolve crumbled into dust. He reached up with the hand that wasn't still pressed to her heart and caressed the dimple in her cheek.

"Is that a yes?" Liss asked in a whisper.

"Do I have a choice?"

Her smile broadened as she shook her head.

When Rhett opened the door, Ciago, Wilsean, Samara, and Jema almost fell into the bedroom. There was some throat clearing, and then Ciago, Samara, and Jema began to grin. Wilsean scowled.

"You cost me a fortune," Wilsean complained to Rhett.

"You can afford it," Rhett replied dryly.

"So, what's the plan, Empress?" Ciago asked Liss.

A jolt went through Rhett, even though he knew Ciago had meant it as a joke. Rhett had given little thought to the idea of becoming emperor, since it was obvious he wouldn't live long enough to take the position. But if he had, what would that have meant for him and Liss?

He couldn't expect her to live in the palace with him when all of her people were elsewhere.

The thought of waking up every morning without her sent a stab through his gut before he remembered that line of thinking was pointless. Rhett wouldn't live long enough to see the end of this brewing war, and he certainly wouldn't live long enough to ask Liss to be his—

"I need a message delivered to the palace," Liss said. "We'll also need to talk about my exit strategy, since it's a little rough around the edges."

Rhett snorted. *Rough around the edges* didn't begin to cover Liss's insane plan.

"Sounds like my kind of plan," Ciago said, rubbing his hands together in anticipation. "Let's get to work."

"I can deliver the message," Jema volunteered, tugging on the hem of Liss's shirt to make sure she wasn't ignored. "If you make one promise."

"Oh?" Liss gave the little girl an amused look.

"You have to let Spence, Mari, and me stay here with you."

"They can have my room," Ciago offered. "I'm going to start staying with the giants. You know, just to keep an eye on things."

Wilsean grinned.

Rhett narrowed his gaze on Ciago. "You're not going to let…whatever this is between you and Winny…get in the way of our alliance with the giants, are you?"

It wouldn't be the first time a woman became violent after Ciago bedded her and then lost interest.

"I resent your implications." Ciago gave Rhett a wounded look. "And for your information, there is absolutely nothing going on between Winny and me."

Rhett wasn't so sure he believed his friend, but he let the matter drop.

"Say yes, Lissy," Jema begged.

"Jema, it's too dangerous," Liss said. "And I don't think—"

Jema jutted out her chin. "Spence, Mari, and I are sick of everyone telling us we can't help out. We can." She crossed her skinny arms. Besides, we don't like that our people are being so mean to the Lagonians. We want to help you."

Jema tilted her head back so she could give Rhett a pleading look. He shrugged at the kid, making it clear all of this was out of his hands.

"You drive a hard bargain, nugget," Liss said, stroking the girl's hair.

"Woohoo!" Jema threw her arms around Liss. Then, to Rhett's horror, the little barnacle attached herself to him.

"Um—" Rhett turned to Liss for help, but she was no longer beside him.

Liss ran across the room, grabbed two vials of potion off the table, and hurried to the door.

"Liss?" he asked.

"Be right back," she called, taking the vials outside.

Rhett was about to go after her, when Mari walked right through the solid oak wall and appeared in the tent's common room.

"Ugh, that potion tastes awful," she said, her orange curls bouncing as she shook her head. She plunked the empty vial down on the table.

The tent's door opened, and Spence and Liss came inside. Spence was carrying his own empty vial of potion and complaining about the taste.

"You guys are not going to believe what I just overheard," Mari said as she accepted the glass of juice Samara offered her.

"What part of *you need to stay in the hideout for your own safety* wasn't clear?" Liss asked the kids, looking exasperated.

Rhett felt a little smug at that. If she was going to torture him with this insane plan of hers, at least the kids were giving her a small taste of her own medicine.

"Someone needs to keep up the spying now that Opal Smoke is retired," Mari said, sinking down onto the couch and sighing in contentment.

Rhett turned away to hide his amusement. Ciago and Wilsean both chuckled. Liss glared at the kids.

"Trust me," Spence said, sprawling out on the couch next to Mari. "You're going to be kissing our feet when you hear what we have to say."

"Spill," Liss ordered.

Spence indicated for Mari to go first while he finished off her glass of juice.

"I was spying on Jaikon, and—"

Rhett saw horror overtake Liss's face at the thought of the kids being so close to the Emperor.

"Now you know how I feel," Rhett muttered to Liss, unable to help himself.

"Anyway," Mari said. "Jaikon is sending all of his invincibles to the Giant Realm to conquer the giants."

Ciago, who had been leaning against the wall, stood up so fast he knocked his head against a low-hanging chandelier.

"Jaikon wants to enslave the giants and force them to become part of his army," Spence explained. "He's going to use them to attack Insorsil so Krozor will surrender to him."

"I have to tell Winny," Ciago said.

"Wait." Rhett put out a hand. He turned his attention on the kids. "Have Jaikon's invincibles left yet?"

Spence shook his head. "I saw them getting their ships ready, so I'm guessing they're leaving soon."

Rhett turned to Ciago. His friend's look of fury transformed to a mischievous grin.

"You thinking what I'm thinking?" Ciago asked.

Rhett nodded. "Take as many rebels as you need to get it done."

Ciago's smile widened.

A dawning light appeared in Wilsean's eyes. "Are you thinking of doing what we did to those cannibalistic humans during the Giant War?"

"Just on a bigger scale," Rhett replied.

"It's going to be excellent." Ciago headed for the door. "I have to go tell Winny."

"I happen to know a beautiful formerly-Insorsiled woman who might be able to hook you up with some necessary supplies," Wilsean offered.

"Does someone want to explain what's going on?" Samara asked.

"Yeah," Liss added. "The three of you look like devious triplets."

"Don't you worry, Lovely Liss." Ciago swooped down and planted a kiss on her cheek. "If all goes according to plan, we'll soon be rid of those invincibles. Permanently."

"But—" Liss began.

"Let Ciago worry about the invincibles," Rhett told her. "We have an emperor and a snitch to murder."

CHAPTER 26

It had taken Burk exactly ten seconds to pack his measly possessions into his filthy travel bag. Now, he was waiting with baited breath for the sound of footsteps descending into the sewer.

Part of him expected this to be another one of Jaikon's tricks. He'd been careful with the language of their bargain, but there was no limit to Jaikon's cruelty.

Then again, Burk had discovered the answer that Jaikon most craved.

It had been a gamble on Burk's part to go into Insorsil during a time of such upheaval. He'd risked his own life to get close enough to the castle to spy on the new king. His efforts had paid off when he overheard Krozor explain to one of his subjects how he controlled Jaikon and the rest of the invincibles.

It was a manipulation spell inside those little gold pins. In order to end Krozor's control over Jaikon and his soldiers, the Emperor would need to destroy the pin from which the others had been created. In other words, the Emperor needed to find a way to convince the warlock king to part with his invincibility pin.

It seemed like an impossible task, but that wasn't Burk's problem.

Jaikon had been so elated to have the information that Burk could have probably squeezed out a better bargain for himself. But if Burk's terms were met, it would be more than he'd ever hoped for.

Burk leapt up from his squalid pallet at the sound of footsteps echoing off stone steps. His pulse was pounding so furiously it made his head hurt.

Burk shouldered his bag and opened the door to his dingy room.

A servant wearing an anti-contagion suit bowed stiffly.

"Sir, would you permit me to escort you to your new accommodations?"

Burk barely managed to keep himself from sprinting up the stone stairs that led out of the sewer and into the palace proper.

The servant led Burk through one gorgeous hallway after another.

"Your room is in this hallway, sir," the servant told Burk.

The walls had chunks of jewels embedded amid the delicate latticework of leather wallpaper. Ornate gilt mirrors and priceless tapestries were hung in the spaces between the enormous bay windows. Burk's heart soared.

The servant bent to unlock a set of double doors before presenting the gold key to Burk.

Burk took the key and stepped into the room.

Up until this moment, he'd still been expecting another one of Jaikon's evil jokes. Only now, as he stood on the threshold of his new suite, did he allow himself to believe that he'd finally…*finally*…achieved what he'd dreamed of from the beginning.

Joyous tears filled his eyes.

There was a sitting room with sumptuous drapes, embroidered upholstery, and hand-woven rugs. The bedroom was even more luxurious. The four-poster bed was canopied, and all the candelabras and wall fixtures were pure gold.

"Perhaps you would like me to draw you a bath, sir?" the servant asked, eyeing Burk and all of his filth.

Burk could have chastised the servant for taking that tone with him, but he'd been fantasizing about a bath for weeks. He stepped farther into the rooms, careful to keep his dirty footprints contained to the far edge of the carpet. He followed the servant into the bathing chamber.

Burk stepped inside and moaned in delight.

The bathing chamber was larger than the most spacious wagon in his old caravan.

The servant knelt on the plush rug to adjust the water temperature. A heavenly smell filled the room as oils and salts were poured into the steaming water.

"So, tell me," Burk said as he watched the servant lay out pristine towels over the lip of the tub. "Who was displaced from this suite when the Emperor gave it to me?"

Burk could only imagine some important foreign dignitary being forced to vacate this suite in order to make it available. The thought warmed him.

"You needn't concern yourself," the servant replied.

"Was it someone terribly important?" Burk pressed.

"Not at all, sir," the servant replied, his attention on the bath. "This suite has been empty since the palace's renovation last year. I'm afraid none of the visiting dignitaries have wanted to stay in this old wing, although I dare say you'll find it quite comfortable."

Burk froze, his feet rooted to the marble floor.

The servant stood. "Just ring the bell in the sitting room if there is anything else you require. Since there are so few anti-contagion suits available and you are Infected, I'll be the only one attending to you." He bowed and left the room.

Burk stayed standing in the middle of the room as steam rose up from the water and fogged the mirrors. A hollow feeling in Burk's chest was making him shiver, despite the humidity in the air.

Jaikon had forced Burk to live in the sewer, even though there was clearly no shortage of available rooms in the palace.

This suite had been empty for more than a year because no one else wanted it. The horrible truth sat in Burk's heart like a smoldering ember.

All at once, every one of Burk's careful plans flashed before his eyes. All of his scheming…all of the people he'd betrayed….

He'd risked everything to get to this moment.

It was a moment that didn't matter to anyone except him.

Burk had thought he'd earned this suite after giving Jaikon what the Emperor most desired. Only now did he realize his mistake. This suite was just another small move in Jaikon's great game.

Despite everything Burk had done to get where he was now, he wasn't really any better off than he'd been back in his tiny room in the sewer.

Burk was still at Jaikon's mercy.

He walked out of the washroom, looking at the suite with new eyes. None of this finery belonged to him. None of it would ever belong to him.

Burk's stomach soured until he was doubled over, clutching at the bedpost for support.

A knock came at the double doors, followed by soft feminine giggle.

"Go away," Burk whispered.

The door handles turned, and two of the most beautiful women Burk had ever seen peeked in. As if on cue, both of them wrinkled their noses.

"Yep, it's him, alright," the blonde said.

"I'll bring the prettiest of us all for our new guest," the brunette offered. She winked at Burk and ducked back into the hall.

"Wait—" he began.

The two women disappeared and were replaced by a third. She wore a long cloak that hid her face.

Burk had never had any interest in Lagonian women. But perhaps a distraction of the female variety was what he needed. Maybe a few hours of mindless diversion would help give him some perspective on the whole situation.

Unlike the other two women, who had kept their distance, this one came right in.

Burk briefly wondered why she wasn't afraid of getting the contagion, but then he remembered that wasn't his concern. This woman was here for him; he needn't worry about her health.

The woman left the door open a crack and sauntered closer. She reached up and pushed back her hood.

A scream caught in Burk's throat.

"Hello, Burk."

Liss drew the knife at her hip. And smiled.

CHAPTER 27

It took hours for Rhett to get from the cape to the palace on foot. If it hadn't been for Wilsean and Dannica helping to keep him upright, he wouldn't have made the eight-mile walk.

Riding Silverbird would have drawn too much attention. The invincibles were down at the docks readying for their voyage to the Giant Realm, but there was still a skeleton crew of slavers guarding the palace. Even they weren't inept enough to miss the sight of a stolen dragon prancing right up to the palace.

Spence, Mari, and Jema had swiped Lagonia guard uniforms for Rhett and his soldiers. None of the slavers who had crossed their path had even taken a second glance at them.

Jennev, one of the women in Jaikon's harem, was waiting right where Liss said she'd be.

Rhett had been more than a little skeptical about trusting Jaikon's women with anything more important than picking out jewelry, but Liss had been confident. Jaikon had recently killed one of Liss's three charges, and the other two were eager for justice.

"This way, gorgeous," Jennev told him in what she must have thought was a seductive voice. She crowded Rhett in the narrow servant's hallway, making sure her voluptuous chest brushed against Rhett more than once.

Rhett barely noticed her. Liss was somewhere in the palace, using herself as bait to lure Jaikon to her. And Rhett was useless to protect her.

He gripped his dagger, not because he'd be able to use it against Jaikon, but because its solid weight was helping him remember how to breathe.

He was sweating, and it had nothing to do with the fever he hadn't been able to shake.

The stillness that came over him before battle was nowhere to be found. Every one of his weakened muscles strained to get to Liss…to protect her. Instead, he was lurking in a servant's passage.

"Just a little longer, big guy," Jennev crooned. Her gaze travelled up and down him like she was determining his market worth.

"You don't look so good," she told him.

"I'm not contagious," he said, before she caught sight of his orange-rimmed eyes and started shrieking.

A bubbly, muffled voice came from the hallway that ran parallel to the one he was in.

"I swear, I saw her come this way," the feminine voice chirped from the other side of the wall.

"That's Mizel," Jennev whispered to Rhett, using the opportunity to brush her lips against his ear.

Sure enough, Jaikon's heavy footsteps filled the adjoining hallway.

It took every ounce of self-control Rhett had to keep from bursting right through the wall that separated them. He wouldn't jeopardize Liss's plan now that it was already in motion. He wouldn't do anything that could put her at any more risk.

As if that was even possible.

He ground his teeth as he thought about the insane plan he'd somehow been roped into.

How the hell had Liss talked him into this?

"Okay, go now!" Jennev gave Rhett a shove. "Make that asshole pay for what he did to Mireille."

Rhett ducked through the narrow door that led from the servant's passage into the main hallway. There was one slaver-turned-guard keeping watch. A slash of Rhett's dagger had the man slumped in a puddle of his own blood. Rhett stepped over the body and went to the double doors that were cracked open.

"You just can't stay away, can you?" Jaikon asked Liss. "Is my former Chief Assassin unable to…satisfy you? If that's the case, then you've come to the right place."

Nausea surged through Rhett. He forced himself to take a steadying breath.

Liss had been worried about Rhett failing to act his part and thus alerting Jaikon to their ruse, but she needn't have worried. Rhett wouldn't have to pretend anything. He was sick with terror and hatred.

Rhett threw open the doors and stormed in, his dagger raised.

Jaikon turned to Rhett and smiled.

"Justice is sweet, isn't it?" Jaikon asked. "I promised that you would see her suffer before you die. I promised I would watch you break before your body was tossed over the cliff." He drew his sword from its scabbard. Cruel anticipation glittered in his ice blue eyes.

Rhett held Jaikon's attention while Liss carefully shifted her body so she was standing between Jaikon and Burk. The filthy Extended man was cowering and babbling. If the fool didn't stand still, he'd ruin everything.

"Leave her alone, Jaikon," Rhett said, stepping all the way into the room.

Just as Rhett knew he would, Jaikon laughed.

"You won't be in such a good mood once you hear how Rhett is going to ruin your plan to enslave the giants," Liss said.

She wore a placid expression, but Rhett knew she was reading the Emperor's soul to make him mad enough to lose control.

Rhett had to fight every instinct he had not to throw himself in front of Liss.

Her movements were so slight, Jaikon didn't notice as she shifted her body. Burk cowered behind Liss to avoid the stare Rhett was burning into the Extended man. Burk didn't even notice when Liss wedged him between herself and the bed.

"What do you know of my plans with the giants?" Jaikon demanded.

Rhett crossed his arms, forcing his eyes off Liss. "I know that your invincibles are never coming back to Lagonia, because my soldiers are better." He stepped closer to Jaikon. "Because they're loyal to me."

Jaikon's face reddened.

"You're fairly chipper for a man who's about to hold his lifeless whore in his arms," the Emperor hissed.

Even though this was part of the plan, Rhett couldn't stop the sick feeling that tore through him. For several seconds, he couldn't think. He forgot what he was supposed to do. All he knew was that he had to get Liss away from this monster.

Rhett started forward, but while Jaikon's eyes were fixed on him, Liss raised her hand and put it over her heart. Rhett went still as they locked gazes. He gave her the briefest of nods, letting her know he understood.

Jaikon laughed softly as Rhett lowered his dagger.

"We've postponed this reckoning for too long," Jaikon said. He ran his fingertip along the edge of his sword, but the sharp blade didn't cut into his skin. Blue light emanated from his pin.

Jaikon raised an eyebrow, as if to remind Rhett that there was no weapon that could harm him.

There was a restlessness to Jaikon's movements that Rhett knew only too well. The Emperor wasn't as interested in playing with his food as he was with eating it.

Rhett tried to give Liss a warning look, but he never got the chance.

Rhett's heart stopped beating as Jaikon thrust his blade at Liss.

She was ready. Just before the sword's point sliced into her chest, Liss threw herself to the side.

Surprise flashed across Jaikon's face, but it was too late for him to change course. His momentum carried him forward.

Jaikon's death blow had been swift, but Rhett had spent months honing Liss's defense skills. For Burk, who had never had any combat training, there was no avoiding the blade that was coming straight for him.

A wheezing gasp escaped Burk as he was impaled on the Emperor's sword.

The Extended man toppled backward onto the bed. Grime and blood smeared across the gold coverlet. Burk glanced down at the wound in his chest, his mouth hanging open in shock.

Liss got to her feet and dusted herself off. Rhett went to her, reassuring himself that she was unhurt. He positioned himself between her and Jaikon. Then, he turned his attention on the Emperor.

If this didn't work…if they had misinterpreted the contract…if Samara had made a mistake about the magic….

"That's for everyone in the caravan," Liss told Burk.

The Extended man tried to speak. Instead of words, blood bubbled out.

Burk's throat bobbed as he choked. Then, with one more gasp, his body went still. His open, sightless eyes were fixed on the gold chandelier hanging above the bed.

Rhett barely noticed. All of his attention was on Jaikon.

The Emperor's sword clattered to the floor. Rhett's heart stuttered back to life.

Jaikon raised his left hand—the one that Liss hadn't crushed weeks ago. The back of his hand was covered in spidery black lines. It was like his veins had been filled with ink. As Rhett watched, the lines thickened and multiplied.

When Jaikon pulled up the embroidered sleeve of his robe, Rhett saw that the black lines went all the way down Jaikon's forearm.

The sharp smell of Insorsiled ink filled the air.

Black lines raced up the Emperor's neck and slithered across his face. Jaikon's blood-curdling screech filled the room.

"Insorsiled contracts are great," Liss said, as Jaikon writhed, "until you break one."

She stepped closer to Jaikon. Rhett moved with her so he stayed between them.

Jaikon's wide-eyed stare found Rhett's. All of the blood vessels in his eyes had turned black.

"Turns out you were right about everyone having a weakness," Rhett told Jaikon. "You were so desperate for power and control, you were blinded into giving up both in the end."

Jaikon was gasping. His chest rose and fell in little bursts, like he couldn't take a deep breath. His legs quivered and then gave out.

"How fitting that you're on your knees," Liss said in a quiet voice. "Since you're looking at Lagonia's future emperor."

Even as Jaikon choked and heaved, Rhett saw some of the rage in his eyes transform into panic.

"This is for Stone," Rhett told the half-brother he loathed. "This is for every Lagonian you've ever threatened, tortured, or murdered. It's for what you did to our father."

Rhett remembered walking into the throne room as Jaikon pulled the dagger from their father's chest. He remembered the smell and feel of the blood as he was forced to clean up the evidence of Jaikon's crime.

With another gasp, Jaikon toppled onto his back. His chest continued to heave as a harsh whistling sound came out of his parted lips. The lines of Insorsiled ink continued to thicken, until there were more of them than of Jaikon's pale flesh.

Rhett stepped forward until he was standing directly over Jaikon.

Insorsiled ink exploded out of Jaikon's chest. The streams of ink twisted and melded together as they continued to pour out of him.

Jaikon tried to scream, but no sound came out.

The tendrils of ink wrapped around Jaikon's torso, like they were ropes rather than liquid. The inky bindings pulled tight.

Jaikon's body jerked off the floor from the force.

Rhett heard the sound of ribs cracking. Jaikon's eyes bulged.

Jaikon was looking at Rhett when he heaved his last, tortured gasp. His eyes, now flooded with ink, stopped twitching. His shuddering body went still.

Without warning, black ink exploded from Jaikon. Liquid sprayed across the room. When a drop landed on Rhett's hand, it slipped off his skin like a bead of oil on water.

Rhett looked back at Jaikon. All that remained of the former emperor was a shriveled, ink-stained corpse.

CHAPTER 28

Lullianna closed her eyes as she chanted under her breath. The incantation was a complicated one, and she was just guessing about most of what she was now attempting. She could almost hear the old warlocks at the academy. If they were here, they'd be droning on about how spells needed to be tested on cadavers first.

Well, Lullianna didn't have a cadaver on hand. But if she didn't figure out a cure for the contagion, her only patient would become just that. She doubted Rhett would appreciate her discovering the formula to cure him…after he was already dead.

Besides, this was the most fun Lullianna had ever had. For years, her life had been a boring montage of school and home. She'd had to live vicariously through Samara, who got to run around the palace having secret love affairs with obscenely handsome and rich Lagonian men. Well, really it was just one man, but still.

Lullianna was ready for her own adventure. Now that it had come, she wasn't going to squander the opportunity by being careful.

"Are you sure this is such a good idea, dear?" Keela asked.

"Shh," Lullianna replied.

Samara had closed herself into her bedroom while she worked on writing the new spell they'd discussed, but it was taking too long. Never one to sit around twiddling her thumbs, Lullianna was doing what she did best. Improvising.

She needed to figure out how much foreign essence could be brought into a body before it shut down. She was using herself as a test subject, siphoning Keela's Extended-ness and using her own magic to sense the way it changed her body's chemistry.

Simple in theory, but in practice….

Lullianna felt the exact moment when she made a mistake. Her chanting hitched as a rush of foreign energy flooded her system. Lullianna's whole body jerked.

"Are you alright, dear?" Keela asked.

The Extended woman's face wavered in and out of Lullianna's view.

Lullianna raced into the kitchen and retched into the sink. She tried to ignore the opal hue of her bile.

Her heart was galloping in her chest. The poisonous essence raced through her veins. Lullianna wheezed in a shallow, agonizing breath.

The fiery pain retreated just enough that it was bearable. Lullianna leaned back against the wall, accepting the glass of water Keela put in her unsteady hand.

"I'm fine," she heard herself saying. "Just need to rest for a minute."

But she wasn't fine, and there was no time to rest. The future of Lagonia—of the entire continent—depended on Rhetteman Loniger surviving. And his survival depended on her.

Lullianna hadn't just come here for Rhett, though.

She wanted what her sister had. She wanted adventure, a change of scene, a chance at finding love….

There was that Extended Runner who was always hanging around— Quic, he'd said his name was. He was pretty cute, and she'd caught him eyeing her over dinner the few times he'd eaten with them.

Samara shouldn't be the only one who got to be a bitter disappointment to their parents by subverting all of their boringly conservative expectations. Lullianna deserved a right to compete for that coveted accolade, and her parents were growing numb to the mischief she caused at the academy.

"So, what do you think?" Keela asked once Lullianna was breathing normally again.

Lullianna shook her head. If she'd had more energy, she might have screamed in frustration.

"Pure Extended essence is too strong," Lullianna explained in a thin voice. "Especially in Rhett's condition. His body would never be able to bear it."

And Liss's essence, as a half-Extended, was too weak. There wasn't enough opal contagion immunity inside her to cure Rhett from the damage that had already been done.

"Maybe we'll have more luck once Samara writes that spell," Keela said without much hope.

Lullianna had no idea if what Samara was trying to do was even possible.

"Come on." Keela wrapped an arm around Lullianna's shoulders. When Lullianna swayed, Keela took her weight and helped her onto the couch.

As she settled against the cushions, Lullianna found herself at eye level with the box of flowers. After her and Keela's disastrous experiments, only three remained.

Three flowers.

Even if she managed to cure Rhett, it wouldn't do the rest of the empire much good if she couldn't figure out how to make more of the immunity.

The flowers in the box were magically frozen in time, presumably so they could survive underground in the grotto without expiring. The spell made it impossible for the flowers to produce seeds or whatever else they did to reproduce. Keela had tried explaining it, but Lullianna had tuned out after the words *can't replicate*.

Once these three flowers were gone, no others would grow.

Keela followed the direction of Lullianna's despondent gaze.

"If only they were made from the earth instead of magic." Keela sighed. "My Extension is itching to be used, but there's nothing in these flowers for it to sink into."

Nothing for it to sink into….

Lullianna sat up so fast she blacked out for a second.

"If I could bring out the organic part of these flowers so it's stronger than the magic part, would you be able to grow more of them?"

Keela traced a finger down her scar as she *hmmed* in thought.

"Yes, I think perhaps I might."

Lullianna patted her cheeks to wake herself up and drive away the remnants of the sick feeling inside her.

"Then, let's get to work," she said.

Once they perfected the formula—a combination of Lullianna's magic and Keela's Green Thumb Extension—they'd be able to reproduce the flowers on a scale large enough to return Lagonians' immunity.

But even if she figured out how to transform the flowers from magic to something natural that Keela could work with, that wouldn't help the thousands who were already sick…already dying.

Lullianna needed to focus. Maybe a healing brew would make the sick feeling in her chest go away.

Yes, a healing brew would take care of the remnants of her latest failed experiment. Then, she could get back to finding a cure for opal contagion.

CHAPTER 29

Rhett and Liss ran through the empty hallways hand-in-hand. Jennev and Mizel were still shrieking at the top of their lungs, drawing every guard in the palace to the Emperor's room and away from the servant's hallway Rhett and Liss were using to escape.

When Rhett heard the sound of Elouicia's voice through the wall that separated them, he started to double back. Elouicia was Jaikon's second-in-command, which meant he had just become the acting emperor of Lagonia.

"Oh no you don't," Liss whispered. "He's still invincible, remember?"

Rhett didn't care. That savage had killed Stone. He'd wanted to torture Liss. The man was a sadist who had no business ruling anything except the inside of the torture cage.

When Rhett continued to lag, Liss wrapped her fingers more tightly around his and gave him a firm tug.

He let her pull him out of the palace, because she was right. There was nothing he could do to Elouicia while the man was still invincible.

Somehow, Rhett's body cooperated enough for him to make the eight-mile run back to the cape. With Elouicia and all of the slavers preoccupied with their dead Emperor, no one stopped them.

Rhett and Liss didn't slow down until they reached the barricade at the cape's edge, where the entire rebel army was waiting for them.

"We did it!" Liss cried, holding up her and Rhett's joined hands. "Jaikon is dead!"

Cheers erupted. Sword were raised in the air as the soldiers chanted Rhett's name. Some of the rebels were even jumping up and down and hugging each other.

"Dinner at our place tonight," Liss shouted, her blue eyes shining in triumph. "We're going to celebrate!"

Rhett lifted Liss into his arms and kissed her.

"Everyone's watching," Liss gasped against his lips as more shouts and whistles surrounded them.

"So?"

He kissed her more deeply.

To his soldiers, it appeared as though he and Liss were celebrating their victory. Only Liss would know the truth about what Rhett was really feeling.

Even though she was safe and in his arms, his body was still shaking. If she'd been one second too slow…if Jaikon's sword had been one inch to the left….

Liss pulled back and looked at him. Her dimple disappeared as her smile turned into a frown. Her face started to blur.

"Rhett?"

He dropped her and stumbled a couple of steps before the ground warped. He went down on his hands and knees as blood spewed out of his mouth.

Someone swore. Liss was on the ground next to him. He tried to tell her to go…to turn away, but more blood was gushing from his mouth. Everything had an orange haze, and the perspiration on his palms had a rainbow sheen.

Between bouts of vomiting, Rhett saw Wilsean sink down onto the ground beside them and pull Liss away. She fought him, but he held her and turned his body to block the sight of Rhett. Dannica was there too, her mouth pressed in a grim line as she used a cloth to wipe the blood and sweat from Rhett's face as he continued to dry-heave.

Rhett forced himself to his feet. His bones felt like liquid, which, if he had passed to the third stage of the contagion, they very well might be. Once there were no more muscles to waste away, the virus got to work on bones.

He met Wilsean's eyes and nodded. His friend let go of Liss.

Rhett tensed, readying himself for her grief. When she looked at him, though, there were no tears. She wasn't hyperventilating. Her beautiful, expressive eyes were dull. Lifeless.

Somehow, it was worse than what he'd been expecting.

"Liss, I'm—" Rhett cut himself off, knowing how stupid an apology would sound. It wouldn't change anything.

"I'm going to talk to Lullianna," Liss said in a monotone that matched the look in her eyes.

Feeling like he'd betrayed her in some unforgivable way, Rhett let her go. He was grateful she couldn't see how it took both Wilsean and Dannica to get him onto Silverbird's back.

"Thanks," Rhett muttered, knowing there was no point in trying to deny he needed their help.

Wilsean walked beside Silverbird and kept one hand on Rhett's leg, like he was a child just learning how to ride.

Wilsean twisted the ring on his index finger. "Ciago and the giants left an hour ago. The invincibles are still loading their supplies, so our guys will have no trouble beating them across the sea." He let out a humorless laugh. "Apparently, the invincibles thought their mission would be canceled after Jaikon's death, but Elouicia went down to the port and told them to carry on."

Rhett nodded, since his throat was too raw to manage actual words. He appreciated his friend's efforts to distract him more than he could ever verbalize.

"Do you think the invincibles will fall for it?" Wilsean asked.

Rhett nodded again. The words, when they came, were so raspy they were barely audible. "There's a difference between invincibility and invulnerability. They all seem to have forgotten that."

"What I wouldn't give to see their faces when they figure out what we've done." Wilsean gave a wistful look toward the sea.

Rhett felt a smile pull at his lips. "If I know Ciago, we'll get a vivid play-by-play as soon as he returns."

Wilsean chuckled. "That I don't doubt."

When they entered the Insorsiled tent, Liss and Lullianna were sitting on the couch together. They were both staring at the single immunity flower that remained. Lullianna was holding Liss's hand and saying something in a soft, apologetic voice.

Another stab of guilt went through Rhett as Liss just nodded. She'd been expecting bad news, but some part of her had clung to hope, anyway.

Rhett thought that might be the cruelest part for her. If there had never been any chance of finding a cure, Liss would have been forced to accept the inevitable. Now, she was stuck in a nightmare where she hovered on a precipice between hope and despair.

Because he couldn't bear the look on Liss's face, he crossed the room to where Samara was sitting at the table with a stack of papers in front of her. A growing pile of crumpled, discarded notes had accumulated on the floor at her feet.

Samara's quill scratched across a paper that was already covered with magical symbols and formulas that were beyond Rhett's comprehension. Keela had one hand resting on the edge of the flower box. Rhett noticed the way the flower's petals were straining in the direction of her skin.

Both women were so intent on their work that they didn't notice him lurking in the shadows. Rhett stood against the wall, letting the solid wood keep him upright, as he watched the women labor over a cure for him.

Lullianna, Samara, and Keela all had dark circles beneath their eyes, and Rhett knew they were straining themselves to the breaking point. Wilsean had needed to resort to threats to get Samara to pause in her work long enough to eat and sleep.

Lullianna seemed especially exhausted. She sagged against the couch the same way Rhett was leaning against the wall, like it was all that was keeping her upright.

Rhett wanted to tell them—all of them—to cut it out. But one glimpse at Liss had him sealing his lips shut.

Samara leaned back in her chair, looking like she was on the verge of tears.

"Why is it so hard to bring life back to these?" she asked, waving her hand at the flower.

"That's a lesson I had to learn early in life," Keela replied. "As a teenager, I tried to use my Extension to bring my father back from death. It…didn't work."

"What happened?" Samara asked in a soft voice.

"It's not a pretty story, I'm afraid," Keela told Samara.

"I have a high tolerance for ugly stories," Samara replied, pausing in her writing to look at the Extended woman.

Keela traced the thick scar that started at her hairline and traveled down her neck. It went below the collar of her shirt. Her next words made Rhett go still as a statue.

"My father became a drunk after Lagonia soldiers killed my mother," she said.

Rhett's chest tightened. He would have been too young to have any part in that particular murder, but he was responsible for plenty of other similar ones. The reminder that he had torn apart families like Keela's was a kick to the gut.

"I was about fifteen at the time," Keela continued. "He'd had too much to drink, and he was antagonizing a group of Lagonia soldiers outside an Insorsil bar. By the time I got there, my father had gotten one of their weapons and was trying to fight them."

Keela absently stroked one of the flower's petals.

"I tried to stop them." Keela's voice got smaller, like she was once again that helpless fifteen-year-old surrounded by soldiers. "My father died quickly. While I was trying to bring him back, the soldiers came after me."

"Why?"

Rhett was just as startled by the question that came out of his mouth as Keela and Samara were.

"Sorry for eavesdropping," he said roughly. "But after living through that, why would you help with this?" Rhett indicated the flower, which could be the salvation of the people who had killed Keela's father and nearly done the same to her.

"I'm a Green Thumb," she said. "We believe all life is precious and should be nurtured. Death in any form, no matter how justified, pains the part of me that wishes to see things grow."

She pressed her fingers into the soil around the flower. Rhett could have sworn he heard the flower let out a contented sigh.

"Besides, if someone doesn't stop the cycle of vengeance, then the killing never ends." Keela gave Rhett another knowing look. "I forgave those soldiers long ago. I decided to value life over death, without exception." She nodded at the flower box. Her expression softened. "And I also happen to be a hopeless romantic. If I can spare Liss a broken heart, I will."

"Lagonia doesn't deserve your kindness," Rhett said, more humbled than he'd ever been in his life.

"Don't start thanking me yet," she told him. "But we'll do our best."

"I'm sorry," he told her, hating those meaningless words. "For what happened to your father. And to you."

I'm sorry for what I've done to your people.

Keela stood and crossed the room to him. She took his hand in hers and squeezed. Even though she wasn't a witchdoctor, her touch eased something inside him.

"I know, dear," she said in a soft voice. "And I think it's time for you to release the burden of guilt you're carrying. Whatever crimes you've committed against my people, you're paying for them."

Rhett turned to the side and caught Liss's eye. He realized in that moment just how wrong Keela was.

He wasn't the one who was paying for his crimes. Liss was.

CHAPTER 30

Jaikon was dead. Burk was dead. Ciago and the giants were dealing with the rest of the invincibles, although Liss still didn't know the particulars of that mission. Elouicia was the only invincible remaining on this side of the sea, but he had left Lagonia with a hundred slavers shortly after Jaikon's death and hadn't come back.

There was so much to be grateful for, and yet Liss didn't think she was the only one forcing a smile onto her face. She caught the rebels' fleeting glances in Rhett's direction, as well as the anxious emotions radiating off their souls.

The Insorsiled tent was doing everything in its power to distract all of them from their troubles. The common room, as well as its furniture, had swelled to accommodate all one-thousand of the rebel soldiers. It was now more like a tent-castle. Liss couldn't even see the other end of the table.

Lullianna had assured all of the rebels that they didn't need their anti-contagion suits with the potion she'd made for Rhett and the Extended. It had taken a fair amount of convincing before the soldiers stripped out of their suits, and even then, there were more than a few suspicious looks thrown in Liss's direction. There were several empty seats between the section of the table where the Extended were sitting and the rest of the group.

The soldiers' distrust wore off as food and drink began to appear on every available place at the table.

Every few minutes, new platters appeared, while the empty bowls and plates just vanished. No matter how much was drunk, goblets full of mulled wine stayed full.

The air was heavy with the smell of herbs and spices. There were platters of steamed fish smothered in citrus and topped with ice berries. Loaves of fresh bread were accompanied by tart jams and honeyed butter. There were also fried potatoes, soft cheeses, and thinly-sliced salted meat. Between courses, they were served foreign fruit cut into the shape of flowers.

And then there was dessert. There were sugar plum pies, layered jellies, and rainbow cupcakes that were only slightly less colorful than Extended skin.

An entire golden cake had appeared on the table directly in front of Jema. Rhett had already needed to rescue her once from suffocating herself as she literally dove in. Her face and clothes were smeared with frosting. The little barbarian had gotten her sticky fingerprints all over the tablecloth and Rhett's sleeves, which she tugged on whenever she wanted to tell him something.

Rhett twirled a lock of Liss's hair around his finger as he nodded and replied to the questions soldiers shouted down the table. As usual, Rhett gave one- and two-word answers, when everyone else needed whole sentences.

"Oh, wow." Mari, who was sitting next to Spence, leaned back and sighed in contentment. "This is the best bite of my life."

"You can't say that for every single bite," Spence informed her.

"I can if it's the truth." Mari speared a forkful of sugar plum pie and brought it to Spence's lips.

In spite of her dark mood, Liss's spirits lifted at the way Spence opened his mouth and let Mari feed him. A drop of plum juice hovered on Spence's lower lip, and Mari reached up with her finger to wipe it. The two of them shared a look that left both of their opal faces shimmering.

"Better put them in separate bedrooms tonight," Rhett said in a low voice in Liss's ear.

No kidding.

"Don't worry," Jema said in a loud voice. "I'll make sure they don't get naked like Wilsean and Samara."

The comment was followed by a great deal of hooting from Rhett's soldiers, and a great deal more blushing from Samara. Wilsean just leaned back in his chair and grinned.

Rhett chuckled, and the sound was like a balm across Liss's aching soul.

Mari and Spence weren't the only ones making eyes at each other. Quic, who had been hanging out in the Insorsiled tent more and more, kept shooting glances at Lullianna. His leg bounced at lightning speed as he fidgeted and tried to flirt.

Lullianna hardly seemed to notice his attention. She looked exhausted. She barely touched her food, and when Samara asked her about it, Lullianna snapped at her older sister to mind her business.

There was too much pressure on her to find a cure, and it was Liss's fault. Until this moment, Liss hadn't given enough thought to the toll others were paying for her misery. Here she was, moping around over Rhett's disease and waiting for someone else to solve her problem.

The realization was a mental slap to the face.

Liss didn't depend on other people to save her. She was the one who got things done. If something was wrong, she fixed it. *I don't know how* had never been a good enough excuse before. How could she let it be one now, when the stakes were higher than ever before?

Just like that, Liss knew what she needed to do. All the food she'd eaten curdled in her stomach, but she ignored the ache.

She turned to Rhett, who had eaten nothing…unless a few sips of water counted as dinner.

Every time she looked at him, she was shocked anew at how gaunt he'd become. He must have lost fifty pounds off a frame that hadn't had an ounce of fat to spare. His broad shoulders had shrunken seemingly overnight, and every time Liss met his gaze, she was startled by the orange halo around his brown irises.

Enough, she told herself as grief threatened to consume her. If she didn't want to live without Rhett, then she needed to find a way to keep him alive. And she knew exactly how to do that…sort of.

She took a steadying breath and rearranged her expression to hide everything going on in her head.

"I'm calling it a night," she told Rhett, kissing him on the cheek and getting to her feet.

Rhett nodded and pushed back his chair.

"What are you doing?" Liss asked, needing to school her features once again so her alarm didn't show.

Rhett gave her a quizzical look. "Going to bed with you."

"No. You need to stay here." She swallowed a sudden surge of nausea. She wasn't sure if it was from lying to Rhett or from what she was planning to do. "Your soldiers need to be with you right now," she added.

"I need to be with you." He gave her that soul-deep look that was difficult to hold and impossible to turn away from.

She forced a lighthearted smile onto her face. "Hang out here for an hour, and then you can come join me."

Rhett hesitated.

"Emperor Rhetteman!" a soldier shouted from farther down the table. "Come drink with your soldiers!"

"Go." Liss gave him a little shove.

While Rhett's attention was elsewhere, Liss bent and whispered to Quic. She waited for his nod and then left the table without another glance.

As soon as she'd shut herself in her bedroom, she took a few deep breaths to calm herself. She was shaking, and the last thing she needed right now was to let her emotions get the better of her. Once Liss had made up her mind, she didn't waver.

There was no other option. She couldn't afford to lose her nerve now.

She went into the closet, methodically layering on warm clothes. She took the dagger off her nightstand and sheathed it at her belt. She gathered up the just-in-case satchel full of jewels she had stashed inside a boot. When she was ready, Liss peered at the thick oak walls that enclosed the bedroom.

"Help a girl out?" she asked the tent.

A few seconds passed, and then a doorway appeared on the wall across from the bed.

"Pleasure doing business with you," Liss said, opening the new door and letting herself out into the frigid night.

CHAPTER 31

Liss's whole world was spinning. Quic had just gotten them from Lagonia to Insorsil in seconds, and Liss's stomach wasn't sure it appreciated the disruption.

"First time's the worst," Quic told her with a grin.

Liss shook off the last of the nausea and gave him a weak smile.

"I'll be back in a little while," she told him, making sure he was comfortably situated in an empty shop.

Then, she slipped into the crowd of night shoppers filling the Insorsiled alley without drawing a second glance.

Her first stop was the witchdoctor who had made the potion that had been her mom's only source of relief for years.

Liss went into the small apothecary, which smelled like dried lavender and the strange pickling liquid the kids referred to as toad juice. Liss waited until the other patrons had finished purchasing their beauty potions and good luck charms, and then she turned the lock in the door.

The crinkled old witch folded her gnarled hands as she regarded Liss.

"I haven't seen you in some time," she said in a voice that always reminded Liss of the dried-out pages of an old book. "I would ask how your mother is, but unless my crystal ball is mistaken, she has grown stronger."

"She has," Liss replied. "That's kind of why I'm here."

The witch listened without interrupting as Liss told her what she wanted. There was no surprise on her face or in her soul, only a gentle kind of pity that irritated Liss almost beyond sense.

Liss took a breath. When the witch didn't say anything, she continued, "I know that warlock's spell made my father immune rather than curing him once he'd already been infected, but I was hoping—"

The witch was shaking her head.

"I will not help you with this," she said, taking an old broom from the corner and starting to sweep the already-spotless floor. "Your friend was correct that dark magic is not to be trifled with. Only the most wicked among us have ever attempt such spells, and it was more miracle than magic that your mother wasn't killed because of that foolish experiment."

"But—" Liss began, but the witch cut her off.

"I remember when I first examined your mother. You can't imagine the damage that warlock's spell did to her. If I hadn't spent the last fifty years studying antidote magic, I never would have been able to make that brew that brought her back from the brink of death."

"I appreciate everything you did for my mom," Liss said, pressing her hand to her heart to emphasize her sincerity. "That's why I thought you might be able to help someone else I love."

"I don't perform dark magic. And I would never strip away one person's strength to feed it to another, even if such a thing were within my skills." The old woman's wrinkled face tightened in anger. "Witchdoctors have an obligation to perform healing magic. What that warlock did was reprehensible. If he didn't have so many friends in high places—"

"Fine." Liss said, uninterested in the witch's ramblings about politics and Insorsiled hierarchy. "Then tell me where to find this shady warlock."

Liss's mom had told her the story about what had happened to her, but she had never mentioned the warlock's name or where he could be found. Liss's mom had probably thought—with good reason—that Liss would seek revenge on the corrupt warlock if she knew his identity.

The witchdoctor gave her another pitying look that had Liss seeing red.

"I will not be party to this nonsense," the woman said. "Many before you have sought to evade the natural order of life and death. They were disappointed on their quest, just as you will be."

Liss opened her mouth, but the witchdoctor wasn't finished.

"Go home to your love. Hold him, comfort him, and then let him go. It is the only choice that remains."

"That isn't good enough."

Liss barely recognized the snarl in her own voice. Her feet brought her across the small shop, almost of their own will. Liss had her knife pointed at the witchdoctor before she'd thought twice about it.

"I'm going to need a name and an address," she told the woman. "Now."

Fear filled the witchdoctor's soul, followed by more pity.

Liss's hand shook on the handle of her knife.

The witchdoctor sighed. And then she told Liss what she needed to know.

"Thank you," Liss said, sheathing her knife and feeling contrite.

"If you go down this road, you will become everything you hate," the witch warned her. "Either that, or you'll be dead. Your brave warrior won't thank you for your sacrifice."

Liss left the shop as fast as she could, but she couldn't outrun the witchdoctor's words that continued to echo in her head.

❄ ❄ ❄

Liss reached the end of one of Insorsil's sketchier back alleys. Her skin pricked hot and cold as she stood outside the small shop. Bunches of herbs and dried rodents hung upside down in the window display. There was also a sign that read, *The only antidote to death is my magic. And your jewels.*

Oh yeah. She was definitely in the right place.

Even though she'd thought she had made up her mind, Liss's hand trembled as she raised it to turn the door's handle.

The inside was dark and dingy. The place was empty except for a skinny old warlock who was bent over the counter. He had bushy white eyebrows and a long, wispy goatee. He was muttering to himself as he separated gold nuggets from semi-precious jewels on the countertop.

He didn't look up, even though the bell above the door jangled to announce her arrival.

There was only one emotion in the warlock's soul: greed.

Good.

Liss strode up to the counter and overturned her satchel of jewels on top of the carefully-organized piles the warlock had made.

His rheumy eyes bulged as he took in the pile of treasure.

"Half now," Liss informed the warlock, who squeaked in protest when she swept half the pile back into her satchel. "And half when the job is done."

"And what is it that you want, my pet?"

The warlock looked her over from top to bottom.

"You're already beautiful, so you can't be after a physical enhancement spell." He leaned over the counter and sniffed the air in front of her. "You aren't pregnant, so no need for a child-cleansing spell."

Liss bit her tongue before any number of sarcastic remarks tumbled out of her mouth. This whole process would go more smoothly if she didn't antagonize the warlock who was about to have her and Rhett's lives in his hands.

"I'm here for something a little darker," Liss told the warlock.

"Ahh." Intrigue washed across his soul. "Perhaps you wish to awaken someone from the dead? A curse to torture your enemy? A death spell?"

Liss hid her disgust at the excitement that filled the warlock's soul.

She cleared her throat. "Twenty years ago, you created a spell that made a Lagonian man immune to opal contagion."

The warlock's interest deepened.

"Don't tell me you're the product of that happy union."

Liss nodded.

"Sorry, girl. I can't undo the spell on your mother. She knew the cost. You'll just have to content yourself with the fact that your father is alive despite being married to an Infected."

He gave her a false smile that matched the emotions in his soul.

"My father's dead," Liss said in an even voice.

"Very sorry to hear it," the warlock said.

He wasn't sorry.

"Can you do it again?"

The warlock's bushy brows furrowed. "You want me to bring your father back to life and kill him again? Well, it would be difficult, but I suppose—"

"The immunity," Liss said through gritted teeth. "Can you make another Lagonian immune to the contagion?"

The warlock looked down his nose at her. "I never forget a spell, unlike some hacks in this kingdom. Any magic I've performed once, I can summon again."

"What about…curing someone who already has the contagion?"

Liss's palms had started to sweat. She leaned against the counter so the quivering in her knees would be less visible.

The warlock tugged on his goatee.

"Perhaps. Never tried it before. There could be some…unintended consequences."

"Could you also make him immune to all strains of the contagion after you heal him?" Liss pressed.

She could worry about unintended consequences after she figured out whether what she wanted was even possible.

The warlock let out a whistling breath. "Anything else you want while I'm at it, girl? The Insorsil throne delivered to you on a gold platter, perhaps?"

Liss lifted a shoulder. "If you can't do it, then I'll just have to take my business elsewhere."

"There is no one else who is capable of performing this kind of magic. None willing to even try it."

"I'm resourceful," Liss said. She started scooping the rest of the jewels back into her satchel.

"Wait, wait, wait."

The warlock's eyes were fixed on the pile of jewels on the counter when he said, "I've never attempted such a powerful version of that spell. It would be extraordinarily difficult."

"But could you do it?" Liss pressed.

She felt the answer on the warlock's soul before he spoke.

"We won't know until I try, but yes, I think I can."

"What exactly would you need from me?" Liss asked.

The warlock squinted at a sapphire on the counter.

"What you're asking for will require magical propulsion, which isn't easily achieved," he said.

Liss waited. Her entire world was balanced on whatever the warlock said next, and for him, this was just an academic curiosity.

"I will need a great deal of your essence. A great deal."

"Okay—"

"At minimum, you'll lose your Extension. Permanently." The warlock pushed up his sleeves, as though preparing to go to work. "Depending on how far gone your Infected man is and how messy the magic becomes, you'll likely die."

Liss couldn't stop herself from sagging against the counter. Her heart was pounding a thunderous rhythm in her chest.

Her Extension…her life….

Liss was a survivor. She'd spent the last twenty years doing everything in her power to stay alive.

And even if she didn't die, what kind of life would she have without her Extension?

Her people rejected her now. What would they do to her if they found out she gave up her Extension for Rhett?

An image filled Liss's mind before she could stop it. Her…lying in a bed…too weak to get up. Sipping from a potion that kept her alive but not strong enough to live….

It felt like a giant was sitting on her chest. She couldn't breathe.

"Did I mention purchase is final upon consultation?" the warlock asked, giving her a sly look. "Now that you've taken my time, you owe me the jewels whether you go through with the spell or not."

Liss rolled her eyes, even though the warlock's payment was the last thing on her mind. Her thoughts were racing. She tore off her cloak, which had begun to stifle her.

She couldn't do this. She couldn't—

She thought of Rhett, on his hands and knees and vomiting blood. She thought about walking out of here. She thought about watching Rhett die and living on without him.

She doubled over, dry-heaving.

"Easy there, girl." The warlock patted her hand. His skin was cold and dry as dust.

Liss straightened and looked at the warlock.

"Do it," she said.

As soon as the words were out of her mouth, she could breathe again. The weight on her chest eased. She could stand without leaning against the counter.

It was the right decision…the only decision. As much as she feared losing her Extension…as much as she feared dying…losing Rhett would be worse. Lagonia needed Rhett. Their world needed him.

She met the warlock's expectant gaze. "I'm ready."

CHAPTER 32

Rhett nodded and contributed to the conversation when it was expected, but his mind was elsewhere. He gave Liss the hour he'd promised. He put Wilsean in charge of making sure the kids were looked after, and then he excused himself from the table.

Liss had perked up a little during dinner, but her smile had barely made an appearance. He decided he wasn't going to give her the chance to be sad tonight, or for any of the nights they had left together. He wouldn't give her time to grieve.

He was contemplating the creative means he would use to wake her up when he shut their bedroom door behind him.

The room was dark. The bed was made and clearly hadn't been slept in.

"Liss?"

He knew even before he called her name that she wasn't here. The natural draw he felt whenever she was near wasn't tugging him in any direction. The smell of wildflowers was absent from the room. Her knife wasn't on the nightstand.

Where the hell—

His gaze caught on the door on the wall…a door that had most definitely not been there before.

Almost wrenching the door off its hinges, he stepped outside and looked around.

No Liss. He forced himself to think, even as a warning travelled down his spine.

He started to jog in the direction of the cape's point, where the surrounding shallows offered the most direct route to Insorsil. He ignored the way his brittle bones creaked and scraped together.

"Sir." The soldier on guard bowed low to Rhett.

"Did you see Liss?" Rhett asked without preamble.

"Yes, sir." She left with that Runner Extended about an hour ago."

Rhett swore. He craned his neck to see into the distance, even though he knew Liss was long gone.

"My apologies, sir." The soldier frowned. "Should I have stopped them?"

"Yes! I mean, no. I mean—Shit."

Rhett stared at the rafts tied to the dock without seeing them. He had a feeling *what* Liss was doing, but he had no idea of the specifics of *where*.

"Did Quic come back?" Rhett asked, already knowing the answer before the soldier's regretful *Not yet, sir*.

"Saddle Jaikon's gold dragon," Rhett ordered the man.

He didn't wait for his soldier's acknowledgement before he started sprinting back to the tent.

"Rhett?" Dannica called. She appeared out of the shadows and fell into step with him.

"Go back to the party, Dannica," he told her.

"If you're going somewhere, you need an escort," she said, unbothered by their run even though Rhett was ready to pass out. "You're the empire's future, and—"

"Let's not pretend I have any future," he managed between gulps of air.

Rhett cursed his failing body, which was an obstacle that was preventing him from getting to Liss faster. If he was right about what she was doing, he didn't have a minute to spare.

"You do until you don't," Dannica replied in a curt voice. "Now, where are you going and what do you need?"

"Liss is gone," he said. "I have to find her before she does something insane."

"Fine, but you're not going alone. Elouicia and the slavers are still at large, not to mention the thousands of Insorsiled who would love nothing more than to put your head on a spike."

She was right, but at the moment, Rhett didn't care.

"Where's the fire?" Wilsean demanded when Rhett burst into the common room with Dannica on his heels.

A scan of the room told him Quic hadn't reappeared from wherever he'd taken Liss.

"The kids," Rhett managed as he tried to catch his breath. "Where?"

"Is something wrong with Liss?" Spence jolted up from where he'd been dozing on the couch. The door to Mari and Jema's room opened, and the two girls hurried out.

"If Liss was going to see a witchdoctor to do something…illegal," Rhett said, "which one would she go to?"

Spence gave him a skeptical look. "Why do you want to know?"

"Which one?!"

"I don't know about the illegal part," Mari said, "but I can tell you who brewed her mom's potions. Liss always trusted her."

"Tell me how to find her."

CHAPTER 33

Liss lay on top of a freezing slab of stone in a back room of the warlock's shop. She stared straight ahead to avoid looking at the dead and pickling reptiles. Glass jars crammed full of the poor creatures were stacked on floor-to-ceiling shelves in front of her. Of all the witnesses she could have for the most terrifying moment of her life, dead snakes wouldn't have been her first choice.

The warlock moved around her, drawing chalk symbols on the stone. He'd made Liss put on a sack-like dress that itched. Every time she tried to wriggle away from the scratchy fabric, the warlock barked at her to stay still.

She was shivering from the cold stone…at least, she told herself that was the reason for her uncontrollable shaking.

She closed her eyes and tried to relax. When she realized she could no longer hear the chalk scratching against the stone or the warlock's incantation, she opened her eyes.

"Everything is prepared," the warlock said in a reverent voice. "Once I begin, there is no going back."

Liss gave him a short nod.

"Very well."

The warlock raised his staff. Liss held her breath.

A faint light began to pulse around her. The symbols turned crimson and peeled away from the stone. They began to move in hypnotizing patterns around her prone body. The warlock began to chant. He raised his staff so the tip hovered an inch above Liss's chest.

She felt an unpleasant sucking around her ribcage. The brighter the light became, the stronger the feeling grew.

Liss was dizzy, and it took every ounce of her concentration to keep from hurling all over the warlock.

Her vision started to go spotty. It felt like her heart was being pulled to the surface of her skin.

Not her heart, she realized. It was her Extension.

The spell was dragging out her soul sorting ability.

Raw panic flooded Liss's entire body. Her insides were in knots. The room started to spin.

Then, the world slowed. Liss's Extension was still clawing its way out of her chest, but the pain didn't even register anymore. The crashing thunder of her pulse in her ears had ceased. Her lungs refused to draw in air.

She was dying.

Liss felt her life leaching out of her. All sensation began to fade away, until she was left with nothing except her panic and a desperate need to draw in air.

Pull yourself together, she ordered herself.

Sweat was pouring down the warlock's face. It was clear this spell was taking every ounce of his energy. She couldn't risk even the slightest distraction.

In an effort to calm herself, Liss thought about Rhett. She tried to bring all of her favorite memories to the surface as the pressure in her chest increased.

She thought about their first kiss in the Insorsiled forest. She remembered their night on the cliff overlooking the flower fields. She thought about every time she'd woken up in his arms, feeling safer and more loved than she'd ever imagined it was possible to feel.

Dark spots gathered at the corners of her vision. Her lungs screamed with the need to draw in air.

It was okay. As wrong as she felt, this was right.

Rhett. She pictured his face. She imagined his arms around her instead of the cold stone at her back. She saw him sitting on the Lagonia throne.

A clattering sound startled Liss and the warlock. The stone's light winked out, and with it, the sick feeling in Liss's chest retreated. The crimson symbols lowered back down to the stone and returned to the chalk drawings they'd been.

Liss's pulse returned. She gasped in a burning breath.

"Goddamn pixies! I'll kill you all—" The warlock stomped to the front of the shop, disappearing behind a dusty shelf that was filled with even dustier potion bottles.

"Seriously?" Liss demanded.

She waited several beats. When he didn't return, she sat up.

"Warlock, I'm not getting any younger over here. Get back—"

The warlock crashed through the shelf of potions. The bottles hit the floor and shattered. Glass and liquid went everywhere. The warlock landed on his stomach, but his face was turned toward Liss.

His eyes were open and unseeing. Blood oozed from a slash across his throat and mixed with the spilled potions.

Liss screamed.

No. No, no, no.

This couldn't be happening. He couldn't be dead.

"Liss!"

Rhett, his dagger dripping with fresh blood, leapt over the destroyed shelf.

Liss looked from his bloody dagger to the warlock.

"You." Liss grabbed her head as the sickening truth settled into her bones. "How could you?!"

Rhett took in the stone slab, the symbols the warlock had painstakingly drawn, and Liss's sack dress.

He crossed the room in two steps and knelt so they were eye-to-eye. Liss was too panicked and furious to know what he was looking for, but whatever it was, he found it. Relief filled his soul.

"Damnit, Liss. What the hell were you thinking?"

"What was I thinking?!" she shrieked. "You just killed the only person who could save you!"

"Good," he shot back. "Do you have any idea what it did to me when I figured out where you were? What you were planning to do?"

Liss shoved him away from her and stood up, wincing as bits of glass cut into her bare feet. "He was your only chance, and you ruined it. You ruined it!"

If only she'd been paying more attention, she might have felt Rhett's soul before he killed the warlock. She might have been able to stop him.

Tears stung her eyes. She tried to run past Rhett, but he locked his arms around her.

"Let me go," she shouted, struggling against him.

"Never."

He lifted her up and sat her on the stone slab, which was the only place free of broken glass. The harder she struggled, the closer he held her. He was speaking in a low, gentle voice, but she couldn't hear anything over the sound of her soul cracking into a thousand pieces.

She'd been so close to saving him. Rhett could have lived. Instead, he'd taken away his own last chance. He'd doomed himself.

At that realization, all of the fight went out of Liss. She collapsed in Rhett's arms and sobbed.

"You'll be okay, Liss." Rhett kissed the tears streaming down her cheeks. "You're the strongest person I've ever known."

Liss shook her head. Her vision swam. "I can't live without you."

"You can survive this." He took her face in his hands, making her meet his gaze. "You can survive anything."

CHAPTER 34

Ciago had to admit, crossing the Brookgar Sea in an enormous ship with a crew of giants was far superior to the dinghy and two-person crew he'd had on his last voyage to the Giant Realm.

As Ciago stood at the helm and let the frozen air blast his face, he tried to rein in his impatience. This was where he needed to be right now, and he trusted his best friends to keep Lagonia in one piece in his absence. The only part he didn't have faith in was that Rhett would still be in one piece when he returned.

"You love him, don't you?"

Ciago turned to find Winny studying him. Her black hair stood out in stark relief against the gray sky.

"I don't know which *him* you're referring to," Ciago told the giant leader, "but I'm not a *love* kind of guy. And even if I was, the lucky recipient of my love wouldn't be a *him*."

He gave Winny a suggestive smile. In Ciago's extensive experience, it was the easiest way to deflect a conversation he had no intention of engaging in.

Winny gave him an unimpressed look. "I meant a brotherly love. And you know who I'm talking about. I can see your worry."

Ciago shrugged. "Rhett's almost died so many times, it's not even newsworthy anymore. Like, oh, it's Tuesday? Rhett probably almost died today."

Winny stared at him for an uncomfortably long time. That was something Ciago hadn't quite gotten used to about the giants. They didn't concern themselves with normal politeness conventions. The effect of

Winny's penetrating look was worse because Ulfrath was sitting beside her. The wolf fixed his unblinking black eyes on Ciago with an expression that seemed very much like hunger.

Winny sighed and put a hand on Ciago's arm. Even with the layers of their gloves, her fur cloak, and his jacket, he somehow felt the warmth of her touch.

"He is strong and a worthy leader," Winny said, leaning over the railing and staring out at the landmass coming into view. "Whatever happens, I do not regret allying with him."

She might change her tune once Rhett died and his promise of gifting the giants with land vanished into thin air.

If Jaikon, or perhaps worse, Elouicia, had control of the throne after Rhett was gone, the giants would be as bereft as Ciago and the rest of the rebels.

"Lady Umbrog." Grub shuffled over to the helm and bowed. "Lord Ciago." He bowed again.

Ciago stifled an amused chuckle. He could tell from the way Winny's lip twitched that she was doing the same.

Bowing was not something the giants had ever done, but Grub seemed especially eager to pick up on the rebels' mannerisms. Ciago had noticed the giant taking more care with his bumbling feet and wild appearance. Grub asked Ciago on an hourly basis whether *Lovely* had noticed his new haircut and clean clothes. Poor giant was smitten.

"We arrive," Grub said, pointing at the harbor where the giants' ships were moored.

Winny turned to Ciago. "Time to put this plan of yours into motion."

The group of giants gathered around Ciago while he explained what they needed to do…again. He spoke slowly and repeated the same instructions he'd given the giants every day since their ship set out from Lagonia. With the exception of Winny, the giants weren't known for their intelligence.

"Take everything," Ciago told his semi-attentive audience for the fourth time. In his experience, that was the ideal amount of repetition. It got into the giants' memories but didn't offend them to the point where they started bashing their mallets around.

It was a narrow line to walk.

"Giants, furs, food, firewood," Ciago continued. "I mean everything. Load it up on the ships and then head back to Lagonia. Do you remember the route we showed you?"

This part was important. The giants needed to stay far out of sight of the incoming invincibles. If the Lagonians sailed in to conquer the Giant Realm, only to witness all of the giants sailing away, their ruse would be up.

The giants nodded. And picked their noses.

"Don't forget," Winny reminded the giants as they began to disembark with the pack of wolves. "Destroy every ice hut. Break apart the ice castle."

"Don't leave anything behind except the snow," Ciago added.

Ciago and Winny watched as the giants splashed and swam through the frigid water to shore.

"Now, we wait?" Winny asked as Ciago took the helm.

He steered the ship toward the far side of the harbor, where the jutting landmass would hide them from the incoming Lagonian ships.

"Now we wait." Ciago patted the package of Insorsiled crystals in his pocket. He shared a knowing grin with Winny. "And then we play."

CHAPTER 35

Samara slipped into the dress that had appeared in her enormous closet an hour ago. It was a little creepy the way the tent seemed to know everything about them, but it was mostly just convenient. She hadn't brought along any clothes that were suitable for dinner with one of the most important families in Lagonia.

Samara was full of guilt at the thought of taking a night off from working on Rhett's cure to go to dinner with Wilsean. Rhett was getting worse and worse, and Samara was no closer to having a workable spell than she'd been days ago. But as Wilsean had pointed out, maybe a few hours without going cross-eyed from staring at magical symbols would freshen her mind.

Samara looked at herself in front of the floor-length mirror. The dress was a soft pink, made out of a gauzy material that swished gently with her every step. The fabric had a shimmer that drew the light every time she moved. Delicate flower petals had been stitched into the bodice.

The dress was feminine without being girly. It fit her like it was made for her, which, she supposed, it was. As she stared at herself in the dress, she felt…well, magical.

"Samara, come on," Wilsean called from the other side of the closet door.

Taking a deep breath, she opened the door and stepped into the main part of the bedroom. Wilsean's jaw went slack.

"Uhhh," he stammered.

"You like?" She spun around, letting the material and her waist-length hair flare around her.

"Forget dinner." Wilsean's hands came around her waist. He started backing her toward the bed while his fingers found the hooks at her back.

"Don't you dare," she laughed. "I don't want you rumpling me before I meet your parents."

"Trust me, I'm going to do a lot more than rumple you." His dark eyes sparked with desire, making Samara's blood heat.

Shaking her head, she put her hands on his chest and pressed him back.

"You have a job to do, remember?" she reminded him.

Lagonia had been on the verge of chaos for weeks. Between opal contagion ravishing the population, and clashes between the courtiers and peasants, the empire was headed for civil war. And now, Emperor Jaikon was dead.

Elouicia, the second in command—and in Samara's opinion, the evilest man in the empire—was the new Lagonia emperor by default.

Rhett had the peasants' loyalty, but once he took the throne from Elouicia, he was going to need the aristocracy's support.

Part of their reason for having dinner with Wilsean's parents tonight was to begin recruiting support from the top of the empire's food chain.

And Wilsean's parents were definitely the top of the Lagonia food chain.

Wilsean scowled. "Yeah, I remember." He straightened his gold tie and offered her his arm. "But don't think you're getting out of being ravished later."

"I appreciate the warning," she told him, trying to maintain a serious face.

Lullianna's Insorsiled bike was already waiting for them right outside the tent. Samara climbed on behind Wilsean, adjusting her dress so it wouldn't get caught or drag. The engine revved, and the bike sped forward.

Their drive to the wealthiest residential street in the empire was a blur. Samara was reviewing everything she knew about Wilsean's parents and trying to remember how to breathe. She never got nervous about meeting new people, but then again, she'd never thought she would be meeting Wilsean's parents.

She tried not to think about how much it meant to her that he'd asked her to come with him, and how much she wanted them to like her.

She'd only spoken to her own parents once in the three years since her exile. It would be an understatement to say that meeting hadn't gone well. Her parents had screamed and threatened her. In turn, Wilsean had threatened them.

Two servants opened the gates that led to the biggest single-family home Samara had ever seen. Wilsean parked the bike in a stone courtyard with a bubbling fountain. Colorful flowers grew around the house in a wild, beautiful tangle. Samara recalled that Wilsean's mother tended the flowers herself.

The servants bowed to her and Wilsean.

Samara smoothed a hand down her dress as she tried to ignore her overwhelming urge to join the servants who were fastening the gates. She couldn't help but think she belonged with them rather than on Wilsean's arm.

"Nervous?" Wilsean asked as they crossed the courtyard to the front porch. He lifted the heavy knocker on the door and let it fall back down.

"Of course not," she replied. "I regularly go to dinner with all of my boyfriends' colder-than-ice parents."

"Boyfriends? As in plural?" Wilsean turned to her.

"Sorry for you to have to find out like this." She grinned, feeling some of her tension ease away.

"At least promise me that I'm your favorite of all of them," he said in a low voice. He was close enough that his breath tickled her ear. She shivered.

"You're certainly one of the top contenders," she teased.

"But I'm the best in the sack," he said, sliding his hands up her sides and smirking at her small gasp. "Admit it."

"Heathen."

The door opened.

"Wilsean, darling." A slender woman stepped onto the porch. Incredibly, she was almost as tall as Wilsean. The gold silk of her gown looked amazing against her ebony skin.

"Hello, Mother." Wilsean kissed her on the cheek without letting go of Samara's hand. "This is Samara."

Samara stopped herself just in time before she curtsied. It was old habit to do so whenever one of the Lagonian courtiers passed her in the palace, but she wasn't a servant anymore.

"It's wonderful to meet you, my lady," Samara said, lowering her head in something that wasn't quite a curtsey but acknowledged their relative positions.

"Call me Druella." Wilsean's mother barely touched the tips of her fingers to Samara's hand. Druella's fingertips were bony and cold.

Samara surreptitiously wiped her hand on her dress, wondering if the look on Druella's face was because Samara's palm was sweaty.

"Haven't I seen you before?" Druella asked.

"She used to work in the palace," Wilsean said smoothly. "Shall we go in, or is dinner being served in the doorway?"

"How right you are."

Druella snapped her fingers, and servants flurried around them, taking cloaks and offering glasses of sparkling wine.

Druella led the two of them through the massive foyer. Wilsean put his hand on Samara's back, and when his mother turned away, he winked at her.

They entered a dining room with a long table, silver candelabras, and enormous family portraits hanging on the walls. A dark-skinned man in a crisp suit sat at the head of the table. Samara immediately saw the resemblance between Wilsean and his father.

He offered Samara a bland smile and shook her hand as introductions were made. As soon as they were all seated at one end of the long table, four servants came forward with covered dishes.

Once again, Samara had to stop herself from getting up to help arrange the plates.

All at once, reality came crashing in on her.

What the hell was she doing here? She didn't belong in this dress…at this table. She was an Empty who had been disowned by her parents and exiled from her kingdom. She was a servant who was masquerading as a lady. She was a fraud.

Under the table, Wilsean traced letters on her thigh.

I-L-O-V-E-Y-O-U.

That small gesture was enough to ease her tension. She took a sip of her wine to hide her smile and relaxed in her chair. Maybe she didn't belong here, but she was with Wilsean. Belonging or not, she was right where she wanted to be.

The conversation was stilted at first. It wasn't easy coaxing a smile out of either of Wilsean's parents, but Samara managed it by the second course. By the third course, she had Wilsean's father belly-laughing as he reiterated stories about Wilsean's childhood antics. By dessert, Samara had stopped worrying and was just enjoying the company.

Wilsean's father put down his wine glass and looked at his son. "I assume you have a reason for coming here, besides gracing us with Samara's charming company?"

Wilsean's expression transformed into the face he wore when he was more soldier than boyfriend.

"We want the councilmen to back Rhett when he claims the throne," Wilsean said.

His father motioned to a servant to clear their plates. Samara tensed in anticipation of whatever he might say.

"Rhetteman Loniger is the rightful heir to the Lagonia throne, but his blood is weak."

That was a slightly more polite way of calling Rhett a bastard.

"His blood is a hell of a lot stronger than Elouicia's," Wilsean said in a flat voice. "But that isn't the point. Rhett is the only one who can keep the empire from tearing itself apart."

Wilsean's father nodded. "And yet, there is concern among the high families that Rhetteman will not have our interests at the forefront of his agenda. Your friend always had a bad habit of running low on his tax collection tallies." He drummed his fingers on the table. "It was a habit I'm certain you took no part in."

"Of course not, Father," Wilsean replied with a smirk.

"There's more to ruling than befriending peasants and assassinating Extended," his father continued. "Elouicia may be a monster, but he understands Lagonia's hierarchy in a way Rhetteman never will."

Samara could feel Wilsean twisting his ring around his finger under the table. To everyone else, he appeared to be the picture of calm. Only she could feel his growing agitation.

"How much of this empire's food supply comes from the Lagonia peasants?" Wilsean asked in a seemingly abrupt change in subject.

"Over ninety-six percent," his father replied without hesitation.

"That's right." Wilsean crossed his arms. "And what happens to a society when food production halts, say because all of the peasants begin protesting at once."

Wilsean and his father exchanged a hard look.

"What are you saying?" his father asked in a soft voice that did nothing to hide the aggression radiating off him.

"I'm saying that unless you convince the other councilmembers to back Rhett, taxes will become the least of your worries."

Several long seconds passed.

"That is…a compelling argument," Wilsean's father said. "And what do you expect me to tell the councilmen?"

"Tell them there's going to be an imminent change in leadership," Wilsean replied. "They can begin preparing for the shift by ceasing all hostilities with the peasants. And they can ready the throne for the rightful emperor."

Wilsean's parents exchanged a glance.

"Elouicia is a very dangerous man," Druella told her son. "Are you certain Rhetteman is strong enough to face him?"

If Samara hadn't been watching Wilsean, she would have missed the twitch of a muscle at his jaw.

"Our entire rebel army has been on Lagonia soil for a week, and Elouicia hasn't even tried to challenge us."

"Yes, Elouicia has been decidedly absent from the empire as of late," Wilsean's father said, rubbing a hand across his bearded chin.

"So has his army of slavers," Druella added. "I heard they've taken up residence in the Insorsil castle, and Elouicia is advising the new king."

Samara and Wilsean exchanged a look.

Why would Elouicia leave Lagonia to go serve another leader? He was power-hungry and bloodthirsty, and he'd just inherited an empire.

Besides, Elouicia was invincible. He had nothing to fear from Rhett and the rebels. So, why wasn't he terrorizing innocent Lagonians with daily floggings and executions?

"Maybe he's trying to verify the strange reports coming from the few merchants who are still travelling to Insorsil," Druella said.

With the opal contagion protocols now in place, no Lagonians should be able to leave the empire. But where there was money at stake, exceptions were made.

"Apparently, the weather has been poor," Druella continued.

"Poor weather," Wilsean drawled, looking thoroughly unimpressed.

"Yes," his mother replied. "Dust storms, for one. A heat wave that went into the triple-digits, for another."

"During winter?" Wilsean spluttered. "The Lagonia rumor mill must be running dry for that kind of nonsense to take hold."

Druella lifted a delicate shoulder. "I'm just telling you what I heard."

Samara made a mental note to ask her brother about these rumors. She hadn't had much contact with any of her siblings aside from Lullianna in the past weeks. After everything that happened with her parents, and the instability in the kingdom following Gatria's death, Samara hadn't wanted to endanger her sisters and brother. If anyone in the king's court found out they were keeping in touch with their Empty sister, they could be executed alongside her.

She hadn't forgotten the sight of those Empty corpses swinging from the gallows in front of the Insorsil castle.

"What do you think?" Wilsean asked her in a low voice while his parents were involved in their own private conversation.

"Sometimes overextending magic can affect the weather temporarily around the area where the spell was cast," Samara said. "I've never heard of it happening on the kind of scale your mother mentioned, though."

After that, the conversation turned to more pleasant topics. By the time they'd drunk their tiny glasses of sherry, Samara was pretty much counting the night as a success.

"Samara, darling." Druella pushed back her chair and stood. "Let me show you my private flower gardens."

Definitely a success, Samara thought, feeling a little giddy as she stood up. The gardens were Druella's pride and joy.

"I'd love to."

"Shall we join you?" Wilsean's father asked.

"No," Druella said.

At the same time, Wilsean said, "Actually, I need to speak with you, Father." He turned to Samara. "If that's alright?"

She nodded, curious about what Wilsean needed to talk to his father about privately. There was a strange, expectant look on his face, and he was twisting the ring around his index finger in the way he did whenever he was worried about something.

"I'm sure we'll find some way to pass the time without your company," Druella said as Wilsean bent to give Samara a light kiss.

When Wilsean turned to follow his father out of the room, Druella smiled at Samara. There was something in her gaze that made all of Samara's easy comfort vanish. Ignoring her sudden urge to run away from this woman as fast as she could, she followed Druella out of the dining room.

CHAPTER 36

Wilsean shut the study door behind him. He shook his head when his father offered him the crystal decanter filled with amber liquid.

Like Samara's eyes, he thought.

Man, Ciago was right. He was totally lost for this woman.

"I have to say," his father said. "I had my doubts about your backing of Rhetteman Loniger, but I'm beginning to think your instincts were correct. If we can play this right with the council, we'll be known as the family that first gave their support to the new emperor. Any harm done to our reputation from you turning traitor on Jaikon will be reversed."

Always about their family's reputation, Wilsean thought, holding back a sigh.

"I'm glad you approve of my loyalties," Wilsean said, being careful not to let any hint of sarcasm come through. He didn't want to unravel the good mood Samara had brought out of his old man. "But that's not what I need to talk to you about right now."

Wilsean met his father's curious gaze.

"I'd like to have the family signet." *Breathe.* "So I can have a ring made for Samara."

His father just stared at him, his crystal glass frozen halfway to his lips.

Only heads of the highest Lagonian families had signets. Bands marked with the family crest were worn by the heir and his or her spouse.

"I'm going to ask Samara to marry me," Wilsean added, even though the clarification wasn't necessary.

Wilsean's father moved to one of the velvet chairs by the fire and sat. "Who is her family?"

Wilsean tensed. He'd known this question would be the first one out of his father's mouth. "The Moonfalls, but you wouldn't know them. They're Insorsiled."

"Insorsiled?" His father began to laugh.

Wilsean clenched his jaw.

"Samara is a captivating young woman," his father said when his laughter had subsided.

"She is," Wilsean agreed.

"But she is not for you."

Wilsean stopped fidgeting with his ring.

"You know you must marry from one of the high families if we're going to maintain our control." He sipped his drink. "In these turbulent times, it's imperative that we don't relinquish our hold on trade routes or supply chains."

So many furious retorts flooded Wilsean's brain that he couldn't give voice to any of them.

His father got to his feet and grasped his arm. "I will relinquish my position as advisor to the Emperor as soon as you wed. At that point, I will also turn over ownership of all our holdings. Our family's assets will belong to you. You'll become the new head of our line."

Nothing his father said came as a surprise. This was the future Wilsean had been groomed for since he was in the womb. He had fought and bled for the empire, and he certainly knew it better than the corrupt old men who made up the Emperor's council. Lagonia's citizens needed an advisor who would speak on their behalf.

And yet, those noble intentions were drowned out by the one and only piece of advice Rhett had ever given him.

If you care about Samara half as much as it seems, you shouldn't let anything else get in the way of being with her.

He cared about her so much more than that. All at once, he couldn't remember why duty and family mattered so much. All he could think about…all he could see…was her.

"Take her as your mistress if you wish," his father said, studying the liquid in his glass. "But you will wed one of our own."

Wilsean shoved his hands in his pockets to resist the urge to draw a weapon against his own father.

"I would never disrespect Samara that way."

"Then give her up," Wilsean's father said. "It's your only option. You'll reap great rewards when you ascend to head of this family, which will more than make up for this temporary loss. You have to take the good with the bad, Son."

Wilsean met his father's stare. "That doesn't work for me."

His father gave him an incredulous look. "You wouldn't really consider choosing her over your own family, would you? Your empire? Your future?"

Wilsean thought about telling Rhett and Ciago he'd lost his position in his family, and with it, his right to serve in the Lagonia army. He thought about saying goodbye to his friends and leaving the only home he'd ever known, since no one in Lagonia would ever sell him property or offer him a job after he'd disgraced his family.

Then, he remembered the brave, determined expression in Samara's eyes when she'd faced off with her parents. She'd been terrified, but she'd stood her ground.

She deserved a man with the same kind of courage.

"I would choose her over all of that," Wilsean told his father.

As soon as he spoke the words, he knew they were the right ones. There was no sense of doubt or hesitation. There never had been. If he'd ever thought things could turn out differently, he'd been lying to himself.

He was in love with Samara. He wasn't giving her up.

"You know the law." His father crossed his arms. "And if you think Rhetteman will be able to change it once he's emperor, think again."

Wilsean knew his father was speaking the truth. The law that required high family heirs to marry and breed with other high family heirs had been written to consolidate and preserve wealth. The lawmakers happened to be members of those same families who benefitted from the law. They would never permit an emperor to change them, and they wielded enough influence in the court to ensure their interests were protected.

"If Rhetteman showed you that kind of favoritism, the high families would rebel against him," his father continued. "He'd find himself with a knife in his back before the month's end."

Wilsean twisted the ring around his index finger for the last time. Then, he pulled it from his finger. In the five years since his parents had given it to him, he'd never taken it off. He felt naked without it. He tossed the ring at his father, whose eyes bulged as he caught it.

"You're out of your mind," his father said. "If you go through with this, I'll be forced to disinherit you. You'll lose our family name and any ties you would have had to the palace. You'll never be able to serve the new emperor."

As he stared at his father, Wilsean felt that same overwhelming sense of calm that overtook him before a battle. It was a peacefulness that came with the knowledge that he was right where he should be, and that he was ready for whatever came next.

His father scoffed. "You think your woman will still want you when you don't have a home or cent to your name?"

The possibility was a knife between Wilsean's ribs. He didn't think Samara cared about his wealth, but the fact that he would be jobless and penniless wouldn't exactly be a turn-on.

"That's up to her," Wilsean said. "But this is my choice."

And with that, he strode out of his father's study.

"Samara," he called. "We're leaving."

He shoved open the double-doors that led into his mother's garden. His mother was sitting on one of the stone benches, pruning a rosebush. Wilsean looked around.

"Where's Samara?"

"How should I know?" his mother replied without pausing in her pruning. "She didn't tell me where she was going before she ran off."

For several seconds, Wilsean couldn't speak.

"What did you say to her?"

The tone of his voice made his mother look up.

"I told her the truth." His mother lifted a shoulder. "I told her you were important, and she was being selfish for trying to distract you. I also told her that you would soon tire of her decorative wiles and come to your senses. I told her if she cared about anything besides your jewels, she'd go peddle her wares elsewhere."

Wilsean's vision went red. "You…said…what?!"

"Really, Wilsean?" his mother retorted, glancing up from her rosebush. "A servant?" She wiped an invisible speck of dust from her sleeve and gave him a disappointed frown. "Even your father has the dignity to only dally among the gentry. You should have more self-respect."

"Screw you," Wilsean spit. "Screw this goddamned family and its goddamned reputation."

Wilsean turned his back on his mother and left his parents' house. He didn't look back.

* * *

The Insorsiled bike was gone from the courtyard. He could have taken his parents' dragon, but that would have involved speaking to them. So, instead, he sprinted the eleven miles back to the tent on foot.

He burst into the common room hours later, ignoring the surprised looks he got from Keela and the kids. He went straight to his bedroom.

It was dark inside. Light spilling in from the common room caught on the sparkly fabric of Samara's gown, which was crumpled in a pile on the floor. There was no sign of the woman who had been wearing it. Samara never left her clothes lying around.

Where was she? Was she alright?

Of course, she wasn't alright. After the things his mother had said to her—

"Wilsean."

He turned in the doorway.

Rhett was slumped on the couch in the common room. Wilsean hadn't even noticed him when he came in. Rhett inclined his head in the direction of his and Liss's room.

Wilsean didn't ask questions. He barged in.

He went still when the point of a dagger dug into his chest. He followed the blade to a hand…to Liss's face. Her eyes glittered with fury.

"Take one more step and I'll drop you," she snarled.

"No." Lullianna prowled over to him. She gave Wilsean a pitiless smile. "I can cause him *much* more pain."

Wilsean barely heard Lullianna's threats or felt the pressure of Liss's dagger. All of his attention was drawn to the small figure curled on the bed.

"Leave him alone," Samara said, sitting up. "This isn't his fault."

Her eyes were red. Wilsean's heart lurched.

This was completely his fault.

"I thought you were cool," Lullianna said, her anger shifting to betrayal. "Dick."

"Get out of here," Liss told him, pressing her knife farther until it cut through the fabric of his jacket. "You've done enough damage."

"I deserve it," Wilsean said, stepping into the blade. Liss's hold faltered, and she pulled back. "But you're going to have to wait to slice me up until later. Samara and I need to talk."

Liss's fierce gaze softened, and then Rhett appeared in the doorway. He leaned against the frame, and even in Wilsean's distracted state, he noticed the bright orange glow of Rhett's eyes. His friend was shivering from the fever that was making perspiration bead on his brow.

"Liss, come on," Rhett said in a hoarse voice.

"His soul is full of guilt," Liss said, glaring at Wilsean. "He knows he deserves this."

Rhett smiled a little.

Thanks, man, Wilsean thought, even though he wasn't really paying attention to anyone except Samara.

"Give us a few minutes," Samara said in a quiet voice. "Please."

Liss and Lullianna looked at Samara, and then at each other. They both glared at Wilsean. Then, they left the room. Rhett shut the door behind them.

"I'm so sorry," Wilsean began as he approached Samara. He moved slowly, like he might spook her.

Samara sat back against the headboard and smoothed her hair.

"You have nothing to be sorry for," she told him. "You're not responsible for what your mother said."

"I never should have left you alone with her." Wilsean wanted to kick himself for being that thoughtless. He'd been so intent on asking his father's permission for something he never should have needed permission for, that he'd abandoned Samara.

Samara gave him a sad smile. Her next words tore the breath right out of his lungs.

"I'm glad for it."

Wilsean choked. "You are?"

Samara nodded, but she wasn't looking at him anymore.

"I think I somehow convinced myself we could keep on being…whatever we were to each other. Tonight reminded me that we come from two different words—"

"No." Wilsean knelt down beside the bed. He tried to reach for her, but Samara pulled away from him.

"It was a fun year," she said, her voice bright even though her eyes were dull. "Now, it's time for us both to move on."

She got off the bed and walked to the door. Wilsean stayed where he was, his knees digging into the hard wood and his heart in pieces.

CHAPTER 37

Rhett left Silverbird at the edge of the road with a bag full of gold nuggets. It was easier to follow the tracks that led deeper into the Insorsiled forest on foot.

He'd been at this for hours, and if it hadn't been for the temporary strengthening spell Lullianna had put on him, he wouldn't have made it even this far.

It was nearly a full moon, but the heavy cloud cover kept the forest dark enough that he could barely see. Every few minutes, the clouds would shift and a ray of silvery-blue moonlight would filter down. If he'd been thinking more clearly, he would have brought an Insorsiled stone to light the path. He'd been more focused on slipping out of bed before Liss woke up than he'd been about the logistics of his search.

Lullianna had told him he had another few days at most. Probably less. He really wasn't looking forward to sharing that news with Liss, so he was postponing the conversation in favor of tying up loose ends.

Elouicia and a few-thousand slavers were unaccounted for.

There had been no word from Lagonia's new emperor and his mercenary army. Rhett wasn't naïve enough to think Jaikon's brutal second-in-command had fallen down some dark hole…along with his entire army. And that meant Elouicia was up to something that would more than likely spell Lagonia's doom.

Rhett was determined to solve this final mystery. Then, he could die knowing he'd done everything he could to give the empire a chance.

As he waited for the clouds to shift and illuminate the tracks on the ground again, he puzzled over what his spies had told him. The Insorsiled were behaving strangely. Well, some of them were. It seemed that the most powerful Insorsiled were exempt from whatever Krozor was doing that left the rest of the kingdom's occupants glassy-eyed and with no memory of how they spent their days. Samara's siblings hadn't been able to discover what was happening, but they'd confirmed what Wilsean's parents had said about the weather.

Rhett wasn't sure what Krozor was up to, but instinct told him it would soon become Lagonia's problem if he didn't find a way to stop the new king. He had a feeling the situation in Insorsil was somehow connected to Elouicia and his slaver army.

Without warning, Rhett's legs gave out. His knees crashed into the frozen ground as the world seemed to tumble over on itself.

Not again, Rhett thought, just as the taste of blood filled his mouth.

Adrenaline and sheer stubborn will kept his blood inside him where it belonged. He leaned against a tree and waited for the dizziness to subside.

Rhett knew he should be grateful. Those two immunity flowers he'd eaten had kept him going longer than most Infected. They'd bought him time for all of his unfinished business.

But as he knelt on the forest floor, he knew it still wouldn't be enough.

A cold wind blew in, helping to cool his fevered skin and pushing down the remnants of his nausea. The wind also parted the heavy layer of clouds. The moon's blue light shone down brightly enough that it illuminated the forest floor, and the footsteps that Rhett could now easily follow.

He forced himself to his feet once more and walk-limped after them.

The deeper he went into the forest, the more warnings began to fire off inside his brain. He passed through a thick tangle of trees and stepped into a large clearing.

The air was scented with freshly-chopped wood and turned earth. There was also a caustic chemical smell that had Rhett tightening his hold on his dagger as he melted into the shadows.

That was when he saw the first hole in the ground. The square trench had to be at least twenty feet in length and nearly as many in width. From where he was standing, he could see two more holes with the same dimensions. Rhett could tell the holes were deep from the piles of frozen earth stacked up all around the tree stumps.

He approached the first trench slowly, his nose burning as the chemical smell grew stronger. He looked down into the hole.

This time, his nausea had nothing to do with opal contagion.

Rhett was standing at the edge of a mass grave.

Bodies in various stages of decomposition filled the hole. They were stacked on top of each other. Their limbs were tangled and splayed in grotesque poses. A white powder that looked like snow, but was the source of the acrid stink, covered the corpses.

Rhett staggered back until he was leaning against a tree. He tried to breathe, but his chest felt like fire.

He was no stranger to death. He'd seen the aftermath of battles and held dying soldiers as they breathed their last. But this—he'd never seen anything like it.

He forced himself to go to the two other trenches to confirm they were also filled with bodies. They were.

Rhett forced aside his horror and sickness. These dead didn't need his anger or grief. They needed him to understand what had happened, so he could prevent any more bodies from being added to this atrocious tally.

It had taken only a glance into the graves to realize the dead were all Insorsiled. Their colorful cloaks and long hair gave that away.

Rhett pressed a hand to his sunken stomach at the sight of all these dead civilians.

Who would do this? More importantly, why *would they do it?*

A flicker of movement caught Rhett's attention. For a second, Rhett thought he was seeing one of the spirits that had almost killed him in Gatria's grotto. But the hand that clawed the dirt was no apparition. The man's skin was covered in angry red welts where the white powder had burned through his flesh.

Rhett knelt down and helped pull the warlock out of the grave.

The warlock was crying and shaking as the two of them sprawled onto the frozen ground.

"What is this?" Rhett asked in a hoarse voice. "What happened here?"

The warlock was crying too hard to speak.

"Don't want," the warlock whispered. "Don't want to die…alone."

Rhett's throat thickened.

"You won't. I'm here." He took the warlock's trembling, blistered hand in his own and squeezed.

The warlock sighed. His shaking grew less violent.

Rhett pulled off his jacket and draped it over the warlock before taking the man's hand again.

The warlock stopped crying. The tremors wracking his body stilled. When Rhett looked at the man's face, he realized the warlock was dead.

Their hands were clasped so tightly it took Rhett several seconds to disentangle them.

Even though Rhett had more need of his jacket than the warlock, he left it draped over the dead man.

Roiling disgust and anger gave Rhett strength. He coaxed his legs into a swift jog.

He needed his soldiers. He needed answers.

His mind was in such turmoil that he didn't immediately notice the prickling sensation at the back of his neck. He had nearly reached the road where he'd left Silverbird, when he finally took note of the buzzing sound that was growing louder by the second.

At first, he thought it was just the pulsating ache in his head. It wasn't until the sound of high-pitched chattering was added to the fluttering of hundreds of small wings that Rhett understood.

"Monster."

"Killer."

"Murrrderrrerrr."

He glanced around, searching for the source of the sounds. All at once, what had looked like leaves on a nearby tree transformed into tree fairies. More trees burst apart, becoming hundreds of fairies. Their voices got louder as they descended.

The tree fairies swarmed and cycloned around Rhett until he was so dizzy he could barely stand.

"Found him. Found him so good."

"Take that, murderer. And that."

The fairies cackled as they stabbed their tiny swords into any part of Rhett they could reach.

"Get lost," he told the diabolical little creatures.

"Nope, nope, nope. Murderers have to pay. Murderers have to *die*."

Before Rhett could swat a path through the fairies, more sounds filled the woods. He caught a glimpse of opal skin and burnt orange hair.

"Hello, Opal Slayer."

An Extended man Rhett had never seen before stepped forward. The look on his face was anything but friendly.

The man raised his arm, and Rhett's dagger was pulled right out of his hand. It flew across the space separating them and delivered itself into the Extended man's waiting palm.

A Metalsmith.

"Time to answer for your crimes," he told Rhett, smiling grimly.

Rhett saw the man's fist flying toward his face. Then, there was only blackness.

CHAPTER 38

The invincibles arrived sooner than Ciago had expected. Then again, invincibility likely had the side effect of increasing risk taking. The Lagonians had evidently braved the quicker, but more dangerous, route through Dead Sailor's Channel. The narrow passage was riddled with icebergs and sea serpents.

Fortunately, the giants had left several hours ago. The fact that the Lagonian fighter ships were still headed this way meant the two hadn't crossed paths.

Ciago pocketed the Insorsiled glass he'd been using to spy on the ships' progress. He moved farther toward the stern, even though there was no way the Lagonians would notice his ship. The invincibles' attention was fixed on the shore.

Winny stood silent and still beside him. They watched the invincibles moor alongside the giant ships that had been left behind. The soldiers were efficient as they lowered anchors, armed themselves, and unloaded the rowboats.

Ciago handed Winny the Insorsiled glass so she could have the pleasure of seeing the invincibles' reaction when they reached shore. When their first shouts of dismay reached Ciago's ears, he felt a smile split his face.

"Ready?" he asked Winny.

"More than ready." Her eyes shone with mischief.

They coasted their ship back out onto the open water, making a wide loop so they wouldn't be noticed as their ship came into the harbor. They dropped anchor, using the cover of the other moored Lagonian ships to hide them from view.

It probably wouldn't have mattered even if Ciago was shouting and shooting up Insorsiled sparks. The soldiers on land were too preoccupied by the lack of any remaining vestiges of the giants to concern themselves with what was happening in the water.

That would soon change.

Ciago opened the bag that Samara's brother had delivered to him right before he left. It was good knowing people in high places.

Ciago took one of the heavy gray crystals from the bag.

"Whose aim do you think is better?" he asked Winny, bouncing the crystal in his open palm.

"Mine." Winny reached her hand into the bag, took out a crystal, and threw it.

The shimmery powder coating the outside of the crystal caught the sunlight as it streaked through the air. Ciago whipped out his Insorsiled glass just in time to see the crystal land on the bottom of the farthest rowboat.

"Not the worst throw I've ever seen," Ciago conceded. Then, he threw his own crystal.

They emptied the bag, making sure there was at least one crystal on every Lagonia vessel and giant ship in the harbor. Once that was done, they got busy hauling up their anchor.

Samara's brother had said they would have ten minutes before the crystals began exploding, and Ambrosius had emphatically suggested they get their own ship away before it got caught in the magic.

By now, the invincibles had begun sheathing their weapons. Because there was no one to fight. There wasn't a single giant left in the entire realm. There also wasn't any food, booze, shelter, or anything at all except for the snow the giants had dutifully left behind.

The invincibles were stranded on an enormous, frozen island. There was nothing else within a hundred miles except for the Brookgar Sea.

Even if the invincibles got desperate enough to try to swim back to Lagonia, it would take years without a ship. They'd get lost in the open stretches of ocean. They'd never make it back to the empire or anywhere else where they'd be a threat.

As Rhett had said, there was a difference between invincibility and invulnerability. Cold, isolation, and purposelessness wouldn't kill these soldiers. But after a few months of this hell had passed them by, their invincibility would become more of a curse than an asset.

Ciago had rid his empire of all the invincible soldiers in one fell swoop, save Jaikon and Elouicia. And it was done without losing a single life.

"Not bad planning, Lagonian," Winny told him. "Not bad at all."

The look of deep respect she leveled on him gave him an extra spring in his step as he readied their ship to return home.

"Funny," he murmured as he and Winny moved around each other, preparing for their voyage. "I never expected an enemy to become my greatest ally."

"I never expected a bumbling Lagonia soldier to become a friend," Winny replied.

He looked at Winny, whose fierce gaze was turned toward the storm-torn sea that stretched out in front of them.

"Also never thought I'd be proud of the giant blood in my veins," he murmured, almost to himself.

Winny scoffed. "You barely have enough to even scent. I'd wager you couldn't even lift a giant mallet."

Ciago raised an eyebrow at her. "Challenge accepted. And don't say I didn't warn you when I embarrass you in front of all your people."

"Pompous Lagonian," Winny said, but she was smiling.

They were still in sight of the harbor when the first crystal exploded. The entire Lagonian ship burst apart with so much force there was nothing left but splinters. The first explosion was followed by another, and another.

Winny held up the Insorsiled glass close enough for Ciago to peer through the lens with her. They stood, cheek against cheek, as they watched the invincibles onshore.

Ciago saw the moment when the soldiers realized what was happening. They weren't under attack. They were stranded in a barren realm with no means of escape.

The expressions on their faces were priceless. Ciago made a point of committing every detail to memory so he'd be able to give an accurate retelling to everyone back in Lagonia.

In the written record that would come after the verbal retelling, the story would be called "The Fearless Warrior who Slayed the Invincibles." Or something like that.

"If you're quite finished gloating," Winny said, raising her voice over the sound of the final explosions, "we should return."

Ciago let out the sails while Winny positioned herself at the helm.

"Sorry for your loss, by the way," he told her.

She'd just watched her ships explode and seen her land overrun by Lagonia soldiers. It was an outcome she'd fought to prevent for two years during the Giant War.

The giant leader gave him a sly smile. "Yes. I suppose the giants are homeless now."

Ciago returned her smile. "Well, then. Let's go win you a new home."

CHAPTER 39

When Rhett opened his eyes, he was no longer beside the mass grave. He was inside the walls of the Extended hideout.

His dagger was gone, and he was trussed up well enough that he wouldn't be able to escape. He noticed that it wasn't rope binding him but orange hair. The hair was attached to the same man who had almost strangled Liss to death with his Extension weeks ago.

Rhett should have listened to Dannica about wandering off alone. If the Extended didn't kill him, she would.

"Well, well, well." The Metalsmith from the Insorsiled forest stepped forward. "I suppose there is some justice to the world, after all. Opal Slayer is dying from opal contagion."

Rhett didn't say anything, since there was no need to speak. The evidence of his disease was in the bright orange halo around his irises.

"Mul, please," a familiar voice said. "If he's going to die anyway, there's no need for us to kill him now."

Rhett recognized Nya's voice before she appeared in the sea of hostile opal faces. Her expression was guilt-ridden and apologetic.

"You and I had a deal, Nya," the Metalsmith—Mul—tsked. "You'd send your tree fairies to find him, and then he was mine."

"But—" Nya began.

"—and in return," Mul continued, "I'd let your daughter live."

Rhett's attention caught on that.

"I know," Nya said, putting out a placating hand. "But I didn't realize at the time that Rhett was keeping our people safe. He ordered the Lagonians not to kill us. Tell him, Rhett."

Rhett didn't waste his breath. He could read the desire for vengeance in ever taut muscle in the Metalsmith's body.

"If you try to deny me this," Mul told Nya in a threatening tone, "I'll go after Liss."

Rhett jerked, forgetting about the hair that held him in place.

"Leave Liss alone," he growled.

"She chose you," the Metalsmith retorted. "She should die beside you."

The hairs binding Rhett snapped apart as he threw himself at the man.

If he'd been his normal self, he could have head-butted the Metalsmith into next week. But Rhett was too feeble. The Metalsmith shoved him, and Rhett went reeling back. He barely caught himself before he went down.

"I'm sorry, Rhett," Nya said. Tears tracked down her cheeks, making her opal skin glisten. "It was the only way to protect Liss."

Rhett nodded, letting her know he was alright with the trade. More than alright. If Liss didn't have to worry about the Extended, then that was one set of enemies she wouldn't have to deal with when he was gone.

"Take Nya's bow and arrows," Mul told the gathering crowd of Extended around them. "Just in case she starts feeling…heroic."

Nya hissed when someone stepped forward to disarm her.

The Metalsmith shrugged. "Fine. Then we'll just send a message to Lagonia for Liss. She can have her dying man if she stays behind in his place."

"Give up your weapon," Rhett ordered Nya, even though Liss's mom was already unstrapping her quiver from her back and handing it over.

"We could let the contagion take you," Mul told Rhett. He held up Rhett's dagger. "But I think it will be more appropriate to slice your throat with the same weapon you used to take so many of our lives."

Rhett kept his expression completely blank. In truth, he was relieved beyond measure. Liss and his friends wouldn't have to watch him rot away over the next two days. It would be a clean death. An easy death.

A better death than he deserved.

Mul stepped up to Rhett until they were close enough for Rhett to smell metal on the other man's skin.

"Look around you," the Metalsmith said. Hatred glittered in his orange eyes. "Look at the men and women you've stolen from. Mothers, fathers…husbands, wives…siblings…grandparents….

"Look hard, Caravan Butcher. Look at all the empty spaces where our loved ones should be standing. Because of you, they're dead and rotting in the ground."

Rhett did look. He had thought he reckoned with his guilt years ago. Now that he was staring at the accusing faces of his victims' families, he couldn't stop picturing all of the lives he'd taken.

He looked at the hatred surrounding him. He saw the naked pain behind that anger.

So many. He'd killed so many, and for what? For an emperor who was dead.

He glanced down at the ground, finding he couldn't hold those unblinking orange stares. That was when he saw the corpses. The ground was littered with the tiny bodies of frozen tree fairy remains.

Their bodies were swollen, and their skin was tinged with the unnatural gold color that was the result of honey poisoning.

Those deaths were on Rhett's hands, too. He'd been the one to tell the Extended how to use honey to control the fairies. He was the one who decided the tree fairies were a worthwhile sacrifice in his war with Jaikon. Just like he'd decided the Extended people's lives were less valuable than his own. It was only after he learned Liss's true identity that his assessment had changed.

If he thought it would do any good, he would have apologized. He would have told the crowd standing before him that he regretted every innocent life he'd ever taken. He would have told them that he should have let Jaikon kill him. Instead, he'd murdered people who had committed no crime other than be born what they were.

Rhett knew there was nothing he could say to ease all the pain he'd caused, so he stayed silent.

He forced himself to face the Extended people's judgment. He accepted their sentence and would take their punishment. He was ready.

The Metalsmith tossed Rhett's dagger in the air. It rose up and came back down, but instead of falling to the ground, it hovered at the height of Rhett's neck. The dagger slowly turned until the sharpened edge was aligned with Rhett's skin.

"No!"

Rhett's peaceful acceptance turned to one of horror as a tiny person sprang up from seemingly nowhere. Jema, who must have been using her Extension to stay hidden, appeared directly in front of Rhett. She raised her small arms, trying to grab the dagger out of the air.

The dagger jerked higher until it was out of the child's reach.

"Jema," Rhett said, trying to keep his voice calm. "You need to leave."

She turned to face him. Her eyes were wide and brimming with tears.

"You're my friend," she said, her chin wobbling. "And Lissy loves you. You can't die."

A strange ache pulsed through Rhett's chest.

"Jema, can you do something for me?" He did his best to make his voice less rough. "Can you take a message to Liss?"

A tear slid down Jema's cheek, but she managed a nod.

"Can you tell Liss that it's okay…that everything's okay?"

Jema gave him a hesitant look.

"Please," he told her, sensing the Metalsmith's impatience.

Without warning, Jema threw her arms around his legs.

"Go now," he told her as the ache in his chest spread. "Hurry."

With a hiccupped sob, Jema tucked her arms against her sides. Her body folded in on itself until she transformed into a white sphere that blended into the trampled snow on the ground.

Rhett watched the little sphere roll away from him and out of the circle of Extended. When she was out of sight, he released the breath he hadn't realized he'd been holding.

It was only once Jema was gone that he was overcome with a desperate urge to call her back.

Would Liss understand what he'd been trying to tell her with that last message? All at once, it seemed far too cryptic for anyone to make sense of. How would Liss know that he was trying to tell her that he'd come to terms with his past and that, finally, he was at peace? How was she supposed to know that he needed her to let go of any sense of obligation to avenge him and live her life? That he didn't care about anything beyond her happiness?

Damnit.

Why hadn't he told Jema to tell Liss that she'd made his life worth living? That she'd been the center of his entire world.

It was too late. Jema was gone, and Rhett's life was seconds away from ending. The dagger was repositioning itself for the final blow.

Steel doesn't know love or despair. It can't be bent or broken. It needs no heart or warmth. I am steel.

Rhett was ready to die.

The dagger sliced through the air.

There was a blur of motion, and then a body was between Rhett and the dagger. Blood splattered across Rhett's face. A scream tore through the hideout.

CHAPTER 40

A scream tore from Liss as she skidded to a halt just inside the Extended hideout. The dagger had been coming for Rhett. Instead, it sliced into a throat with opal skin.

Her mother's throat.

A small, red slash appeared on the side of Nya's neck. The moonlight illuminated her mother's blood as it leaked onto the snowy ground.

Liss started for the mob of Extended who stood between her and her mom. Before she made it a step, she felt Quic's arms come around her. In less than a second, she was standing inside the ring of Extended beside Rhett. He'd thrown off the hair that was wrapped around him and was in the process of catching her mom.

Quic let go of Liss and blurred out of sight. He was back just as fast.

Liss choked on a sob as her mom reached out a shaking hand for her weapon. Quic handed over Nya's bow and arrows.

Her mom was alive, but the wound was gushing blood. It was coating her neck and soaking the front of her shirt.

"Mom—"

"Move," Nya ordered.

Rhett let go of Nya, who was on her knees. Then, her arrows started to fly.

From her vantage point on the ground, Liss saw the first of her mom's arrows hurtle through the air toward Mul.

The Metalsmith put up a hand, trying to control the arrow's metal tip.

The arrow slowed, but it stayed true on its course. The missile struck Mul's skull and passed through two others who had been standing behind him.

"Back up," Nya told the onlookers in a hoarse voice.

"Drop your weapons," another voice called.

As she and Rhett stood, Liss saw a row of soldiers in anti-contagion suits had appeared between them and the Extended.

Quic was transporting the rebel soldiers at lightning speed until the entire army was there with them. Dannica, who was the first to figure out Rhett was missing, now held her sword to an Extended man's neck.

The rest of the rebels raised their weapons in a silent threat. The Extended, outnumber and outmatched, backed up.

Liss barely noticed. She fell to the ground beside her mom.

"Lullianna!" Liss shouted at Quic. "Get Lullianna!"

Liss tore off the bottom half of her shirt and started putting pressure on the wound on her mom's neck. The cut wasn't deep, and yet Liss's hands were instantly covered in blood.

"I'm going to save you," Liss told her mom, looking into orange eyes that were starting to go unfocused.

"Oh, sweetheart." Nya offered her a wobbly smile. "You've been saving me since you were a little girl. This time, it was my turn to save you."

Tears burned Liss's eyes. She wiped them away furiously, refusing to accept what was happening.

Rhett handed Liss a length of cloth. Only then did she realize the shirt she'd just put to her mom's neck was already soaked through. She'd barely started applying pressure with the new fabric when it, too, was drenched.

"Where's Lullianna?!" Liss shrieked.

"Liss." Rhett, who was kneeling beside her, shook his head.

Out of the corner of her eye, she saw Quic. He was panting and his opal skin gleamed with sweat.

"I'm tapped out," he said in a miserable voice. "I'm sorry, Liss."

Liss disregarded him immediately. She pointed to two of the rebels.

"Get Lullianna. Now!"

A tiny voice in her mind argued that Lagonia was half a day's dragon ride away, and that her mom didn't have an hour…let alone half a day. The louder voice in her head was screaming for her to help her mom…to save her.

"I'm sorry," Nya said as Liss adjusted the rag to try and slow the flow of blood. "I sent the tree fairies after Rhett. I told Mul he could kill Rhett. I thought I was protecting you, but then I realized…." She coughed.

"Shh," Liss told her mom. "You're going to be just fine."

Nya waved an impatient hand.

"I realized you love him the way I loved your father," she continued, her voice growing hoarser. "I couldn't let you lose your true love."

Small sprays of blood seeped around the cloth, no matter how Liss tried to adjust it. When she glanced at Rhett, she saw the apology in his eyes.

"Just this once," Nya said. "Let me take care of you."

"Mom, please," Liss begged. "Just hold on. Please just hold on."

"You look so much like him," Liss's mom told her. She reached up to touch Liss's face, but her arm fell back against the ground.

Liss lifted her mom's hand and cradled it against her cheek.

A breath shuddered out of Nya. Her eyelids closed and her shallow breathing grew even shallower.

"Mom? Mom!"

Rhett's arms came around Liss.

"No, she's not dead." She wrested herself from Rhett's grip. "She isn't dead!"

Nya's soul was cloudy in unconsciousness. Liss could sense the faint hint of peacefulness across her soul.

"Liss," Rhett said in a soft voice.

"I'm telling you!" Liss felt a little crazed. "Her soul. It's—she's—"

Liss turned back to her mom. She saw how all the shine had leached out of her mom's opal skin. When Liss tried to sort her mom's soul, there was nothing.

"No," Liss choked. "Mom, please."

She let Rhett gather her against him. There was no stopping the tears, so she let them come.

She had no idea how long she stayed there, kneeling on the bloodstained ground with Rhett's arms locked around her. She cried until the sun was rising and she was empty of tears.

CHAPTER 41

As Rhett watched Nya bleed out and tried to ease Liss's helpless grief, he relived his loss of Stone all over again.

If it hadn't been for Nya's sacrifice, he'd be dead. He knew Nya had died for him for the same reason why Stone had died for Liss.

Knowing the reason didn't make him feel any better about the fact that Nya had lost her life. It was even more of a waste because Rhett would be dead in a matter of days, anyway.

Rhett and the members of Liss's old caravan helped dig a grave for their fallen leader. Rhett's soldiers stood over all of the Extended, silent but watchful. The gleam of their weapons reminded the Extended not to attack.

Once Nya had been enclosed in her shallow grave, Rhett and the others backed away, giving Liss privacy to say her final goodbyes. He watched her kneel over the covered mound and wished there was some way to ease her pain.

He knew from personal experience there was nothing he could do or say to make her loss less raw.

When Liss got to her feet and walked back to him, her spine was straight and her eyes were free of tears. He saw courage and determination in those blue depths. Impossibly, he felt himself fall even harder for her.

Liss glanced at him, and then she stared out at the crowd of Extended. Rhett could feel the tension as both the Extended and rebels readied for a fight. He felt his soldiers' eyes on him, waiting for an order. He watched Liss, ready to follow her lead.

"Well, go on and get it over with," an Extended man said, looking from Rhett to Liss.

"Get what over with?" Rhett asked.

The Extended man sneered at him. "One of ours hunted you down. Mul was going to kill you. Now, Liss's mother is dead and your soldiers surround us. Don't pretend like you're not going to slaughter us all."

"We could do that." Liss scanned the crowd. "Or, we could put aside our differences to defeat an enemy that's trying to kill us both."

"Why do you think we'd ever trust you?" a different Extended demanded, her orange-rimmed eyes boring into Liss. "You're one of them." She pointed at the group of Lagonia soldiers.

"No, I'm not," Liss replied.

"You certainly aren't one of us," the same Extended woman snarled.

Several seconds passed. Rhett tensed.

Liss laughed. It was a soft sound that held no humor.

"I'm so damn tired," she said in a voice that was too quiet for anyone but him to hear. Louder, she said, "I've been trying to figure out who I fit with—the Extended or the Lagonians. The truth is, I don't belong with either."

Rhett wanted to argue with that, but he kept his mouth shut.

"I have an Extension, but I look Lagonian," Liss told the Extended. "My existence is as deadly to any Uninfected as the rest of you." Her voice hitched a little. Rhett saw her swallow. "I grew up in a caravan just like all of you. I'm a Soul Sorter, and I spent most of my life stealing from and fighting the Lagonians.

"I grew up hating the Lagonians as much as any of you. But then I befriended some of them." Her eyes locked on Rhett's. "I fell in love with one."

The way she looked at him when she said those words made his heart grow impossibly huge.

Liss turned her attention back on the crowd while Rhett tried to get control of his stuttering pulse.

"So, yeah, I don't fit in with either group. And that's the reason why all of you are still alive."

"You won't win our love with threats, girl," an older Extended man said.

"I don't need your love." Liss's voice grew stronger. She stood to her full height, seeming more confident and sure of herself than Rhett had ever seen her. "In fact, I don't need anything from you. But you need me."

For weeks, Rhett had seen Liss trying to reconcile her loyalty to her people and her love of him. He'd seen how deeply it hurt her when her own people treated her like the enemy.

That wasn't the case anymore.

That's my girl, Rhett thought, unable to stop the burst of pride that went through him.

"Explain to us why we need you," the Extended man said.

Liss held the man's challenging stare. "Rhett and I killed Emperor Jaikon, but now there's someone even more evil, and he's coming after all of us. We," she gestured to Rhett and the rest of the rebels, "will help you fight against King Krozor and the Insorsiled who want to kill all of us."

Rhett nodded. He thought of those mass graves in the Insorsiled forest. He thought of the warlock who had crawled out of a pile of bodies, only to die on the frozen ground.

"We're safe in the hideout," another Extended argued. "We don't need your protection."

"The hideout won't keep out magic," Liss told them, just as Rhett opened his mouth to say the very same.

"We're in this together," Liss told the group. She began to pace back and forth, like she was a commander addressing her troops. "Krozor wants to destroy all of us. If we're going to have a chance against him, we're going to need to fight him instead of each other."

Rhett watched as the Extended absorbed her every word. Even the skeptical ones were rapt with attention. They couldn't help themselves.

At that moment, Rhett knew Liss was going to become the Extended leader. She would turn them into a force to be reckoned with.

He wished he'd be around to witness it.

"What about the Viper?" an Extended asked, pointing a finger at Rhett. "He still needs to die."

"And he will," someone standing nearby replied. "In a day or two at most. He'll get his justice. It'll probably be worse for him if we let him die slowly, anyway."

It was the truth.

Liss's face blanched. Rhett tried to give her a comforting look. He saw her steel herself and turn back to the waiting crowd.

"Let's make an agreement here and now. We'll put aside our differences, at least until Krozor is dead."

* * *

Hours later, there was a tentative agreement between the Extended and rebel Lagonian army. Rhett arranged for a rotation of guards to stay at the hideout and then left Dannica in charge.

He pulled Dannica aside to deliver a much-deserved thanks and apology. She accepted both only after he swore not to be an idiot again. The necessary promises were made, and Dannica turned her attention onto organizing her soldiers so they'd be able to make the best use of their numbers.

Quic was designated as the go-between for the two groups, so that Rhett and Dannica could easily stay in touch.

Rhett sent a group of his most hardened soldiers to keep watch over the graves in the Insorsiled forest. They would report back on any activity.

By the time Rhett, Liss, and the rest of the rebels started back for Lagonia, the sun was high in the sky.

Silverbird was waiting where Rhett had left her—a small miracle, since Rhett knew he wouldn't be able to make the walk on foot.

"Are you okay?" Rhett asked Liss in a quiet voice as they rode.

"No," she told him, and Rhett realized how stupid the question had been. "But I will be."

"I'm sorry," Rhett began. "Her death was…such a waste."

Liss shook her head. "Don't say that." She tugged on Silverbird's reins and turned to face him. She rested her cheek against his beating heart.

As Rhett held her, he was overcome by a desperate wish for a future with her. All of the peace and acceptance he'd felt when he was about to die abandoned him. He wanted to live.

"I guess we're even now, huh?" Liss gave him a small smile.

"How do you mean?"

"I snuck away from you to find that warlock, and you gave me the slip to track Elouicia."

Rhett suppressed a shudder at the memory of those mass graves. He tightened his hold on Liss.

"So, is this the part where we agree never to leave the other one behind again?" he asked, reaching up to touch her cheek.

"I guess it is." Liss offered him a smile before she pressed her lips to his.

And just like that, their bargain was sealed.

As much as he hated the idea of Liss and his friends watching him die, Rhett decided then and there that he wouldn't slink off to die alone in some dark corner. He also wasn't going to disrespect his soldiers by trying to take down Elouicia's army single-handed. He owed his people more than that.

It was half a day's ride back to the cape. By the time they made it to the Insorsiled tent, it was taking all of Rhett's concentration to keep from stumbling in exhaustion.

Before the contagion, he could go for days on no sleep without losing his edge. Now, every waking moment felt like a fight...one that he was losing.

"Rhett!" Jema came out of nowhere and barreled into him with enough force that he almost lost his balance.

She attached herself to his leg and hung on for dear life.

Rhett patted the girl's back, trying to figure out what he was supposed to say. He'd never really had much contact with kids, but he couldn't deny this one was growing on him.

"I tried to give Lissy your message," she told him. "I rode Lullianna's bike as fast as it would go, but by the time I got back here, Lissy was already coming to save you."

"There you are." Mari ducked out from under the tent's flap and jogged over to them. "I've been looking all over for you."

"What's wrong?" Liss asked.

"Nothing." She grinned. "They figured it out."

"Who figured what out?" Rhett asked, trying to gently separate his leg from Jema.

Spence appeared just behind Mari. The two of them exchanged a conspiratorial look before he said, "Just come inside. It's better if you see for yourselves."

Rhett followed the others into the tent. Lullianna and Keela were sitting at the table. The flower box was between them. The last flower was still there, but it wasn't alone. The dark soil was dotted with small buds.

The only sound in the room was Lullianna's voice as she murmured a soft incantation. The only movement came from Keela. She alternately stroked the soil and waved her hands in a complicated pattern in the air above the flower box.

As Rhett watched, the tiny buds began to grow. White stems appeared. A flicker of rainbow light reflected across the tent's ceiling as a single, tiny opal petal unfurled.

A small sound escaped from Liss. She put a hand over her mouth.

Rhett slid an arm around her waist. They were all silent and unmoving as Lullianna and Keela worked.

The temperature in the room had Rhett's teeth chattering, but both women were sweating. Lullianna's hands were shaking and her voice was hoarse.

Someone gasped.

There were now two fully-formed immunity flowers in the box when, before, there'd only been one.

"You did it," Liss breathed.

Keela gave Liss a tired smile. "Lullianna figured out the magic that grows the immunity flower, and then she infused it with earth magic so it would respond to my Extension."

Both women looked like they were having trouble staying upright in their chairs.

"We just need to figure out a way to make enough without burning ourselves out," Lullianna added.

"Can you do it?" Rhett asked, hating the exhaustion and strain that growing a single flower had caused both of them.

The women exchanged a glance.

"We're certainly going to try," Keela said in a kind voice. "But this is still only a prevention. We have yet to discover a cure."

Rhett nodded in understanding.

"Once you grow more," Liss said in a tentative voice, "could he just keep eating them to reduce his symptoms?"

Lullianna shook her head. "The contagion's progressed too much for that. The virus is in his bones, and a thousand of these flowers couldn't undo that kind of damage. I'm sorry."

Rhett held Liss more tightly. He was trying to think of what to say to her, when the door to the tent opened. A blur of opal color flew in with a flurry of snowflakes. Quic stood in the center of the common room. His orange hair was a wild tangle, some of it frosted over.

"What's happened?" Liss asked, tensing in Rhett's arms.

Quic turned his attention on Rhett.

"Dannica wanted me to tell you. Elouicia brought a cart full of dead Insorsiled to the graves in the forest." Quic swallowed. "A group of us followed him back. He and the slavers are in Insorsil, but we couldn't get close enough to see what they were doing. There was some kind of magical shield that kept us out."

Rhett nodded. He'd suspected as much, since so little information had made it out of Insorsil.

"But while we were waiting to see if Elouicia or any of the slavers would come back, something crazy happened." Quic's gaze darted around the room. "The air got really hot. Boiling, actually. And then the temperature dropped. I swear it got fifty degrees colder in a second." He snapped his fingers for emphasis.

When no one spoke, Quic let out a nervous little chuckle.

"It sounds crazy, huh?" Quic asked. "I thought it was crazy, and I was there. The ground started shaking, too. After a few minutes, everything went back to normal. Except for the smell of burning in the air."

"That's from the magic," Lullianna said. "When Insorsiled use too much of their magic, or lots of witches and warlocks are doing spells at the same time, it smells like fire."

Quic nodded. "We couldn't see what was happening through the shield, but we could hear a lot of cheering." He looked at Rhett. "Whatever King Krozor is making with all of that magic, it's almost ready."

CHAPTER 42

King Krozor Ragnor Mantis stood on the rickety outlook that rose over the pit. The hole was massive enough to contain a hundred Insorsiled who were filling it with their magic. Sparks and the murmured hum of a hundred incantations filled the air. Cloudy swirls of reds, blues, and greens filled the pit.

The sight was glorious to behold.

The pit formed a necessary physical barrier to contain the magic being brewed within. It also kept the thousands of untethered spells away from prying eyes. Krozor had constructed a strong magical ward around the perimeter, so not even his own subjects would happen upon the pit uninvited.

Krozor stared through his monocle at the Insorsiled working feverishly around the pit. Their eyes were glazed over as they added spell after spell into the collection in the pit.

Everything was nearly ready.

The dead were piled up and awaiting the carts that would transport them to the graves in the Insorsiled forest. The new curfew Krozor had instituted would ensure no one saw the carts.

Krozor looked at the stack of bodies awaiting transport. The sight made him want to weep. Every magical life was precious, and even though he had been careful to only select the weakest of his people for this task, it was still a burden to see any Insorsiled expire. But he'd had no choice.

When Insorsiled pushed their magic beyond its limits and died mid-spell, a magical burst of energy was left behind. It was a combination of the partially-completed spell and the witch or warlock's spirit.

Krozor was harnessing this effect.

Every time an Insorsiled burned himself out, Krozor whispered the words that would gather the witch or warlock's spirit to him. The magical energy was drawn into the orb at the top of his staff, which was glowing. It radiated heat from all the magic contained within.

The incomplete spells filtered down into the pit.

All for the good of Insorsil, Krozor reminded himself. Everything he did would safeguard their magic. Nothing was more important.

"We've done everything you asked." Elouicia, his face and hands caked with dirt, pulled himself up the ladder that led to the outlook. "Give me what I came here for so I can return to my empire. There are people who need killing."

"No," Krozor replied. "I still have uses for your soldiers."

"I am Lagonia's emperor," the assassin snarled, baring his sharpened canines. "The only reason I came back here was for more pins. I have no interest in serving you."

Krozor gave the magic in Elouicia's pin a fierce tug. He made pain lance through the Lagonian's chest, reminding him of who held the power. Elouicia hissed and limped away.

Like a dog with its tail between its legs.

As he'd been doing for the last several days, King Krozor sent out the magic that linked his pin to all the others. The spell in his pin sought out the rest of the invincibles.

Still nothing.

Krozor didn't understand how Jaikon had evaded his order, or why he could no longer sense the invincible soldiers' whereabouts. With the exception of Elouicia, it was like the rest of the invincibles had just vanished.

Krozor adjusted his own pin on his cloak. There were exceptions to every spell, and it was possible that something had caused the soldiers to lose their invincibility and succumb to death. It was also possible that they'd traveled so far they were out of Krozor's range.

He could order Elouicia to tell him what had happened to the rest of the invincibles, but he wouldn't risk admitting that his hold on the pins might have limitations. He wasn't interested in Elouicia getting the idea that he might be able to resist Krozor's hold over him. Krozor also just didn't care.

In the end, it made no difference.

He adjusted his monocle and peered at the woman who was attempting a spell that was far beyond her abilities. Predictably, her magic left her in a great gust. She tottered around mindlessly, chanting *I can't, I can't, I can't.*

Krozor tapped into the power of his artifact. The magic blazed within him.

The witch's babbling cut off. Her eyes went blank. Then, she poured all of her energy into the spell she'd been afraid to complete moments before.

It was too much for the witch's overwrought magic. She died.

The dead woman's spirit separated from her body. Krozor held up his staff, absorbing the burst of magical energy that would likely have caused an earthquake if he hadn't captured it in his staff. The orb flared brighter as the new magic was added to the store of energy already roiling within.

The remnants of the witch's incomplete spell sunk down into the pit.

Elouicia tossed her empty body onto the growing pile.

Krozor felt a stab of grief at the loss of another one of his people. He had to remind himself that, with her magic having been burnt out, she was almost as bad as an Empty…almost as useless. And there was nothing else to do with Empties besides dispose of them.

A shudder of disgust ran down Krozor's spine. Fury followed on its heels.

Move faster, he thought, fixing his gaze on the Insorsiled down in the pit.

Krozor had waited decades for Gatria's exit from the throne. He was done waiting. He was done with sharing land and resources that had belonged to the Insorsiled before the other races had even existed.

Krozor would reclaim all of it for his people.

As another Insorsiled died and Krozor captured the magical energy that was released, he thought about how fitting this particular spell was. All of these Insorsiled were contributing, even if they didn't know it. When Krozor's spell took down the un-Insorsiled across the continent, it wouldn't be just his victory; it would belong to his entire kingdom.

Krozor turned his face into the wind, catching the scent of magic. Soon, his spell would be strong enough to release.

Then, the storm would begin.

CHAPTER 43

Samara tore the paper down the middle and threw the scraps across the room.

Useless. It was useless. She was useless.

After twenty-one years of trying to convince herself that possessing magic and value as a human being weren't the same, she realized she'd been deluding herself. Maybe if she was a witchdoctor like Lullianna or a transfiguration expert like Ambrosius—

Distraction. Unsuitable.

Druella's words from the other night filled her head, even though she'd done everything she could to block them out.

Empty.

That had to be the most hateful word in any language.

Except now, it seemed like a fitting description for what she was…how she felt.

She blinked against the sting in her eyes. She hadn't shed a single tear, and she wouldn't start now. Rhett had only a day at most. Samara wasn't going to stop trying to save him just because she'd been overwhelmed by a bout of self-pity.

She tore another sheet from the pad with more force than she'd intended. It ripped. She tried again. This time, the paper came away cleanly. She put her quill to the top line and heard a small snap as the tip broke off.

Samara sat back on her heels and cursed with all the venom she could muster.

She looked up from her blank paper and broken quill, blinking furiously. She focused on the two narrow beds that Mari and Jema slept in. She had holed up in their room because she needed the solitude to concentrate. And because she was a coward.

Walking away from Wilsean had been almost impossible. She didn't think she had the fortitude to face him after that. So, she would stay in this room until she had a cure for Rhett.

Except she only had the one quill, which was now useless.

Sighing, she got to her feet, ignoring the way her stomach rumbled and her head swam from dizzy exhaustion.

A quick glance out the window told her it was midday, which meant the only ones who would be in the tent were Keela and Lullianna. She could grab a new quill and maybe something to eat, and then lock herself back in the kids' bedroom.

Samara opened the door and tripped over…Wilsean.

"What are you doing?" she demanded, pressing a hand to her throbbing chest.

"Waiting for you."

His voice was so achingly familiar. So was that rich smell of pine and mint.

"How long have you been here?" Samara asked.

"Oh, not long." Wilsean winced a little as he got to his feet and stretched his legs.

Samara looked around. The common room was empty.

Gulping, Samara tried to duck past him on her way to the spare quill lying on the table. Wilsean caught her elbow before she made it a step.

"Please," he said. Something about the way his voice hitched made her go still. "Hear me out."

The tortured expression in his bloodshot eyes split her ragged heart apart even more. He waited for her nod before letting go of her.

"Samara, I'm so, so sorry," he began. "Leaving you alone with my mother was unforgivably stupid."

"I already told you, I don't blame you for what she said to me."

Exploiter. Parasite. Disgrace.

More of Druella's words crowded into her mind. Samara shook her head until the ugly words fell back into a dark corner of her mind.

Wilsean started to twist the ring on his index finger, the way he did whenever he was stressed. But then he dropped his hands to his sides.

Samara noticed his ring was gone.

She'd never seen him without it. He didn't even take it off to bathe or sleep. There was a band of lighter skin in the place where his ring belonged, but no sign of the ring itself.

"Where is it?" Samara asked.

Wilsean's brow furrowed, and then understanding dawned as he followed the direction of her gaze. He put his hand behind his back, hiding it. Samara knew from the look on his face she wasn't going to get a straight answer.

Damn. Where was Liss? Samara could really use a Soul Sorter.

"I wanted to ask you something," Wilsean said. He reached for his ring again before seeming to remember it was gone. He let out a quiet curse.

Samara had never seen him so agitated.

"Yes?" Samara asked warily.

"Once the new emperor is throned and things settle down, I'm going to be leaving the continent."

Samara's eyes jerked up from where she'd been studying the floor. She looked at him to see if he was joking. One glance into his eyes told her he was deadly serious.

She was still trying to come to terms with that piece of unexpected news, when he hit her with another.

"And I'd like you to come with me." He swallowed. "I mean, will you come with me? Would you consider coming with me?"

He swore again, hitting his forehead with his closed fist.

"I—don't understand," Samara stammered.

Wilsean gave her a little smile. "What? Do you think you're the only one who's allowed to get kicked out of their family and banned from their home?"

Samara gasped. "They didn't! They couldn't—"

Wilsean shook his head. "It was me. My choice."

The tears Samara had sworn she wouldn't cry bubbled to the surface.

This was why she'd walked away from him the other night. She hadn't wanted to come between Wilsean and his family…his future.

"Samara." Wilsean pulled her hand down from her mouth, linking it with his own. "I'm okay with all of this. Seriously."

Then, he told her everything. He told her why he'd wanted to bring her to his parents' house, and what he'd asked his father. By the time he got to the part where he relinquished his place in his family, ensuring he'd be a permanent outcast from Lagonia society, she couldn't stop the flow of tears. When he told her about how he'd cursed out his mother, Samara was laughing and crying.

"I love you, Samara." Wilsean lifted their joined hands and used his thumb to wipe the tears still coursing down her cheeks.

"I don't have a penny to my name, and I'll probably have to get work as a lumberjack across the sea—"

Samara choked out a laugh.

"—but I want to spend the rest of my life with you."

"I want that, too," she managed.

"I know you have a life here, and I wouldn't expect you to even consider following me until I've established myself. But once I do, will you have me?"

Samara tackled him. They fell back onto the couch, with Samara splayed on top of Wilsean.

"Yes!"

His eyes widened and filled with warmth. His arms locked around her, pulling her even closer.

"Yes?" he asked, like he needed to make sure he'd heard her correctly.

"But—" Samara faltered. "I don't want to be the reason why you lose your reputation." She swallowed. "Marrying an Empty won't exactly help your social status."

Wilsean grinned at her. "Given that my social status was recently downgraded to *outcast*, it's far more likely I'll be the one dragging your reputation through the mud."

Samara giggled at that.

Wilsean's expression sobered. "I was serious about getting work and saving enough for a house before I come back for you."

Samara shook her head. "I have plenty of money from all the magic I've sold over the last few years." She nuzzled his cheek before whispering, "We're rich."

The point was moot. She wasn't letting him get away ever again.

"Well," Wilsean gave her an affronted look. "If I'd known I'd be a kept husband, I would have proposed to you sooner."

Samara leaned down for a kiss, but Wilsean was frowning.

"In all seriousness, I'd drive you insane if I didn't have some kind of job. Would you really be okay with leaving Lagonia?"

"I was planning on leaving myself before I fell in love with you," she admitted. "I was going to travel the world until I found a place where I didn't feel like an outcast."

Wilsean's face brightened. "We'll be outcasts together."

"Those have to be the most romantic words ever spoken," she said, only half teasing.

"Are you seriously hooking up on our common area couch?" Ciago, his huge fists balled on his hips, stared at them in disbelief. He seemed more amused than offended.

"You're back," Wilsean said, sitting up. "How'd it go with the giants?"

"All according to plan with the invincibles," Ciago said. His brow furrowed. "But the rest of the giants should have been back already."

"Maybe they got lost," Wilsean said. "It's not like the giants are known for their sense of direction."

"True," Ciago conceded. "Winny's worried, though."

Samara had never been out to sea herself, but Wilsean had told her stories about his own crossings. She could see the worry on Ciago's face, even though he tried to hide it behind a mask of humor.

"You should know the kids are outside." Ciago gave Wilsean and Samara a suspicious look. "You might want to put your sexy time on hold before the kids walk in and are scandalized for life."

Wilsean scowled. "We're both still fully clothed, in case you haven't noticed."

Ciago shrugged. "I don't judge."

Wilsean rolled his eyes, and Samara laughed.

"Did Rhett kill Jaikon?" Ciago asked.

"Sure did." Wilsean cracked a grin.

"I can't believe it." Ciago shook his head in amazement. "That's just…wow. I can't believe it."

"Liss said ink exploded out of Jaikon," Wilsean added.

Both men chuckled in appreciation at the mental image that conjured.

Ciago sauntered past them and into the kitchen, still muttering to himself about exploding emperors.

Wilsean turned back to Samara. "I'm sorry I don't have a ring." He gave her a sheepish grin.

"We'll get bands made for both of us," Samara said. "We can make our own crest."

If she and Wilsean were going to ignore some of the rules, they may as well ignore the rest, too.

"Perfect." Wilsean got up and lifted Samara into his arms. "So I guess all that's left is to consummate our engagement."

"That's after the wedding, man," Ciago called from the kitchen.

"Who says it can't be both?" Wilsean winked at Samara as he carried her toward the bedroom.

Ciago chuckled. "Glad you both finally figured out you're two halves of the same whole. Congratulations."

Halves of the same whole.

That was almost like—

Samara gasped and flung herself out of Wilsean's arms.

"Samara, what the—"

She raced into the kids' room and began gathering up the scraps of paper she'd torn earlier.

"What's going on?" Wilsean asked, looking both confused and alarmed.

Clasping the shredded papers to her chest, she felt a smile stretch across her entire face.

"I think I know how to cure Rhett."

CHAPTER 44

Liss should have known Krozor's monocle had a purpose other than giving the warlock king that classic trying-too-hard look.

Quic had just come from the Extended hideout to deliver Dannica's message. One of Rhett's soldiers had seen Krozor's monocle slip from his eye. All at once, the fogged-over expressions had vanished from the Insorsiled people's faces. As soon as the monocle was back in place, the witches' and warlocks' faces had become blank again.

Liss sat on one of the couches in the common room next to Rhett. The kids were at the table finishing breakfast. Lullianna was doing something complicated and magical with the box of flowers. Samara was going back and forth between Gatria's spell book and a paper she was marking with symbols.

"That explains so much," Samara said.

"It does?" Lullianna raised her eyebrows. She paused with her fingertips hovering over one of the three new immunity flowers Keela had grown.

"I couldn't figure out the spell Krozor was using to control those Insorsiled, since it was obviously so much stronger than a normal compulsion spell," Samara said.

"What does it have to do with his monocle?" Liss asked.

"Our oldest records describe artifacts that were made by the first witches and warlocks. They intensify a person's magic and grow stronger over time."

"How come I've never heard of these artifacts?" Lullianna asked.

Samara lifted a shoulder. "There's never been any evidence that they actually existed. I only came across mention of them when I was learning about archaeological digs that unearthed ancient spells."

"Sounds riveting," Lullianna quipped as she turned her attention back to the flowers.

"Krozor's an archaeologist," Samara said, ignoring her sister's sarcasm. "He must have believed the artifacts were more than legend and found one. That explains why a hermit who is hundreds of years old would suddenly make his move to become king." Samara looked down at the spell book in front of her without seeming to see it. "If I'm right and this really is one of those artifacts, he'll get stronger every day he has it."

"Well then, we have to take it away from him," Liss said, stating the obvious. "Fast."

"He'll still be powerful without it," Samara warned. "Just not the kind of powerful that would allow him to control people's minds *and* keep his hold over the invincibility magic in all those pins."

"It'll be a start, anyway," Liss said.

"If you do manage to get your hands on it," Samara said, "you'll want to destroy it right away. If what I read is true, those artifacts will start to mess with your mind."

Liss suppressed a shudder at the thought of those mass graves in the Insorsiled forest. When Rhett had told her about them, it had been almost impossible to wrap her mind around that much evil.

Liss had thought killing Jaikon would solve their problems. As it turned out, they'd just made way for an even more evil leader to take innocent lives.

"You'll just get yourself killed if you try," Lullianna told Liss in her no-nonsense voice. "Krozor probably put some fusing spell on it so it won't fall off again."

"Not likely," Samara replied, her attention back on the spell book. "Any modifications to the artifact, magical or otherwise, will weaken it."

"Maybe so." Lullianna put her hands on her hips. "But it's not like he's going to let Liss snatch it right off his face. Especially if it's as valuable as you say."

Lullianna muffled a dry cough.

"Are you alright?" Samara asked her sister.

"I'll get you some water," Quic offered, disappearing in a blink and reappearing just as fast. He sloshed most of the glass's contents on the floor in his eagerness.

Lullianna waved away everyone's concern as she tried to hide another bout of coughing.

"Lul—" Samara began.

"Just been sniffing too much pollen from the flowers," Lullianna announced to the room, which had gone quiet. At the worried look she got from Samara, Lullianna scowled. "If I was sick, I think I'd know."

"You're the witchdoctor," Samara muttered.

"And don't you forget it," Lullianna shot back.

"We'll take the monocle by force," Rhett said, speaking for the first time. "I'll get together a team."

"You aren't going anywhere," Lullianna informed him. She came over to the couch and hovered her hand over Rhett's heart. She closed her eyes for several seconds while her lips moved. "He's ready for the brew," she announced a few seconds later.

Liss tamped down the hope that surged up from deep within her.

Lullianna, Samara, and Keela had been maddeningly vague about what they were up to. A new door had appeared off the common room this morning, and since then, the three women had barely come out. Liss had needed to resist all of her thieving instincts to pick the lock and see what they were up to. Instead, she'd contented herself with sensing the optimism and anticipation on their souls.

"So this monocle," Spence said, moving his hands in an impatient gesture. "How do we steal it without getting ourselves killed?"

"We'll need a distraction," Liss replied. "A really, really good distraction."

"You're not thinking what I think you're thinking," Spence said, raising an eyebrow at her.

Liss's grin was all the answer he needed.

Mari clapped her hands together, while Jema squealed in delight.

Liss's smile broadened. "I think it's time for our thieving crew to work some of our own magic."

* * *

It was easier to track Krozor down than Liss had expected. He was standing on one of the castle's lower balconies, looking down at the Insorsiled who were amassed below. The entire kingdom seemed to have turned out to hear Krozor's speech.

It had been a tight squeeze fitting herself and all three of the kids on Lullianna's flying bike, but they'd made it all in one piece. Liss hid the bike behind a pile of garbage in a nearby alley. She made sure the kids' cloaks were drawn tight to hide their orange hair and opal skin. Then, the four of them melted into the crowd of Insorsiled.

"I think every person in the kingdom is out here right now," Mari grumbled, giving a warlock a dirty look when he stepped on the hem of her cloak.

"This is perfect," Spence replied, glancing around and smiling at what he saw.

He was right. If what they were hoping to pull off was going to work, they'd need lots of witnesses. Especially if Krozor was as prideful as most Insorsiled.

The trick Liss and the kids were about to attempt was one they'd used back in their thieving days. It offered a distraction that allowed them to make off with whatever valuable they were after. Plus, it was great for a laugh.

They'd never tried it on such a powerful target, though. If everything Liss had heard about Krozor was true, the warlock was anything but stupid. Liss could be walking the kids into a trap they'd be unable to escape from.

"What are the rules?" Liss asked the kids for the fifth time in the last hour.

Spence and Mari rolled their eyes. Jema parroted, "If anything goes wrong, we run straight back to the bike. We fly back to the tent without waiting for you. *No* exceptions." She put her hands on her hips and glared, doing her best Liss impression.

"Smart ass," Liss muttered before raising her voice enough for the kids to hear her. "We ready to do this?"

Liss, Spence, and Jema waited at the edge of the crowd while Mari scoped out the castle. Her Extension, which allowed her to walk through walls, enabled her to map out the guards' positions and get the lay of the castle's interior.

She reappeared less than an hour later, guiding them to a servant's entrance at the back of the palace.

They were all covered up to their knees in mud by the time they made it to the door, but at least it was better than the garbage chute Liss had crawled through the last time she infiltrated the Insorsil castle.

They were careful to stay out of the Insorsiled crowd's direct line of sight, but they probably could have waltzed right through the front doors without anyone taking a second glance at them.

Everyone's gazes were riveted on Krozor. Most of the onlookers didn't even seem to be blinking.

Samara hadn't been kidding when she said the artifact would get stronger over time. It seemed like Krozor had the entire kingdom under his thrall.

Krozor was droning on about the superiority of Insorsil and how the lesser, uncivilized races needed to be annihilated. Liss was sure the only reason why every Insorsiled in the crowd wasn't rolling their eyes was because of that monocle.

Mari slipped through the castle's wall, and then a few seconds later, the lock on the servant's door clicked.

Liss found herself inside a dim hallway with a guard posted on either end.

"Hey, you're not supposed to be here," one of the guards said.

Liss raised her hands. "We surrender."

She gave him her most alluring smile.

As soon as both of the guards came close enough, Spence touched one and then the other. The warlocks dropped like stones.

By the time they reached the balcony, Liss had lost track of how many snoring guards Spence had left in his wake. His opal skin had lost its lustrous sheen, and his soul was heavy with exhaustion.

"Good work." Liss squeezed Spence's arm. He and Mari slunk into a dark corner behind a set of velvet drapes.

"Ready, nugget?" Liss asked Jema.

In answer, the little sphere on the ground rolled forward and nudged Liss's foot.

Alright, then. It's show time.

Liss shook out her hair and pasted a smile on her face. Then, she parted the drapes that led out to the balcony.

"Oh my." She covered her mouth to hide her fake giggle. "I must have taken a wrong turn."

Irritation filtered into Krozor's soul. From what Liss could tell, he'd just reached the zinger of his speech. The warlock king was less than happy about being interrupted.

Liss only hoped the crowd's enthusiastic cheers were a side-effect of the monocle and not a result of their actual opinions. Their souls were muted from the effect of Krozor's magic, so Liss couldn't tell how any of them really felt about their king's bigoted speech.

"How did you get up here?" Krozor hissed.

Liss giggled and sauntered over. When she pulled out her knife, he sneered.

"Go ahead and try," he challenged. He yanked aside the collar of his dirty brown robe. He tapped the golden pin fastened to the threadbare brown shirt beneath.

"As you command, King Krozor." Liss curtsied. Then, she whipped her blade up, slicing through the ties that held the warlock's outer robe together. Before Krozor could react, Liss yanked the material away.

She pivoted out of the way so Krozor was standing directly in front of the crowd when Spence yanked his pants down.

The Insorsil king stood before all of his subjects, naked from the waist down.

Krozor might be a king and the most powerful Insorsiled ever to live. But when faced with the problem of flashing a crowd, he reacted the same way as everyone else.

He fell all over himself, trying to reclaim his pants. In his haste, the monocle slid away from his eye and dangled from its slender chain.

Laughter filtered up from the crowd below as Krozor cursed and fumbled with his pants.

Liss palmed the monocle and let it drop into the awaiting sphere on the ground before Krozor had covered himself. The king was so busy with his pants he didn't even notice.

Jema and the monocle rolled back off the balcony and disappeared into the castle.

Embarrassment and hatred filled Krozor's soul.

"Guards!" the king roared.

When no one appeared, Liss offered the king an innocent smile.

"I think your guards decided to take the rest of the day off," she announced.

Krozor's shocked outrage began to transform into something far more dangerous.

Liss saluted the king. Mari peeked around the curtain to bow. Spence gave him the finger.

"You bitch!" Krozor shrieked.

He lunged for Liss.

The warlock's eyes bugged. Liss stepped to the side as Krozor fell flat on his face.

The laughter from down below got louder as Krozor's legs flailed, displaying Jema's handiwork. The warlock's bootlaces were knotted together.

As much as Liss would like to continue antagonizing this monster, it was time to leave.

Liss ushered the kids back into the castle just as Krozor's first spell crashed through the stone wall beside them.

It took mere minutes for Liss and the kids to exit the castle and lose themselves in the crowd. Jema popped back up beside Liss and handed her the monocle.

Liss let the small glass disc fall from her hand and onto the ground. Then, she crunched it beneath her boot.

All at once, Liss was assaulted by the emotions from the thousands of souls that had been dulled by Krozor's spell. It was like a heavy fog had lifted off the crowd of Insorsiled. All of them seemed to take a deep breath at once. They looked around, as though trying to remember how they'd gotten there. Then, understanding took hold. The Insorsiled knew their minds had been tampered with.

And they weren't happy about it.

"He's been manipulating us!" a witch nearby shrieked.

"Guess Krozor was exposed in more than one way," Spence said, grinning.

Liss laughed at that.

"Imposter king!" a warlock shouted.

"Tyrant!" another called.

"Let's kill him!" cried a third, raising his staff into the air.

A mass of angry Insorsiled were surging toward the palace. Liss grabbed Spence and Mari's collars and hauled them away as spells began to fly through the air.

Liss glanced back once, just in time to see Krozor reach up to his face. She saw the exact moment when he realized his monocle was gone.

The king tipped his head back and bellowed. Magic sparked from his fingertips, and Liss could swear she saw actual steam coming out of his hairy nostrils.

The crowd was getting close enough to the castle that some of their spells were nearing the balcony. One spell hit the railing. There was an explosion of red sparks, and then blocks of stone were flying into the air.

Krozor raised his hands. White smoke billowed around him. And then, without warning, the smoke disappeared.

The Insorsil king had vanished.

CHAPTER 45

Rhett forced himself to stay still, even though every shredded muscle in his body demanded that he go tearing after Liss. She had gone to Insorsil to steal from the king, and Rhett was sitting here on the couch, sipping a watery brew and being completely useless.

Lullianna was sitting beside him and chanting in a soft voice as she pressed her hand to his chest. They'd been at this for hours, and if anything, Rhett only felt weaker.

It was obvious this incantation was taking its toll on Lullianna, too. Her skin was sallow and dotted with perspiration. Earlier, when he'd suggested she take a break, she'd just about bitten his head off.

Rhett felt his eyes beginning to close of their own accord as Lullianna's voice drew him into a state of semi-consciousness. From what he'd been told—which was next to nothing—Lullianna had to prepare his body so it wouldn't reject the cure she was going to attempt. Samara had written the spell, which was a combination of various magical components.

It all sounded very complex.

Rhett had his doubts that whatever they tried would work, but he kept those thoughts to himself.

"Alright, that's enough for the moment," Lullianna said, a little out of breath. "Your essence is already strained enough. If I do any more, you won't make it through the spell."

Lullianna tipped her head back against the cushions and closed her eyes.

A flash of color drew Rhett's attention. He thought he'd imagined it, but then it came again. Lullianna's skin flickered from bronze to opal, and then back again. Rhett jerked away from her.

"What is that?" he asked, just as a round of dry coughing had her doubling over.

Rhett got up, ignoring the way the small motion made his brittle bones threaten to crack under his weight. He grabbed the glass of water that appeared on the table and brought it back to her.

Lullianna's hand shook a little as she held the glass.

"You're sick," Rhett said, immediately wanting to take back the obvious statement.

"Just worn out," Lullianna replied, setting the empty glass down. "I'll be fine once all this is over. Now sit back down before you fall down."

Wilsean liked to tease Samara about how she was a terrible liar. It was clear that Lullianna shared that quality. She couldn't even look at Rhett when she spoke the false words, and she fidgeted with her hands as her cheeks reddened. Rhett narrowed his gaze at her.

Was this more than just too much work and too little sleep? Had he somehow infected her?

Horror crept through him at the thought.

"Do you have opal contagion?" he asked.

Lullianna scoffed. "Insorsiled aren't susceptible to the contagion. Duh."

"Then, what—"

"Rhett, I like you." Lullianna crossed her arms. "But if you try to mother me, I'm going to use one of Ambrosius's transfiguration potions to turn you into a chicken. And then I'll chop off your head."

"Okay, then." Rhett put up his hands in surrender.

"I just need a healing brew, and I haven't had time to make one."

Lullianna got up and walked over to her cauldron on unsteady feet. Rhett was watching her and saw the moment her eyes rolled back in her head.

He managed to cross the room before she collapsed. He caught her, his whole body bowing under the added strain, even though she was as light as a feather.

He set his jaw and made it back to the couch, where he gently lowered her onto the cushions.

"Rhett?" she blinked up at him.

"What do you need?" he asked, his alarm growing by the second. Something was very wrong with Lullianna.

"Promise me something."

He nodded. After everything she was doing for him, he was in no position to deny her anything.

"Don't tell my sister."

Rhett and Lullianna both jumped when the new door off the common room opened. Keela, her hands cupped around something, stepped through the doorway.

Ever since Rhett had heard Keela's story about how she got her scar, he'd had trouble meeting her eyes. Keela didn't have the same problem. In fact, she seemed incapable of holding a grudge against anyone.

The Green Thumb offered Rhett a smile and tossed him the small object in her palm. Rhett opened his hand reflexively and caught it. He looked down at the round, opal-hued seed he was now holding. It was warm to the touch and caught the light coming through the window until it seemed to glow from within.

Rhett stared at Keela.

"You did it?" he finally managed. "You figured out how to make enough of the immunity flowers?"

"Better than that," Samara said, following Keela into the common room. "We enhanced the spell, so eating one flower will be enough for lifelong immunity."

"Only one flower for a lifetime of immunity?" Rhett asked, his mind trying to wrap itself around what that would mean for the empire.

Samara smiled. "That's right."

All words failed Rhett as he tried to process the enormity of what these women were casually telling him.

Keela inclined her head at the closed door. "If you're up for it, I can show you."

Rhett was on his feet in an instant. Samara took his place on the couch beside her sister.

Keela unlocked the new door that had appeared in the tent, which no one except for the three women had been allowed to go through.

He stepped inside the room and froze.

He was standing inside a greenhouse. Except for a few narrow footpaths, the entirety of the large space was crammed full of live immunity flowers.

Rhett had to squint against the blinding brightness of all the rainbow light. A breeze coming from a fan on the ceiling caught the delicate petals, making the light flicker and shimmer with even more force. There had to be tens of thousands of flowers growing in this one space.

The petals blended together until they looked more like an opal-hued river than individual flowers.

"The flowers prefer more space to stretch their roots," Keela said as Rhett stared in stunned silence. "But we decided to grow them here for now, where no one will be able to sabotage them. There should be enough for everyone in the empire, and now that we have the seeds, you'll be able to grow more for newborns and anyone else who needs them."

Rhett tore his attention away from the flowers to focus on Keela.

"This is…incredible."

Incredible didn't even begin to cover it. What they'd accomplished…it changed everything.

"We'll be able to eradicate opal contagion from the continent," Keela continued. "After that, perhaps we can figure out how to get the immunity across the sea so no one else ever needs to worry about the virus."

"How?" Rhett managed.

Keela gave him a knowing smile. "It was a group effort. Samara wrote the spell to fuse the magical and organic parts of the flowers, Lullianna made the magic, and I made them grow."

"I don't know how we'll ever repay you for this," Rhett managed. "Anything I can give—"

"This isn't a bargain, Rhett," Keela told him. "It's a gift."

"Why?" Rhett looked at her in stunned disbelief. These flowers were what his empire needed above all else. It was the single most valuable commodity in all the realms.

"Life is not something to be bargained for," Keela replied.

Rhett sunk to his knees before Keela.

"For as long as I live, I will be in your debt," he told her.

Realizing those words weren't meaningful given his rapidly-declining health, he modified his vow. "I'll make sure every Lagonian knows what you've done for us. My soldiers will be at your command and will give their lives to protect you and yours."

"Thank you, dear," Keela replied. "Now, I suggest you get your people to start distributing these so no one else suffers needlessly."

"I have to tell my soldiers," Rhett managed.

"I already sent Quic to bring all of them here," Keela replied. "They can each have a flower, and then we can all work on distributing them to the rest of your people."

"Thank you," Rhett said. "Truly. Thank you."

Keela patted his arm as she moved past him. "You're very welcome."

✳ ✳ ✳

Some time later, Rhett's entire army gathered in the common area of the Insorsiled tent. The room had expanded to hold all of them, and the entire wall that separated the greenhouse from the rest of the tent had slid away.

Rhett's soldiers gaped at the flowers while Rhett repeated what Keela had told him.

His soldiers were careful as they entered the greenhouse one at a time and knelt down to pluck a single flower for themselves. Rhett's soldiers, usually as reserved and stoic as he, couldn't contain their emotions. There was a great deal of throat clearing and sniffing.

Tears ran unabashedly down some of the soldiers' faces. Rhett couldn't blame them.

"Let's get these distributed to our people," he said once all of his soldiers had eaten one. "Make sure they know they were a gift from the Extended and the Insorsiled."

To Dannica, he said, "Open up our borders. From now on, the Extended are under our protection."

With a crisp nod, Dannica turned and went to carry out his orders.

His soldiers were efficient as they harvested the delicate flowers. Keela stood over them, ensuring the flowers were handled with the utmost care.

After the greenhouse had been cleared out, all that remained was a single immunity flower.

Keela had told him that, if the spell Samara and Lullianna were going to attempt to use to cure him worked, then he'd need to take a flower to make sure he didn't contract the virus again.

The flower seemed so small and insignificant now that it was the only one.

Sunlight streamed in through the clear ceiling panels. The air was warm, almost uncomfortably so. Still, Rhett couldn't stop shivering.

He heard footsteps and felt a presence beside him. He knew without looking it was Ciago. Rhett opened his hand, offering his friend the seed. No words were needed between them as Ciago's palm cradled the tiny, precious seed.

Ciago gripped Rhett's shoulder as they stood side-by-side and stared at the single immunity flower. Neither of them spoke, but Rhett knew they were both sharing the same thought.

Salvation had come for their people. But for Rhett, it was too late.

CHAPTER 46

Liss sat still as stone, hardly daring to breathe.

Even though the common room was crowded with people, it was silent except for Lullianna's chanting. Lullianna sat next to Rhett, who was stretched out on the couch. Samara stood behind her sister.

Wilsean, Ciago, Keela, and Liss sat at the table. The kids sat cross-legged on the thick rug. They were as still as everyone else in the room.

An immunity flower rested on the table, its roots still clinging to bits of dirt. If the spell worked, then Rhett would eat the flower and become immune to the contagion for the rest of his life.

If the spell worked.

It seemed like everyone was holding their breath as their eyes stayed glued to Lullianna, who was hovering her hands over Rhett's chest and filling him with magic. They'd had to start the spell over twice because Rhett had thrown up blood partway through.

Liss chewed the inside of her cheek raw.

Samara was quietly murmuring to Lullianna in the pauses in her chanting. Samara was reading off a paper covered in Insorsiled symbols that looked like gibberish to Liss.

Samara had promised to explain everything afterward…if the spell worked. All Liss knew was that Samara had created some kind of new spell that Lullianna was now implementing. It had something to do with essences. For some reason Samara hadn't explained, Liss and Ciago were involved in the spell. The vile aftertaste of the potion the two of them had drunk earlier lingered on their tongues.

Liss felt a little dizzy, but other than that, she hadn't sensed whatever else the potion had done to her.

Samara had assured Liss and Ciago the potion wouldn't hurt them, even though neither of them had asked any questions before downing the liquid. If this spell saved Rhett, Liss didn't care what it took away from her.

While everyone else was watching Lullianna, all of Liss's attention was on Rhett. She saw the exact moment when his eyes went from orange back to brown. She dug her fingers into her thigh to keep from reacting.

If she let her hope run away with her and this didn't work—

Rhett sucked in a breath. Liss was on her feet.

Samara held up a hand to stop her.

"Take off your shirt," Samara told Rhett.

He hesitated, his gaze flitting to Liss.

"Lullianna needs to get to your heart, and this spell will make fabric catch fire," Samara said in an urgent voice. "Take it off. Now."

Rhett lifted his shirt over his head.

Liss couldn't stop the strangled sound that came out of her. Ciago jerked, making the whole table vibrate.

Rhett's stomach was sunken, and his ribs seemed ready to burst out of him. But that wasn't even the worst part. His skin was covered with pustules.

Some of the blisters were black and scabbed over. Others were oozing blood and infected pus.

Bile rose to the back of Liss's throat.

Rhett was looking at her, but she couldn't stop the silent tears pouring down her cheeks. She'd known the way the contagion's stages progressed. She'd seen the virus steal Rhett's strength day by day. But none of that had prepared her for what she was now witnessing.

Liss felt a thickly-muscled arm come over her shoulder. She didn't turn to look at Ciago, but she could feel his soul was as full of horror as hers. Wilsean, who was sitting on her other side, covered her hand with his. The three of them sat frozen in disbelief as they stared at the gruesome sight.

As Liss blinked past her tears, she noticed something was happening to Rhett's skin. The pustules stopped leaking. The hideous, scabbed blisters smoothed out and sunk back into Rhett's skin. All that was left were dark scars all over his arms, chest, and stomach.

Lullianna hovered her palms over Rhett's torso. Her chanting grew louder, and as it did, a white light started to pulse from her fingertips. The light bathed Rhett's skin in a translucent glow.

Lullianna sucked in a harsh breath and swiped at the perspiration on her face. The glow receded from Rhett, revealing skin that was no longer a sickly yellow color. He was pale, except for his scars. There wasn't a hint of opal sheen.

Rhett looked from Liss to Lullianna. His breaths were coming short and quick.

Lullianna had her eyes squeezed shut. Her blonde hair was dark with sweat, and she was trembling.

Samara had her arms around her sister and was whispering in her ear. Lullianna's voice was hoarse, but she didn't stop chanting the spell.

Rhett took a deep, shuddering breath.

"Take the flower, Rhett," Samara ordered. "Now."

Liss's fingers closed around the delicate stem. She handed it to Rhett.

Their eyes met as he put the flower in his mouth.

Lullianna's voice faded until it was nothing more than a whisper. Then, there was silence.

For several moments, no one spoke. No one even moved.

"Well?" Lullianna asked in a thin voice, giving Rhett a questioning look.

Rhett's eyes met Liss's when he answered. "I feel…better."

Liss let out a choked sob. She had no memory of moving. All she knew was that she was no longer sitting at the table. She was on Rhett's lap, and his arms were around her.

Incoherent sounds came out of her. She felt the rumble of Rhett's voice as he spoke, but she was crying too hard to hear a word. After what felt like seconds but was probably minutes, she forced herself to move so Wilsean and Ciago could hug Rhett.

"Thank you!" Liss threw herself at Lullianna and Samara next. She wrapped an arm around each and squeezed the life out of them. "Thank you, thank you, thank you!"

By the time they were finished, the only dry eyes in the room where Rhett's. He seemed more bewildered than anything. Liss was pretty sure he'd never been hugged by so many people in his life. His soul was also heavy with exhaustion.

"Your bones and organs are back in working order," Lullianna said in a tired voice. "But you'll have to get your muscles and weight back naturally."

"We can help with that," Wilsean said, slapping Rhett on the back. "It's about time you ended your little vacation and went back to training."

There was some shaky laughter as they all tried to get their minds around the fact that Rhett was healed. Liss could hardly believe it. She kept her eyes glued to him, half-convinced that if she looked away, the contagion would sneak back inside him.

It was all too impossible. Too impossibly wonderful.

Rhett was alive. He was healed. He had a future.

Samara went over to the cauldron in the corner of the room, dipped a mug inside, and brought it back to Lullianna.

After a few sips, some of the color returned to Lullianna's cheeks.

"How did you do it?" Liss asked, wiping at the tears that hadn't stopped falling.

Samara and Lullianna exchanged a knowing glance.

"Tell them, Sis," Lullianna said, curling up on the couch.

Wilsean brought a blanket in from the other room and covered Lullianna with it.

"Well." Samara grinned. "It all started with Ciago."

"When is that *not* the case?" Ciago asked, earning another round of giddy laughter from all of them.

Samara continued, "Ciago mentioned Wilsean and I being two halves of the same whole." She paused to give Wilsean a look so full of love that it squeezed more tears out of Liss.

Samara turned her attention back to the group. "Lullianna and I had been trying to write a spell that would replicate our own immunity, but pure essence can't be transferred from one race to another.

"That's when it occurred to me that maybe we could combine two essences that contained Lagonian *and* immunity properties."

"Ciago and me," Liss said with a surprised laugh.

Samara nodded. "It's also how I came up with the idea to strengthen the immunity flowers. It was Gatria's original spell, which we modified to contain partial giant and Extended essence. And then Lullianna added earth magic so that Keela would be able to use her Extension to make more of them."

Liss shook her head, hardly able to comprehend everything Samara was saying.

"So, are you saying that some of me is now inside Rhett?" Ciago asked.

"Sort of," Samara replied. "It was a replication of your essence, rather than your actual essence."

"You lucky, lucky man," Ciago told Rhett, shaking his head. Ciago gave Liss a shameless grin. "Don't be surprised if Rhett suddenly gets really good at certain stuff, if you know what I mean." He waggled his eyebrows at her.

Rhett rolled his eyes skyward. Liss laughed.

"How are you feeling?" Lullianna asked Rhett, hovering her palm over his chest again.

"Hungry."

More laughter filled the tent.

"Let's get this party started," Ciago announced.

As if the tent had just been waiting for the signal, music filled the common room. Plates of food sprung up on the table. The tent, which had been silent for hours, was full of smells and sounds. Everyone was talking at once. There was a great deal of shuffling as they settled themselves at the table and sprawled out on the comfy chairs.

Liss felt weightless, like if the tent's ceiling wasn't there, she'd float away. After losing her mom, and coming so close to losing Rhett, the impossible had happened. His opal contagion was cured. He was alive.

She looked up, only to find Rhett was already staring at her. He smiled. Her heart felt so enormous she wondered how she didn't collapse from the weight of it.

He opened his arms to her. She went without a moment's hesitation.

She reached up on her toes and pulled his mouth down to hers.

"Are the scars going to bother you?" Rhett asked when they separated.

Liss laughed at that. "Never." She tilted her face up to meet his gaze.

"Besides," she said. "Whatever extra abilities you've inherited from Ciago's essence should more than make up for a few little blemishes."

Rhett scowled. Ciago pressed a hand to his heart and called, "Marry me, Lovely Liss!" which only made Rhett's frown deepen. Liss laughed, feeling a little drunk.

"Let's get some food in you," Liss said when Rhett bent down for another kiss. Her cheeks hurt from so much smiling, but she couldn't stop.

Rhett, Wilsean, Ciago, and the kids started digging into the meal that had appeared. Liss held back a laugh when Jema clambered onto a very surprised-looking Rhett's lap. After a moment of paralysis, Rhett wound one arm around Jema to keep her from falling off as she began to reach for bowls.

Too excited to eat, Liss dragged her chair over to Samara.

"I'm so sorry I haven't been…mentally present the last few days," Liss told her best friend as they embraced.

Samara had been heartbroken over what happened with Wilsean's parents, but with everything else that was going on, Liss hadn't really been there for her.

"And holy hell." She gave Samara an incredulous look. "You're engaged!"

Samara beamed. "I am, aren't I?"

Liss was going to say more, but she caught sight of Lullianna slipping into her cloak.

"Where are you going?" Liss asked.

"Even heroines need to sleep," Lullianna announced.

"Are you sure you don't want to sleep here?" Samara asked, worry filtering into her soul. "We can make you another healing brew and take you home in the morning."

"Nah. Mom and Dad are probably having a fit about how long I've been gone. Time to go and face the music." There was a twinkle in her eyes, like she was looking forward to the confrontation. "I need a night of normal after saving an entire empire from utter annihilation."

"My humble sister, ladies and gentlemen," Samara said with a grin.

"Facts are facts," Lullianna replied with an immodest shrug.

"Let me take you back," Wilsean said, getting to his feet.

"You stay with your bride-to-be." Lullianna gave Wilsean a quick hug. "I've got my bike outside, and it's more comfortable than your dragon."

There was another round of thank-you's and goodbyes before Lullianna made it to the door. Liss followed her out into night. The moon was full, and everything was bathed in a blue glow.

"Thank you, Lullianna. I'll never be able to repay you for what you did, but if there's ever anything I can do for you—"

"Actually, I think there is." Lullianna's tired expression turned mischievous.

"Oh?"

"Put in a good word for me with Quic." She leaned closer to Liss and confided, "He's pretty cute."

Liss laughed as she threw her arms around Lullianna for the second time.

"He's into you, too," she informed Lullianna.

"Really?"

Liss nodded. "I saw it on his soul."

* * *

Liss had never taken so much pleasure in watching someone sleep. As she watched Rhett's chest rise and fall under the blanket, she was overwhelmed with so much gratitude it was almost unbearable. His soul was at peace. The tent was quiet, filled with the people Liss loved most.

So much that had been wrong in her world was right now.

There were unpleasant things she would need to deal with soon. Like how, with everything else that had happened, she hadn't had a real chance to come to terms with what her mom had done for Rhett. It was almost impossible to comprehend that her mom was gone.

There were other problems that would have to be dealt with, too.

The tentative peace between the Extended and Lagonians would only last until Krozor was defeated. The Insorsiled might be free from Krozor's mental manipulations, but that didn't mean they were free from him. He was still invincible, and he was still planning to kill all the un-Insorsiled.

But those were tomorrow problems. All of today's problems were solved. She had never felt more at ease.

Liss settled back onto her pillow, curling herself around Rhett. Her eyes were just starting to close when the bedroom door flew open.

Samara, her corresponder clutched in her hand, ran into the room. Wilsean was on her heels. He was sliding knives into the straps on his chest and stuffing arrows into his quiver.

"What is it?" Liss demanded, hardly able to think over the frantic clamber of their souls.

"My brother just called," Samara said in a breathless voice. "Krozor arrested Lullianna for helping un-Insorsiled." A ragged sob tore free from her. "She's being executed at dawn."

CHAPTER 47

Rhett stared down at the enormous hole in the ground. It was deep, but the moonlight illuminated the space almost as well as if it was day. Colorful swirls of magic wafted through the hole without dissipating.

Krozor had maintained his control over the throne since he was still the most powerful person in Insorsil, but after his monocle was destroyed, all of his subjects were freed from their king's manipulation. That meant Rhett's spies began to hear talk of this hole, which Krozor referred to as the *pit*.

Krozor had requested the presence of every person in Insorsil at the pit the next morning. He'd taken down the ward that had kept the place out of view, since whatever he'd been doing here was apparently finished. He would be explaining everything to his subjects in the morning.

But that wasn't the reason why Rhett and Wilsean were here now.

Rhett's people had reported that gallows had been constructed just over the pit the day before. Samara's parents had confirmed through bribes that this was where Lullianna would be hanged in the morning.

There was no question their sources were right. A makeshift wooden platform had been erected beside the pit. A single noose hung from the beam.

Rhett studied the gallows. There was a lever connected to a pulley system. When the lever was pulled, the noose would be yanked upward, wrapping the rope around the upper beam.

The thought of Lullianna hanging had Rhett clutching his dagger and fighting the urge to storm the Insorsil castle. Instead, he forced himself to breathe and focus on their plan.

As soon as they had found out about Lullianna's execution, Rhett, Wilsean, and Samara had come straight to Insorsil on Jaikon's winged dragon. Liss and Rhett's rebel soldiers had gone to the Extended hideout to rally the Extended. With any luck, Liss would convince the Extended to use their wagons to transport the rebels to Insorsil faster than they could arrive on foot.

If they'd have any chance of rescuing Lullianna and getting out of here alive, they'd need all the backup they could get.

Ciago had delivered a message to Winny, who was still searching for her fleet of missing giants. Rhett had no idea whether Winny would get the message in time, and if she would even heed their call.

The giant leader had been beside herself since she found out her giants never made it across the sea.

Wilsean had given Liss his corresponder so she and Samara could stay in contact, but being separated from Liss still made Rhett uneasy. There was too much at stake, and too much that could go wrong.

Samara had convened with her siblings, who were plotting and gathering their magic. They were in charge of creating a distraction so no one would notice when Rhett and Wilsean freed Lullianna from the gallows.

Rhett would have preferred to get Lullianna out of the Insorsil dungeon while most of the kingdom was still asleep, but Krozor had clearly expected that. Samara's family had learned that Lullianna wasn't being kept in the dungeon with the other prisoners. They didn't know where Krozor was keeping her, and the kingdom was too big to search all of it without being discovered. So, Rhett and Wilsean had come here to hunker down and wait for dawn.

Given the late hour and the curfew Krozor had instituted for his subjects, no one else was around.

Are you sure about this?" Rhett asked Wilsean as he stared down at the swirling magic in the pit below. A burning smell lingered on the air.

"Not in the least," his friend replied grimly.

No one had been able to figure out what the magic in the pit was for. All they knew was that the spells were unformed. According to Samara, that meant the magic shouldn't be able to hurt them.

Rhett generally liked to have more assurances before he dove headlong into danger. Given the situation, though, they didn't have much choice. There was nowhere else for Rhett and Wilsean to hide that would give them a clear view of the gallows.

Rhett and Wilsean attached their grappling hooks to the edge of the wooden platform. Rhett gave his rope a tug, making sure the hastily-built structure would hold his weight. Then, he repelled down into the pit.

Rhett's skin pricked with heat as the magic washed over him. He hit the bottom a few seconds later. A cloudy haze of magic hovered just overhead. The smoke screen wasn't thick enough to block their view of the gallows, but it was dense enough that it would hopefully keep anyone standing above the pit from seeing them. With their dark clothes that made them blend into the dirt wall, no one would notice them unless they were really looking. That was the hope, anyway.

When Wilsean spoke, it was startling in the silence, even though his voice was barely above a whisper.

"I owe you an apology," Wilsean said.

"For what?" Rhett asked. He couldn't imagine a single reason his friend would have for apologizing.

The cloud of magic filtered out the moonlight, and Rhett could barely make out his friend's profile.

Wilsean blew out a breath. "Things didn't go well with my parents when I told them I was proposing to Samara. They…disinherited me."

"I figured as much, since you're not wearing your ring anymore."

Wilsean let out a soft chuckle. "You didn't say anything, so I wasn't sure if you'd noticed."

Rhett hadn't seen any point in bringing it up. As Wilsean's friend, he hadn't wanted to pry. As his commander, it hadn't mattered. Rhett had assumed he'd be dead before he could ever take the throne or appoint advisors.

That wasn't the case anymore. With a jolt, Rhett realized he had a future again.

Ever since he'd gotten the contagion, Rhett's every action had revolved around trying to lessen the impact of his passing on the people he cared about most. Now, he needed to recalibrate.

The thought of taking the throne and trying to rule Lagonia without one of his two best friends was almost incomprehensible.

"Maybe we can convince the high families to change the law," Rhett said.

"Not likely, man," Wilsean scoffed. "And by that, I mean no way in hell."

Wilsean was right. None of the high families would agree to amend a law that had been instituted to maintain their power. If Rhett tried to change the law without the council's permission, the empire's most influential subjects would be liable to instigate a civil war.

Maybe someday Rhett would have the kind of power needed to sway the most prominent families in the empire, but by then, years would have passed.

Rhett made sure none of his growing anxiety showed on his face. He respected Wilsean's decision and was happy for his friend, and yet—

Rhett wasn't a politician. He'd never had any tolerance for the deceitful and greedy old councilmen. How the hell was he supposed to become emperor without Wilsean by his side? How was he supposed to navigate all of the subterfuge without one of the few people he trusted?

"I would have been honored to serve as your advisor," Wilsean said, breaking into the tumult of Rhett's mind.

The honor would have been mine, Rhett thought, but couldn't bring himself to say out loud. Wilsean likely already knew what he was thinking. It had always been that way between Rhett, Wilsean, and Ciago.

"I wish it didn't have to be this way," Rhett said. "But I'm glad for you, and I understand."

"You were right," Wilsean said. "All the stuff I thought mattered so much stopped being important when I weighed it against her."

"You don't need to apologize for that," Rhett told his friend.

Wilsean laughed a little. "We all know you could have used my expertise, and it's going to kill me not to witness firsthand you putting those entitled old schemers in their places."

Rhett's tension eased a little.

"I'm sure Ciago will keep you appraised of my every blunder."

"That's something to look forward to." Wilsean reached out in the dark and clasped Rhett's arm.

They passed several moments in companionable silence.

Wilsean chuckled softly. "So, do you think Samara and Liss are going to plan a double wedding, or something?"

Rhett's heart stuttered.

"I—don't know what the future looks like for Liss and me."

The words sounded stiff…formal. Wrong.

"You're joking, right?" Wilsean asked incredulously. "Please don't tell me you're not sure if she's that serious about you."

"It's not that." Rhett forced out a calming breath. "I assume she's going to become the Extended leader. I couldn't ask her to give that up to live in Lagonia." And if Rhett gave up the throne to be with her, the empire would dissolve into a bloody battle between every Lagonian who had ever desired the seat of power.

Countless innocent lives would be lost in the struggle, and the empire as a whole would suffer.

"That's tough, man," Wilsean said in sympathy.

Rhett didn't reply. He was trying not to think about it. He couldn't imagine only seeing Liss when they could escape their respective duties. A coldness filled him.

Focus, Rhetteman, he could almost hear Stone ordering him. *A distracted soldier is a dead soldier. Find the threat. Eliminate it.*

Before he succumbed to regret—a useless emotion—he turned his mind to a far more pressing issue.

Rhett looked up at the wisps of magic swirling overhead. What could Krozor possibly be doing here?

Rhett's spine tingled in warning every time he glanced at the magic.

As the first rays of sunlight filtered through the cloud of magic, he still didn't have any answers.

* * *

The Insorsiled began showing up just before dawn. Rhett and Wilsean stood against the wall and went still as statues so they wouldn't draw attention. The higher the sun rose, the more sheer the cloud of magic became.

From his vantage point at the bottom of the pit, Rhett could see that the witches and warlocks moved stiffly. Their eyes swiveled around in fear. It was obvious they hadn't come here out of a desire to watch one of their own hang. They were here because they were afraid of the consequences if they weren't.

A black kind of anger took hold of Rhett. He was so damn sick of corrupt, power-hungry leaders using fear to manipulate their people.

His blood turned to liquid fire when he caught sight of the Insorsil guards leading Lullianna through the crowd. His pulse thundered in his ears.

Rhett had to hold Wilsean back from bursting out of the pit here and now. Rhett didn't want to wait, either, but there were too many of the Insorsiled and too few of them. Besides, Rhett wasn't exactly in fighting shape. They needed to wait for Samara's distraction to give them some cover.

Krozor climbed onto the platform. The sun rising behind the king brought the gallows into sharp focus. The Insorsil king faced the crowd, which ringed the pit where Rhett and Wilsean were hidden.

"I know you all have questions," Krozor began. He had enspelled his voice so it carried and was impossible to tune out. "You all know that I intend to save magic from those who wish to dilute and steal it from us."

He paused to let the Insorsiled stare at the magic swirling around in the pit. Rhett and Wilsean pressed themselves farther against the wall to avoid being seen.

"The storm is coming, and it will destroy all of the un-Insorsiled," Krozor continued. "I have asked you here to witness the beginning of our triumph. But first, we must conclude a small bit of unpleasantness."

Rhett tensed as guards escorted Lullianna onto the platform. One of the warlocks knelt down and did something to the wooden boards at their feet, but Rhett was too far down in the pit to see what it was.

"Come on, Samara," Wilsean muttered.

Rhett put a hand on Wilsean's arm to steady him. He had no idea what kind of distraction they were waiting for, but given the little he knew about Samara's siblings, he expected it wouldn't be quiet.

The warlock king continued to speak. He condemned Lullianna as a disgrace to the Insorsiled. He called her a traitor for associating with Extended and Lagonians. Krozor emphasized the need to eliminate the *lesser* races so the Insorsiled would be able to focus on their magic without fear of it being stolen.

Wilsean was grinding his teeth with enough force that they squeaked. Rhett punched him in the arm to silence him.

Through the swirling wisps of magic floating above their heads, Rhett saw the guards lower a noose over Lullianna's neck. He estimated he had five more seconds before Wilsean forgot all sense of caution and started the rescue, with or without backup. Not that Rhett could blame him. Lullianna was a friend, and she'd also saved his life. There was nothing Rhett wouldn't do to rescue her.

"It pains me to execute a powerful witch," Krozor called out to his audience. "Only the unmagical deserve death. It is my hope that this execution will serve as a warning to any other traitors, and we will not need to endure any more of this unpleasantness."

"Enough of this," Wilsean growled. "I'm going."

Rhett didn't argue. He grabbed his rope and began to propel himself up the side of the pit as fast as he could.

They swung themselves out of the pit just as Krozor's words were drowned out by a louder, clearer voice.

"I am the most powerful Insorsiled in the kingdom," a familiar voice called. "And I challenge Krozor Ragnor Mantis for the Insorsil crown in a duel to the death."

Rhett looked at Wilsean, whose mouth was hanging open.

Samara, her white-blonde hair whipping back in the freezing wind, hovered in mid-air over the pit.

"What the hell is she doing?" Wilsean hissed.

Rhett didn't have a clue. He didn't know how an Empty was giving every appearance of being a witch, and a powerful one at that. More importantly, he had no idea what Samara would do if Krozor agreed to the duel.

"Accept my challenge and fight me," Samara said. She tilted her head up to display a fierce, terrible, un-Samara-like smile.

Her amber eyes flashed as the rising sun spilled across the sky.

"You are a fraud, Krozor Ragnor Mantis," Samara called. "You are not the most powerful among our people. I am."

Samara raised her hands to the sky. And then magic erupted from her palms.

CHAPTER 48

A ball of fire flew through the air and exploded in the exact spot where Krozor had been standing moments before. A puff of silver smoke extinguished the fire, and then Krozor was running. He dodged more fiery sparks that flew from Samara's hands that just missed his trailing cloak.

Rhett didn't stop to ask how Samara was managing to wield magic.

He and Wilsean raced to the platform as the crowd dissolved into chaos.

Krozor was gone, but there were still five guards who had held their positions. There was one on either side of Lullianna, one in front, another behind, and the executioner.

Rhett took out the front and right guards, easily dodging their spells. Wilsean got the back and left.

In seconds, it was just them, Lullianna, and the executioner whose face was covered by a black hood.

"Don't!" Lullianna shouted as Wilsean raised his knife and started toward the executioner.

Lullianna's wild eyes went down to the wooden boards at their feet, where Rhett noticed a chalk circle was drawn around her and the executioner.

"The circle's enspelled," she hurried on. Her voice was barely audible over the yelling all around them, but Rhett's attention was fixed on the threat before him.

"If you or anything of yours crosses the circle, you'll die," Lullianna explained. "You need to get out of here."

Rhett coldly assessed the situation.

Lullianna's wrists were tied with an Insorsiled rope that had been knotted tight enough to draw blood. There was no way she could do magic with her hands tied up like that.

The executioner chuckled. The sound raised the hairs at the back of Rhett's neck.

The executioner kept one hand on the lever that would raise the crossbeam and simultaneously tighten the noose. With his free hand, he reached up and pulled off his hood.

Elouicia smiled, displaying his jagged fangs.

A low growling sound was coming from somewhere. Rhett realized it was coming from his own throat.

Rhett didn't even realize he was moving forward until Lullianna screamed.

"Stop," she begged. "Don't come any closer. The spell—"

Rhett looked down and saw he was inches away from the chalk line. He turned to Wilsean.

"Don't even think about it," Wilsean said. "I'm doing this."

"You aren't." Rhett gripped Wilsean's arm and positioned himself between his friend and the chalk circle.

"Like hell—"

"I didn't save your life so you could throw it away!" Lullianna yelled, on the verge of hysterics.

Elouicia's grin widened. Rhett's vision went red with fury.

He forced his attention back on Wilsean, who was getting ready to barrel past Rhett.

"As your commander," Rhett began.

"Don't do this," Wilsean said.

"I order you to stay here." Rhett lowered his voice. "As your friend, I'm telling you to go home to Samara."

"Listen to me," Lullianna said, her words tripping over themselves. "Even if you step over the circle, it won't change anything. I'm still going to die."

Rhett looked in her eyes and saw only truth.

"You know I'm sick," she hurried on. "I infected myself with Extended essence when I was experimenting with different spells for the cure. I'm rotting on the inside, and there's no way to undo the damage."

Rhett couldn't breathe. Nausea, even worse than it had been when he'd been sick with opal contagion, turned his stomach inside out.

"You're…Infected?"

"This isn't your fault," she told him in a stern voice that reminded him of Samara. "I knew the risks, but I was impatient." A small smile flitted across her face. "The truth is, I was in a rush to leave my mark on the world." She shrugged, making the noose around her neck flop. "Now, I won't have to worry about people forgetting my name when I'm gone."

"Lullianna," Wilsean said in a broken voice.

"I can't let you do this," Rhett said, his voice splintering.

Elouicia's grin widened.

"You have to," Lullianna told them. She was the image of perfect calm, while Rhett was burning up from the inside.

"No," Rhett decided. "Even if you die, you're going to do it with your family by your side."

Not by a noose with Elouicia as company.

Rhett breathed out, readying himself. He'd have to move fast, and there was still the fact that Elouicia was invincible.

"Aren't you going to bow to your emperor?" Elouicia asked, running his tongue along the sharpened points of his teeth.

Rhett shoved Wilsean back so he wouldn't get any ideas. "Tell Liss—"

Moving so fast he barely saw it, Lullianna put her hand on top of Elouicia's and yanked the lever.

The crossbeam shot up. Screams filled the air.

Lullianna's body went limp. Her neck was broken.

The chalk circle vanished. The sound that tore out of Wilsean didn't even sound human. He ran forward and started to hack at the rope that was tangled around Lullianna's corpse.

"I'm so sorry, Lul," he cried as he cradled her limp body in his arms.

Elouicia drew his sword and launched himself at Rhett.

CHAPTER 49

Samara's brilliant, magical sister was dead. Through vision blurred by tears, Samara saw Wilsean gathering Lullianna's lifeless body in his arms.

It should have been her up on those gallows.

If anyone had discovered her as the Empty she was, Samara would have been hung. Instead, she was down here in this hole Krozor referred to as *the pit*, facing down the warlock who was responsible for her sister's murder.

"I took no pleasure in executing a young witch with so much promise." Krozor inclined his head up in the direction of the gallows.

"Don't you talk about her," Samara choked.

"I do not wish to kill you, either," Krozor said as they faced each other. He let his staff fall to the ground in what he must have thought was a conciliatory gesture.

"Oh, you won't kill me," Samara told the warlock king.

All she wanted to do was curl up in a ball and sob. But her sister's murderer was standing right in front of her. Samara wouldn't fall apart until she'd gotten justice for Lullianna.

Wisps of raw, untethered magic swirled just overhead. The reds, greens, and blues were shot through with rays of sunlight, making the air shimmer all around the pit.

Samara could sense the magic whirling around them was restless. It made her uneasy.

From what her siblings had been able to find out, the unstable magic was the result of hundreds of Insorsiled who had died in this very pit.

Because their spells had been unfinished when they died, their magic still tethered a part of them to the living world.

The only other time Samara had seen a similar phenomenon was in those spirits down in Gatria's grotto.

Except, there was nothing in this pit that looked like a spirit; it was just raw magic swirling around with nowhere to go.

"I'm the stronger Insorsiled," she said, turning her attention back onto the only thing that mattered.

Liss had told Samara everything she'd seen inside Krozor's soul when she stole his monocle. Now, Samara knew the Insorsil king's insecurities and what to say to draw them out. Samara could tell from the pinched look on his face that Liss had been right.

"Fine," Krozor snarled. He rolled up the sleeves of his dirty brown robe. "Then let us fight."

He drew his hand in an arc overhead. A blue, shimmery veil spread above them, expanding outward until there was a translucent bubble over the top of the pit. The shield spell would prevent anyone else from coming into the pit, or them from leaving, until the duel was complete.

Samara was on her own.

It had been her siblings' magic, made to look like her own, that had gotten her down here. She'd used everything they'd given her to get Krozor's attention and draw all eyes away from the platform. Now, she was down here, facing the Insorsil king without any magic.

Empty.

Samara forced down her fear and all thoughts of Lullianna. She ignored Wilsean, who was clawing at the shield spell in an effort to get to her. She cleared her mind of everything except for the warlock in front of her.

Krozor might be more powerful than Samara in every way, but she had one advantage.

Samara had grown up surrounded by arrogant, self-important Insorsiled who thought their magic made them superior to her. Krozor wasn't much different from a hundred other warlocks who had teased, belittled, and looked down on her.

She knew how he would react when she needled his weak spot. More importantly, she knew which spells he was most likely to rely on in a fight to the death.

Samara wasn't a warrior like Wilsean, or fearless like Liss. She didn't have any of the magic her siblings had been born with.

But that didn't make her useless.

She might not be able to create any magic, but she'd spent a lifetime studying it. She could call to mind just about every offensive and defensive spell ever recorded.

Now, she just had to make sure Krozor used the only one that would give her a fighting chance against him.

"You're pathetic," Samara goaded the Insorsil king. "I haven't seen a single worthy spell come out of you yet. I don't believe you're as strong as you say you are."

Krozor reached up to his left eye to adjust his monocle before remembering it was no longer there. His lip curled.

"You have no idea how powerful I am, girl," he growled.

Samara lifted a shoulder, resisting the urge to back up a step as the king came closer. "I know that you gave *our* magic to the Lagonians." She let her disgust for the warlock show on her face. "You helped our enemy's emperor become invincible."

Krozor scoffed, but Samara could see his skin turning scarlet beneath his patchy beard. "I gave Jaikon the invincibility magic because it would enable me to use the Lagonians before I disposed of them."

Samara gave the warlock an unimpressed look. "When I defeat you and become queen, I won't need to make the Lagonians my pawns." She spoke the next words slowly, making sure they sunk in. "I'm powerful enough to take what I want…what our people deserve." She forced herself to take several steps toward Krozor until she could see the individual hairs springing out from his nostrils. "It will be my name that goes down in our history as the monarch who eliminated the un-Insorsiled. And you'll be dead."

Fury sparked in the warlock's eyes.

"You have no idea what's coming," Krozor hissed.

Samara faltered.

"What are you talking about?" she demanded, her voice sounding shrill.

Krozor's lips quirked in a cruel smile. "I suppose I have my predecessor to thank for everything. After I learned about Gatria's spirits down in the grotto, I got the idea to use a similar magic to create all of this."

Krozor stretched his arms up at the swirling magic overhead. "All of the lives lost in this pit weren't in vain. As the Insorsiled who were casting these spells expired, their energy was left behind." He inhaled, like he was taking in the magic. "They will be part of Insorsil's victory, even though they're no longer with us." His smile broadened. "You'll understand what I mean soon enough."

Samara refused to let Krozor distract her from her purpose. There would be time to unravel the mystery behind the pit's magic later. Right now, she needed to take this warlock down.

She pushed past her fear for one final attempt to direct Krozor's ire where she needed it. She pointed up at the people circled around the pit and staring down at them.

"Imagine what they will say when I defeat you." She closed her eyes and breathed deeply, as if she was living in that moment. "They will all bow down to me. They will shout my name. The entire kingdom will know without question who is the most powerful Insorsiled to ever live." She gave the king a pitying look. "Honestly, I'm embarrassed for you."

Samara might not have the power to create a magical illusion, but she'd created her own kind of illusion. She'd made Krozor believe she was a powerful witch. She'd displayed magic, and Krozor had seen what his eyes were telling him. He'd made assumptions about who and what she was that he never questioned. And thanks to her parents' humiliation at bearing her, only their closest family friends knew Samara was an Empty. Even if Krozor put it together that Samara was Lullianna's sister, he had no reason to suspect she was less powerful.

It would never occur to Krozor that a lowly Empty would challenge him.

"You're embarrassed for me?" Krozor demanded through clenched teeth. "You're about to understand true embarrassment." His fingertips sparked with magic.

Samara thrust up her hands, like she was casting a spell. Krozor reacted at the same moment.

He shouted two words.

Samara didn't let relief show on her face. It was the spell she'd been hoping for…the one she needed.

A jet of green light shot out from Krozor's hand. It flew straight up into the air, hit the blue dome of the shield spell, and hurtled back down.

It was a magic-dismantling spell.

Samara could smell the acrid burn of its strength as the green light shot toward her.

The spell was powerful, as she'd known it would be. For a magic-dismantling spell to be completely effective, it had to override whatever inherent magic the intended recipient possessed. Krozor's spell was strong enough to destroy an immense amount of magic.

The spell went right through her, feeling like a gust of warm air.

Krozor looked at her in expectation. His unkempt eyebrows drew together when she didn't collapse from the force of her magic being torn away from her. Samara felt no pain…because she'd never had any magic to begin with.

The spell should have stripped her of every bit of magic she possessed. She should have been left empty and broken, probably writhing on the ground. Except, she was already an Empty.

Empty, but not broken.

The spell didn't splinter or fracture, since there had been no magic inside Samara for it to cling to. Instead, it just passed straight through her. The green light zinged toward the far wall of the pit.

Then, just as Samara knew it would, the spell ricocheted. The spell had been directed at her, so that's where it had gone first. But there had been nothing for it to cling to. So, the spell latched onto the only person with magic in this confined space.

Krozor.

The green light flew at him.

It didn't pass through him like it had with Samara. The light pierced Krozor's chest.

The warlock king jerked. Then, green light erupted from his entire body.

Krozor screamed. Light poured from his skin, his fingertips, and even his eyes. It looked like an uncontainable fire was burning inside him.

The small gold pin on the king's robes flared blue for an instant, but the light was swallowed up in a flash of green. Krozor had dismantled all of his magic, including his invincibility.

Krozor's own spell was devouring his magic. The light grew brighter…brighter…so bright that Samara had to turn away before she was blinded.

The light winked out. Krozor collapsed on the floor of the pit, but he wasn't dead.

He was Empty.

With grasping finger, he reached for his staff. Samara lunged for it, but Krozor got to it first. He lifted it up and smashed the crystal orb on a rock.

There was a flash of light. A wisp of smoke escaped from the shattered pieces. The smoke wound up through the cloud of magic in the pit and into the sky.

Samara held her breath. Seconds passed, but nothing happened.

Krozor flopped onto his back, defeated.

Samara unsheathed the knife she'd borrowed from Liss right before they parted ways. She crossed the distance that separated her from the Insorsil king. He was writhing on the ground and weeping.

Samara had never been a violent person. But this was the warlock who had killed her sister. Samara wasn't going to lose a single night of sleep regretting this death.

"Ironic, isn't it?" Samara asked as she looked down at the warlock who was now as devoid of magic as she was. "You lost to an Empty. In a way, I guess I wasn't lying. I defeated you, which makes me the most powerful person in Insorsil."

Krozor managed only a small whimper before she brought the dagger down.

CHAPTER 50

As their group neared the ward surrounding the Extended hideout, she couldn't shake the feeling that something was wrong. Very wrong.

The cold breeze had disappeared, and the air had gone unnaturally still. The usual animal sounds were absent. It felt like the whole forest was holding its breath.

"What's that?" Ciago pointed up at the sky.

Silverbird snorted and pawed at the ground in agitation. Liss absently patted the dragon's scales as she stared in the direction Ciago was pointing. There was a faint trail of smoke that stood out against the bleak winter sky.

"It's moving too fast to be a cloud," Winny observed.

The giant leader was right. As they all watched, the wisp of smoke seemed to gain speed and substance. It also seemed to be coming right for them.

"Look at what it's doing," Dannica, who was standing on the ground beside Silverbird, said.

The single wisp of smoke was growing and snaking across the sky. As they watched, it expanded outward. Except, unlike normal smoke, it didn't dissipate. It grew larger and darker until it formed what appeared to be a huge, dark storm cloud.

"It's coming from northwest Insorsil," Dannica noted, squinting up at the sky.

Northwest Insorsil was where Rhett, Samara, and Wilsean were now.

What the hell was going on over there?

Liss had no idea why a single cloud should make the hair on her arms stand on end. All she knew was that her instincts were ordering her to get away as fast as she could.

"We need to get to the hideout," she said in a sharp voice. "Whatever that thing is, we need to get the Extended out of its path."

She dug her heels into Silverbird's sides.

The giants and rebels crashed through the path behind her. Their footsteps were deafening amid the eerie silence that gripped the rest of the forest.

"Look!" one of the rebels cried.

Liss hauled on Silverbird's reins. As the dragon dug her claws into the frozen earth, Liss stared up. Her mouth went dry.

The storm cloud had doubled…no, tripled in size. It was darker and glowed purple around the edges. Thunder boomed, making both Liss and Silverbird flinch.

"That's no ordinary storm cloud," Ciago said, breaking the unsettled quiet.

As though to emphasize his words, bolts of teal lightning began to shiver across the cloud's surface. Liss could feel the crackle of energy in the air. The static lifted her hair straight up. When she tried to flatten it back down, she felt an unpleasant zing go through her fingertips.

The nine giants, who had come as soon as they received Ciago's message, gathered around Silverbird and gripped their mallets. The wolves began to growl, the whole of their attention fixed on the dark cloud.

"Smells like magic," Winny said, sniffing the air.

She was right. The fresh pine smell of the forest was overpowered by the distinct burning scent.

"I don't like the feel of this," one of the rebels said in a nervous voice.

There was a blur of opal color, and then Quic appeared.

"We need to get the hell out of here," he said, uncharacteristically out of breath. "There's a storm coming, and I swear everything is heading straight for here."

He had barely finished speaking when the wind started back up. It wasn't the normal frosty wind that came with a winter storm. This wind was heavy with moisture and something more ominous than Liss had ever felt.

Dannica, who was standing next to Liss, drew her sword.

"That's not going to help us now," Quic told her in an impatient voice. To Liss, he said, "Come on!"

He raced ahead and disappeared through the ward. Liss and the others followed as fast as they could.

Hurry, hurry, hurry.

The word ricocheted in Liss's head every time Silverbird's claws struck the ground.

They rushed through the ward just as a jagged streak of teal light burst out of the dark cloud. It shot straight down and hit the hideout's wall.

Chunks of stone and wooden beams exploded outward.

The soldiers flung themselves out of the way of the debris. Silverbird let out a piercing shriek. Ciago shouted something, but his words were lost as another unnaturally strong gust of wind blasted them.

Screams came from the other side of the wall as another lightning bolt struck the wall. More stones flew outward. When another vicious gust of wind swept past, Liss was almost thrown off Silverbird's back.

A huge gap had been opened up in the thick wooden wall. Liss could see the Extended were racing around and trying to gather their loose belongings. Tents, food, and even people were rolling across the ground as the wind buffeted everything in its path.

"What the hell is going on around here?" an Extended shouted.

Excellent question.

Then, the sky opened up. Balls of ice began to pelt them from above. At first, it was just an unpleasant barrage of painful stings every time the ice connected with Liss's skin. But with every second that passed, the balls of ice grew in size. Soon, they were large enough to draw blood.

Lagonians and Extended clustered together under tree branches, trying to shield themselves.

Liss's pocket began to vibrate. She remembered the corresponder Wilsean had given her before they parted ways, and she wrenched it out of her pocket.

As soon as she held up the glass sphere, Samara's face appeared amid the white smoke.

Even in miniature form, Liss could see her friend's terror. Liss held the corresponder as close to her face as she could get it. She swore when a ball of ice the size of her fist smacked her arm. She crouched underneath Silverbird, whose scales protected both of them from the ice.

"It's the storm he's been planning," Samara said before Liss could even open her mouth. "Krozor was containing it in his staff, and he released it right before I killed him."

"You killed Krozor?" Liss asked, focusing on the one thing Samara had said that actually made sense. Liss had to shout to hear herself over the fierce gale. All around her, rebels and Extended were struggling to stay on their feet.

"Yes, and the spirits of the dead Insorsiled are fueling this attack," Samara hurried on. "Krozor collected the energy they gave off as they died. It's making a storm that's going to kill all the un-Insorsiled. It's going to where there are the most people without magic first."

Liss looked around at the group of Extended and Lagonians. Then, she stared up at the dark cloud, which seemed even more massive than it had been a few minutes ago.

"What do we do?" Liss asked Samara.

A shout came from somewhere on Samara's end. Samara turned her head, and then white smoke began to fill the corresponder. Samara's face disappeared. When the smoke settled, Samara was gone.

For several seconds, Liss stood amid the pandemonium surrounding her. Several people were lying on the ground, unconscious from being struck by the ice balls. The Lagonians were trying to herd the Extended away from the crumbled wall and under tree branches.

The hundreds-year-old trees creaked and groaned as the wind and ice buffeted them. Some of the trees had already started to fall.

Soon, they'd have nothing to protect them from the elements.

Liss looked across the icy field, to where the wagons were parked along the far edge of the wall. There was no ice or lightning over there. In fact, the sky over the wagons was clear.

"There!" Liss yelled, pointing.

Her voice was barely audible over the raging wind, but the people around her got the point. They started to run away from the storm and toward the wagons.

Cries of dismay echoed all around Liss as the storm followed them. The dark cloud hovered directly overhead, pouring down ice and lightning wherever they were.

There was no escaping.

And if they brought the storm to the wagons, the elements would tear the vehicles apart.

"W-what do we d-do now?" Arom the Aromatic, whom Liss hadn't even noticed until this moment, gave her a pleading look.

She wanted to tell him she had no clue what they were supposed to do about a magical storm that was going to kill all of the un-Insorsiled. She glanced around to see if the others had any ideas.

Liss started. Everyone was looking at her.

Like she had some idea about how to fight this storm.

Worry about today's problems now, she ordered herself, trying to keep her mind from spinning in a hundred different directions.

Right now, all that mattered was getting all of them to Insorsil. Once she was back with Rhett and they had all of their people in one place, they'd be able to face this new threat together.

She stared at the Extended huddled around.

"Flooders," Liss said, her mind moving a dozen steps ahead of her mouth. "Can you control the falling ice?"

Men and women from different caravans began to step out from beneath their trees. They raised their hands to the sky.

"Flamers," Liss said, flinching away from another lightning bolt. "Can you melt the ice that gets past the Flooders?"

Freezing rain was unpleasant as hell, but at least it wouldn't kill them or tear apart their wagons.

Flamers gathered around the Flooders. Fire crackled along their palms, and sparks shot into the air. Liss looked up and got blasted in the face by a slushy glop of ice-snow.

"This storm's strong," one of the Flooders said, his forehead beaded in perspiration. "We won't be able to hold it off for much longer."

"We just need to buy ourselves time to get some distance from it," Liss replied. "Energizers, get the wagons ready to go."

"Air Extended might be able to help with the wind," an opal-skinned man said. He stepped out from beneath his tree and sucked in a breath. All at once, the rushing wind around them seemed to quiet.

More Airs came to join the first and did the same, sucking the wind into themselves. They turned their faces up at the sky and exhaled.

Wind, ice, and rain shot up and away from them.

All that was left was the lightning, which was still wreaking havoc on the hideout's wall and splitting trees right down their center.

"Metalsmiths!" one of the Extended called. "Give all of your weapons to the Metalsmiths!"

Quic appeared out of nowhere and began collecting knives, swords, and metal-tipped arrows. The Lagonians seemed more than a little reluctant to part with their weapons, but when a jagged streak of lightning struck a tree that was shielding a group of them, the soldiers began to offer up their swords.

A small group of Metalsmiths were huddled together. Their arms were at their sides, but all of the weapons Quic had collected were floating around them.

The weapons arranged themselves end to end. The line of metal began with a single sword anchored into the ground and grew up and outward. It looked like a metal tree, with branches that split off in every direction.

The next lightning bolt that came down seemed drawn to the metal tree. It struck one of the sword branches. Teal light shivered down the metal and disappeared into the ground.

For several precious seconds, the storm seemed to still. The lightning retreated, like it knew it had been beaten. The wind had quieted. The balls of ice had been transformed into nothing more than a gentle rain.

"Wagons," Liss ordered the Energizers. "Now."

Uncertainty filtered into the Extended people's souls. They looked from her to the ruined wall.

"We've been safe here," an Extended man said in a tremulous voice. "Maybe we could just wait things out in our wagons and let the storm pass us by."

"This storm is here for us," Liss told the man, barely able to rein in her impatience. "It's going to kill all of the un-Insorsiled."

Liss's people wavered.

"Do something before you lose them," Ciago muttered in a low voice.

He was right. She could feel the fear and indecision on their souls.

Lightning zig-zagged across the cloud overhead. The wind began to howl. Liss knew they had minutes…maybe less…before the storm overwhelmed them again.

Since no grand speeches filled her mind at that particular moment, she just let the truth spill out of her.

"I don't know about all of you," she said, "but I'm tired of being told that we're inferior. I'm not going to wait around for some dead king's magic to come for me."

"I'm with you, Liss," Quic said.

"M-me too," Arom agreed.

Ciago raised his fist into the air.

The rest of the rebels and giants did the same. A cacophony of shouts mixed with the wind, which was getting stronger by the second. Slushy, frozen rain began to slop down onto their heads.

There was so much noise Liss almost didn't notice the emotions radiating from her people's souls. Their fear and reluctance were gone. Her people were angry.

"The Insorsil king wants a storm?" an Extended man called out. "We'll show that dead warlock who has the real power. We'll rain down hell like no one's ever seen before!"

Liss could barely believe what she was seeing as the Extended began to race to their wagons. The Energizers already had the vehicles humming with power. But they weren't preparing to flee. They were going to fight.

As Liss watched the Extended gather their scattered weapons, she was filled with a fierce pride. Her people had been beaten down, oppressed, enslaved, and murdered for as long as she'd been alive.

They'd come together and turned the hideout into a sanctuary. Now, their sanctuary was broken. Instead of falling to pieces along with the ruined wall, Liss's people were banding together. They weren't weakened. They were stronger.

Ciago gave Liss a fierce smile. "Looks like we're going to make our own storm of sorts."

With the rebels' war chant and the buzzing of the wagons, it really did sound like a storm was brewing.

"Not just any storm," Liss corrected as she turned to watch her people clamber into the wagons. "An *opal* storm."

CHAPTER 51

Krozor's severed head hit the ground. Then, the rest of his body collapsed in a graceless heap at the bottom of the pit. The blue dome that had covered the pit disappeared. All of the spells Krozor had still been controlling died with him.

Rhett turned to Elouicia and smiled.

The assassin's face paled.

"What's the matter?" Rhett asked. "Feeling a little…mortal?"

Usually, Rhett let his blade do the talking for him. Liss must be rubbing off on him more than realized if he was provoking his enemy.

But Elouicia wasn't just any enemy. He'd killed Stone. He would have done worse to Liss if given half a chance.

Rhett leapt onto the platform and swiped his dagger at Elouicia. The other man blocked, but Rhett's blade nicked his arm. Blood spurted.

Elouicia curled his lip. He raised his arm and licked the blood.

Rhett's only reaction was to crouch down in expectation of the attack he knew was coming. It did. Elouicia threw himself at Rhett.

Rhett deflected the graceless blow.

Elouicia was rattled. He looked to his left and then to his right. There was no one there to help him.

Rhett glanced across the pit, where the Insorsiled were tangling with the thousands of slavers who had dug the graves of their friends and families. Wilsean and Samara were in the midst of all of them, trying to organize the Insorsiled.

"I don't think they're going to be able to save you," Rhett noted.

No question Liss was rubbing off on him.

The few slavers who escaped from the Insorsiled were fleeing as fast as their legs would carry them.

From his vantage point on the raised platform, Rhett could see all the way to the road that led into inner Insorsil.

Rhett glimpsed Silverbird streaking down the road. Even at this distance, he knew the figure on the dragon's back better than he knew the sight of his own reflection.

Liss.

There were hundreds of wagons hurtling down the road behind her. The nine giants came last, sprinting behind the wagons with their wolves on their heels.

An enormous storm cloud trailed directly behind their group, and Rhett could have sworn it was moving with the wagons. Bright blue lightning splintered through the cloud, which looked nothing like any storm cloud Rhett had ever seen before.

He didn't have more time to consider it.

Elouicia was prowling around and trying to get a clean path to strike out. Rhett never gave him the chance.

"Don't worry," Rhett said, easily blocking another sloppy jab from Elouicia's blade. "I'll tell everyone you died pitifully."

Rhett had a moment of satisfaction when he raised his dagger and Elouicia cringed. But Rhett didn't slice his throat. That death was too merciful for this man. Instead, Rhett reached up for the now-empty hangman's noose that had been used to kill Lullianna.

Rhett forced down his pain and guilt at the thought of Lullianna's senseless death. With one flick of his hand, the noose settled around Elouicia's neck.

The assassin's face registered surprise for a second.

Then, before Elouicia could disentangle himself from the rope, Rhett dove for the lever and yanked it.

Elouicia's body lurched up.

Rhett saw the exact moment when Elouicia's neck snapped.

The assassin's head lolled to the side. A fierce wind had kicked up, and the man's heavy body made the wooden beam creak and the rope groan in protest.

Rhett stared up at the corpse. Then, he turned his back on the man who had been Lagonia's emperor for only a few short days. He leapt off the platform.

He was halfway around the pit when his eyes caught on a glint of gold in the sky.

Jaikon's gold dragon dipped out from between the black clouds and soared straight for him. Rhett recognized Dannica on the beast's back. Her black hair was coming loose from its tight braid in the wind.

The gale was getting stronger by the minute. Dirt particles on the ground were being stirred into a frenzy.

Dannica gave the reins a firm tug, bringing the dragon down to the ground. She stared up at Elouicia's corpse. The man's dead weight was making the unsteady platform rock from side to side.

Rhett and Dannica watched in silence as the gallows came unhinged from whatever primitive stand had kept it in place. The whole structure leaned forward.

For a second, Elouicia's swinging body hovered over the edge of the pit. Then, another fierce gust of wind sent the corpse swinging forward. The momentum was enough to drag it, and the entire gallows, down into the pit.

Rhett glanced down. The swirling wisps of magic parted amid the disturbance. Rhett had a clear view down to the bottom, where a corner of Elouicia's dragonhide jacket peeked out from a pile of wooden beams. Krozor's head was still visible from where it had rolled away from his body. The rest of the warlock's corpse was buried beneath the gallows.

Rhett thought he heard Dannica let out a satisfied sigh, but the wind was too loud for him to be sure.

When he turned back to her, her eyes blazed in satisfaction.

Dannica handed the dragon's reins to Rhett. Her normally serious expression softened into a smile.

"I figured you'd be wanting your dragon, Emperor Rhetteman."

* * *

Rhett managed to coax the temperamental winged dragon to land in front of the row of parked wagons. He jumped off the creature, tossed its reins to one of his soldiers, and ran.

Liss leapt off a still-moving Silverbird.

Rhett was too weak to lift her off the ground, so he wrapped his arms around her and crushed her against him. He kissed her like it had been days rather than hours since they'd seen each other.

"We've got a problem," Liss said as soon as they paused to take a breath. Even though they were pressed together, she had to shout to be heard over the wind.

As Liss relayed everything Samara had told her about Krozor's storm, the black cloud moved in. Blue sky was replaced with an ominous shadow.

The Lagonia soldiers, Extended, and Winny's giants surrounded them. Rhett could sense their anxiety was growing with each passing second.

"Wait a second," Rhett said, when Liss had finished explaining. "I thought if an Insorsiled died, then their magic died with them."

"Samara said the storm is made out of magical energy rather than a spell. And there was something about all the Insorsiled who died, but I didn't understand what she was talking about."

"We barely outran it," Ciago said, joining them. "Even if we keep going, we won't be able to stay ahead of it."

"Little late for that," Quic noted.

The Runner was right. The storm was here.

"Where is Samara, by the way?" Liss asked.

Rhett motioned with his chin to the opposite side of the pit. "Dealing with her new subjects."

The last few hours had been a blur. Rhett hadn't even spoken to Wilsean and Samara since Lullianna's death.

Ulfrath, Winny's fearless wolf, tipped its snout up into the air. He let out a long howl, and then he took off. The rest of the wolves were on his heels. The entire pack raced down the road that led out of Insorsil.

Winny let out a piercing whistle, but the wolves didn't glance back. In seconds, they were gone.

"Useless muts," Ciago muttered.

"I think they actually had the right idea," Quic said, looking up at the storm cloud and frowning.

Rhett didn't give the wolves a second thought. The wind was strong enough that some of Rhett's smaller soldiers were having trouble staying on their feet. Thunder rumbled across the sky, and then pellets of ice began to come down on them.

Someone screamed as a bolt of lightning struck within feet of the huddled group of rebels.

"That's our cue," Liss yelled over the wind. She pulled up her hood, winked at Rhett, and disappeared into the crowd of Extended.

Rhett watched in awe as the Extended rallied around her. Then, like they were as much of an army as his own soldiers, the Extended battled the storm.

Flamers threw fire at the ice pellets, and Flooders repelled the water away from their huddled mass of people. Air Extended redirected the wind so it was less fierce. Metalsmiths pulled silver rods from nearby shops and used them to absorb the lightning.

Rhett couldn't take his eyes off Liss. She was everywhere at once, giving her people exactly what they needed to draw out strength they didn't even know they had.

"They won't be able to keep this up for long," Ciago said.

He was right. Rhett could see the Flamers' fire sparking out. The Flooders sagged, and the wind was already starting to return.

"Emperor, what are your orders?" one of the rebels asked, wincing as an ice pellet bounced off his armor and slashed a bloody mark across his cheek.

What were his orders?

This wasn't an enemy he could fight. His dagger was useless. So were his past experiences in battle. He'd never fought the weather before.

"The only way to fight magic is with magic," Winny called. Her voice rose above the raging tempest. Unlike everyone else, she didn't cower or cringe as the ice struck her. She was a statue amid the chaos, and her steadiness helped ground Rhett.

Rhett turned to look at the Insorsiled. Some of them were chasing the remaining slavers down the road and out of sight. The rest were taking up positions around the pit. That was when Rhett noticed that the colorful swirls of magic inside the pit were trying to escape.

Tendrils of magic floated into the air. The Insorsiled ringing the pit seemed like they were trying to contain the magic. Every time one of the colorful wisps rose out of the pit, the storm worsened.

"The Insorsiled don't answer to me," Rhett said.

"No, but they'll listen to their queen."

Wilsean parted the crowd, reaching a hand back for Samara.

The few Insorsiled who were nearby sunk to one knee, even amid the madness.

"Samara, I'm—" Rhett began, thinking about how he'd failed both her and Lullianna.

Samara shook her head, seeming to know what he was about to say. She was right. Now wasn't the time for apologies or grief.

Samara was about to speak, when am older warlock who shared her amber eyes and white-blonde hair cut through the crowd to them.

"Samara, the magic's too strong for us to hold," the warlock, who must have been Samara's father, said. "We need to flee until the storm subsides. It won't harm us if we put distance between us and the un-Insorsiled."

"I'm as much of a target for this storm as the Lagonians and Extended," Samara told her father in a cold voice Rhett had never heard her use before.

"The magic in the pit is too volatile to control," Samara's father persisted. "It can't be harnessed, and we're going to burn ourselves out if we try."

The two of them were locked in a battle of wills. Wilsean reached inside his jacket for a throwing knife.

"You're addressing your queen," Wilsean told Samara's father. "I'd choose my next words very carefully if I were you."

Samara put a reassuring hand on Wilsean's arm. To her father, she said, "The Insorsiled are the reason why this storm exists, and we're going to do everything we can to end it."

Shouts from the Insorsiled around the pit drew Rhett's attention away from Samara and her father.

The magic was escaping. Swirls of red, green, and blue lifted on the wind that was buffeting them from every direction. The acrid burning smell of magic filled the air. The magic rose up from the pit.

The colorful strands of magic began to weave together in a way that Rhett could tell wasn't random. He could also tell the Insorsiled on the ground had no control over whatever was happening.

A blinding flash of lightning split the sky, illuminating the shapes the smoky tendrils were taking on. The magic was transforming into people.

Except, they weren't human.

Enormous beings made out of the storm's elements began to take shape in the air overhead. The green streaks of magic seemed drawn to the wind. All of the colorful wisps were absorbed. Translucent soldiers made out of wind stood in their place.

Lightning fused with the blue streams of magic and transformed into soldiers made out of pure, crackling lightning. Finally, the pellets of ice combined with the red magic. Ice people appeared in the air.

"Spirits," Samara whispered.

These looked nothing like the ghostly spirits they'd faced down in the grotto. These ones were solid. And they radiated pure evil. They had no eyes, and yet, Rhett could sense the way their attention zeroed in on every non-magical person in Insorsil.

All at once, the storm spirits lowered themselves to the ground.

Rhett saw his battlefield with perfect clarity. He saw the enemy they were up against. The cold, rational commander in him understood the truth. His side was grossly outmatched. They were all going to die.

The spirits let out a war cry that raised the hair on the back of Rhett's neck. Then, they attacked.

CHAPTER 52

Liss stared at the rows of storm spirits. There was a whole army of them, except it was unlike any army Liss had ever seen before. These soldiers weren't human.

They were shaped like humans, but they weren't made out flesh and bones, and they certainly didn't have souls.

Some of them were made out of lightning. Others were wind. The rest were ice. They carried no weapons, because they were the weapons.

Liss knew instinctively they would all be equally impossible to kill.

"Retreat!" someone shouted. "Seek shelter!"

Liss watched in a daze as a group of Extended and Lagonians sprinted for the nearest tangle of shops. They crammed themselves inside until people were hanging out of the doorways. Through the fogged-over windows, Liss saw opal faces pressed against the glass.

The storm spirits turned toward the shops. Their movements were identical and so calculated it made Liss shiver.

The wind spirits didn't walk. They whirled across the ground, sending up a flurry of dirt and debris as they went.

Liss raced toward them. She didn't know what she could do to help; all she knew was that she couldn't leave her people to face the enemy alone. Rhett fell into step beside her.

Liss's attention was so fixated on the people crammed into the nearby shops that she didn't notice the wind spirit coming up behind her. Rhett pushed her out of its way, his momentum throwing both of them to the ground.

Rhett broke their fall with his hands, not even seeming to notice when his palms scraped against the cobbles.

"You okay?" he asked as they scrambled to their feet.

Liss didn't have a chance to respond. The wind spirit had almost reached their people.

Liss shouted out a warning, but it was too late. The spirit blasted right through the line of shops. Brick and plaster disintegrated in a puff of white smoke. Then, an ice spirit descended on the survivors who were stumbling out of the wreckage and choking on the dust.

Liss couldn't hold back her cry as the ice spirit attacked. The creature drove its fist right through a group of Extended and Lagonians. Blood sprayed. People were thrust into the air and crumpled to the ground dozens of feet away. They didn't get back up.

Liss started forward. She drew her knife, even though she knew it would be useless against this enemy. Rhett stopped her with a hand on her shoulder.

"My soldiers will draw them away," he told her. "See if your people's Extensions can do anything while we keep the spirits busy."

Before Liss could reply, Rhett was charging toward the storm spirits head-on.

Ciago, Wilsean, and Dannica were close behind. The giants and the rest of the rebels followed.

Rhett's dagger flashed, and an ice spirit lost its head.

The rest of the spirit's body collapsed onto the ground. Rhett turned to the next spirit. Before he could even lift his dagger, the headless ice spirit stood back up. It reached down for its head and placed it on its ice neck. There was a crack as the spirit tilted its head, sealing it back in place. The spirit turned to Rhett. Then, it attacked.

Liss screamed as Rhett ducked away from the ice fist that came within inches of his skull. He backed up slowly, dodging one lethal blow after another as he drew the ice spirit away from the Lagonians and Extended.

More of the ice spirits split off to surround Rhett.

Panic crawled its way up Liss's throat. Rhett wouldn't be able to avoid all of them.

She was about to abandon her own task to help him when a flash of opal appeared beside Rhett. Quic grabbed Rhett's arm, and then they were gone. They reappeared several feet away, on the outskirts of the group of ice spirits.

Quic did the same for the other Lagonians, pulling them away just before they were attacked and repositioning them so they could lead the storm spirits farther and farther away from the rest of their group.

Liss shook herself.

"Flamers, Flooders," she shouted at her people, who were as paralyzed as she'd been moments before. "Get those ice spirits." She spun in a circle, frantic. "Airs—"

Her people were already exhausted from outrunning the storm, and the ones who had fought the ice pellets and wind back in the hideout were close to tapped out. If the rest of them didn't find a way to make their Extensions useful, they'd all be dead in a matter of minutes.

"Fight them!" Liss shouted. "Use whatever you've got."

She led the charge with her knife raised. She slashed at a wind spirit that came at her.

She was knocked off her feet by the force, but she heard a distinct hiss as her blade sliced across the spirit. Her entire arm went numb, but the wind spirit staggered…at least for a few seconds.

Since soul sorting wasn't useful against this enemy, Liss used her Extension to help her people. She gravitated to the Extended who were most paralyzed by fear and fought alongside them. She slashed at the spirits with her knife, giving her people a few precious seconds to fight back.

Beside her, Mari's four Fighter brothers pummeled ice spirits with their fists, smashing the creatures into oblivion.

The ice spirits reformed, but not as quickly as they did after a blow from a knife or sword. Each time the Fighters destroyed the spirits, the creatures came back weaker than they'd been.

Someone nearby let out a high-pitched shriek as they were struck by one of the lightning spirits.

The sound made the ice spirit coming for Liss hesitate. It almost seemed like the spirit flinched.

That gave Liss an idea.

"Minstrels," Liss called out in a hoarse voice, not even sure if they would be able to do what she had in mind. She'd only ever known Minstrels to use their Extension to sing beautiful songs. "Can you break the ice spirits with a high enough pitch?"

Her answer came when the air filled with a piercing sound that made her ears ache.

The Minstrels' voices rose so high in pitch that Liss couldn't hear anything else. And then, just when she thought she'd go deaf, the ice spirits began to explode. All around her, chunks of ice flew outward.

With the spirits in pieces, it was easier for the Flooders to transform the ice chunks into pure water. They gathered the water into a great wave that rose from the ground.

They were pushing the water toward the pit, where it wouldn't hurt anyone. At the last second, Liss stopped them.

"Send the water at the lightning spirits," she ordered.

When the water and lightning collided, sparks exploded into the air. The lightning spirits burst apart.

"It's working!" Ciago called from nearby where he was dueling two of the wind spirits. "Keep at it."

Liss knew without having to ask that her people had nothing left. Only a handful of the storm spirits were down, and her people were exhausted.

"Block out their magic!" Samara's voice called.

Liss couldn't see her friend, but Samara's voice was loud enough that it must have been enspelled to carry. All at once, the Insorsiled were fighting alongside Liss's people. They shouted incantations and raised their staffs.

The storm spirits' movements slowed. Some of them crumpled. Most kept on attacking the Lagonians, who were falling at a terrifying rate.

More of the Insorsiled converged around them. They wove magical shields that kept the storm spirits back. Perspiration streamed down the witches' and warlocks' faces as the inhuman creatures clawed at the translucent shields.

It was taking all of their people to keep the storm spirits from overwhelming them. They were all on their last reserves of energy. Soon, they'd have nothing left to stop the spirits.

Liss looked around, searching for answers. Her gaze locked on the hundreds of wagons parked on the road.

They couldn't outrun the storm, but maybe—

"Energizers," she called out, praying her desperate idea would work. "Attack the spirits with the wagons!"

Liss got a few strange looks from her people, but then she heard the telltale creak of wooden axels and wheels.

The line of driverless wagons began to move. Liss and the others had to leap out of the way as the wagons barreled down the cobbled road. The Energizers made the vehicles stretch out and converge on the storm spirits, like the wagons were themselves an army.

There was a tremendous crash as the two forces collided. Wagons were swallowed up into great gusts of wind. Others split apart from the force of the ice spirits.

The lightning spirits were the most terrifying. As soon as the teal bolts of energy touched the wagons, they burst into flames. The wood turned black and disintegrated. In seconds, there was nothing left of the wagons except splinters.

Liss stared. Her people's homes…all of them…were gone.

She had caused the ruin of the only homes her people had ever known. And now that the hideout was destroyed—

"We did it," one of the Energizers called in a hoarse voice. He turned to Liss, his eyes bright with wonder. "You saved us."

Looking back, Liss saw that the collision that demolished the wagons had also shattered the spirits. She felt her face crack into a smile. They'd done it.

Victorious shouts began to erupt all around her. Liss was so wrapped up in everyone's jubilation that she almost missed a shadow rising from the wagons' rubble.

One shadow turned into two. Then, all throughout the rubble, shadows were rising.

Not shadows, Liss realized. *Spirits.*

"No." The word came out as a whisper. Liss couldn't even hear her own voice over the shouts of victory all around her.

Her people's congratulations began to die off as her people saw what she saw. The storm spirits were reforming from beneath the broken wagons. Some of them were missing limbs or heads, but with each second that passed, they seemed to grow in size and strength. The broken parts repaired themselves.

Liss's knees felt rubbery. All around her, shouts of victory transformed into cries of despair.

The storm spirits turned their attention on Liss's broken, battered people. Then, they attacked.

CHAPTER 53

These storm spirits wouldn't die. That was the only thought in Rhett's mind as he dealt blow after useless blow. If this wind spirit was a human, it would have been dead a hundred times over. Instead, the damn thing kept getting back up and coming for more.

He leapt onto his gold dragon, using the creature's bulk to help scatter some of the storm spirits. The dragon's height gave him extra leverage as he attacked the spirits.

Winny and Grub fought on either side of his dragon. They bashed at the storm spirits with their mallets.

The Lagonians were fearless. They knew as well as Rhett they were battling an enemy they couldn't defeat, and yet, not a single one of them abandoned the fight. They were doing everything they could to keep the spirits distracted long enough for the Extended and Insorsiled to take them down, but it was taking too long.

All around, Rhett's soldiers fell.

The ice spirit he'd just beheaded was coming back for him.

Apparently, the one human quality these creatures possessed was the ability to hold a grudge.

Ciago jumped between Winny and an ice spirit, slashing out with his sword again and again. He was as focused and tireless as Rhett had ever seen him.

"If we're going out," Ciago said between sword strokes, "at least we're doing it together."

"Yeah," Wilsean said, throwing three knives in quick succession. "I wasn't sure we'd get the chance to fight together again."

Rhett spared his friends a grin. "You weren't going to get rid of me that easily."

Rhett turned to the next storm spirit, but his hand paused halfway to the creature's neck.

"Um, Rhett?" Wilsean asked, staring at the wind spirit in front of them. "Is that your jacket?"

It was. The wind spirit was wearing Rhett's jacket…the jacket he'd placed over the warlock who had crawled out of the mass grave and died beside Rhett.

The spirit reached out a hand. Rhett took it, just as he had when the warlock was dying.

Rhett gritted his teeth against the bone-deep chill that seeped into his body the moment his skin came into contact with the spirit.

"Rhett," Wilsean said uncertainly.

Rhett kept his gaze fixed on the spirit. It had no eyes, but Rhett could sense its attention was on him. He knew instinctively that this storm spirit wasn't like the others. This one didn't want to hurt him.

"Our magic created the storm," the wind spirit said in a raspy whisper. "And we became part of the storm when we died."

"Why aren't you like the others?" Ciago demanded.

"A kind act in the last moments of my life tethered my soul to my spirit." The wind spirit placed its free hand over the jacket it wore. "The rest won't stop until all of you are dead."

"Is there any way to fight them?" Rhett asked.

The spirit tipped its ghostly face up at the sky.

"The cloud holds the storm's power. When it is destroyed, the spirits will fall."

A witch who had been fighting beside Winny blasted an ice spirit that had been coming for Wilsean. Without pausing, she turned her staff on the spirit wearing Rhett's jacket.

"Wait—"

A burst of fiery sparks engulfed the wind spirit. Rhett's jacket caught fire, and the whole thing disintegrated along with the spirit.

When the spirit reassembled itself, it no longer had the jacket. The spirit looked at Rhett without any recognition. That was when Rhett knew it was no longer an ally. Without any tether to the living, it was as soulless and single-minded in its purpose as the rest.

"Get Samara," Rhett shouted to Wilsean.

Wilsean disappeared into the crowd of clashing soldiers and spirits. Seconds later, he was back with the Insorsil queen.

"Your people have to destroy the cloud," Rhett called over the mayhem.

Samara squinted up at the cloud, which had grown larger and more ominous-looking during the course of the battle. She just nodded and turned to the Insorsiled around her.

"You heard him," she said in a calm voice that somehow carried over all the other sounds. "Focus all of your magic on that cloud. We have to destroy it."

"Keep the spirits distracted a little longer," Rhett told his own soldiers.

Liss was nearby, telling the flagging Extended the same.

They needed to buy enough time for the Insorsiled to destroy the heart of the storm.

The Insorsiled poured their magic into the sky. Bursts of light shot upward as the witches and warlocks tried to destroy the storm cloud.

Rhett didn't need to be a warlock to know that their spells weren't reaching their mark.

Puffs of smoky magic shot into the air and fizzled before even reaching the storm cloud.

"Your people need to get their magic closer," Rhett told Samara.

Samara shook her head. "The cloud's too far away."

"Here is where the giants can help," Winny announced, just as everyone else began to despair.

The giant leader struck her enormous mallet against the ground, causing a minor earthquake that brought all eight of her giants to her.

Winny nodded to Grub. The giant strode up to the nearest warlock. To the shocked screams of all the other Insorsiled, Grub threw the warlock straight into the air.

"Winny, what the hell?" Ciago demanded.

Winny didn't respond. Her face was tipped up toward the sky, where the warlock's bright green robes stood out against the black cloud.

The warlock's body went high enough that he almost came into contact with the cloud. A streak of lightning missed him by what looked like inches. Then, his body hurtled back down.

"Winny," Ciago said again, this time more urgently.

Grub leaned forward and held up his arms. Calmly, as though he was reaching up to pluck a falling feather, Grub caught the warlock around the waist and brought him back down to his feet.

The warlock let out a strangled squeal.

"W-what was that?" the warlock screeched.

Liss stepped back and covered her nose as the strong scent of urine wafted off the man. Arom's nose wiggled, and then the air around them took on the scent of lemons.

"This time, when you're thrown up there," Winny told the Warlock, "do something besides shriek like a newborn babe."

The warlock's terrified cry was cut off when Grub threw him up into the sky again. This time, the warlock's hands flashed.

One of the crackling lightning bolts winked out when the warlock's magic touched the cloud's edge. As the warlock fell back down, Rhett noticed a small chunk of the dark cloud had been carved away.

Grub caught the warlock as easily as he had the last time.

"What are you waiting for?" Winny barked at the Insorsiled who were staring at the giants in white-faced terror. "Find someone to throw you and fight the storm."

Rhett watched in a state of partial disbelief as he stood in the midst of the giants. All of them were tossing Insorsiled up at the cloud. Some of the giants had an Insorsiled in each hand, making it look like they were juggling. It seemed more like a bizarre game than a fight for their lives.

While the giant-tossed Insorsiled fought the storm clouds, the ones on the ground threw up more shield spells to protect the giants from the storm spirits.

The Extended and Lagonians were doing whatever they could to help keep the spirits at bay long enough for the Insorsiled to take down the heart of the storm.

Rhett helped by flying as many of the Insorsiled up into the storm as his dragon would carry. He was starting to find a rhythm with the creature beneath him, where Rhett stopped wrestling with the reins and the dragon consented not to burn or drop its riders.

Slowly but steadily, the Insorsiled were wearing down the cloud.

The storm spirits were weakening. Their movements were slower, and they were fighting with a new kind of desperation. A spell caught hold of the entire storm cloud and made a tremor run through it. The storm spirits let out a chorus of ghostly shrieks that sent a shiver through Rhett's body. The spirits started to back away from the Extended and Lagonians.

"They're retreating!" someone called.

More people began to cheer, but Rhett ignored them. All of his attention was fixed on the spirits.

They weren't retreating. They were…combining. They moved closer and closer together until it was no longer possible to determine where one ended and the next began.

They climbed on top of one another and melted into each other. In seconds, the army of storm spirits was gone. In their place, a single spirit remained.

It was four times as big as the tallest giant. The storm spirit was made out of ice and moved like the wind. Bolts of lightning crackled up and down its enormous body.

"Not good," Ciago said as the massive spirit loomed over all of them. "Not good at all."

The being crouched, and Rhett knew it was about to charge. He opened his mouth to shout a warning, but before he could, a tremendous rumbling shook the ground.

At first, he thought it was some effect of the storm. Then, he saw movement in the distance, along the main road that passed through Insorsil.

Winny's pack of wolves came first. On their heels were…giants. Hundreds of them.

All of the giants who had been lost on the Brookgar Sea were here.

Ciago let out an ecstatic whoop. Winny exclaimed something Rhett couldn't make out over the sound of pounding feet. Then, she was running toward her giants.

Rhett trusted Winny, but the sight of all those giants hurtling straight toward his people was…unsettling.

When he turned to Ciago, he saw his friend was grinning. The next moment, the giants were all around them.

Rhett was overcome by another surge of nervousness when one of the giants lifted Ciago off the ground and pulled him into a bone-crunching hug. There was laughter and booming exclamations.

"We got lost," one of the giants announced, giving Winny a daft smile.

"You're just in time," Ciago was saying as he managed to free himself from the giant's grip. "See that enemy?" He pointed at the enormous storm spirit.

The giants rumbled in the affirmative.

A fierce expression lit Ciago's face. "Get it."

The giants didn't have to be told twice. They threw themselves at the storm spirit, bashing it with their mallets over and over again.

For as big as the spirit was, it couldn't get out from under hundreds of giants who seemed to have endless reserves of energy.

While some of the giants turned the storm spirit into pulp, the rest of them tossed the Insorsiled into the air to finish off the cloud.

The magical storm was no match for the hundreds of giants and all of the Insorsiled people combined.

The sky rippled. A wave of humidity rolled over them. Then, the heat was replaced by icy air. The dark cloud, pierced with holes from the Insorsiled people's spells, seemed to wobble.

And then it burst apart.

Lights of every color flashed across the sky. There was a tremendous cracking sound, and then the remnants of the cloud turned to smoke.

The towering storm spirit was next. First, the lightning bolts disappeared. Then, the ice melted and was absorbed into the ground. Then, even the outline of the wind was gone. The whole creature turned to smoke.

Rhett thought he heard a sound like dozens of people sighing in relief.

The remaining wisps of smoke that filtered down to the ground were harmless. The wolves snapped at the passing tendrils, which were all that was left of the magical storm.

The pervasive smell of burning disappeared.

A cold, natural wind swept through and carried away the fragments of smoke. When Rhett looked up, he saw only the winter-gray of the sky.

"We did it," someone said. "We defeated the storm."

Rhett glanced around. He was surrounded by giants, Insorsiled, Extended, and his own soldiers. It had taken all of them to defeat the evil that Krozor and Jaikon had left behind in their wake. But they'd done it.

A silence heavy with anticipation had fallen. Rhett moved past his own soldiers to face the giant leader.

"Thank you," he told Winny, offering her his hand. "You have more than upheld your end of the bargain. We'll draw up official documentation that gives you ownership of Lagonia's eastern farmlands. My soldiers are at your disposal, but no one will bother you. Ciago will make sure you have anything you need for building."

Winny offered him a solemn nod. She took the hand Rhett offered, gripping him hard enough to make his bones grind together.

"Thank you, Emperor Rhetteman."

The title sounded strange, but not wrong.

Knowing that his soldiers were watching his every move, Rhett went to Samara next. Loud enough for their audience to hear, he said, "Thank you for saving us, Queen Samara."

Samara gave him a brilliant smile. Ignoring the hand he offered, she threw her arms around him. As he hugged her back, cheering filled the air around them. Rhett understood they were changing the course of history.

The alliance between Insorsil and Lagonia had always been strained—based on mutual need rather than anything deeper. That wouldn't be the case anymore.

When Samara let go of him, Rhett turned to his soldiers. The Lagonians looked at him in expectation.

"The immunity flowers that have saved all of us were made by Insorsil magic, grown by an Extended, and contain giant essence," he told his soldiers. "These people are our allies and saviors. We will never forget it."

Rhett turned to Liss last. When she looked at him, her blue eyes were sparkling.

She was so beautiful.

Rhett swallowed. "Liss, as leader of the Extended, I want you to know that your people will always find allies in Lagonia. I—"

Whatever else he was going to say flew right out of his mind as Liss wound her arms around his neck. When she kissed him, he forgot about their audience. Everything around them disappeared. He knew nothing except the feel of her in his arms and the way her lips moved against his.

CHAPTER 54

Liss felt like she hadn't had time to take a breath. So much had happened so fast—losing her mom, Rhett's recovery, Lullianna dying, Samara killing Krozor…. And then there was the fact that they'd just won a battle against a magical storm. She could barely process all of it.

Everyone was congregated in the center of Insorsil on the stretch of lawn outside the castle. Most of the kingdom had been left untouched, since the storm had been drawn to where all the un-Insorsiled were gathered at the pit. Liss stood with Rhett and the kids a short distance away from the funeral pyre.

Samara and the rest of her family faced the pyre. Her brother handed her the torch, and Samara dropped it onto the wood.

Rhett stood beside Liss, as motionless as a statue. Liss knew there was nothing she could say to lessen his guilt. Instead of trying, she threaded their fingers together.

She tore her attention off the pyre as she felt a nearby soul's heartbreak. She turned to see Quic, who was on his knees. Tears streamed down his face as he watched Lullianna's body burn.

Mari, Spence, and Jema surrounded him. Mari and Jema had their arms wrapped around him, while Spence murmured soft words to the Runner while he cried.

Liss looked up to where Samara and her siblings were locked in each other's arms. They were all shaking from the force of their sobs.

Liss's throat was thick with her own tears. She thought about what Lullianna had sacrificed for people she barely knew. She thought about her mom's sacrifice.

Even with his own soul full of grief, Rhett seemed to sense what was going through her mind. He wound his arm around her shoulders, drawing her against him.

They stayed locked together as smoke rose into the air and Liss cried for everyone they'd lost. She thought about what all of their dead had given up so the rest of them could live on. So they'd have a chance at a future that was about more than just surviving.

It was beginning to snow. What had been a dusting of white powder turned into a flurry of snowflakes. There was nothing evil or magical about this storm, only natural beauty. Liss turned her face up to the sky, letting the snow gather on her lashes and melt on her cheeks.

Her sadness wasn't gone, but its raw, bitter sting had made way for something else. When she looked at Rhett, her soul overflowed with the emotion. It was hope.

* * *

The next day, Liss was helping to clear away the rubble strewn all over the Extended hideout from the storm. Ciago, Winny, and Grub worked beside her. More of the giants were scattered around, helping to make short work of the heaviest stones and wooden beams.

Keela was already regrowing the gardens that had been destroyed by the wind and ice. Her work was slowed because she had to keep shooing away curious and hungry giants. She didn't seem to mind the distraction, though, especially when one of the giants pointed at Keela and said "earth goddess."

Samara and Rhett sat against an uprooted tree as they put the finishing touches on an agreement between them to make the hideout officially-recognized Extended land. The Insorsiled forest didn't technically belong to anyone, but it was generally accepted that Lagonia and Insorsil had joint jurisdiction over anything that happened there.

It had been Rhett's idea to officially give the hideout to the Extended, since all of the wagons had been destroyed.

The Extended had been living in the hideout for weeks, and yet, nothing about it was permanent. The only signs of life inside the hideout were the tents, haphazard stock of food and firewood, and other utilitarian objects.

Now, Liss watched Rhett's soldiers lay the foundations for houses…actual houses…with an open-mouthed kind of wonder.

It had been Liss's dream for as long as she could remember. Her people had never had permanent homes. They'd never had property or a means of engaging in legitimate trade, since they hadn't been able to produce anything of their own. Now, all of that would change.

"Something feels wrong," Ciago said.

Liss was reaching for her knife before she caught the teasing smile on Ciago's face.

"Oh, that's right." Ciago snapped his fingers. "No one's trying to kill us anymore."

"Don't forget that you're no longer a traitor to your empire," Liss pointed out. She grinned. "Provided that your new emperor pardons you, of course."

Ciago scowled. "Don't remind me. Do you know how much mileage I planned to get out of the whole bad boy routine?"

Liss and Winny exchanged an eye roll.

"What about you?" Ciago asked Liss, his teasing veneer sliding away. "You going to be welcomed back by the Extended with open arms?"

Liss didn't have an answer to that.

Her people had accepted Liss's authority since the storm began, both because she was her mom's daughter and because she had been the only one willing to lead the Extended during the battle. And yet, as they worked to clean up the hideout, the Extended left more space around Liss than was necessary. She caught more than a few wary glances as well as mistrust radiating off nearby souls.

Liss wasn't quite sure what would happen once the dust settled.

She was saved from having to answer Ciago when Rhett said, "We're ready for you, Liss."

She wiped her dirty hands on her pants and went to sit beside Samara. Liss took the thick paper her friend handed her, careful not to smudge the still-wet Insorsiled ink.

As she read over the terms, Liss felt her chest expand. Samara and Rhett hadn't just given the Extended the land around the hideout. The entire Insorsiled forest would now belong to the Extended.

The road between Insorsil and Lagonia, which all of the merchants used, would also be considered Extended territory. That meant her people would have control over trade they'd previously been banned from participating in.

"Thank you," she whispered, blinking furiously.

Samara looped their arms together and rested her head on Liss's shoulder. "I'm sorry it took this long for the Extended to get the treatment they deserve."

Liss looked at Rhett. "Won't your councilmen and courtiers be furious that you're giving away control of their trade routes?"

Rhett shrugged. "I'm told that I have the unwavering support of the entire Lagonia army and all the peasants. Between them, and the five-hundred giants who are now my sworn allies, the gentry won't give me any trouble." His expression grew more serious. "But politics aside, we owe your people everything. This is just a small step in that direction."

Samara's eyes twinkled with mischief. She said, "What Rhett actually means is that he's madly in love with the Extended leader."

"Well, there is that, too." Rhett offered her the barest hint of a smile as he handed over the quill for her to sign the contract.

As Liss's fingers brushed Rhett's, the sadness she'd felt on his soul for the last hour deepened until she could barely catch her breath. She'd thought it was because of Lullianna, but now she wasn't so sure.

"What's wrong?" she asked.

"Nothing." He shook his head.

Liss lowered the quill to the paper but paused before she signed her name. At the last moment, she looked up. Rhett had gone completely motionless. His soul, on the other hand, was a riot of emotions. His face was blank, but he was staring at her with such intensity she couldn't hold his gaze.

Liss glanced down at the paper on her lap.

There had been no discussion about her taking over her mom's position as the Extended leader. She had been the only one willing to take charge when her people had needed it, and that had been that.

But now that she was about to embark on her first leadership task that wasn't a fight to the death, she wondered if she was really the right person for the role.

Some of the Extended couldn't see past her Lagonian appearance and probably never would.

She knew she could get her people through the upheaval of the next few weeks, but after that?

Liss's specialty was crises. When it came to the day-to-day responsibilities, she wasn't sure she would be the right leader. Was she really the best person to gently coax the timid Extended from their generations of running and into a life that was more integrated with the rest of the world?

The answer was painfully obvious.

Liss almost laughed at the realization that, for once in her life, she was thinking ahead to tomorrow and all the days beyond. Maybe there was hope for curing her impulsivity, yet.

"Hold on a minute," Liss told Rhett and Samara, even though neither of them had spoken.

Samara gave her a quizzical look. Rhett seemed like he was holding his breath.

She brought the contract and quill across the field to Keela. The Green Thumb was busy directing Mari, Spence, and Jema about how far apart to dig holes for seedlings.

Keela smiled at Liss.

Liss held out the contract. "You're the reason why the Lagonians owe the Extended everything," she told Keela. "Also, you're less likely to chop off people's heads when they annoy you."

Keela raised her eyebrows.

"What I'm trying to say," Liss clarified, "is that I think you would be a better leader for the Extended. If you want it."

The moment the words were out of her mouth, Liss knew they were the right ones. She only hoped Keela would accept.

Keela took the contract, her eyes widening as she scanned the terms.

"But don't you want this?" Keela asked when she'd finished reading. "It's your right, as your mother's daughter."

Liss shook her head. "I think I would be a better advisor. I can represent our people on the Lagonian council, or something."

"That does makes sense," Keela said, nodding in thought. "You are likely the only person who has a true vested interest in both groups."

Liss opened her mouth and then closed it. Keela was right.

Liss had spent so long worrying about how she didn't fit in with either the Extended or the Lagonians, that she hadn't even considered how her position might be a strength rather than a weakness. She had loyalties to both groups. She saw the good and bad in both.

That stretched feeling, like she was being pulled between the Extended and Lagonians without truly belonging to either of them, fell away. Liss was so overcome with relief that she laughed.

"I would be honored to lead our people, if they'll accept me," Keela said.

Liss had no doubt they would. Keela was the kindest and most generous person Liss had ever met. She couldn't think of anyone better to help the Extended grow their new future.

And Liss would be there to help. She just wouldn't be the one in charge.

Keela motioned for Liss to turn around so she had a flat surface to sign the contract. As the point of the quill tickled Liss's back, she caught Rhett's eye.

The sadness in his soul was gone. His lips curved into a full, rare smile.

CHAPTER 55

Rhett should have known everyone in Lagonia would be more interested in the enthronement ball than the thousand more important issues their empire needed to address. But none of Rhett's subjects seemed to care about politics or the logistics of their new trade agreements.

There was nothing Lagonians loved more than a party, and Rhett's official enthronement ceremony had the whole empire in a tizzy.

Rhett couldn't wait for it to be over.

He'd hoped to have time to slip away during the whirlwind of preparations to make a few arrangements of his own. Unfortunately, his soon-to-be subjects were under the mistaken impression that he gave a damn about decorations or cake flavors.

Actually, he did care about the cake. He'd requested Lagonia's famous golden cake, since that was Liss's favorite. As soon as he'd expressed an opinion on that, a torrent of servants had descended on him.

So, he'd been forced to set his plans aside until later. Usually, impatience wasn't a quality he suffered from. And yet, when it came to the conversation he wanted to have with Liss, the notion of *later* was becoming more and more intolerable.

He hadn't had a second alone with her since she'd given up leadership of the Extended. All he wanted was to steal her away this minute and—

"But it's an emergency!" a servant wailed as Ciago dragged her down the hall.

Rhett's attention snapped up at that.

"What is it?" he asked, causing her shoes to stop squeaking across the granite floor when Ciago let her go.

The servant gave Ciago a look that could kill. She adjusted her skewed bun and turned to Rhett. "Your Majesty. I simply needed to ask how you would like the Emperor's suite to be redecorated."

"That's the emergency?" Rhett demanded.

"Want me to take her down to the torture cage?" Ciago asked.

One of Rhett's first acts as Emperor-to-be had been to demolish that evil place, but the servant's lower lip trembled nonetheless.

"It *is* an emergency," the servant persisted, raising her chin in defiance. "The Emperor shouldn't have to spend the night in a room with his predecessor's drapes and linens."

Ciago snorted.

Rhett thought about Jaikon's room, with its black granite floor and the enormous gold bed where untold horrors had been done to the Emperor's women.

No, Rhett didn't want to sleep in that room. More to the point, he didn't want to sleep with Liss in a room that had once been occupied by Jaikon.

"I'll take any other room," Rhett told the flustered servant. "Just not that one."

He would have just carried on in his room in the guards' hall, but that space was outfitted for one person. And he hoped—

"There are so many choices, Majesty. There's the red room, with the beautiful gardens. But then, His Majesty might prefer the—"

"Ask Liss," Rhett said, cutting the woman off. He was already late for his next meeting with Jaikon's old councilmembers, and he had some last-minute preparations he needed to make.

If Liss had it her way, they'd probably live in Samara's Insorsiled tent for the rest of their lives.

As soon as the thought crossed his mind, Rhett wondered if they actually could. The tent was more secure than any room in the palace, and it was small enough that they could pitch it anywhere. Now that Samara had a whole castle, she likely wouldn't have any use for it....

Ciago ushered the servant away just as a mob of noblewomen appeared in the hall. The ladies were dressed in their most formal attire, and the smell of priceless Insorsiled oils filled the air. Rhett fought the urge to duck into a hidden passageway, but he needn't have worried. The women weren't there for him.

They swarmed Ciago.

Lagonia's anti-giant sentiment had shifted overnight. Ever since the news had spread about giant essence being the reason behind Lagonians' lifetime immunity to opal contagion, feelings toward their former enemies had reversed.

Rhett watched in amusement as Ciago tried to extricate himself from the women. As Rhett observed the group, he noticed the trend that had taken hold. All of the women had shaved patterns in their hair. They were also taller and broader than most Lagonian women. Rhett had a feeling Insorsiled illusion potions were to blame for the sudden increase in their size.

At that moment, Winny entered the hallway. She took one look at Ciago, surrounded by women who seemed incapable of taking *no* for an answer, and shook her head.

When the women caught sight of Ulfrath, they began to coo and try to pet the enormous wolf. Ulfrath quickly put an end to their ministrations when he growled and snapped at their hands.

Rhett hoped there wouldn't be a new fad of courtiers attempting to capture wolves from the Extended forest and trying to tame them. There was really no limit to the lengths the Lagonia gentry would go to when a new trend had taken hold.

Winny took one look at the ladies' new hair style and scowled.

"I hear imitation is the highest form of flattery," Rhett told the giant leader.

Winny's frown deepened. "What's next? Will these peacocks start carrying around mallets?"

Rhett chuckled at the image that conjured. "Not likely," he told the giant leader, although again, he wouldn't put anything past Lagonians who had discovered a new kind of fashion.

A few hours ago, Samara had called Rhett on the corresponder Wilsean had given him. Wilsean no longer needed it, since he'd be living in the Insorsil castle with Samara. Samara had warned Rhett that Lagonians were getting into debt with shady warlocks to illegally magic their family records. Apparently, all of his new subjects now wanted to boast about having giant blood in their lineage, regardless of whether or not it actually existed.

Rhett had promptly put his new head of the Insorsil-Lagonia council in charge of clearing up that mess.

The council had been Liss's idea to skirt around the law that prevented Wilsean from serving as one of Rhett's advisors now that he was no longer a Lagonia citizen. Technically, Wilsean was an Insorsiled emissary who represented Insorsiled interests. And if that meant Wilsean needed to make weekly trips to Lagonia, then that was just a consequence of the new alliance between their two realms.

Rhett and Winny watched Ciago try and talk his way out of the gaggle of ladies.

"If those women succeed in eating him alive, I may need to appoint a new head of security," Rhett told the giant leader.

It didn't escape Rhett's notice that Ciago, while basking in the attention, hadn't flirted or accepted a single one of the women's solicitations. He'd have to give his friend hell about it later. After all the times Ciago had busted Rhett and Wilsean for being love sick and tied down, some payback was in order.

Rhett and Winny squeezed past the giggling, preening women. Rhett mouthed *Sorry, man* to Ciago before leaving his friend behind to deal with the horde.

Rhett had a few more important issues on his mind at the moment. Winny went into the throne room ahead of him. Instead of following, Rhett let the doors close behind the giant leader. He stood just outside and tried to summon his inner stillness. It felt like a swarm of insects had gotten loose inside his stomach and were buzzing around. Or tree fairies.

Thinking of the creatures made a flair of guilt spark through him. After all of the honey-related deaths, Rhett had tried to make amends. He'd dedicated a team of Lagonia physicians to developing a synthetic honey, which had the taste and texture but none of the poisonous qualities of the fairies' favorite treat.

Arom, Liss's Aromatic friend, was setting up a tree fairy sanctuary in the Extended forest. From everything Rhett had heard, Arom's ability to infuse the area with the scent of honey pleased the fairies almost as much as the actual stuff…without the added effect of killing them.

Rhett shook his head in an attempt to clear it. He took a few steadying breaths, trying to ignore the way his heart rate had picked up.

Steel doesn't know love or despair. It can't be bent or broken. It needs no heart or warmth. I am steel.

He straightened his spine and opened the throne room doors.

CHAPTER 56

Liss sat at one end of the long table inside the throne room and tried not to fidget. She was beginning to wonder whether she'd made a huge mistake.

She couldn't help but notice the resentment pouring off the councilmembers' souls. She breathed a little easier when Winny entered the room, and some of the old men's ire was redirected to the giant leader.

Still, Liss wished Rhett would hurry up so they could get this meeting over with. She wasn't even sure what was on the agenda. All she knew was that all of the most powerful people in Lagonia were sitting at this table, and she was a very unwelcome addition.

When Rhett finally did come into the room, he was…hassled. Rhett was never hassled.

Liss raised an eyebrow at him. He gave her a small shake of his head and offered a gruff apology to everyone already waiting in the throne room.

The councilmembers, a bunch of old men dripping in jewels and finely-embroidered robes, assured Rhett his tardiness was more than alright. Liss figured Rhett didn't need her to tell him that their smiles were as false as their Insorsiled good looks.

As Rhett passed behind her chair, he let his fingers glide across her shoulder and through her hair. He made no effort to hide the caress, and more than one offended gasp echoed in the lofty room. Not that Lagonians were usually opposed to far more explicit displays of affection, but this crowd seemed more uptight than the typical Lagonian.

Rhett went to the empty seat that was waiting for him at the head of the table. He didn't sit right away, though. He dragged over another chair so it was directly next to his own at the head of the table. Then, he inclined his head at Liss in invitation.

Liss tried not to let her mouth hang open like a fish. She felt every councilman's eyes boring into her.

"Liss, will you join me?" Rhett asked when she didn't move.

With no other choice, Liss pushed back her chair. She winced at the screeching sound it made as the legs scraped against the marble floor.

"I'm going to kill you," she whispered to Rhett when she was seated beside him.

Rhett didn't respond, except to rest a hand on her leg beneath the table.

"Majesty," one of the councilmen began. "This is a very large table for such a small group. Might I suggest we conduct this meeting in the war council room, instead? It's a much more intimate space."

The throne room doors opened before Rhett could respond. Ciago, Dannica, and a dozen of Rhett's other soldiers came into the room. They ignored the appalled stares they were getting from the old men who were already seated. Rhett's soldiers sat at the table without any hesitation. Even after they had settled themselves, there were still several vacant chairs.

When Liss caught Ciago's eye, he winked at her.

"Majesty, what is this?" one of the old men croaked.

"My advisors," Rhett said. "I know I'm new at this, but I figured they should be present during a meeting when I'm getting advice about the empire's future."

Liss choked back a laugh at the offense that flooded into the councilmen's souls.

"Your Majesty, this is a private meeting," another councilman spluttered. "We are discussing sensitive issues. This is highly inappropriate."

Liss exchanged a glance with Rhett. His expression remained blank, but amusement filled his soul.

Rhett turned a hard look on the old men sitting around the table. He didn't speak, and it was only a few seconds before the councilmen began to squirm.

"Shall we commence?" one of them asked after the awkward silence had stretched on.

"We're still waiting on a few people," Rhett said, indicating the empty chairs around the table.

Liss did a quick count. There were nine empty seats.

The next time the doors opened, Liss couldn't hold back her delighted laugh. Keela, followed by Spence, Mari, and Jema, entered the throne room.

The kids gaped openly at the opulent room. They took in the gold statues, black diamonds embedded in the walls, and magnificent chandeliers.

Keela sat at the other end of the table, and Mari and Spence took seats on either side of her. Jema trotted down to Liss's side of the table.

Liss was pushing back her chair in expectation of one of the little girl's hugs, but Jema only gave her a wave. She went to Rhett and hopped onto his lap.

Rhett's eyes widened, but he recovered quickly. He wrapped an arm around Jema to keep her from sliding off.

"Majesty," a red-faced councilman said through clenched teeth.

Rhett held up his free hand to silence the man. A second later, the throne room doors opened once again to reveal Wilsean and Samara.

"So sorry we're late," Wilsean announced. "Can you believe I got lost in my own castle? If Samara hadn't come to find me, I'd probably still be wandering around the attic."

"The Insorsil castle doesn't have an attic," Samara said with a shake of her head.

"My point exactly," Wilsean replied.

Wilsean's cheerful expression hardened when he locked gazes with one of the councilmen. The older man had dark skin and the same handsome features as Wilsean.

Liss realized the man had to be his father…the one who had said Wilsean couldn't marry Samara because she would drag his reputation through the mud. Now, because he'd refused to obey his parents, Wilsean was married to the Insorsil queen.

Bet you're feeling foolish now, Liss wanted to gloat.

Liss leaned closer to Rhett. "Why didn't you tell me council meetings were this much fun?" she whispered.

"It's only fun because I'm here," Jema replied, none-too-quietly.

After Wilsean and Samara had seated themselves on Liss's right, there were still four empty chairs. One of them had probably been for Jema, since Liss doubted Rhett had expected her to sit on his lap for the meeting's duration. But she couldn't imagine who the other three could be for.

"We're all here," Rhett said. He gestured to the three vacant chairs. "Those are for the people who should be at this table but are no longer with us. One is for Stone." He looked at Wilsean and Ciago, who nodded at Rhett.

Rhett pointed to the next chair. "That one is for Lullianna. Without her, I wouldn't be here."

Samara bit her lip. Wilsean leaned close and whispered to her.

"And the last seat is for Nya." Rhett turned to Liss. "I owe her my life and so much more."

Liss took in a deep, shuddering breath. She gave Rhett a look that she hoped expressed how much the gesture meant to her.

Rhett waited several seconds before speaking again.

"Before we get into the regular agenda," Rhett said, motioning to the papers stacked in front of each one of the councilmen, "I would like to present my new second-in-command."

Dannica pushed back her chair and stood. She lowered her head in a slight bow to Rhett before sitting back down.

"We've never had a woman Chief Assassin," one councilman said, aghast.

"She's not an assassin," Rhett replied, as calm as the councilman was flustered. "Since we no longer have any enemies on the continent, Lagonia has no need of a Chief Assassin. Dannica's my second-in-command."

Liss had to stop herself from sighing in satisfaction as the councilmen exchanged appalled looks.

"So, what have you got for us, gentlemen?" Ciago asked, leaning back in his chair until it creaked dangerously.

"Um…taxes," one of the older men stammered as he shuffled through the papers in front of him. "We're proposing a two-percent increase in the peasants' taxes."

"The peasants can't afford the amount they already have to pay," Dannica said, earning her share of the councilmembers' dirty looks.

"Agreed," Rhett said. "Let's halve the amount they need to pay." To Dannica, he said, "You'll keep me appraised if we need to lower them more?"

Dannica couldn't completely hide her smile as she nodded.

"But Majesty," the same councilman said. "We simply can't afford to reduce taxes. The empire will collapse."

Rhett raised his eyebrows at Dannica, making it clear she was the expert on this matter.

"We actually can afford it," Dannica said, "since we no longer have to fund an ongoing war with the giants."

"Good," Rhett said. "Next topic?"

There was more throat clearing and paper shuffling. Liss tensed at the emotions that filled the councilmen's souls. Whatever was coming next, it wasn't going to be pleasant.

"Perhaps, you'd rather ask your…mistress to step out for this part of the conversation?" one of the men suggested. He sniffed delicately, like speaking that word offended him.

Rhett's expression went eerily blank. His body stilled. To anyone who didn't know him well, he looked like the embodiment of complete calm.

Liss reached under the table to squeeze Rhett's hand as fury spiked in his soul.

"Liss stays," he said, his voice a deadly quiet.

More uncomfortable glances were exchanged among the councilmen. One brave soul at the other end of the table stood up.

"Majesty, it has come to our attention that you spend your nights with your…er…Liss."

The emotions that filled Rhett's soul were too chaotic for even Liss to make sense of.

"We, as your most loyal servants—"

Ciago turned his snort into a cough. Winny punched him in the arm. Liss had to cover her mouth to hide her own guffaw.

"—believe you should put more thought into the kind of talk that sort of behavior will stir up."

"That kind of talk," Rhett repeated in a bland voice.

The emotions in his soul were anything but bland. If the councilman knew what was good for him, he'd cut his losses and scamper out of the throne room as fast as his chubby legs would carry him.

Apparently, the man didn't know what was good for him.

"Having…relations…with someone like her isn't…advisable."

The man sat back in his chair and wiped the sweat on his brow with an embroidered handkerchief.

Rhett leaned over the table, fixing the councilman with an impenetrable stare.

"Help me understand," he told the old man. "Is the problem that we're having sex, or that Liss is Extended?"

Jema giggled. "Rhett said *sex*." She giggled again.

This time, Liss couldn't stifle her laugh.

The horror that filled the councilmembers' souls was like a cleansing spring rain. After a regime full of subterfuge and false niceties, Rhett's bluntness must feel like the mental equivalent of taking a dip in the frigid Brookgar Sea for the poor councilmen. They seemed like they were on the verge of some kind of collective fit. Their faces were beet-red, and the men were all clutching their wine goblets like they were a lifeline.

"Jaikon was a full-blooded royal," the councilman who had spoken before said, breezing past Rhett's pointed question. "Since you're—"

"A bastard?" Rhett offered.

The councilman's cheeks turned a plum shade. Liss was starting to worry about the man's health. Between the color of his skin and what was happening to his soul, Liss wondered how much longer it would be before he fainted.

"All I'm saying is that your position isn't as strong as your half-brother's," the councilman persisted. "We're trying to protect you."

"We believe a marriage to one of the high family heirs will better solidify your hold over the empire," a different councilman said.

"Oh, no thank you," Ciago said, holding up his big hands. "Rhett is *not* my type."

"Shut it, or I'll shut it for you," Dannica told Ciago.

At the same time, Rhett said, "Enough, Ciago."

A councilman at the far end of the table passed down a long piece of parchment. Liss caught sight of a list of names…female names.

"We've taken the liberty of putting together a list of women who will elevate your position and make up for any deficiencies in your bloodline." The councilman gave Rhett a benevolent smile. "We need to ensure nothing and no one can threaten your long and profitable reign."

When Rhett made no move to reach for the paper, one of the nearer councilmembers generously positioned it directly in front of Rhett.

The councilmen mistook Rhett's silence as invitation. One of them added, "If you are overwhelmed by the choice, Majesty, we'd be happy to make a selection for you."

You're going to want to stop talking now, Liss thought as the man smiled at Rhett like he wasn't about to get his tongue sliced off. Or maybe his entire head. With the emotions filling Rhett's soul, the latter was seeming more and more likely.

"Let me make myself perfectly clear," Rhett said. An uncomfortable silence filled the room as he made eye contact with every one of the old men. "I will marry Liss, if she'll have me. Or I'll never marry at all."

Liss's gasp wasn't the only one in the room.

Rhett's eyes slid to her for only a second before returning to the councilmen.

"Now, get out," he said in a low, threatening voice. "You've already intruded on what was meant to be a private conversation."

"But—"

"You heard the Emperor." Ciago knocked back his chair and jumped to his feet. He stalked over to the nearest councilman. "Get out, or Winny and Dannica will throw you out a window."

"You have two hands," Dannica grumbled. "You can do your own throwing."

The councilmen couldn't get out of the throne room fast enough. Some of them actually ran, tripping over the hems of their extra-long robes on their way. Rhett's soldiers followed them. Dannica motioned for all of the servants to leave, as well.

Jema jumped off Rhett's lap and raced over to Mari and Spence.

"Rhett's going to kiss Lissy now," Jema crowed as she looped one arm through Spence's and the other through Mari's.

Keela gave Liss a knowing smile before ushering the kids out of the room. Liss was too stunned to do anything except stay seated.

"Ciago," Rhett said in a voice that was so quiet Liss almost missed it. "I'm going to need—"

"I got you, man." Ciago slapped Rhett on the back, grinned at Liss, and jogged out of the throne room.

Wilsean and Samara were the last ones to leave. They were both all winks, smiles, and suggestive eyebrow waggles.

Liss stood up from her chair, because if she didn't start moving, she'd be in danger of combusting. Rhett's words were circling around in her head in an endless loop.

The throne room doors shut, leaving the two of them alone.

"I had a plan," Rhett said, standing before her.

"A plan?"

Why did she sound like she'd just sprinted a mile?

Rhett nodded. "I was going to bring you up to our cliff overlooking the old flower fields and ask you there, but since these idiots ruined it—"

Rhett laughed when Liss threw herself into his arms. The sound was deep and husky, and Liss felt it vibrate all the way through her.

Rhett cupped her face in both of his hands. He kissed her until Liss's head was swimming and they were both breathless.

"Yes," she said against his lips.

"But I haven't even asked," Rhett said, his lips curving into a smile.

At that moment, the doors to the throne room cracked open.

"Rhett," Ciago called.

A small box came sailing through the air.

Rhett caught it one-handed without taking his eyes off Liss. Ciago ducked back out of the throne room, even though he looked like he really wanted to stay.

"I don't just want you to be my wife," Rhett said. "I want you to be Lagonia's empress."

"I still want to help the Extended," Liss said, hardly able to believe the turn this boring council meeting had taken. "Will it be a problem if I go see them once a month or so to check on everyone?"

"I'll go with you," Rhett replied without hesitation. "And we'll have rooms in the palace for Keela and the kids so they can stay here whenever they want."

"Marrying me is bound to cause some waves among your courtiers," Liss warned him. "News travels fast around here, and I'm pretty sure your subjects aren't going to ignore the fact that I'm Extended."

"I don't plan to ever let them forget it," came Rhett's gruff reply.

He opened the small box resting on his palm and held it out to her.

A surprised laugh bubbled up from Liss's throat. It wasn't a plain band with the royal seal, as Lagonia tradition called for. There was a thin band of platinum. In its center was a large, flawless opal.

"Liss, you're my other half…my better half." Rhett slid the ring onto her finger. "My soulmate."

Liss choked on something that was between laughter and tears.

As she met Rhett's gaze, realization struck Liss. All her life, she'd feared loving someone so much that she would give away her soul and lose herself in the process. With her hand in Rhett's and his smiling eyes fixed on hers, she realized she'd been wrong.

In loving Rhett, she hadn't lost herself. She'd gained an equal and a partner. The love of her life. Her soulmate.

THE END

✳ ✳ ✳

Because reviews are so important for a book to be successful, please consider leaving a brief review on your favorite retailer if you enjoyed *Opal Storm*. Many thanks!

* * *

Sign up for Stephanie Fazio's e-Newsletter to learn about upcoming books at:
https://StephanieFazio.com/subscribe/

Acknowledgements

Thank you to all of the people who helped me finish this series. It was such a fun process, and I couldn't have done it without you!

To Andrew Brodsky, Keith Tarrier, and Ellen Schaeffer. Thank you for being part of the team that made this book possible.

To Bob Brodsky, Rhoda Schneider, and the rest of my ARC team, for seeing new ways to bring my characters and stories to life.

Thanks to Two Steps From Hell, Sebastian Böhm, and Thomas Bergersen for your beautiful music. This series would never have been finished without you.

To my amazing friends and family, who have supported me every step of the way.

To my readers. Thank you for giving me a reason to write.

To Andrew. Thank you for being you.

About the Author:

Stephanie Fazio is a fantasy author. She grew up in Syracuse, New York, and prior to writing full time, she worked in the fields of journalism, secondary education, and higher education. She has an undergraduate degree in English from Colgate University and a Master's degree in Reading, Writing, and Literacy from the University of Pennsylvania. Stephanie lives in Austin with her husband and crazy rescue dog. When she isn't writing, she's getting lost in parks, hosting taco nights, or ironically and miserably losing at word games, but having fun while she does it.

Connect with Stephanie Fazio:

Visit her Website: https://www.StephanieFazio.com
Sign up for her newsletter: https://StephanieFazio.com/subscribe/

Discover other books by Stephanie Fazio

Opal Contagion Series

Opal Smoke

Opal Slayer

Opal Storm

The Fount Series

The Prince's Chosen

The Forsaken's Choice

The Chosen Union

Bisecter Series

Bisecter

Halve Human

Dusker Dark

Captain Harkibel

Mags & Nats Series

The Nat Makes 7 (Sept 2020)

www.ingramcontent.com/pod-product-compliance
Lightning Source LLC
Chambersburg PA
CBHW051631180726
48284CB00006B/1687